Abbot Bonifaccio of [   ] man; austerity plays little part in his life. The Abbot is more concerned with material than spiritual matters, and when Brother Ieronimo's latest vision of the virgin suggests to him that a gift is on its way to the Abbey, he's determined not to be unprepared. When monks working in the infirmary bring him a priceless bejewelled cross found on a patient, he has no doubt that this is the intended gift – and he will use all his cunning to keep it. Setting out for the town of Rocca for painful discussions on taxes with the Duke, he proudly displays the jewel, ignoring Brother Ieronimo's dramatic warning: 'Blood! Blood! Don't go, Father! Blood waits for you in Rocca!'

When the Abbot is found murdered, Ieronimo by his side clutching the axe that killed him, it seems that the mad monk has taken direct action to ensure his prophecy is fulfilled. But where is the cross? The Abbot is not the first to die for the sake of the treasure, and there are many possible assassins to hand.

The Duke of Rocca knows that only the former mercenary Sigismondo can unravel the mystery. With his seemingly half-witted servant Benno and the scruffy dog Biondello Sigismondo accepts the Duke's commission – but Sigismondo has his own enemies, including some who believe he has the cross about his person. In days when life is cheap, time is not on Sigismondo's side as he undertakes the search for justice . . .

Axe for an Abbot

Elizabeth Eyre

HEADLINE

First published in 1995
by HEADLINE BOOK PUBLISHING

First published in paperback in 1996
by HEADLINE BOOK PUBLISHING

10 9 8 7 6 5 4 3 2 1

ISBN 0 7472 5163 0

Printed and bound in Great Britain by
Cox & Wyman Ltd, Reading, Berks

HEADLINE BOOK PUBLISHING
A division of Hodder Headline PLC
338 Euston Road
London NW1 3BH

Contents

People in the Story

Olivero Pantera, a rich merchant
Lydia, his wife
Ferondo, his brother
Elisavetta, Ferondo's wife
Bernabo, their uncle
Donna Costanza, their grandmother
Donna Irina, their aunt
Gian, their cousin
Elena, Gian's wife

In Pietra
Felicia, a merchant's wife
Agostino da Sangallo, her husband
Perpetua, her maid
Nuto, the groom

Abbot Bonifaccio
Father Torquato, his secretary
Brother Filippo, his treasurer
Brother Ieronimo, a visionary

In Rocca
Duke Ludóvico
His wife, the Duchess
Roderigo Ranieri, a courtier, friend to Gian Pantera
Ugo Bandini, a merchant prince
Cardinal Pontano

In Rome
Pope Honorius
Cardinal Pantera
Cardinal Tartaruga } One of whom becomes
Cardinal Lepre Pope Felix
Cardinal Bufera
Brunelli, an artist
Barley, an opportunist
Gemmata, a prostitute

In Scheggia
Giovanni Falcone, host to pilgrims

In transit
Angelo, friend to -
Sigismondo, a soldier of fortune
Benno, his servant
Biondello, his dog

Chapter 1

'He Was Murdered!'

'Sigismondo! I'd have known you anywhere.' The blow of recognition landing between the shoulders made no difference to the man he greeted; he had not fallen on his face, or even staggered, as most others might; nor was it any great feat of remembrance, taking into account the man's shaven head. 'What are you doing here?'

Here was the square of a small town, crowded today with stalls, people chatting and chaffering and bawling strident inducements and prices, exchanging news from one side of the square to the other. Sigismondo held out a peach, furry, warm from the sun, to show what he was doing there, and paid the stallholder. His voice was deep and easily heard under the din. 'And you? Olivero Pantera. Surely this town's too small to find a bargain in?'

Olivero had an explosive laugh. 'I live here, man. Just outside the town. Come and dine with us – my brother Ferondo and me – today, now. I'll take no refusal. God's Bones, we've fought brigands together, you're as much my brother as Ferondo is. He'll want to meet you.' He hung a bear-like arm round Sigismondo's neck and led him through the square. A disreputable little man followed at a discreet distance, carrying Sigismondo's other purchases and leading the horses, and himself followed by a little one-eared dog carrying in his turn a long sausage not yet missed by a stallholder.

1

The Pantera villa was within walking distance of the little town, further up the hill where a few houses clung at the edge of the woods, but not so far as to tire the little dog although the road took its toll of the battered sausage.

The door was opened by a deferential porter. Olivero ushered his guest in. The guest's servant was swiftly dispatched to the stables and thence made his way, hopefully, to the kitchen, but dinner had been waiting for the master's return and was being served. Benno had only time to run his fingers through his hair and beard before he was hustled upstairs to wait behind his own master's chair at table.

From there he had an excellent view of Olivero, seated opposite, and he formed the opinion that it might be better to fight alongside him than as an enemy. The short-cut beard did not disguise the mouth's truculence; the dark discs of the eyes showed no pupil and stared as though looking were in itself a weapon.

'Tell Ferondo of the fight. They came down on us from the hills, brother, and this man hurled an axe at the leader.' Olivero's hands came together in a triumphant clap at the memory, startling the servant filling his cup, and the fourth at table, a priest, cast down his eyes as though to deprecate the slaughter. 'Ah, Ferondo, you should have seen it.'

Ferondo was a less aggressive version of his brother, a little younger, vaguer, more sly in looks – someone who perhaps did not always need to fight to gain what he wanted; yet he was willing to regret his absence from a fight Olivero recalled with such affection. Benno, receiving the flagon of wine and pouring for his master, saw Olivero shoot a glance at his brother. It was a glance full of meaning. Sigismondo certainly had not missed it and might even know what it signified.

'Were they all killed?' Ferondo, shifting his gaze to Sigismondo, showed a detached interest that ignored the bloodshed involved. Brigands asked for what they got; in this case an axe.

'To the last one.' Olivero skewered a piece of meat from the dish with his knife. 'I strung up the last one myself, on a handy tree. But it was all over from the moment our friend here planted his axe in the first. Let's drink to that axe.'

Cups were raised, though the priest left his on the table. The Church does not as a rule drink to axes. Ferondo lifted his cup with enthusiastic words. Olivero's eyes, even while he drank, dwelt on Sigismondo.

'Have you the axe with you, now?'

Sigismondo took the question as seriously as it was spoken. 'Certainly. Why should I travel without it? Why do you ask?'

This was not a question Olivero was ready for. The dark gaze switched to Ferondo for support, which was instant.

'No reason. No reason. Of course a man must be prepared at all times.'

Benno, passing a dish back to a servant, saw that Olivero's cup was being filled again. The conversation moved on, and it became evident that Olivero, a merchant dealing in fine silks and carpets, had not much to offer as small talk. He concentrated on eating and drinking, doing both with intensity and leaving Ferondo to make polite inquiries about how Sigismondo had been passing the time since fighting off brigands at Olivero's side.

'Hey – I've been travelling, that's all, as I was when I met your brother. Into France last year; Burgundy; where my sword takes me.' Sigismondo was slowly finishing his plate of pasta baked in layers with walnuts, sultanas, dried

3

figs and apples. Benno, trying not to dribble, hoped there would be some of it left for the servants' meal afterwards. In his opinion, Sigismondo's account of his activities singularly lacked the details that lent them interest – matters like being useful to a couple of dukes and a prince or two. Sigismondo's wits as much as his sword were what people hired him for. 'And you?' Sigismondo said to Olivero. 'I said goodbye to you in Turkey. Are you off to the East again soon?'

Olivero took his time about answering, for a servant put a dish of braised pigeons before him. Another pushed into Benno's hands a platter of hare in red wine, and he put it down beside Sigismondo, who helped himself and sat back. Benno handed the dish to the servant, who was mopping his face with the napkin he carried. Late afternoon sunlight, low through the windows, shone on the display of gold plate on the credenza shelves. The priest received the platter happily. There were traces of past meals down the front of his habit. Perhaps being chaplain to the Pantera brothers had its consolations.

'No, I don't go abroad just yet.' Olivero pulled a pigeon apart and ate, glancing at the priest. 'Things have happened here requiring my presence. I can't travel so freely – I am head of the family here since my father's death.'

'Your father died recently?' Sigismondo's voice had the right tone of sympathy for bereaved sons. Olivero's remark was not of the sort to be passed over without comment.

'*He was murdered.*' Olivero's savagery made the priest drop his spoon and then cross himself. 'Murdered by his own brother not a month ago. What do you say to that?'

Not a lot you *could* say, Benno thought, fetching the wine to refill Sigismondo's cup. If the father or the uncle had been anything like Olivero, you couldn't really be

4

surprised either. Sigismondo was making suitable sounds of shock.

'We had to bury him in the family vault, of course.' Ferondo seemed to think this point ought to be made, though its reason was not clear. He elucidated. 'In spite of our uncle Gianmaria being buried there the day before.'

Sigismondo paused, holding his cup, the better to clarify this.

'Your uncle died too, then.'

The priest shook his head and muttered about a curse, earning himself a glare of dislike from both brothers. 'God punishes covetise and wrath.' He caught Olivero's look and hastily filled his mouth with meat.

'My uncle was killed by my father. Little chance, indeed, had he against such a man.'

Sigismondo did not ask how, if he were so redoubtable, Olivero's father had in fact got himself killed. 'A terrible thing. Is your mother alive?'

'Died giving birth to me.' Ferondo's tone suggested this was quite to her credit; a redeeming feature, so to speak, of a life otherwise without repute. Olivero was draining his wine and his eyes were moist, from either the wine or filial regret.

Benno wondered whether the uncle, surely just as much murdered as the father was, had left a wife. The dinner had turned into an uncomfortable meal, possibilities of talk having been killed as dead as the unlucky subjects of the discourse. The sunlight too had left the gleaming dishes and the room had acquired a sombre look. At last only the priest ate on, until the weight of Olivero's hostility brought him to realize that it was time for him to say the blessing after meat.

Olivero got up with a well-controlled stagger, and went off to the closet. As the table was cleared and taken down,

Olivero, returning, said, 'You'll stay the night, Sigismondo. No, we insist.'

Ferondo took up swiftly. 'We insist. Stay a week, a month. You fought beside my brother. The house is yours.'

'You're kind, sirs. I should be glad to stay tonight, at least.'

Benno, watching the men group round the carpeted table at the end of the room, wondered what exactly this cordial hospitality in this strange household was about. Unaccountably, a cold wind was catching him at the back of the neck as he followed the servants downstairs. Murder had merely been discussed that evening, but Benno felt in his bones they'd be lucky to get away from this place without something bad happening.

Chapter 2

'The Guilt Is Yours!'

Olivero would not consent to Sigismondo's limited acceptance; he leant across the table promising that a prolonged stay at the villa would be amusing. 'We can hire jugglers from town. There's a bull-running there in a few days that always kills a few. There's hunting. There's the festival saint's day only the other side of the hill in a week's time. A man can't spend all his days slaughtering brigands.'

The chaplain did not even raise his eyes at this statement, occupying himself with the wine and the sweetmeats. The sound of his sucking and chewing was the accompaniment to conversation from then on.

Sigismondo smiled in answer, not in any way committing himself. Nobody at the moment laid claim to his services and the Pantera hospitality was better than any the local village could offer. The price of his supper was his playing audience to the brothers arguing over where exactly they had bought the Turkey carpet on the table, and how much they had paid for it, which led to prolonged reminiscences about bargains they had acquired in the past. As Sigismondo glanced round the room during this, he found plenty of evidence that the Panteras were successful in their bargaining.

Merchants like to display those riches which can give them a status even princes must respect, and the brothers were not reserved in their display. The credenza against one panelled wall was ranked, shelf on shelf, with silver-gilt dishes and cups, flagons and covered bowls, that a duke might not disdain. A tapestry, showing Hercules embroiled with the Nemean lion, probably came from Genoa and might well have cost the worth of a small house. Sigismondo's eye was drawn to something that suddenly glittered and flashed when the servants had brought in candles and closed the shutters on the summer dusk. Facing the window, in pride of place between two portraits, hung a cross in the Maltese form, the size of a man's palm and alive with jewels.

'Our treasure.' Olivero observed Sigismondo's gaze. 'An heirloom.' Wine had made his voice thick and he spoke with exaggerated emphasis. 'The luck of the family. Which we guard with our lives.'

'There are those,' Ferondo had the same intensity, 'who would like to take such luck from us . . .' He caught Olivero's eye and mumbled something into his winecup.

'I'm sure,' Sigismondo bent his head politely, 'that you are both well able to protect your possessions.'

Olivero suddenly heaved himself to his feet, almost toppling as his hand slipped on the polished carving of his chair-arm, and lurched forward to pick up the double candlestick. He swung round with it, and Ferondo stepped back to avoid the flying molten wax.

'Your bed, man. Let me show you to your bed. I had them make it up in the room next to this. We sleep the other side.' He tapped his nose, nearly missing it. 'Can't be too careful these days.' Perhaps he was referring to the guarding of his possessions, but from the trouble he, and Ferondo as well, were having in the managing of their feet, the gold plate would have to rely on the security of

8

the villa itself, the grilles on the downstairs windows and the barred oak door.

Olivero's candlestick wavered in his grasp, and its flames flickered and swam as he flung open the door on the next room. It too had shuttered windows, more fine panelling, and a bed whose old-fashioned tester hung from the ceiling, with light summer curtains of bleached linen. There was a chest, with more silver-gilt plate on a blue linen cloth, next to which lay Sigismondo's pack and his sword and short-handled axe, the very one of which Olivero so approved.

'Where's your man?' Olivero peered about as if he expected Benno to erupt from the floor.

'I don't need him.' Sigismondo, hand swiftly raised, prevented Olivero's imminent shout for servants to fetch Benno. 'He can sleep below. I'm a campaigner, sir, not a merchant-prince to need attendance.'

Olivero and Ferondo, who would both obviously need help in getting to their beds, commended Sigismondo to the saints for a good night's rest, and found the door at their second try. They could be heard making a complicated success of crossing the sala, a sliding clash with the credenza rattling a dish or two. Doors shut; a song rose in duet, inaccurate, swelling and then dying away.

Sigismondo undid a shutter and looked at the afterglow in the sky, and breathed the air, listening to the frogs by some pool, and a distant barking. He withdrew and turned to the small bedroom shrine, bent his head before it for a minute or so, crossed himself and, taking off boots and doublet, lay down on the bed and slept.

It was less than an hour later that he woke, and instantly turned his head to listen for what had woken him.

Somewhere near at hand a board had creaked. All

houses have their own sounds, of the fabric settling after
a day's heat, a shutter shifting in the night wind, and he
was in a house whose sounds he did not know. This had
been different. It was a sound of stealth.

The board creaked again, the sound released with
painful care. Sigismondo slid off the bed, his hand closing
on his sword. He had left the shutters open, and moonlight
through the round panes made silver discs on the floor.
Sigismondo trod through them on silent feet.

The almost imperceptible knock of Sigismondo's door
latch lifting was covered by another complaint from a
floorboard in the sala and by a remote but ferocious burst
of snoring.

The shutters in the next room let the moon just alleviate
the darkness. Sigismondo held the door almost closed for
a moment, taking in what was happening.

A long wedge of light from a dark-lantern on the floor
showed a man in the act of reaching up to take the cross,
the Pantera treasure, that shimmered above his hand.
Sigismondo flung the door wide and advanced, sword
ready.

The man wheeled, at the noise and the change in light,
and seemed to make a gesture in protest, a hand thrown
up against the sword that threatened him – and then,
inexplicably, he came lunging forward at speed. So fast
did he come that Sigismondo's withdrawing sword still
took the man's weight with all the ease of its sharp point,
sliding past the breastbone.

Sigismondo, down on one knee, caught the man by the
shoulder as he collapsed forward but he was too late – the
blade was already far in. Blood, hot and soaking, poured
on to the sword hand; the man, as Sigismondo braced him
and tried to draw out the blade, coughed more blood and
got out a word.

'Scheggia . . .'

His head drooped on Sigismondo's left arm. There was no longer need for care and Sigismondo jerked his sword free. He was holding the dead man's head on his arm as he knelt, and wiping away blood from the man's beard when Olivero, blear-eyed and stumbling, came in with a candle to investigate the noise he had finally heard.

'God's Bones.' Olivero's first action was to thrust the candle towards the face of the corpse. '*Uncle Bernabo.*' He raised his voice to a shout. 'Ferondo, it's not Gian after all! It's Uncle Bernabo!' He crouched by Sigismondo, in a miasma of sour wine, reefing up his bedgown of soiled brocade and staring. 'He's dead.'

Ferondo, who had appeared in the doorway yawning loudly, strode forward and then saved himself from sliding headlong into the group of them only by clutching Olivero's shoulder.

'Candle wax all over the floor . . .'

Olivero took up Sigismondo's sword and was examining it with detached interest. 'You killed him with this?' He sounded as if he would have preferred the axe. Sigismondo removed it from him and did not reply. He watched Ferondo go up to the cross and touch it as if for reassurance.

'Old slyboots Bernabo – sneaking in here when we didn't expect him . . .'

Olivero had got to his feet and was scowling. 'I'll kill Tomas! He must have let him in.' Both brothers left the room, gowns trailing after them, and went, shouting and precipitately, down the stairs to interrogate and punish their porter. It was Sigismondo who picked up Bernabo Pantera, carried him through to the other room and laid him on the bed he himself had just left; the dead man had his eyes closed for him respectfully and a prayer said over him by a stranger, if a man whose sword had been so intimate with his lungs could be called a stranger.

By the time Olivero had untied Tomas, found bound, gagged and partly conscious on a bench in the entrance lobby, the commotion had roused the servants, Benno among them, who crowded out to watch and exclaim.

'Fool! Idiot! What the devil possessed you to let him in? You knew him, surely?'

Tomas's eyes were still wandering, but fear brought some of his wits back. Olivero's idea of resuscitation was a brisk and forceful slapping of the porter's face to and fro, and it was not right away that he could get out his jumbled story: a scratching at the postern, news for the brothers of their grandmother who was ill . . .

'She's been ill since Noah beached the Ark.' Olivero gripped the man by the throat and collar-fronts, shook him as a dog shakes a rat, and flung him down. 'You fell for that? You never thought what might happen? What in the name of hell do you think you were here for?'

Benno was wondering what actually *had* happened, what all the fuss was about and, more urgently, where his master was, when Sigismondo appeared on the stairs at the heels of the chaplain, who made straight for Olivero, accusing.

'Your uncle! May God forgive you! Did I not tell you God's curse would fall on the one who next shed blood in this family? The Bishop will keep his word: he will excommunicate you for this. Oh God forgive us all.' This was a different man from the nonentity who had scarcely spoken until now. Here he was on sure ground.

'Amen.'

Sigismondo's deep voice undercut the hubbub raised by the servants. He came forward into the lantern light. His right sleeve was scarlet. He said, 'The sword was mine.'

'You!' The chaplain swung round, unappeased. 'I knew your kind from the start. You man of blood! You pretend to have come here by chance but I knew, I could see. They hired your sword for this. The guilt is yours.'

Chapter 3

Storm to Come

'No – no! An accident! You're in no way to blame.' Olivero strode to Sigismondo, clapped a hand on his shoulder and would have shaken it but found him immovable. 'He came to steal – thief in the night – you did us the office of a friend.' To the chaplain he said, 'There was no *hire*.'

'Your uncle. Your kinsman.' The chaplain, so silent before, having been spurred into speech was not to be halted. 'What will it do to your grandmother? This third and last of her sons to be victim of this curse!'

Benno shrank further back among the crowd of servants, sheltering Biondello in his arms. A curse could take any shape and this one seemed to have extended from the Panteras to his master, standing there so sombre with that blood-soaked sleeve. What uncle was this, here in the middle of the night – *stealing*? But his master would not kill, and particularly not a stranger, without provocation; the uncle must have attacked him. It was his bad luck to choose the night Sigismondo was here, for neither of the brothers had looked capable of killing anything that evening unless they fell on it.

The death of their uncle had apparently sobered them up without in the least depressing them. Olivero now took up the chaplain's words.

'Why, yes! Grandmother! Grandmother shall have what she asked for. It's not what she wanted but yes! She shall

14

see what her greed has got her. She put him up to this – she's been his guts since the day he was born.'

He had pushed the chaplain aside and seizing a servant with a lantern propelled him up the stairs.

Ferondo seemed more concerned than his brother about Sigismondo's involvement in the matter. 'We're obliged to you, sir, really we are.' Olivero's feet trampled overhead, and Ferondo hesitated, becoming aware that thanks for saving their treasure sounded like nothing so much as thanks for dispatching their uncle. 'I assure you we were not expecting *him* at all. A terrible thing indeed. A dreadful accident. He should really not have been there.' Plainly he deplored his uncle's intrusion more than his death. 'By night, you know, and by stealth . . .'

'Make way there!' Olivero, preceded by the lantern-bearing servant, was carrying what in the shifting shadows looked like a roll of carpet. The appalled chaplain, hurrying forward, knew what it was.

'You cannot, sir! Your own kin to be treated so . . . Have you no respect for the dead?'

Olivero's opaque eyes gave him no more than a glance. Still with his uncle draped over his shoulder, arms and hands swinging – and spreading the strong smell of blood as he passed – Olivero was chivvying servants, numb with shock, to open the postern door. It creaked wide, admitting a wash of moonlight. Olivero stepped over the ledge, miscalculating the clearance needed for a corpse so that his uncle's head hit the jamb.

'Ho. You there! Bernabo Pantera's servant, were you?'

Very likely the past tense escaped the notice of the man across the road under the trees, but he came at the summons, leading two horses. Olivero went to meet him, and slung the body over the saddle of the better horse, which stamped, backed, and tossed its head at the sudden awkward weight and a smell that scared it. The groom made matters worse by dropping the reins in his horror, and Olivero had to seize them, control the horse and keep its burden from slipping, while he shouted to his servants for rope. The one who brought a coil of it made such a poor hand at securing the body that Olivero, infuriated, had to do it himself. Everyone had crowded out of the door and stood staring, in broad moonlight not yet threatened by the bank of dark cloud that lay in the sky to the east.

Olivero finally gave the groom his message to his grandmother.

'Tell Donna Costanza from me, she's got her son back. Let her not send for anything else from our house or I'll bring her own death to her.'

He slapped the reins back into the groom's hand and turned to herd the rabble of servants into the house. Crowding back in retreat, carrying their torches, they parted round Sigismondo and crammed themselves in through the postern, leaving only Benno by the wall. Ferondo had followed his brother out; he took Sigismondo by the sleeve and let go hastily when he realized why it was caked and stiff.

'Won't you come back to your bed, sir? You are our guest.'

'No. Benno, the horses.'

'Brother, tell him he can't leave now, in the middle of the night . . .'

Olivero, standing in the road, wrapped his bedgown round him again. He had been listening to the retreating hoofbeats and his face was in shadow. He did not appear to have heard his brother, but turned abruptly to step over the threshold and into the house.

Ferondo said, 'We hoped you'd stay a long time. We are in need of friends like you.' He waited a moment, then seeing no change in Sigismondo's face, he followed his brother.

Sigismondo had not moved by the time Benno came round from the stables leading the horses. He had got Sigismondo's pack, axe and sword, and Biondello was trotting beside him.

Ferondo, leaning from the doorway, made a last appeal: 'Can we not talk of this in the morning, sir? We need your help. You cannot leave us like this.'

Sigismondo mounted. Benno thought, as he swung to the saddle, I'll bet you need help. Nothing like having a stranger come and kill your uncle for you, lets you off the hook with the Church and you didn't even have to hire it done . . . He felt strongly that his master had been very badly used, and this thought made him far more resentful than if he himself had been ill-treated. The sight of Olivero carting off his uncle's body to lash it to a horse and consign to sender was not one Benno would forget. He was glad to have seen the last of the Panteras.

Sigismondo rode in silence, and a glance showed Benno that his stern face reflected the darkening sky. There was going to be a storm in more senses than one.

They stopped in the small square of the little town where Olivero had hailed Sigismondo not so long ago.

Sigismondo dismounted at a wall where a stone lion's head spouted water, glittering silver in the moonlight, into a basin beneath. A dog or two barked, but then the sound of water was the only one in the silence of the town.

Sigismondo pulled off his shirt and plunged it into the basin, then plunged his arm in almost up to the shoulder. The water flowed dark from the basin along the gutter, as Sigismondo washed. Benno, between glances at his master, had ferretted in the pack for a shirt. Sigismondo wrung out the wet one, Benno shook it and fastened it

17

over his saddlebag as Sigismondo put on the dry one and mounted. He still did not speak and Benno, looking at his shut face, did not ask or comment, even though he longed to know exactly what had happened at the unlucky Pantera villa.

When the stony track divided, Sigismondo dismounted and examined the ground before choosing the left-hand fork. It came to Benno suddenly, as he followed, who it was who had ridden off before them that night. The groom carrying the body of Bernabo Pantera might well have come this way. Surely it was not possible Sigismondo was going to see the mother of the man he had killed?

Chapter 4

'Scheggia?'

Benno did not reckon they were as much as half an hour behind the groom with the uncle's body, but it depended how fast he was travelling. He might be reluctant to face his mistress with the body of her son or he might be stimulated by disaster and eager to get back with the news.

Dawn was lining the slatey clouds in the east with vivid gold as they rode down into another little town, small enough to be called a village save that it had a square with a central fountain, and several quite grand houses presenting blank faces to the square.

Dawn was not too early for those at the fountain getting water, for stalls being set up, and for groups, growing by the minute, of people with their heads together, some with clothes half on, listening and exclaiming, glancing at one of the houses. Sigismondo distracted them, and drew eyes as he rode slowly across the square looking at house fronts.

It was not hard to find the Pantera house. It was the one people were giving those covert glances. Over the great oak door was a coat of arms in stone where the shield displayed an animal, a spotted cat courant on a barred ground. Benno, no hand at heraldry, knew his master could read a shield just as easily as he made sense of equally incomprehensible written words. As Sigismondo slowed before the house, a pair of hands emerged from the window slit above the coat of arms, holding swathing that was shaken free to hang over the stone panther. It was a black banner.

For a moment there was no sound from the people – only the fountain, pigeons, some remote birds, and a distant grumble of thunder; then, echoing this, a murmur arose from the square.

But the life of the town went on. Shutters were thrown back or drawn in. Carts came jolting past Sigismondo who had dismounted and tied up his horse; Benno released Biondello while he saw to the horses and looked about for a bucket to borrow to give them water. Then he followed to where Sigismondo was sitting, on a stone ledge along the wall of the Pantera house.

'You reckon everyone knows?' he asked in a low voice. 'That groom must have made something of a din getting back earlier on, rousing the house.'

'Mm.' Sigismondo was disinclined to talk, but Benno judged he was no longer so angry. He seemed calm, absorbed in his thoughts, and as if he had come to a decision.

Very clearly, news of Donna Costanza's bereavement was spreading, as people were gathering before the house with sprays and bunches of greenery in their hands. They regarded the strangers sitting there, and also scanned the increasingly black sky which looked prepared to weep for the Panteras.

Before long they parted to make way for a priest, stout, with a face of shocked concern as he knocked at the door. As he waited, his robes flapping around his legs in the wind that was getting up, he too inspected the strangers. The scrubby little fellow with a black greasy beard was of course half-witted; he dismissed him from consideration. The other, with the shaven head and the air of contained power, was a different matter. Men like this were uncommon hereabouts; the news of Bernabo's murder made one aware of the forces of evil abroad; this stranger had the air of one who had witnessed, and played a part in, terrible things.

The door opened, and there was the frightened, tear-stained face of Donna Costanza's maid. The priest uttered a resounding and firm blessing as he entered the house.

Soon others were being admitted. The sky had now got so black that stallholders were packing up and crowding into the arcade that bordered one side of the square. Those waiting to pay their respects surged into the entrance or pulled up hoods and shawls. Time passed and people emerged from the house. The first big drops of rain began to splash, and Sigismondo, brushing down his leather jerkin, got up and took his place among those still waiting.

A maidservant, her eyes swollen, mopping her cheeks with her apron, bobbed to each guest in acknowledgement of their courtesy, and was too distressed to take notice of two she did not know. Those ahead were climbing a flight of steep stairs to the *piano nobile*.

There, in a room lit only by candles, Bernabo's body lay on a long table. The brocade cloth over him was invisible under sprays of leaves, rosemary and even flowers. His jaw had been tied up with a lawn cloth and there were silver coins on his eyelids. There was a sound of weeping now, and a mutter of prayers. Outside, the rain had begun to drum on the shutters urgently as if it, too, wanted a place by the bier.

Sigismondo stood at the foot of the table; while Benno extinguished himself by the door, Sigismondo made no effort to be inconspicuous. At the head of the bier stood a thin woman in black damask and a headdress of black silk. The visiting townsfolk approached her and exchanged a few soft-spoken words. One or two asked after Donna Costanza. It seemed she could see nobody and the priest was with her. The woman stood very straight, her hands clasped before her – tightly clasped – and she did not move. The dazzle of the torchères either side of Bernabo's head prevented sight of her face, but she could evidently see Sigismondo; for when the final visitor had departed, she raised her voice enough to ask, in a tone of challenge,

'Who are you?'

Sigismondo did not answer. Instead, he questioned.

' "Scheggia?" '

Chapter 5

A Curse

'Scheggia?'

She came round the torchères with quick, decided steps and halted before him. 'What about Scheggia? Did Bernabo tell you?'

Her eyes stared, deep-set under black eyebrows, fierce. She seemed satisfied with Sigismondo's bending his head to her question, but her hand gripped her arm as if she would protect something or would hold back from the moment. There was silence as they both looked along the table at Bernabo, who was not going to tell anyone anything again. Benno, pressed against the open door, was busy cancelling himself in case the fiery eyes found him. If his master was going to get any confidences from this woman she would want them to be for his ear alone.

'Come.' The eyes had found Benno and, disconcertingly, not dismissed him in spite of the specially vacuous expression he had summoned. She moved towards the window, motioning with her head for Sigismondo to follow. There, in the spectral light coming through the veiled lunettes, and against the drumming of the rain that made the shutters vibrate, she faced him again and spoke beneath her breath. 'You know, then, why he went to his nephews' house?'

Sigismondo raised his arms from his sides and let them fall. 'And with this bitter result.' The deep voice was a murmur, but clear enough under the beating of the rain. 'Why did he do such a thing?'

She did not notice, as he had framed what he said, that if he knew why Bernabo had gone to his nephews he would not need to ask; she took it as a protest against Bernabo's wilfulness.

'He thought they would be too drunk to hear!' In a ferocity of protest she had raised her voice, and glanced swiftly at Benno. In reassurance, Sigismondo tapped his temple but she still lowered her voice again as she went on. 'Murderers! Right sons of their father! May *their* sons, if La Feconda grants them, be blind and deformed.' Her energy was the more forceful for being repressed – no witch could have put more venom into a curse. Sigismondo felt her breath hot on his face. 'He told you, then, what he hoped to do? Stop the bloodshed, heal the hatred for ever?'

It did not look as if her hatred would be easily healed; but Sigismondo again used a significant silence and accordingly she continued. 'I told him it was useless. That the thing brought a curse, not a blessing; leave it to work its will! What luck did it ever bring us? My mother,' she glanced across to the room beyond, 'had sons, it is true enough, while we had the cross in this house. But what has happened to them now? Bernabo was her last. Last of her sons. And what use am I, a daughter, a childless widow, to her? She is dying, now, from the news of his death.' A thin hand went briefly over her eyes. 'He thought he could bring her peace. Well, she will find it soon.'

She shut her mouth hard and her head went back. Sigismondo waited until she had controlled her feelings, and then put a hand on her arm.

'And Scheggia, my lady?'

'Scheggia! How did he think he could get it there, with

24

those two after him? Sooner or later they would have realized where he was heading. He'd have been lucky indeed to be able to offer it to the shrine before they caught up with him. Devils. Murderers! And now it will be Gian's turn.' Her hand covered her eyes again.

'Gian?'

She dropped her hand to stare, suddenly suspicious.

'How do you know Bernabo, and not know who Gian is?'

Sigismondo shrugged. 'I fought with him, once. He did not tell me much.'

Her face tightened. 'Men! And it is true, he rarely spoke of his family. Ashamed, and with good reason.' A lull in the rain made her voice seem louder but by this time she had forgotten Benno. 'You may think Bernabo a thief, going in the night to steal the cross, but Olivero and Ferondo stole it first. Olivero's wife cannot bring a live child to birth.' There was scorn in her voice and Benno wondered what had happened to her own children. 'And Ferondo! His wife has had children but they lived only weeks. La Feconda can bring children, it seems, but does not guarantee their living. Both Elisavetta and Lydia have been sent to Rome by their husbands to pray for better success, to bear murderers' sons!'

'And Gian?' The deep voice reminded her. Something in her altered, and her expression changed, softening the fierceness like a film over a hawk's eye.

'My nephew. Gianmaria's son. Abroad now, but expected home at any time. And when he returns . . .' she shook her head. 'He will want revenge. He loved his father dearly, and his uncle Bernabo hardly less. And now my mother . . .'

As if on cue, a maid came pattering from the inner room, and stopped, her knuckles to her mouth, looking around, then came almost hysterically calling out.

'Madam, she's going! Donna Costanza is going! Father's anointing her now!'

'I'm coming.' She moved to the door in a soft rustle of damask, the stranger forgotten. Sigismondo and Benno were left alone with the corpse, in a house that was shortly, it seemed, to have another.

Sigismondo did not stay, in such circumstances, to take his leave. As they stepped out into the driving rain, a high keening came down the stairwell from above; Donna Costanza had found the peace her last son had sought to give her. Benno, his hood pulled well over his face, and struggling with the wet reins of the horses looped into the iron ring, had an uncomfortable thought: his master had been the cause of Bernabo's death, which in turn had caused Donna Costanza's. That cross certainly must have a curse attached to it.

Chapter 6

A Thief in the Night

They paused in the town for a long visit to the smith, and to buy food. Then, heads down against the rain, they picked their way through deserted streets over the sluiced stones and the runnels, back to the road by which they had entered it. Benno hadn't liked the road the first time, and what troubled him as they proceeded was that Sigismondo took none of the turnings off it. If they went on, they would arrive back at the brothers' villa. Benno had heard only some of the talk between Sigismondo and the fierce Pantera woman and he had not yet worked out why his master had thought it necessary to track Bernabo's body back to its source, as it were. He was wholly baffled by the realization that they still had not finished with the horrible Panteras. He watched the rain running down his master's hood and shoulders and, hitching Biondello into a more comfortable place, he pursed his mouth in apprehension.

He felt hope when they veered off the track before they came to the village – the place where Olivero had greeted Sigismondo, and where his master had washed his shirt in the early morning – and he rode more cheerfully until his master reined up in some woods and, looking round, Benno saw buildings not half a mile below them and recognized what they were: the Pantera villa.

Sigismondo led the way on foot. They went deeper into

the woods, with the horses' hooves plashing in wet leaves, the hiss and patter of rain all about them, until they came on a fallen tree. Under its mighty trunk some ground was dry and Sigismondo put down his pack there and, taking axe in hand, set off among the trees. Benno saw to the horses, putting their saddles under the tree, finding them fodder; and when his master came back carrying branches, he helped him to build a bivouac. He hoped they would not be there long. Because of the villa so short a distance off, he was troubled, his mind full of questions. Benno was an inveterate asker of questions and Sigismondo discouraged them severely enough to prevent most of them from being uttered aloud. Today Sigismondo's silence kept Benno silent too. They ducked into their shelter and Benno got out the bread, the cheese and the peaches, and laid them out in their leaf wrappings.

Sigismondo gestured, *eat*. Benno, who could never remember lacking an appetite, was heartily chewing his third mouthful when he saw that Sigismondo was not eating but had produced the bundle of herbs he always carried and, turning them over, carefully chose two and laid them in his piece of bread. Benno could smell, after a moment, the bitter scent of the herbs.

There was no room to stretch out. Biondello crouched under the arch of Benno's knees and wrestled with the pig's trotter Benno had bought for him, but Benno himself sat elbow to elbow with his master and that was how he became sure that something was wrong. Not only, in the chill of the wet evening, did Sigismondo's body give off heat as from a fire, but he was also shivering. The thing Sigismondo had returned to the brothers' villa to do must be condemned to failure. He was ill.

The rain stopped before midnight. Benno, who had fallen

into an uneasy, half-aware sleep with his head drooping forward on his chest, woke with a start at a chinking sound beside him. In the dim light from a sky washed clear by storm, he could just make out Sigismondo rummaging in his scrip again. There was once more the sharp bitter smell of herbs but the nightmare impression of his master's illness had lifted. Sigismondo's movements were swift and confident as he hitched a coil of rope over his shoulder and hid the axe's gleam at his belt.

'Come, Benno.'

Benno's question got out before he was awake enough to prevent it. 'What are we going to do?'

Sigismondo was on his feet and out of the shelter, stretching his back and looking down the hill towards the Pantera villa. Benno, events so far coming together in his mind, saw with horrified misgiving just what Sigismondo's undertaking might be. He had to swallow hard, because he felt his heart had jumped into his throat. He stood up, stiff in damp clothes, and went for the horses. Admire and trust Sigismondo as he did, he was not without apprehension. Olivero was a formidable foe, his brother was not to be trusted a finger's breadth; and Sigismondo might be in health now but only a few hours ago . . . Benno saddled up, fastened the packs, put a crust of bread in his mouth and, chewing, led the horses downhill after Sigismondo in philosophical gloom.

They tied the horses just inside the wood. Sigismondo led on, coming to the villa where a high garden wall met the house wall, black against the sky. Beyond the house somewhere, a yard dog gave a questioning bark, and Sigismondo stood unmoving for a long minute before he went on.

Benno had been trying to make out what his master was carrying, and now he could see it clearly – an object with three splayed hooks, a grapnel, product of that visit to the smith.

He was tense as a bowstring, but Sigismondo seemed to move with easy deliberation, hefting the grapnel, judging the height, swinging it, launching it into the air.

It did not catch, and the thud of it startled the yard dog again, and others within the buildings. Sigismondo became once more an unmoving statue; Benno tried to believe it was safe to breathe but his heart thumped so that he thought it might deafen Biondello stowed so near to it. He prayed to the saints for their protection, a frantic formless prayer.

The dogs at last fell silent. Sigismondo tried again; when the grapnel caught, he tested its hold and began to climb. He used the rustication of the big cornerstones of the house wall as footholds, and reached the top of the wall.

Benno saw him glance down and then round; then he was out of sight. Benno crouched among the scrub weeds at the base of the wall, next to the dangling rope, and listened.

The sounds of the night magnified themselves to him – frogs, some night bird chirring, a disturbed pigeon making a clatter of wings; a dog far off; the horses shifting. Time went by.

A step had taken Sigismondo from the top of the wall to the roof tiles, and he crossed the shallow slope, testing with his hands before he trod, over house leeks and lichen, until he was looking down on the courtyard. He let himself down over the edge of the roof and, by way of a carved ornate pillar, came to the gallery. Moonlight did not reach down into the pit of the courtyard. The silence was not complete – raucous snores came from somewhere. It was not, though, the erratic duet of the night before. Only one succession of clogged breaths sounded out. Only one brother slept for sure. The other might be absent tonight, or he might sleep quietly – or he might be awake.

The door from the gallery to the sala was bolted or locked. Sigismondo moved to the next door, that of his bedroom of the previous night. This yielded, the latch almost silent but the door creaking like a cry of distress. He stood still, holding the door open, listening. He heard the yard dog rattle its chain somewhere, but this sound within the house did not alarm it. He entered.

The shutters were open, showing the bed stripped where he, and then Bernabo, had lain. He crossed, to pause at the door of the sala. What he heard was not reassuring: the click of a dog's claws on wood, and a snuffling.

Sigismondo felt in the scrip at his belt and brought out a napkin, which he shook loose and held in one hand as he opened the door with the other. The dog, a big hound, came snaking through. Sigismondo held out the napkin and shook it, and the dog went for that. He gave a swift, short kick under the cloth and the animal grunted, reared and fell sideways. He caught it, eased it to the floor, and listened.

He carried the dog into the sala, and put it down; he trod forward, transferring his weight with care, making no more noise on the creaking boards than a roaming dog might make – the brothers, by introducing the dog, had in a way eased the intruder's progress. He moved towards the two portraits. It had occurred to him that the brothers might have taken the cross away, perhaps to the bedroom of one of them, if they expected Gian still to try for it. The glint of jewels in the reflected light showed they had not.

The snoring abruptly stopped.

Sigismondo stood still, and listened. The sleeper next door stirred, moaned, and was silent. Sigismondo took the cross from the wall and went back the way he had come.

The dog began to rouse, its paws twitching as he passed it; if a live dog was let out of the sala in the morning, the brothers might not think to check on the cross; if it was dead, they certainly would and the chase would be up. He had been deliberate in his kick, for time was what he would need from now on.

Benno waited. The moon had shifted, brilliant on the wall, giving the rope a sharp shadow, when Sigismondo appeared at the top. He climbed down, unhurried, and joined Benno on solid ground. He held out his hand and showed the Panteras' cross, briefly, on his palm.

'And now for Scheggia.'

'Scheggia?' Benno breathed.

'And we must get there before they get to us.'

Chapter 7

The Search

The smoke of incense in the small church was so overpowering as to make the eyes water. For some whose tears did not come easily it was a blessing. There might be more curiosity than grief among the townspeople crowding in to pay their last respects to Donna Costanza and her son Bernabo, both being buried this day in the family vault. There was sympathy, certainly, for Donna Irina, widowed, childless, mourning her mother and brother together; but there was universal curiosity over what would become of the Pantera house, what would become of the Pantera fortunes. Donna Costanza had been well enough liked, her natural arrogance excused on account of her birth, her age and the procession of tragedies that had afflicted her. The church was as full of rumours as of incense: what was the real cause of her son's death that had precipitated her own? The groom who'd ridden back escorting her son's body had told with horror how Olivero had roped his uncle's corpse to the horse, and it was generally believed that Olivero and his equally murderous brother would not be anxious to show their faces at the funeral. It would be very interesting to see what form justice would take.

Many of the townsfolk, signing themselves and genuflecting as the Mass proceeded, were wondering when the excommunication, promised by the Bishop upon the next shedding of blood in the family feud, would take place; and would it be possible to make a day trip to the Cathedral to attend it?

Olivero and Ferondo were, as it happened, nearer than any of the congregation suspected. Their horses' reins were tied to the very ring which Benno had used for Sigismondo's and his own. The brothers had availed themselves of the open and even unattended door of the Pantera house – for such servants as were not at the church were resentfully and furiously preparing food for the guests after the interment. The preparation of a lot of food is an activity provoking recrimination, and the exclusion of these particular servants from the chance of an emotional jaunt to the church had doubled bad feeling. Therefore the brothers were in luck as the servants banged the pans about and shrieked at one another, ignorant of the presence of surviving Panteras.

Both brothers were for once entirely sober; this did not render them any more capable of co-operation or organization. Taking merely elementary precautions against being heard, they ran up the stairs to the *piano nobile* and, entering the room so recently vacated by the body of their grandmother, started to search at random.

Olivero flung open the chest at the foot of the bed and hurled out carefully folded clothes in all directions, the apples placed to scent them hitting the floor, rolling all over and being crushed underfoot. Ferondo looked at the shrine and, finding nothing of interest there, dragged off the bedclothes. Olivero drew his knife and slit the pillows and mattress, releasing clouds of feathers that made them lurch about, cursing and sneezing, while they rummaged the bedding. It was Ferondo, feathers frivolously lodged in his beard, who found the strongbox in the wall cupboard and forced its lock. Together they slung its jewels, its gold

34

spoons and toothpicks, its silver-gilt table ornaments on to the bed where they raised miniature storms of feathers as they fell. It was Olivero who led the way into the next room, where Sigismondo had talked to Donna Irina beside Bernabo's body.

There they had no better success. They ripped up cushions from the benches and window seat, ransacked another store-chest, and emptied the coffin-shaped boxes under the window seats of all sorts of ancient wall sconces, toys such as tops and cup-and-ball, broken carvings and objects lost for ages. Olivero, glancing impatiently round, caught the eyes of a wooden Christ regarding him from a tall crucifix on the wall and, seized by an idea, struggled, with Ferondo's puzzled assistance, to take it down. Propping the foot of the crucifix on the floor, he examined the back hopefully but found no sign of anything concealed within. As Olivero rushed into the next room, Ferondo turned the crucifix round, crossed himself before it apologetically, and hurried after his brother.

Empty bedrooms offered no better scope, nor did the brothers expect to find what they sought in rooms not frequented. In the kitchens, a screaming altercation over the blame for a burnt piece of pork came to a sudden halt at the sound of booted feet clattering down the stairs. It is a fact that disappointed men make more noise than hopeful ones, and it is also a fact that servants on the whole feel unqualified to deal with robbers. Moreover, those in a house because they are not attending a funeral have no wish that the next should be their own.

So the Pantera brothers departed unchallenged from their grandmother's house, partly since they left by the front door, as they had come. Had they chosen a more furtive exit by the back door they would have met the mourners who, with a lifting of spirits, were coming through the garden from the adjoining cemetery and heading for the feast spread on the terrace under the pergola of vines.

The servants had, by consensus, agreed that the feet on the stairs must have belonged to relatives arriving late and looking for Donna Irina. Much better not to upset anyone with tales of robbers when there was grief enough to go round. Besides, there was plenty to do hurrying to and fro with dishes and flagons to console the mourners without thinking of anything else, let alone sparing the time to look upstairs.

Fortune was both smiling and frowning on the Pantera brothers, offering them opportunities and frustrating them. They had found the door of the family house open – so was the door of the tomb. Donna Irina had left it unlocked so that she could return to pray alone when she had done her duty in making the guests welcome at the feast. Olivero, who had been very willing to smash the lock, took it as a sign from above when Ferondo tried the handle and opened the door on the chill of the family vault.

For a moment they hesitated, as the light of the watch-candles flickered through incense smoke and made huge shadows dance on the marble walls. Then Olivero, with a truculent jut of his chin, stepped over the threshold and gestured to Ferondo to shut the door behind him. What they were going to do now should have no witness save the dead.

Chapter 8

'Who Put a Sword in Him?'

Donna Irina received the commiserations of the mourners with dignity. She knew that many of them were discreetly looking about, perhaps counting the windows on the house viewed from the terrace, covertly assessing the quality of the grapes overhead. The large man who gripped her hand to press a moist kiss upon it, moister than his eyes, had been threatening Donna Costanza only a week ago with forcing her to sell up part of the estate to meet what she owed him. Now, with Bernabo gone too, how was she herself to avoid the sale? In any other family she might have raised a loan or accepted a gift, to keep the estate intact and enable the Panteras to hold their heads high. Only her nephew Gian might be willing to help; he was abroad on business and could well return too late to be of use – and then blame her for selling family land.

At least, whenever he might return, it would not be too late for him to revenge the deaths of his father and of his uncle. If God were merciful, she would live to see another funeral, that of Olivero and Ferondo. She would have been surprised to know they were already in the family vault, though not in the condition she would have wished.

They were in fact paying their disrespects to their grandmother. Donna Costanza lay, arms crossed on her breast, a black veil covering her from head to foot, on a carved, stone platform between that of her husband and

37

of her son Bernabo. The watch-candles burnt at the head and at the foot, the flames dwindling and flaring as the brothers moved, making their shadows into those of giants or sending disturbing gleams into the vault's far corners where other, less recent, Panteras lay. Ferondo kept his back towards where his other uncle, Gianmaria, lay, the pall over him concealing the fatal wound dealt by his brother, Ferondo's father, over whose body they once more vowed revenge. Family feuds fill family vaults. Ferondo tried to keep his mind on what they were there to do, but he shuddered as Olivero pulled aside Donna Costanza's shrouding veil. He could not rid himself of the fancy that she might suddenly sit up and catch them a box on the ear with a bony, dead hand.

'Try *him*.' Olivero had uncrossed the icy hands, found nothing beneath, had even felt at the neck for a chain under the black brocade. Irritated by Ferondo's gaze, he gestured at the body beyond: Bernabo, so neatly killed by the useful Sigismondo. Ferondo had fewer scruples over this and was bent over his uncle, feeling under his hands, when the candle flames dipped violently as the door opened.

Donna Irina stood there, eyes huge in a white face so like their grandmother's, a bunch of rosemary sprigs, tied with black ribbon, in her hand.

Before she had time even to open her mouth to reproach, Olivero plunged towards her, threw an arm round her waist and clapped a hand to her mouth. The candle he had passed blew out and dark came one step nearer in the tomb.

'*Where is it?*'

Olivero, grasping a live body, his rage fuelled by the frustration offered him by dead ones, began to shake his aunt to and fro as if she were a doll. Muffled noises under his hand brought him to notice he was choking the very answers he was anxious for, and he released her, kicking the door shut with a clang that woke sonorous and alarming echoes in the vault.

'Where is *what*?' Donna Irina spat out a fragment of Olivero's soiled cuff and regarded her nephews with disdain. Her courage did not permit her to consider that she was shut in alone with those she believed to be her brother's murderers, in a place where no one would dream of interrupting her prayers for some time.

'The cross, Aunt, the cross! Tell us where it is and we'll go at once – we'll trouble you no more.'

Donna Irina had long rated Ferondo's ingratiating ways as more disgusting than Olivero's belligerence. She ignored him as she turned to his brother.

'Why ask me about the cross? Has God taken it from you - no doubt in punishment?'

Olivero scowled. Seizing her arms, he shook her again, making her drop the rosemary at their feet. 'Tell us where she put it. Tell us or—'

'Or you will kill me as you killed your uncle. Why should I tell you murderers anything? You are excommunicate in all but the rite itself; and your presence here—'

'We didn't kill him, Aunt!' Ferondo came forward, agitated at the accusation in that place, before his uncle's body. 'I swear we are innocent of his blood.'

Donna Irina regarded him and Olivero – who had stepped back from her – with the same inimical, disbelieving gaze.

'*Innocent*? Who put a sword in him? Who sent him home like luggage roped to a horse? Did he come to your house merely in order to kill himself then?'

'He came to our house to steal our cross, as you well know. And now you've sent someone again to steal.' Olivero advanced his face close to Donna Irina's, snarling. 'You took the cross and you've hidden it. We'll find it wherever it is and we'll take it again, you can swear on that.'

'But,' Ferondo was at his brother's elbow, tapping his arm, placatory towards his aunt, 'we *are* innocent, you know. We can swear to that, here.'

Donna Irina's fierce eyes turned towards him.

'Here?'

She swept past Olivero, sending a candle flame horizontal as she went, and stood by her brother Bernabo's body. 'Very well. On his wound you shall swear. Both of you. Be mindful that if you should lie, before the dead and before God, his blood will flow again.'

This belief was rooted in all of them, a belief older than the vault in which they stood, nearly as old as the ground beneath their feet. So the brothers – Olivero having reluctantly concluded that nothing could be got from their aunt unless she believed in their innocence – came to stand by the body. She bent over Bernabo and tenderly kissed his forehead. Then her inexorable fingers undid his doublet and shirt and laid bare the wound. Both placed their right hands on Bernabo's breast, and swore, on their hopes of Heaven, that they were not guilty of his death; their voices hollow in the vault and their ancestors listening. The three living watched the wound. No blood flowed. She looked up at them, still unappeased, her eyes glittering.

'Who then? If you did not kill him, who did? You were there. Was it one of your servants? If so, you are still guilty . . .'

'A stranger did it.' Ferondo was babbling in his relief. It may be he had expected his uncle's blood to recognize equivocation and come out to say so. 'It was an accident – he lay in the room next door and he thought Uncle Bernabo was a thief—'

'He *was* a thief!' Olivero pointed at the grey-white empty face on the slab between them. Tired of exoneration, he had not forgotten his purpose. 'But for that stranger, your mother would have succeeded, and she failed and so she sent another. *Where have you hidden it?*'

Donna Irina was looking thoughtful. She went to pick up the rosemary from the flagstones, and brought it to place on Donna Costanza's breast under her fingers, then carefully laid the veil over the haggard face once more, while Olivero fretted and Ferondo crossed himself. The dank chill of the vault seemed to have increased, as if the dead themselves exuded it and it sank into the flesh of the living.

'This stranger. Had he a shaven head?'

Olivero raised his eyes sharply. He and Ferondo looked at each other.

'Has he been here? Sigismondo here?'

'Sigismondo . . . He killed my brother? Then I can tell you where to find him.'

Chapter 9

The Way to the Cross

Donna Irina returned from what all supposed to be a prolonged period of prayer at the family mausoleum, to find that the mourners, having finished the feast provided and having drunk generous quantities of wine to fortify themselves against the misfortunes of others, had discreetly left. She stood for a while in the late afternoon sunlight which dappled the table under the vines, looking at the mess that remained, the dishes with scraped bones, the stains of wine and sauces on the cloth, the oil, the empty dishes and drained cups. Two servants were dawdling at clearing away, one tipping a cup over her mouth for the last drops, the other, hands on hips, so busy passing on gossip overheard from the guests that she did not notice Donna Irina standing behind her until the drinker, lowering the cup, suddenly saw her and curtseyed.

'Take the dishes and go. No, leave the rest.' She did not want them bustling round her, even in sympathetic silence. Once alone, she sat at the head of the table, where she had sat only at the beginning of the feast. A flagon had been left, and she found wine in it. They had taken her cup, but she found another, shot its dregs on the stones, wiped the rim with the edge of the cloth, and poured. Only now did she realize how weak she felt after the encounter with her wretched nephews.

But she was not finished with nephews for that day. As

she sat drinking under the vines she heard a distant thundering at the street door and then voices, one of which she thought she knew, and hurried footsteps coming through the house. She had risen in anticipation, and stood with one hand supporting her on the chair-back, when the man she had hoped and dreaded to see came out on the terrace, dismissing the ushering servant with a swing of his arm.

'Gian! I've so longed for your coming . . .' Aunt and nephew were in each other's arms, weeping. The tears Donna Irina only now let herself cry fell on Gian's dusty jacket. 'Poor child! You have heard everything? We buried them both today, only a month after your father, God rest his soul.'

They stood there together, Gian unable yet to speak. Then she released him, led him to a chair, made him sit, filled the cup again and made him drink. The sunlight showed the dust on his face, streaked with his tears – a handsome, intelligent face with large thick-lashed eyes and a full mouth. Only the determined chin and the quick frown reminded Donna Irina of her less favourite nephews. He was, not surprisingly, frowning as he put the cup down, and his question was about those cousins of his.

'Where are they? Olivero! Ferondo! I will kill them! I came home and found – what you know . . .' Yet he had to rehearse it. 'My father murdered . . . I went to their house, those fiends, and found nothing but an ant-heap of servants telling me they had come here after La Feconda. Do you have it?'

He had gripped her hand, on the table, with as much violence as Olivero had used, and she paused a moment before she replied, as if to calm him; then spoke deliberately.

'No. The cross is not here. They will not find it.'

'Then you know where it is.' He leant forward in avid question, but she stayed silent. 'How did you get it back? They said uncle Bernabo was murdered as he tried to take back what was ours – the porter told me a man with a shaven head was hired to lie in wait and kill him.'

Donna Irina shook her head. 'No. I don't believe that. He – his name is Sigismondo – he was here too. I believe I know what he wants to do.'

Gian leapt to his feet, sending the cup flying to dent itself on the flagstones. 'What he wants to do? What *they* want to do! Hire a bravo to kill our uncle because they don't dare excommunication!' He leant over Donna Irina, his face as close as Olivero's had been so short a time ago. 'He came here? Where did he go? Has *he* got the cross?'

It was a shot in the dark but, he could see from her face, an accurate one. She rose and walked past him to the edge of the terrace, where she stood with her hand on a trellis post, running her palm over the smooth wood as if in consideration, looking at the slope of orchard beneath, at the vineyard and, beyond, the blue hills of the distance.

'Your uncle Bernabo wanted an end to this bloodshed, to this terrible killing. Both his brothers! I don't want to lose you too.' Her voice faltered but she did not turn. She did not look at him. 'He wanted to take the cross where it belongs—'

'It belongs with us!'

'It belongs to the Virgin of Scheggia. Don't forget the story. My grandfather took it from the German pilgrim who died of fever in this house. He was taking it, in thank offering, to Scheggia.'

'A thank offering for a flourishing family – for prosperity. He didn't need it any more. We do.'

Now she did turn to look at him. 'We don't need the hatred, the killing that has gone with it. It brings wealth

44

and good harvests – ' she gestured at the orchards in the sun – 'But, as you know, wealth can be gambled away. Bernabo was good man, but he liked games of chance. When he lost he became desperate and pledged your grandmother's lands in advance of her death—'

'Uncle did *that*?'

She hit the pillar with her palm, sharply. 'He was afraid we would lose everything—'

'*Because he had not got the cross*. It was with me until those brutes stole it. Where did that man, that bravo, take it?'

She came towards him, her face still stern but her voice almost pleading.

'I told Olivero and Ferondo he had taken it to France, to give him time. I believe he is a good man and means to fulfil Bernabo's dying wish.'

'An assassin take a jewel like that to a shrine – when he can get good money for it anywhere? Especially if it's known it contains La Feconda.' Gian was striding to and fro. 'We must get it back. And I know where he'll have taken it. Rocca! The Duchess is talking of a pilgrimage to Scheggia soon and the Duke has sent offerings to Rome for prayers for a son. That's where he'll go. I'll catch him. And once I've got the cross I'll attend to those devils my cousins.' He came to clasp his aunt's hands, locked together unyieldingly at her waist. 'Never fear. Uncle shall be avenged, Father shall be avenged.' He kissed the cold cheek. 'It was clever of you to send them astray. Next time they are here it will be for their funeral, I promise.'

She drew back from him. 'Promise me *nothing*. I have had time and reason to think, this morning. Those bodies in the tomb ... What pleasure would it be to me to see the bodies of my brother's sons? Take care that it is not your own funeral that comes next – this Sigismondo is a man to be respected; not a fool, however dangerous, like your cousins. Why don't you heed me? What need do you have for La Feconda, you with a young wife, a baby son—'

'Who is dead. That is what I returned to, from my travels. My father murdered, my son dead of a fever only days before I arrived.' Gian picked up the hat he had cast down and crammed it on his head. Its scarlet plume seemed as if it, too, had flushed with rage. 'I must have La Feconda whatever lies in my way.'

Whatever obstacles he had imagined, he had certainly not known how close two of them were. Olivero and Ferondo, unluckily for Gian, judged others as people do: by themselves. They would have lied, therefore their aunt lied. They wanted the cross, naturally she wanted it too. It was clear, as Olivero explained to Ferondo, that Sigismondo had come to drive a bargain with Donna Irina once he had realized what he could make out of the situation. Finding she could not pay anything worth his while, he had taken the cross all the same and left, so she said, for France.

Here Ferondo narrowed his eyes and interrupted.

'Wouldn't *he* have lied?'

Olivero drank again from the flask he carried at his saddlebow. They were sitting their horses in the shade of a little copse just off the main road out of the town. This was as near as they had got to France.

'Why would he bother? A man like Sigismondo? No, he'd tell her where he was going, he wouldn't care if she did send after him.'

'You think she'll send Gian.'

Olivero stoppered the flask, then hit Ferondo's arm with it and pointed.

A man, head bent to his horse's neck, rode furiously out

of the town, a storm of dust behind him. Even with his face half-hidden, they knew him. Olivero, grinning, urged his own horse forward.

'She'll have told *him* the truth. We'll let cousin Gian show us the way to the cross.'

Chapter 10

'You Need Anyone Dead?'

It was Benno who saw him first. He had thought for some minutes there was a familiar timbre in the voice, light yet clear, the slight foreign accent, singing a ballad – a mixture of sentiment and bawdy that hit the audience where it lived. The inn was crowded. A crossroads town, however small, has plenty of travellers. The innkeeper did not provide entertainment but he welcomed singers and jugglers who could help keep the customers drinking. The ballad singer could count on a free meal that day.

Benno had not seen the singer until now because Sigismondo's shoulders blocked his view; his master, hunched over his wine, was saying nothing, seemed not to hear the song, seemed in fact to be in another world where Benno hesitated to disturb him. Yet when the song ended and the group round the singer broke up, clapping, stamping, calling for wine for him and more for themselves, and Benno caught a glimpse of the singer, he had no option. He leant forward and pressed Sigismondo's arm, nodding beyond him.

'Look who it is.'

He knew better, by now, than to name the singer aloud. The young man Sigismondo was turning to look at probably travelled, as Sigismondo often did, under a selection of aliases, but the one Benno knew was most

48

appropriate to his face; perhaps not to his character. Now, as he took off his cap of rubbed blue velvet, and wandered from group to group holding it out for coins, the long golden hair shone in the torchlight, and only the crooked teeth in his smile could preclude the belief that Gabriel was come, with a ballad instead of one of the more conventional messages from on high.

When he reached Sigismondo his expression did not alter. No one looking at him, thought Benno, could have supposed them acquainted, from a murderous first meeting to appreciative collaboration – for cash, as, in spite of his resemblance to a visitor from Heaven, Angelo was strictly practical. Benno hoped he was of a mind to throw in his lot with them for a while: his master, whether he admitted it or not, needed help.

'Thank you, kind sir.' Angelo favoured them with the teeth. He picked out of his hat a meagre coin Benno was sure was not Sigismondo's contribution, and examined it with his head on one side. He said loudly, 'If this is the best you can do, you owe me a drink.' He sank down beside Sigismondo, who made room and called for more wine. 'You've far to go, sir? Saving your money for the whores when you get there?'

After the general laugh this produced, Angelo dropped his voice and said conversationally, 'So what's new? You need anyone dead?'

Sigismondo hummed in appreciation. 'Every life can be improved by the deaths of an enemy or two.' A flagon and a cup were handed over his shoulder by the server and he set them out and poured for Angelo, who watched him attentively.

'You want to tell me about them, or are there too many?' He was busy vanishing the coins from his cap to various places on his person. Benno did not fancy anyone's chance of finding them unless with full permission of the management.

Sigismondo was wiping the back of his neck, and his head, and his face, with his shirt sleeve; true, it was a hot night but Sigismondo did not as a rule run with sweat and Benno was afraid. He had seen Sigismondo's hand shake as he poured the wine and he rather thought Angelo had too.

'Too many for comfort, Angelo – as things are.'

Shouts rose at the gateway, with the wild whinnying of a horse and the sound of blows and yells of protest. Sigismondo listened intently and, as the innkeeper pushed past and descended the few steps from terrace to courtyard, he took Angelo's empty cap and covered his own bare head with it. 'And I believe there are two, just arrived.'

Angelo stood up, joined those seeking further entertainment at the edge of the terrace, leant on someone's shoulder and cheered the fight below. It seemed that a patron objected to a newcomer's flinging an ostler across his table, and had taken the matter up with the flinger. The innkeeper, the potential loss of a pair of customers on his mind, was trying to mediate, but the ostler-hurler only broke off to kick the ostler round the courtyard, scattering drinkers from their benches and making the horses at the gate stamp and rear. Several dogs joined the uproar very heartily.

Sigismondo was on his feet, Benno had caught up Biondello from the floor where he was trawling for leftovers and had stuffed him inside his jerkin, by the time Angelo returned. Sigismondo bent to murmur in Angelo's ear. Angelo nodded, and took back his cap with another coin in it that gleamed more warmly than had any of those before.

There was no further need for the disguise of Angelo's cap as Sigismondo, picking up his doublet, led the way through the kitchen. A large woman with a ladle barred his way, and Sigismondo enfolded her in one arm, humming like a delighted bee, and kissed her, earning a blow on the arm with the ladle, a simper, and free passage. Benno felt Biondello struggle in excitement as they went by a hot side of meat being hacked by a kitchen boy, and he hurried after Sigismondo to prevent the little dog erupting in quest of a share. Sigismondo was putting on his doublet as he went to the stables. A coin to the ostler in the rich-smelling dark, while he complained at doing the work of two, and they were leading their horses out of the back way, past a wagon loading empty casks of wine.

'That was the Panteras, wasn't it?' Benno was securing the saddlepacks. 'How'd they find out about you?'

'We don't know that they have. If they were looking to catch me unaware they wouldn't risk a brawl to draw all eyes.' Sigismondo was silent for a little, muffling himself in his cloak though there was scarcely a breeze. 'We must hurry. Angelo will hold them up for a bit.'

They led the horses down a narrow alley and through a little square where children were playing cloth-stone-knife and so threaded their way on to a road out of town, and there they mounted. As they rode off, Benno tried to suppress his anxiety. It was not like his master to avoid trouble. Surely he could take on even that dangerous pair of brothers? It must be to protect the cross that he was going to these pains. Yet Benno could not help wishing that Angelo, who could be trusted to hold up Olivero and Ferondo – if necessary, he thought, at the end of a rope – were travelling with them. Glancing sideways he could see Sigismondo's profile, the hawk nose, the full mouth, whose lips were now tightened and Benno knew why.

The fever was on Sigismondo again and whatever they did would be done at a disadvantage.

Chapter 11

A Lodging for the Night

The messenger with the letter was admitted no further than the secretary. Proper acknowledgement was made, perfunctory courtesies were exchanged, the messenger was led away to be offered some of the excellent Abbey wine. The letter was taken on a journey into the heart of the Abbey until it reached its destination.

Abbot Bonifaccio was a man of great presence. Even the innocent faltered before him; no one who knocked on the door of his private study and heard that harsh voice bid them enter could possibly obey without a moment's hesitation, no matter that he was familiar to them. His secretary, bearing the letter, crossed himself quickly before going in.

'From the Duke, my lord.'

The words were unnecessary; a dangling red seal with the arms of Rocca told the news. The Abbot took the letter in silence, broke the seal with the silver knife the secretary handed him and unfolded the smooth, crackling vellum. He scanned it without expression and then, suddenly, violently, threw it from him into a corner of the room. The secretary started but made no effort to retrieve it; he had held his post for some time and he knew the Abbot.

'*No right*. The Duke tells me I have *no right*. No right in my own lands? The Duke questions *my actions*? Does

53

he set himself against Holy Mother Church?'

These questions were certainly not meant to be answered. Even soothing noises might be dangerous. The secretary stood with head bowed and hands clasped beneath his scapular, only sliding his eyes sideways to judge when it might be imperative to speak.

The Abbot rose, an operation frightening in itself. Seated, he majestically overflowed the high-backed chair with his white robes; as he paced about the room it could be seen that the robes were not responsible for the overflow. The Abbot was a massive man and one whose bulk imparted very little confidence in his austerity of life. What Abbot Bonifaccio had really mastered was austerity of discipline – of others. His secretary uttered no word until the Abbot stopped pacing and wheeled to face him.

'Well? What would *you* do in my place?'

The question had peculiar poignancy. The secretary was a man of burning ambition and he longed for the kind of authority the Abbot had. With the Abbot's eye upon him, however, he inclined his head yet further and spoke meekly.

'Surely, my lord, there is no need to do anything. You have his Grace's goods secure in your warehouses. He needs those goods if his trade is not to suffer. He especially needs those luxuries he is importing for the coming celebrations and in the end he will pay the increased dues and then you will have your precedent. Next time you will charge the same and cite his payment as proof that he accepted the new rate.'

'My son.' The Abbot dropped a heavy hand on the young man's shoulder and very briefly smiled. 'You will go far. We think alike.' He returned to his chair and made it creak at his weight. Nodding at the roll of vellum in the corner he added, 'He refuses to pay, yet he asks my prayers. Does he think me a fool?'

No one who knew the Abbot was likely to make that mistake but, to the secretary's mind, the mischief lay in that the Duke was no fool either. He was refusing the Abbot's increased charges and yet asking favours. Formal favours they might be, but had the Duke some card up his sleeve; was Cardinal Pontano of Rocca perhaps closer to the Pope since his last visit to Rome? Was the Cardinal with the Duke in this matter of the dues?

A tap at the door interrupted the secretary's reverie and the Abbot's indignation. Before permission to enter could be given, a monk had slipped in, discreetly as a shadow, his voice a breath to match.

'Your pardon, my lord, but you asked to be informed. Brother Ieronimo has had another vision.'

Benno found Pietra stimulating. So much was going on that it almost distracted him from his worry about his master. It was somehow comforting to be back in his own state of Rocca, where he had been born and where he had lived all his life until he met Sigismondo. Most people spoke with an accent he knew, since Pietra was only a score of miles from the city of Rocca itself. Of course, in a port like this, you heard all manner of foreign speech; he wondered whether his fondness for travel had come from perhaps having a sailor for a father. He would never know, his mother having lost no time in abandoning him on the steps of a church whence he had started his career by rolling all the way down into the nearest gutter. At the moment, after that drenching in the storm a few nights ago and a stumble in Pietra mud, he looked as if he had not ever got out of it. His master, wrapped in his black cloak even in the noonday sun, and with a hat like a dead bird concealing his head, seemed for his part worthy of such a servant.

Also their luck was out, as if Fate were treating them according to face value. No boat was going to Scheggia that day; no boat was likely to go for quite a few more. It did not seem to help that Sigismondo showed a coin that belied his appearance – that you might think would make any sailor grab the nearest oar and set out at once. The sea captain in the rowdy little quayside tavern was quite firm: God, not gold, was in charge of the weather. Other pilgrims had offered as much but no boat could reach Scheggia against the onshore wind that had been blowing steadily for days. The Virgin of Scheggia was taking a rest – she didn't want to be bothered for a bit. Let them go to the Abbey and pray to her to give a right wind, and then come back and ask about a boat.

As they emerged on to the quay, with the scream of gulls overhead and the loud slap of water against the stones, Benno looked up at the great walls of the Abbey dominating the town, solid, unlike the expanse of dancy water. The last abbey he had seen was in Borgo, where the Abbot was a friend to Sigismondo. If the Abbot of Pietra could be got to add his prayers to theirs, they would surely soon get to Scheggia. Sigismondo, though, showed no signs of seeking the Abbot's help. Instead, he seemed to be brooding as they walked back through the narrow, crowded streets. Perhaps he was wondering, Benno thought, how long it would be before Olivero and Ferondo managed to free themselves from whatever trap Angelo had set for them. It was really a shame Sigismondo was not more ruthless. Benno knew Angelo, and was sure that the addition of another coin like the first he'd been given would have had the Pantera brothers stopped for ever in this world, even if the Devil with his pitchfork kept them moving in the next.

Then there was another Pantera called Gian, who was expected back from foreign parts any day, said Sigismondo, and who might contribute his bit of trouble. The brothers might be tracking Sigismondo or they might not, but they were too close for comfort while Sigismondo had to hang about in Pietra. Sooner or later people would come to look for him and for the cross he was carrying. Benno knew where it was, not round Sigismondo's neck where someone might expect it if they were looking, but bound low on his stomach where only a person intimately interested in him could find it. Benno reckoned that his master, still somewhat in the grip of fever, was not likely to give himself into the hands of any such.

In this, as it turned out, he was wrong.

They were strolling through the market, Biondello at their heels and Benno much distracted by the wares set out: a row of brown shiny pies, fruit in polished piles, the scent of red and gold apples, little yellow melons, downy peaches. Sigismondo stopped so abruptly Benno almost cannoned into him. At first alarmed, and peering about to see if any nasty Pantera faces were on view, Benno saw no one looking their way, and Sigismondo had only picked up an apple and was sniffing it, under the idle regard of the stallholder.

'D'you see the woman buying silks?'

Benno gaped absently round. A shop on the ground floor of a house opposite was a draper's, and a woman, her maid at her elbow, examined lengths of a rich red brocade being shown to her. Benno glimpsed her profile against a length of deep purple velvet hanging from a rod over the counter open to the street. She had suspiciously bright golden hair plaited with ribbons under her cap of lilac gauze, long lashes, a tip-tilted nose, a rosy mouth and a curved chin which would one day have a spare to take over. Though she frowned over the brocade it was a face more used to laughter, and not devoid of intelligence.

'Mmm, Benno, we have our lodging for tonight.'

Chapter 12

Two Visions

Benno transferred his vacant gaze to his master's face, but Sigismondo was biting into the apple and putting a coin down on the stall. He handed another apple to Benno and slowly crossed the square. The black, crumpled hat gave him a different air Benno found disconcerting.

The woman bought the brocade, had it measured off and began her leisurely progress home; if she knew she was being followed she certainly did not show it. It was her maid who seemed conscious of the possibility, turning more than once to simper at Sigismondo over the roll of brocade she was carrying; that, Benno thought, was because she fancied him. She had a large slab of a face and it was very much to be doubted that she would often be fancied back. It did not cross Benno's mind that she might have recognized his master, because he was as yet working on the theory that Sigismondo intended to buy the privacy of a night with a high-class courtesan instead of risking further notice in a tavern possibly swarming with Panteras. It did not for a moment occur to him that they were following a perfectly respectable woman to her husband's home.

He began to have doubts as they came into a gloomy part of town among houses whose barred lower windows gave them a prison air. No prettily painted girls leant on balconies to catch the eyes of passers-by; there were not even any passers-by when the maid stopped, produced a key worthy of a jailer, and unlocked one of the more forbidding doors in the narrow street. Her mistress went in without looking back but the maid, turning, said abruptly, 'What are you loitering about for, rascal?'

Benno was startled. Used to being addressed like that himself, he found this was being said to his master and endorsed by a push at Sigismondo's chest.

'Get along with you round to the back – I've some work if that's what you're after.' The simpers were no more. They hadn't really suited the large plain face, better matched to this severity. 'You too, you rogue.' The push, ineffective on Sigismondo's chest, was administered again and now encountered the living resistance of Biondello snug inside Benno's jerkin and provoked him into one of his rare barks. The maid gave a corresponding yelp, backed into the house and shut the door, leaving them to find the back door down a side street just wide enough for a wagon.

A wagon in fact was already there. Two men had just finished lowering barrels of wine into the cellar. As Sigismondo and Benno arrived at the back door, the wooden leaves of the cellar door on the ground were being fastened and a manservant waved off Sigismondo on the step.

'You're too late. If you want work you'll have to turn up when there's work to be done, and not when it's all . . .'

Suddenly the oblong slab of the maid's face appeared over the man's shoulder. She twitched him aside. 'That'll do. You know nothing about it; in with you, rogue, wasting time on the doorstep.'

She wasted none. She took Sigismondo by the arm and drew him into the huge kitchen and its stone-flagged cool. A girl with her hand inside a plucked chicken, her apron all feathers, turned to stare as Benno ran after his master whom the maid was ushering at a great rate into the dimness beyond the kitchen. A flight of worn marble steps led them to the *piano nobile* and the door of another room, opened by the maid to Sigismondo and immediately barred to Benno. She stood, arms folded, and looked him over with mounting disapproval.

'You weren't with him before. You could do with a wash. Or two. Is that a dog you have in there? Both of you skipping with fleas, I'll be bound.' She came closer. 'Let's have a look at him.'

Biondello, as if he perfectly understood the requirement, poked his head out and put it on one side to regard her.

'Oh-oh . . . Whatever became of his ear?' Her face was melted granite. She put out a cautious finger and Biondello licked it. 'Ah, he's hungry, poor little fellow. Let's be having him.'

Biondello had been a cause of lasting anxiety to Benno ever since his abduction by a court lady, but there was as little choice now as then. Plucked from Benno's bosom, he was carried off, the maid's cheek pressed to his wool, endearments flowing. From halfway down the stairs she called, 'Don't *you* want anything to eat, then?'

She had a room of her own, a large cupboard into which they all crammed, and to which she fetched a great bowl of broth. Benno was allowed first go at this before Biondello, with some bread still warm from the oven to dip into it. The maid told him her name was Perpetua; she watched them both eating with a maternal expression, arms once more folded.

'That's right. Eat up. Your master will be getting a meal soon and then I'll bring you a bite more.' She patted Biondello, who revolved his tail as he cleaned the inside of the bowl one more time. 'Lucky your master has come to Pietra on a day *my* master's still away, or there'd be murder done and no mistake. When my lady first met your master – oh, years ago – her husband was overseas and that was a lot safer. More bread?'

Benno accepted the bread and, as he chewed, wondered how far off the master of the house was at this moment, and hoped Sigismondo really had chosen the safest of refuges.

'And now, my son, tell me slowly, and in your own words, what you have seen this time.'

Even under the scrutinizing gaze of Abbot Bonifaccio, which most of the brothers went to great lengths to avoid, Brother Ieronimo showed neither fear nor hesitation. He stood, tall, slightly stooped, with his head held as if listening to something only he could hear, and smiling slightly as if the message was a cheerful one.

'Oh, they'll be my words, my lord. I haven't got any others but the Offices and psalms. You see, she didn't speak to me this time.'

The Abbot pressed his fingertips on the edge of the table until the nails turned white. It was necessary not to hurry this ramshackle old dunderhead; one must try to remember how God often chose the strangest instruments for the exposition of His will. Brother Ieronimo was at least a servant of the Abbey and under the Abbot's nominal control.

'Our Lady appeared to you again, my son, and yet she said nothing?' What in the name of the saints made the mooncalf beam, as if this were an especial favour? 'In what form did she appear?'

'Oh just like herself,' Brother Ieronimo hastened to assure him, his smile broadening happily. 'In blue, with a white veil over her hair like the picture in the chapel.

With her hands out, like this.' He spread large and bony hands towards the Abbot, and took up a rapt pose, inclining his head and freezing his smile.

'Her hands out? She was giving something? Did you see what it was?'

Brother Ieronimo stopped being the Virgin and thought, hands now hanging at his sides. 'No. Nothing. Couldn't she have been asking for something?'

The Abbot frowned. It was for him to interpret. A vision might well be vouchsafed to one as simple as Brother Ieronimo, but the business of interpretation must belong to the intelligent mind.

'Very well, my son. Speak to no one of this. And pray that Our Lady continue her favours to you. You may go.'

Brother Ieronimo made his obeisance. At the door he turned back with that idiotic smile again lighting up his face. 'I forgot, my lord. She was coming over the sea. Waves moving under her feet. There was thunder too, I think.' His smile, incredibly, became even wider, and he was gone, shutting the door more quietly than seemed possible to such awkward hands.

He left the Abbot frowning. The Virgin coming over the sea? Clearly from Scheggia and the shrine there. What did the Virgin of Scheggia intend to give to the Abbey? There was plenty needed, certainly, after the terrible harvest for which even the raised dues on Ducal imports would hardly compensate; supposing the Duke consented to pay them. It was clear that the Virgin was aware of their troubles and that they could count on her help, whatever shape it might take. At this moment it came to him that moving her shrine from Scheggia to the Abbey would be a brilliant stroke. This he must consider.

A bell rang, clear and sonorous, in the Abbey chapel,

and the Abbot heaved himself to his feet and went to the wall shrine by the window, crossed himself before the image and began a prayer. The future would not find him unprepared.

Chapter 13

'Fell – As If He'd Been Axed'

In another part of the city and later in the night, it was the past that concerned Donna Felicia and Sigismondo as they drank their wine in her room. Rain was slashing the balustrade of the loggia and flooding its marble floor, but they sat within the lamplit room and, discussing the past, celebrated the present. Donna Felicia's golden hair, perhaps more golden than when Sigismondo had last seen it, lay unbraided on her shoulders, and he put out a hand to caress it while she smiled and poured more wine.

'You're in Pietra for long?'

'Until the weather changes.'

She glanced at the window just as lightning whitened all the rain. 'If it does! What winds and rain we've been having. The Abbey harvests are ruined, the Abbot says.'

'Do you know the Abbot?'

She shrugged opulent white shoulders. 'I presented the Abbey with an embroidered altar frontal and he admired it and sent for me to commission a hanging for his room . . . and I could have pleased him in more ways than that if I'd chosen, as he let me see; and I knew his reputation, of course.'

Sigismondo waited for the thunder to rumble into the distance before he said, 'I'm not the one to blame him. Did you plead your husband and your honour?'

'I told him the truth: that Agostino is madly jealous

and would stop at nothing if he thought I'd put horns on his head; that he would very likely kill me and find a way to kill him . . .'

'Madam! Madam!' Perpetua, horribly agitated, burst into the room to the accompaniment of a loud crack of thunder. 'The master! He's below changing his wet clothes—'

Sigismondo had sprung up. Donna Felicia pushed his cloak into his arms and his winecup into Perpetua's ready hand. 'Get him out by the back way. Quick!'

Rain swept across the loggia in a fresh gust as Perpetua thrust Sigismondo before her across an anteroom and down the spiral staircase past the garde-robe. He was putting his cloak round him and pulled up the hood as he crossed the kitchen, and a gust of wind blew his hood back and billowed the cloak hugely round him as he stepped out into the storm.

In Perpetua's little store-room, Benno half woke at a crack of thunder, curled himself closer to Biondello, who was nervous of storms, and slept again. His last waking thought was envy of his master, no doubt comforting something whiter and more beautiful than Biondello. He would have been horrified to know that at that very moment Sigismondo was standing in the shelter of an arcade, waiting for him, already drenched to the skin and racked by shivering.

Rain on the roof is one of the most soothing sounds to those who know their roof is in good repair and who do not have to go outdoors. Benno was not bothered by the first nor aware of any necessity for the second. Well fed and warm, cuddling Biondello, he slept on until, shortly after first light, Perpetua opened the door on him and exclaimed in horror.

'God and His saints! I'd forgotten all about you.'

Benno was astonished to see that her slab-like face was ornamented by a black eye. Without explanation, without breakfast, he was hauled out clutching Biondello and, to an accompaniment of scolding and prayer, dragged across the kitchen and hurled into the street, where he sprawled into an old woman carrying a rushbasket of apples which fountained in all directions. Benno, and an urchin who had been squatting in the gutter, picked them up. Benno gave what he retrieved to the old woman, who clouted him but accepted the small coin he offered.

By this time he felt battered as well as apprehensive. From Perpetua he had managed to understand that her master had returned the night before. He whistled up Biondello and went to look for Sigismondo in a town still gleaming wet from the storm.

Small though Pietra was as a town, perhaps half the size of the capital, Rocca, it was well supplied with narrow streets and alleys. Benno had not Sigismondo's sense of direction. Sigismondo would expect him to come, by their standing arrangement, to the main marketplace, where it was easy to stroll about without being conspicuous. He could see the Abbey tower over the roofs and he made for it, thinking he remembered that it overlooked the market square. In fact, when he finally wound his way there he discovered that it overlooked a high-class square with a fountain where women drew water and chatted. A more distant noise and bustle led him to the marketplace further down the hill. He was held up by ox-carts laboriously creaking and impassable in the streets.

Sigismondo was not in the market square. Benno searched as unobtrusively as he could but with mounting panic. Had the Panteras got to him? Then remembering Perpetua's black eye, Benno had a vision of Sigismondo surprised and set upon by a raging husband, being thrown into the street as he had been himself, and then attacked by raging Panteras. He had to tell himself that, even if Sigismondo, from compassion towards Donna Felicia, forbore to kill her husband, he was a match for any Pantera, however savage; nor could it really be supposed that Olivero and Ferondo would be patrolling the streets of Pietra by night. Benno had the happy thought that Sigismondo might have been smuggled out of the house in time to find lodging in a tavern. He would be paying the reckoning now and would shortly arrive in the marketplace looking for Benno and breakfast. Reassured a little, Benno found another small coin and bought a handful of roast chestnuts, and a piece of sausage to share with Biondello.

He sat down on a stone ledge, now dry and warm from the morning sun, and listened to stallholders talking as they set out their wares.

'Fell – as if he'd been axed.'

'I thought someone'd put an arrow through him. Big man, too. Take something to knock him over. Couldn't speak when they got to him – making no sense and burning like fire.'

'Lucky those brothers were passing. It took both of them to get him away . . .'

'He looked unconscious by then.'

Brothers, Benno thought, rigid.

'He'll be well looked after. The Abbey infirmary's a good place. There's none so clever as the brothers. I thought he was one of them at first, all in black and with a shaved head . . .'

Benno had dropped all the chestnuts, and sat with open mouth. Biondello first ate a couple of them and then, looking up at his master, paused, and barked sharply.

Chapter 14

'Justice, Your Grace!'

The Duke of Rocca was not a patient man. Incapable of suffering fools gladly, he was not so good with the intelligent either. That the young man at his feet looked far from witless was therefore no recommendation.

The Duke had only just returned from the hunt. He was tired and he was thirsty. Before he heard anyone's petition he wanted to be washed and to relax with a cup of wine. His chamberlain, well aware of this, was attempting to get the young man off his knees and was being energetically resisted.

'Justice, your Grace! Justice in the name of all the saints!'

The face was not only intelligent. It was attractive, with thick-lashed dark eyes and strong chin; the young man's clothes were of quality, the brown velvet not rubbed, the shirt of fine linen embroidered at the neck. Perhaps an interesting story lay behind his plea, and Duke Ludovico had curiosity as well as impatience. He held up a finger and the chamberlain let go of the young man's shoulders.

'Your name?' The question, in the Duke's harsh voice, did not encourage.

'Gian Pantera, your Grace. From Montesacro.'

'Montesacro? Why are you here demanding my justice? Go to your own Duke.'

'It's a matter concerning your Grace and your Grace's honour. I beg you to hear me in private.'

A Duke's honour is by its nature a very public commodity; any slur on it had better be heard by the least possible number of ears. A gesture from Ludovico, and the courtiers who had hunted with him withdrew, the chamberlain shut the great doors and stood by them, and only the guards with their pikes, and the Duke's own notorious speed with a dagger, were left to protect him against the stranger, in case murder were contemplated.

Murder was on his mind, but not the murder of the Duke. It appeared, as he expounded – still on one knee on the anteroom's flagstones – that a quantity of his relatives were dead. Ludovico collected a gold winecup from a waiting page and roved across to sit on the brocade cushions of a window seat. Now that he had consented to listen to the story, he would hear it out. He drank, still regarding the young man with disconcertingly blue eyes. He broke through the account to ask a pertinent question.

'This is about a feud. We have more than a sufficiency of those in Rocca. What do you ask of me?'

'I came to warn your Grace against a man called Sigismondo.'

The blue eyes abruptly narrowed.

'*Sigismondo*? Has he another name?'

'I have not heard of one, nor have I seen him. I'm told he is tall and well built and has a head shaved all over, just like some wrestler.'

'I know this man. He has done me some service in the past. What's your complaint of him, and why do you warn me rather than any other?'

Gian, watched disapprovingly by the chamberlain, rose and ventured nearer to make his point with some intensity. 'He may seek to sell you a thing he has stolen, a thing for which he killed my uncle.' Gian had wanted to present his narrative more dramatically, but he was discomposed by the force of the Duke's regard. Moreover, the Duke was now frowning.

'Sigismondo has *stolen* something to sell to me?' The Duke did not add that Sigismondo had received from him only a few years ago a gold chain of such massive splendour that it would have taken exceptional and applied dissipation for its owner to need more funds yet than its sale would provide. 'What is this thing?'

'A cross, the property of our family; a cross of great value and possessed of holy powers.'

'Holy powers.' Characteristically, the Duke seized on the important point. '*What* holy powers, and why should Sigismondo suppose I am in need of them?'

For the first time, Gian hesitated. How, exactly, does one intimate to a Duke that he needs holy intervention in order to get children? True, he had an heir by his former wife, but the boy had been ill; and even outside Rocca the world knew that Ludovico's present Duchess had not yet presented him with any infant, boy or girl, despite offerings to various shrines. There were even rumours that it was Divine punishment on the Duke for the murder of his former wife. True, another had borne the blame at the time, but who knew? Not surprisingly, the punishment of dukes was considered best left to God.

Inspiration came. 'Your Grace, the holy powers reside in a jewel in the centre of the cross. It is called La Feconda, bringer of fertility.'

The Duke's eyes showed that he understood. He flung himself back against the stone embrasure and stared. To Gian's amazement he began to smile. 'So. That is your story. This Sigismondo, a man to whom I would trust my life, who has saved my duchy for me, who snatched my beloved daughter from death and disgrace, takes it upon himself to murder – murder, you said? – your uncle, was it? – in order to steal property of yours which is in itself a sacred object, so that he may come and screw a price out of me for a chance to get a son?'

He leant forward so suddenly that Gian flinched. The smile was a snarl. 'I tell you that if Sigismondo had come by that cross and thought I needed it he would *give* it to me. What have you to say to that?'

Gian swallowed. He had heard that Ludovico of Rocca was one on whose justice men could rely in a world full of corrupt and wicked rulers. No one had thought to tell him that this justice was no mild affair, that the Duke might see himself obliged to be even-handed also to one's enemies. Gian had been quite sure that his story would carry conviction, that the passion he felt would impress the Duke with his truth, that the creature Sigismondo would be found and forced to return the cross. Now a horrible suspicion had come to him. What if the Duke had been pretending ignorance and had known the story all along? What if he had heard of La Feconda? If this murderer and thief Sigismondo were so high in the Duke's favour, what more likely than that he had been commissioned from the beginning and that the Duke had been amusing himself all this time ... Suddenly Rocca had begun to feel not a safe place to Gian.

Chapter 15

A Spy

'It is to be feared the man is a thief.'

They had got him, with some difficulty because he was neither light nor slender, into one of the coffin-shaped beds in the infirmary and, well acquainted with fever, they had sponged his face and chest with water and tried to get him to drink a bitter concoction Brother Infirmarian kept made up for such patients. He tossed and turned too much for them, however, and when they had him held down and trickled physic into his mouth, as they had been taught, they discovered fever had not sufficiently weakened him for their purpose. He struck Brother Marco's hand aside, splattering his habit with the drink, and abruptly uttered what, to their amazed ears, sounded like excellent Latin – '*Abstineas manum!*' A moment later, he had returned to gibberish. Brother Marco, not one of the more learned monks, did not recognize Greek.

It was the violent movement accompanying the gibberish that startled them. It had also torn away the shirt to which they had stripped him, showing a linen bandage round his body. Expecting a wound, they undid this, and stared.

A cross of exquisite workmanship, set with rubies and diamonds that glittered as the man breathed ... They might not be experts but they knew something of great value when they saw it.

'He cannot have come by such a thing honestly.'

'Brother, we may be doing him a wrong. We shall have to question him before we draw conclusions.'

The difficulties inherent in questioning a man talking gibberish silenced them both.

'If the cross were his, surely he would wear it round his neck.'

Brother Marco shook his head. 'He, too, may fear thieves. If such a thing were seen it might provoke attack.'

'Who would attack a man who looks so well able to take care of himself? Don't forget, he had a sword and a hand-axe with him. No, brother, the man is a thief. We must take the cross to Father Abbot.'

That almost stopped them. Neither of them had any wish to approach the Abbot. As they hesitated, another shadow fell across the man tossing on the bed.

'What is taking you so long? Is the man a leper?'

Brother Infirmarian, perhaps as a result of several years of reliance on a keen sense of smell and touch for diagnosis, was a little short-sighted. He bent over to stare until his nose nearly touched the cross, and then drew back with a speed that suggested the thing were red hot.

'The Abbot must know. This cross is worth a fortune.'

The Abbot was in conference with the Abbey treasurer and his own secretary when Brother Infirmarian asked permission to speak to him on a matter of urgency. Nothing at that moment seemed urgent to the Abbot compared with the wretched state of the Abbey finances, laid out before him with explanatory figures and facts by Brother Filippo. He was therefore about to say that the Infirmarian must wait, when he remembered the possibility of very bad news indeed.

The plague had kept its distance for the last few years, nowhere near Pietra, but a port is always vulnerable. In the Abbey chronicles, an entry dated a century ago recounted how a boat had put into Pietra with a corpse at each oar, before people realized that Death himself had rowed in. After that entry in the chronicle came a long gap. The monk who wrote it had died. Most of the monks had died. The Abbot of that day had died. A third of the city's inhabitants had died and been shovelled into the plague pit, lucky if there was a priest able to say the last prayers.

'Let the Infirmarian enter.'

'Your pardon, my lord. I knew you were occupied, but it seemed to me that you should see this.'

The Infirmarian knew how to make an effect. Extending an arm over the Abbot's table, he allowed the cross to slide from the darkness of his sleeve on to the polished chestnut surface like a star fallen from the night sky. There it lay, glittering quietly, almost mesmerizing the men who stared at it. The Abbot broke the rapt silence.

'What is this? Is it a gift to the Abbey?'

The thick voice had lost its harshness. Almost it was reverent. People had given such gifts, had left their goods, chests full of coin, in the desire for spiritual benefit. This cross could certainly buy a lifetime of Masses.

'It was concealed on a patient brought in with a fever. I fear,' said the Infirmarian, 'that he had stolen it.'

The Abbot's soft white fingers caressed the cross, lifted it, turned it to catch the light, sending rainbow sparks across the ceiling and waking the fire in the heart of the huge ruby in the centre.

'What workmanship . . . Did you question the man?'

'My lord, his words made no sense. The fever – he may be foreign.'

The Abbot let the cross fall to the table. Secretary and treasurer exchanged a glance over his head.

75

'Fever? Is he from a ship?'

'My lord, there were no pustules, no darkening of the skin, no rash. We necessarily searched him – hence we found this. I am inclined to think he has a marsh fever, a tertian fever. The man is strong and in the prime of life. I believe he is in the second or possibly the third day of this attack and he will throw off the effects soon when he has taken the draught I have ordered for him. A mixture in preparation of *achillea millefolium*, *trigonella foenum graecum* of course, perhaps *agrimonia eupatoria*, ruled by Jupiter, when he . . .'

'Bring him to me.'

Startled, the Infirmarian looked at the Abbot without comprehension. 'He's sick, my lord. In bed and, when I left him, in delirium. He cannot be moved.'

The Abbot clasped his hands benignly across his stomach and directed a look under his eyebrows at the Infirmarian.

'You have brothers and lay brothers working for you; let him be carried. I must know how he came by this cross. If he is a thief, he shall hang. Why should we have care for his body when it will end on the gallows? It is his soul we should think about.'

The Infirmarian made his obeisance and left the room. Only a fool would make further objection; he was far from being a fool. He did not think the man would die from being moved but the cross disturbed him; there might be good reason for carrying so valuable an object in hiding. Plainly the Abbot coveted the cross and had already decided the man was guilty. The Infirmarian crossed himself: he was acting under obedience and the sin of covetise could not be laid at his own door.

In the Abbot's study, the secretary and the treasurer were being permitted to handle and admire the cross, which the Abbot was already treating as Abbey property well on the way to becoming his own. The treasurer, Brother Filippo, was particularly loud in his praise.

'A piece of exceptional beauty. Surely made for a Prince of the Church. We must make inquiry as to whether any Cardinal has been robbed of it.'

In the silence that followed, the secretary suppressed a smile. Brother Filippo was beginning to qualify his suggestion when a scratch at the door interrupted him. The Abbot growled a command and the door opened, admitting two lay brothers supporting the sick man. There was no problem getting the man to kneel as his legs gave way at the moment the Abbot gestured.

'I know that man!'

It was the secretary, swiftly pointing. His face, as a rule sly but submissive, had gone white and taut. The Abbot, regarding the shaven head bent before him as the lay brothers held the arms, was interested. Was the fellow a renegade priest? Hanging, in that case, was too good for him.

'Who is he?'

'An agent of Duke Ludovico. *A spy.*'

Chapter 16

The Virgin's Gift

A smile spread, terribly, across the Abbot's large features. It is even more proper to hang a spy than a thief. He put a heavy hand over the cross, eclipsing its glitter.

'From whom did you steal this?'

The man raised his head slowly, without speaking. The Abbot, about to repeat the question impatiently and with a threat, paused. This was not the face of a common criminal nor of a man easily intimidated. The dark eyes were steady in their regard although the face was pale. The Abbot was particularly aware of the contained power there; these were not the features of a man who could easily be made to talk if he did not choose to, and the Abbey possessed neither dungeons nor torturers. Diplomacy might be quicker. The Abbot had summoned up a quite benevolent smile, when the man spoke.

'I am taking the cross, Father Abbot, to its rightful owner, at the request of a dying man.'

The fellow had at least recovered the power of speech, though in an accent faintly foreign. What he said, however, was specious entirely.

'This . . . dying man. He had stolen the cross, then?'

The regard of the dark eyes was unwavering. 'The cross did not belong to him and had already been stolen.'

'I want no riddles, man. I am not to be played with.'

Everyone in the room heard the threat in the deliberate

voice, but the kneeling man did not appear affected by it.

'My lord, I tell the truth.' He swayed and the attendant brothers increased their grip under his arms.

The Abbot picked up the cross and presented it towards the man, as if exorcising evil. 'By this holy symbol of Our Lord's suffering, I conjure you to tell me who is its rightful owner.'

The man bent his head in respect.

'My lord, I will. The rightful owner is the Virgin of Scheggia.'

The Abbot's lips opened involuntarily, but no words came. Of all answers, he had not expected the one he got. If the cross were intended for the Virgin of Scheggia, to confiscate it would be as heinous as to rob a pilgrim. How unlucky, too, that all those in the room, including the lay brothers, had heard this preposterous claim. Still, sarcasm was always a good weapon.

'The Virgin of – Scheggia?' The Abbot smiled a little. 'Did the Virgin herself tell you this?'

The man was not to be thrown. 'Our Lady has not so honoured me. It was the dying man of whom I spoke, who with his last breath wished her to have it.'

The Abbot leant forward over the desk, laying his hands either side of the jewel. 'Our Lady has not honoured you, fellow, but the one she has honoured is a brother here. She has told him her wish.'

The dark regard was very nearly disconcerting in its continued steadiness. The Abbot's hands moved together over the cross. 'She has visited a monk of this Abbey.'

Sudden acute attention from Brother Filippo and the lay brothers was evidence that Brother Ieronimo had kept silence as bidden. Brother Filippo at one side was breathing through his mouth. At the other side, his secretary was like a statue. The Abbot put out his hands, palms upwards and cupped, and infused his voice with a practised solemnity.

'The Virgin, in this vision, was approaching across the sea towards her humble servants in this Abbey, holding her hands thus, offering a gift. What gift that might be we did not know, but your words have made it clear. She wishes us to have this cross.'

If he had been an actor in a theatre, they would have applauded. As it was, there came a murmur of reverent gratitude. The only man unimpressed was the provider of the cross, whose face had indefinably hardened. The secretary, who had been watching the man closely since identifying him, now ventured to speak. 'And the thief, my lord? What of him?'

The prisoner's eyes turned to the secretary for the first time, then back to the Abbot, who was ready with his answer. 'Our Lady has brought us the cross, but she gave us no revelation about this fellow. He has sought to impose on us with his tale of the dying man, but we must remember the mercy Our Lord showed upon the penitent thief.' He paused. 'For true penitence there must be suffering. I shall commit him to the hands of the Marshal of Pietra to be flogged; after that the Marshal may decide whether or not the man deserves hanging.'

The soft white hands were making a dismissive gesture. The lay brothers got a more comprehensive grip and hauled Sigismondo to his feet. The secretary was now at the Abbot's side, whispering, and as they got Sigismondo to the door the Abbot spoke again.

'You were agent for Duke Ludovico, I am reminded. There is more to this tale of the cross than you have told. The Marshal has men who will find it out from you before you hang.' Again the bass note of solemnity returned. 'Let the truth purge your soul before you die, my son.'

The door had not closed behind Sigismondo before the Abbot had taken off his pectoral cross of damascened gold and amethyst, and was threading its chain through the loop at the back of the cross of the Virgin of Scheggia. He hung it round his neck. Such a gift must have a worthy resting place.

Chapter 17

Stampede

Benno was received at the monastery's alms-door with more charity than he expected. He had forgotten that monks were used to people who looked a great deal worse than he did. However, although they at once gave him a flat loaf of bread and a cup of rough, watered wine, they were astonished at any idea of his visiting a patient in the infirmary. He made the mistake of saying his master had a fever, and any chance of seeing Sigismondo was gone. Fever patients were kept apart until the fever's cause was determined.

Benno could have kicked himself and, when he persisted in pleading, it was clear that Brother Porter was ready to do the job for him.

'Off with you! Come back in three days. If your master still lives, you might be let see him. Be thankful he's in good hands. Besides, if he dies, he'll be sure of the last rites here.'

Benno was amazingly unconsoled by this. He stuffed a bit of the bread into his bosom, where a convulsive gulping of his jerkin showed that Biondello appreciated the Abbey's charity. Then there was nowhere to go that was better than anywhere else.

He was tormented by thinking that he had let Sigismondo down; that if he had woken when Perpetua got Sigismondo out of the house, if he had been there in

the square when his master collapsed he would have
stopped the monks from carrying Sigismondo away.

But he might have died if they hadn't.

But he might die anyway.

A deep almost instinctive distrust of doctors had been
instilled in Benno somehow. Doctors who were monks were
no different. Besides, his master shut up inside those walls,
unable to communicate with Benno, was as good, or as
bad, as in prison.

Benno, wandering round the Abbey precincts, had no
idea how close he was to the facts. It was by pure chance
that he was dragging his feet along past yet another door
of the great sprawl of buildings, and saw it open to admit
four men in uniform colours, and badges on front and back
of their tunics who, had he known it, were officers of the
Marshal. Benno, weary and aimless, leant on a tree and
waited just to see if they would come out again. He hadn't
long to wait before they did.

Two ducked out of the wicket first and turned to give a
hand to the other two, who were getting a man over the
high threshold.

The man was Sigismondo and his wrists were manacled.

'And I was going to ask you where he was.'

It was a breath in his ear, but Benno knew at once
whom the breath belonged to. Only Angelo could
appear from nowhere like the conjurer he was. Never
was such magic more welcome. Shocked at seeing
his master so pale, and in chains, hauled about by
those men, Benno almost turned to grab Angelo for
reassurance. A steely grip on his arm from behind
prevented him. He remembered his training and gazed
vacantly at the dreadful scene.

'Lucky I came. Let's organize something. Go ahead of
them.'

An idiotic smile of relief was all Benno could organize as he stumbled off. It wasn't difficult to keep ahead of the men, for they were having trouble with their prisoner. He seemed incapable of helping himself and had to be pulled, hauled, and half lifted, half dragged. Benno, turning to see the small crowd that had gathered to see the fun, hoped that Angelo had taken Sigismondo's weakness into account. How to rescue a man who couldn't walk?

Cattle, however, could be made to run. Angelo had disappeared once more, but Benno now caught sight of his slender figure in the cattle market as the escort came through with their prisoner. At the end of the square, heading for a narrow street between blank walls and grilled windows, the escort stopped to send off the idling crowd, and Benno kept ahead along the narrow street. He was not halfway down, and the four men with their prisoner were a dozen paces behind, when two things happened together.

Angelo emerged in front from a narrow side alley and came strolling towards them, and a drumming of hooves and a disturbed lowing sounded from behind. Benno turned. The escort turned.

The street was packed with cattle behind them, gathering speed and thundering forward. One of the guard, probably a countryman, held his ground a moment, brandished his pike and yelled. The first few cows may have faltered but the press behind drove them on. The escort, dragging Sigismondo who looked as if he might fall forward at every step, ran. Angelo ran, Benno ran. Biondello, shaken free, ran too. Angelo ducked into the side alley. Benno and Biondello followed. The escort, seeing this refuge, followed. One of them met Angelo, gasped and fell. Benno, grabbing up a stone from the street, struck another. Angelo kicked one in the groin and Sigismondo, raising his arms, brought his manacled wrists down on the fourth man's neck. Biondello, at a safe distance, was barking himself off his feet.

The cattle were running past the alley down the street. Their smell invaded the alley, their staring eyes looked only ahead.

Angelo was searching the recumbent guards. He came up with a bunch of keys of which the second he tried unlocked Sigismondo. Benno was amazed to see his master upright and steady, circled by Biondello who wagged his rump, pleased at the reunion. Angelo kicked the head of a stirring guard and said, 'Can you run?'

'Not yet. You know this city?'

'Well enough.' Angelo set off up the alley, through a courtyard and into a long archway. Halfway along this, he turned down some steps and pushed open a door into a small dark room smelling of wine and sweaty clothes and full of excited talk that centred on a dice game under the only window. Angelo indicated a bench against the wall, and Sigismondo sat. He leant back, and looked at them both. Only his breathing and his pallor betrayed his recent fever.

'Mmm. I'm in your debt, Angelo; and cattle are expensive. And I've been robbed.'

Benno, meeting his master's eyes, realized with dismay what he meant: the cross as well.

Angelo ordered wine, and came back to sit by Sigismondo. 'I came to Pietra to tell you the Pantera brothers are out of jail. They have no money either. I robbed them.'

'What were they in jail for if you robbed them?' Benno asked.

'A gold cup belonging to another traveller went missing.'

Angelo shrugged. 'Found in their luggage. And they'd no money to bribe anybody into thinking they were honest.'

Sigismondo put down his cup. 'I have something more for you to do.'

Chapter 18

Blood Waits in Rocca

It is not every day that angels visit mankind with messages, so it was not surprising that the maid sweeping the yard at the back of Agostino da Sangallo's house was at first too stunned to take in what was being said to her. She gripped her broom, staring into the glass-grey eyes of the angel until he sharply repeated his demand: to speak to Perpetua. Reluctantly, the maid, still looking at the angel and therefore walking sideways, blundered into the kitchen and into Perpetua herself. A jerk of the head, an awed whisper, and Perpetua was advancing magisterially on the beautiful messenger. His origins did not appear as heavenly to her as they did to the kitchenmaid. Perpetua noted the rubbed velvet of the blue cap so politely taken off as she approached, the crooked teeth in the smile she was offered. She even suspected the gold of the hair — how often had she tried for that shade when tinting her mistress's hair! She folded her hands over her stomach and defied any efforts to charm.

After half a minute of listening to the young man's words, charm was forgotten. The man she had smuggled out into last night's storm was inquiring in some anxiety after her mistress, and her treatment at her husband's hands. Perpetua's own black eye had ripened to sinister aubergine, but she had worse news of poor Donna Felicia. On no account could such a risk be run again. Her mistress had not only a swollen face but a bruised back, and had taken to her bed. She wasn't likely to be allowed out for some time except in her husband's company. God alone knew why the master was so sure his wife had entertained a lover last night. Perpetua had over and over protested that the man he had glimpsed going into the street from the kitchen was a bald brocade-seller come to deliver stuff they had bought earlier. For some reason he was not convinced. Steer clear of the house, keep off altogether until the master goes abroad again.

A few words from the beautiful stranger and Perpetua nodded. Certainly she knew of lodgings where no one would ask awkward questions. Who better than her own cousin in the Via Condotti? He kept a clean house and a shut mouth and they could say she sent them there.

Perpetua came back into the house, to the interested audience of the kitchenmaid and the cook, chuckling to herself and with the purple hues round her eye set off by a flush on the sallow cheeks, where the angel had saluted her in parting. It is possible to succumb to charm even when one sees through it.

Impossible to question Perpetua about what had passed or, indeed, about her curious behaviour in ignoring the drink she had come down to get for Donna Felicia and instead bustling upstairs to return with a bundle under her arm. She went through the yard to the alley at the back and disappeared from view. She returned a moment later, without her bundle, her cheeks burning even more brightly, and she wore a silly smile, which changed to a glare when she met the gaze of kitchenmaid and cook, and she scolded them thoroughly for idleness. Angels cannot bring happiness into everyone's life.

It was not long afterwards that the same angel, now playing the tender and considerate son, escorted his ailing mother to the lodging-house on the Via Condotti. She seemed a large woman to have given birth to so slender a son, and larger still for the broad-brimmed straw hat on the head swathed in linen wimple and kerchief. Perpetua's cousin was as taciturn and obliging as she had promised, very willing to provide a room and a meal for pilgrims waiting for the right weather for a ship for Scheggia. He even gave the scruffy servant a bone for the little one-eared dog. His cousin Perpetua was only too certain to inquire whether he'd done his best by them.

'What are you meaning to do about the cross?'

Benno, watching Biondello fighting a bone that was almost as big as he was, felt grateful again that Angelo had no hesitation in asking Sigismondo the questions he himself would never dare to ask. Sigismondo had taken off the hat, but the face turned to Angelo was curiously transformed by the femininity of the linen around it, that brought out the darkness of the eyes and the curve of the mouth in a way that might deceive anyone accustomed to the strong features of Tuscan matrons. It was the pallor that worried Benno, but he was relieved to hear a return of energy in the voice even though Sigismondo spoke softly.

'I must wait. What can I do? Rob the Abbot as I robbed Olivero and Ferondo? Not at the moment, I think.'

'I could do it.' Angelo was confident, and Sigismondo smiled.

'You could rob a saint of his halo and not even the Devil be the wiser. But I'll not send you to do what I can't. When I have my strength again it will be another matter.'

'You've had these fevers before?'

'Too often. They're like the marsh fevers in Rome but I had them first in Egypt – a few miles from here and over the sea, Benno – and I've not died of them yet. A soaking can bring them on but good wine, like this, restores me in no time.'

He had his scrip unrolled and was choosing herbs to put in his cup. Not wine alone would bring about his recovery.

Angelo spooned up stew with relish and remarked, 'Better be well by tomorrow. The Abbot goes to Rocca then, to meet the Duke. I don't suppose he'll leave the cross behind if he's as devoted to it as you say.'

Sigismondo nodded, and drank. 'Rocca then. I can ride a horse tomorrow. Have you money, to hire?'

Angelo tapped his chest, where the main part of his money must be. His habit was to distribute coins about his person as a safeguard. 'Olivero and Ferondo were very generous. They seem to have brought plenty of money, enough for horses. And the cross is a cause close to their hearts, from all you say.'

Sigismondo began on the stew. 'Too close to too many hearts at the moment.' He was not to know how true this was in the literal sense. 'It remains to be seen whether Duke Ludovico will remember past services.'

The Abbot of Pietra was going to visit the Duke of Rocca. This was therefore a State visit, conducted with all the considerable pomp the Abbey could muster, because it was absolutely imperative to impress upon the Duke that the Abbot was someone to be reckoned with, someone to whose words it was wise to attend. The Abbey had been putting its collective mind for days to presenting its Abbot to the greatest advantage.

In the city it was known that the cause of contention between Abbey and Duke was the raising of the port dues. The Abbot had every right to raise them: the harvests on Abbey land had been abysmal and its famous vineyards had been visited by the ruinous rains of this summer at a crucial time. Some, viewing the great preparations for the Rocca visit, thought a bit of holy poverty might be more convincing than so many sleek mules and gold tassels; others did not think the Duke's heart would be any more easily touched or his purse opened did the Abbot arrive in sackcloth and ashes. Besides, the Abbot need not present his case with pathos. His advantage bulked in the shape of a quantity of the Duke's goods in the Abbey warehouses, not likely to be released unless the Duke paid up.

Others still argued that the Abbot's going to Rocca at all suggested that he was not confident that the Duke would pay – that the journey itself was a confession of weakness. The Pietresi, although they were not fond of their Abbot – who could be fond of Abbot Bonifaccio? – would be sorry to see him lose any quarrel with the Duke. It was their Abbey. Its prosperity was bound up with that of the port in general.

Because it was a port, there were a number of foreigners such as sailors, merchants, travellers and pilgrims for Scheggia among the crowd that gathered to watch the Abbot's departure, and the natives were ready and proud to expound while these wondered at the manner of it.

To begin with, the Abbot was not travelling by mule. A horse that would take his weight was out of the question for a churchman, and the mule had not yet been bred whose legs would have failed to snap under such a burden. The problem was decently, even flamboyantly, solved by a caretta, a kind of wagon, a room on wheels, fitted up with a couch, a cupboard, even a chest on which an attendant could sit opposite the Abbot. It was protected from the sun by hoops covered by a canopy of white silk, embroidered in gold and scarlet with the arms of the Abbey and of Abbot Bonifaccio with all the quarterings of the family connections that had helped to make him Abbot. White silk cushions, tasselled with gold and embroidered in the same way, were being piled on the couch against the joltings of the road, as the crowd watched. A team of mules, harnessed with silver and purple leather, were hitched up and the accoutrements checked by the grooms.

Benno was in the crowd, his mouth open to drink it all in. He would be going on the same journey himself shortly, though in nowhere near such style and by a different route. Angelo was at this moment hiring the horses, and Sigismondo, much restored, had paid Perpetua's cousin from the money so generously contributed by the Pantera brothers. Benno was to meet them at the east gate in an hour's time and had meanwhile come to look at the Abbot, the man who had intended to have his master hanged. The Marshal's men had been everywhere in the city looking for a sick man with a shaven head, though how sick he was caused them some puzzlement as he appeared to have knifed one of the four in charge of bringing him to jail and to have disabled the others. Benno was not afraid he would be recognized as having been at the scene, because those who might recognize him were most likely still groaning on a pallet somewhere, if they weren't awaiting burial. As for Angelo, true to his magician's nature, it was to be doubted he'd been seen at all; the only man who could have sworn to him was quite certainly dead.

'Here he comes. That's him now.'

No question. The Abbot had emerged from the shadowed portal, a canopy of white silk held over his head by four monks, his bulk moving with majestic deliberation that gave the crowd plenty of time to appreciate his dignity. One does not clap or cheer Abbots as one does secular personages, but a confused roar arose. The Abbot acknowledged this graciously, and with his plump right hand raised in blessing. Some of the many prostitutes Pietra supplied for its visiting sailors had forced their way to the front of the crowd and, conspicuous in their dresses of brilliant scarlet, pink and purple, shuffled forward on their knees to try to catch and kiss the Abbot's robes as he passed, which his escort indulgently permitted. As he turned, one velvet-shod foot on the step of the caretta, to give a final blessing to the crowd, Benno's eye was caught by a scintillant flash on the Abbot's chest. There was no mistaking, even at that distance, the Pantera cross with the deep glow of La Feconda.

Benno thought now he could tell Sigismondo there was some point in following the Abbot to Rocca, since he certainly wasn't leaving the cross behind. Suddenly all attention was sharply drawn away from the Abbot. After him crowded the monks, both those going and those staying. One of them, tall, gangling, with untidy white hair and wild eyes, had cast himself on his knees, raised his arms to heaven and was babbling words Benno could not catch. In common with most of the delighted crowd, Benno surged forward to hear better while at the same time everyone's speculations prevented hearing.

'He's having a fit . . .'

'He's praying.'

' . . . asking God to protect the Abbot.'

'From what? From the Duke? Nah, that's a fit.'

'A fit, I say. He'll roll on the ground next.'

Obligingly, the monk at this moment did fling himself face forward with arms spread, making a human cross in the dust.

The Abbot had got into the caretta, but delayed the signal to start as he observed what was going on. Benno noticed that none of the other monks attempted to haul the prone man to his feet or stop him singularizing himself like this in public. Whatever he was doing, the others treated him with respect.

The crowd's movement forward had stopped and people had fallen silent as the monk lay still. Now he pushed himself upright to his knees, and his words came, indistinct but audible.

'Blood! Blood! Don't go, Father! Blood waits for you in Rocca!'

In this way did Brother Ieronimo declare the auspices for Abbot Bonifaccio's journey.

Chapter 19

St Anthony Stumps Up

Rocca was the goal of more than one traveller. The Abbot of Pietra, and his party which now prudently included Brother Ieronimo, was already halfway there. If Brother Ieronimo continued to have awkward visions, he had better have them under the eye of the Abbot – who had blandly interpreted the rain of blood, so publicly and inconveniently foreseen, as an omen for his enemies and not himself. The Abbot's private thought was that the rain of blood symbolized his feelings about the Duke and his fiscal recalcitrance. Were there not rains of blood in the Bible and did they not fall upon God's enemies? Was not God's representative on earth His Holy Church and was the Abbot himself not the Church in Pietra? Therefore what more likely that He intended to punish the Duke for denying the Abbey its rightful dues?

The Abbot, trundled along the dusty road in the caretta, fanned by an assiduous attendant behind silken curtains, toyed with the thought of mentioning the rain of blood to the Duke if he should prove contumacious. He might remember other curses by association. A plague of frogs might be possible at this time of year; indeed, if God so chose to arrange things, of course anything might happen . . . The Duke might consider how God had afflicted the intractable ruler of Egypt with the death of the first-born. Ludovico's son was ailing . . . The Abbot smiled as the air stirred by the fan dried the sweat on his jowls.

Rocca was also the destination of a widowed lady, her son and servant, who had availed themselves of the time given by contrary winds that held up their pilgrimage to Scheggia to take the chance of visiting Rocca. Their journey was uneventful, but enlivened for them and for other travellers by the charming tenor of the widow's son, who had at his command a quite amusing repertoire of ballads, not all of them suitable for those of a religious turn of mind but to all of which the scruffy servant enthusiastically bore the refrain.

Others who had already reached Rocca would have been decidedly interested in these pilgrims had they met and been able to recognize them. Here was a matronly widow, strong features softened by the old-fashioned wimple of full mourning, head covered by linen and a straw hat. Where was the doughty fighter who had so usefully dispatched their uncle? Here was the widow's son, respectable in good brown cloth, last seen in particoloured blue and yellow and singing in a tavern. They would not have known that the singer had let them in for their recent spell in jail or that they had paid for his good clothes with their lost purse.

Angelo was responsible too for the bad mood both Olivero and Ferondo were in as they looked for lodgings in Rocca. It irked them severely to owe money to the fellow-merchant who had rescued them from jail, vouching for them to the authorities. It irked them more to have had to borrow extensively to replace the stolen money. Worst of all, the whole incident had so delayed them that they were now sure they would not find Sigismondo before he sold the cross. Once they got out of jail, it had been easy to track Gian to Rocca; he was far too intent on getting there to think of concealment.

They had all along doubted Gian's ability to get the cross from Sigismondo; they had offhandedly mentioned between them the pleasant possibility of his finding out something about Sigismondo's axe that he could not know beforehand. In this chase, their cousin was in the way and it would be obliging of Sigismondo to cancel cousin as well as uncle.

Meanwhile, who had the cross? In their exploration of Rocca in search of lodgings they had caught no sight or word of either Sigismondo or Gian, but that meant nothing. If the cross were already in the Duke's possession, Sigismondo would have money and he might have left the city. It hardly mattered where Gian was, though of course it would be nice if he had met Sigismondo and been forwarded to the family vault.

Olivero had already spent some time in a tavern on the palace square, washing the dust of the journey from his throat and the rankling memory of jail from his mind. The only mitigation for him there, providing some temporary amusement, had been the occasion when a rat had eaten the greater part of Ferondo's plumed cap, and it was under a new one that Ferondo entered with the news that the Abbot of Pietra was arriving. At first this did not interest the brothers greatly, but the swelling murmur of the crowd gathering in the square drew both men, first to the tavern window and then outside to view the spectacle, pushing their way forward.

In fact, it was worth the effort. The Duke's trumpeters, the green and white banners of Rocca swinging from their trumpets, were deployed on the palace steps, awaiting the precise moment for their fanfares. There was intense speculation and laying of bets among the crowd as to the meeting of Duke and Abbot. Would the Duke descend the palace steps to greet the Abbot? Would he kiss the Abbot's ring in deference to the Church? General opinion favoured this. As their Duke was in the right to refuse payment of arbitrarily increased taxes on his own goods, he could, people thought, afford to be magnaminous.

'Kiss his ring and kiss his arse.' A confident little sharp-featured man beside Olivero held, as he did, a large cup from which he drank as he surveyed the scene. 'Give that fat priest a penny and he'll not rest till he's bled you every ducat you own and then charged you for the prayers to keep you out of Hell. *Kick* his arse, I'd say. You can't miss.'

Olivero drained his cup. Abbots didn't concern him. Indeed, his only concern with the Church was to keep out of its hands for as long as possible. Nevertheless, he did not care for the little man's remarks. Not to antagonize the Church had always been his own policy; it had weapons such as excommunication. The Pantera brothers had never been described by any friend or associate as religious, but they were definitely superstitious, as instanced by their pursuit of the cross. Both were therefore prepared to bend the knee for any blessing of the crowd by Abbot Bonifaccio.

The procession came through the crowd, the white top of the caretta swaying, and the Abbot prepared to descend. The Duke appeared in the palace doorway and the trumpeters blew a fanfare that sent every pigeon in the square clattering up into the air to wheel overhead. The Duke began slowly to descend the steps, his cloak of gold brocade, lined with ermine, softly following five steps behind. The Abbot stood to bless the crowd, as if unaware of the Duke's concession, and as the whole populace sank to its knees the sun in its turn blessed the Abbot, the tonsured head, the white robes, and the thing of rainbow fire sparkling upon his breast. The Panteras, dumbstruck, kneeling automatically, stared at their cross, at La Feconda winking a signal at them from a few feet away.

Had they been able to release their gaze from that sight, they might have been able to identify another: the face of their cousin. Gian Pantera was confused and apprehensive after his failure with the Duke, getting neither news of the cross nor an assurance that it would be restored to him if the villainous Sigismondo attempted to sell it to the Duke. He had decided that morning to put his problem before an even higher authority than the Duke. He had gone to the Cathedral, a fine building in green and white marble, dedicated to St Agnes, where he prayed before the altar and the shrine holding the saint's bones. It occurred to him that, given the history of the cross, it might be tactless to address his prayers to the Virgin, since the jewel had originally been intended for her shrine at Scheggia. Thinking about the difficulty of his search, therefore, Gian petitioned St Anthony and St Jude. If the cross were found, he promised them each a wax candle the size of a man's wrist.

Now, standing on the cathedral steps, blinking against the flood of sunlight, he too caught a flash of brilliance as the Abbot turned, generously broadcasting his blessing.

St Anthony and St Jude had come up with the goods.

Chapter 20

'That's La Feconda!'

'They say Abbot Bonifaccio has an eye for the ladies, your Grace.'

The Duchess grimaced at her image in the looking-glass; she saw a neat, small face full of curves and character. 'How disgusting. If he has an eye for *me* I shall spit in it.'

Both ladies-in-waiting laughed sympathetically. They all knew that a duchess may not express her real feelings in public, especially if they are hostile. Her only chance must depend upon her husband's taking the lead. No one at court could be unaware how matters stood between the Abbot and the Duke, but diplomacy must be given a chance.

The long ropes of pearls were at last plaited into the Duchess's long brown shining hair, and the lady finished it with a gold clasp.

'Will your Grace wear the blue and silver?' The lady presenting the bodice for approval was a well-built girl, and the tiny waist held up against her sturdy form exaggerated the smallness of the Duchess who, considering the dress, was struck by this and frowned. Once she had never objected to being slight and elegant, but now that tiny waist reminded her yet again of failure. She was failing, in the one department where it was vital she should succeed. The Duke had one son, true, but this summer's illness of the little Lord Domenico had agitated the whole state, not to mention the Duke. If she could produce an heir ... if she could only produce a *child* it would be a relief for all Rocca. It was over a year! She waved the dress away, impatiently.

'No! The rose and gold.' As the girl turned away from her, folding the bodice with a rustle of metallic thread, the Duchess went on, 'This Abbot. I wouldn't have to see him if I went to Scheggia, would I?'

'I think your Grace would have to stay in Pietra until you could take ship for the island. Were you thinking to go?'

The Duchess made another face at the glass. 'What is there left? I don't want to go to Rome at this time of year, and leave his Grace. I must have made offerings at every shrine there is, so I suppose I must face the sea at last. Isn't there a mountain to be climbed as well?'

The large lady-in-waiting, carrying an armful of rose and gold, brought comfort too. 'It'll be worth it, your Grace. The Virgin of Scheggia has great power to grant favours. You could be carried up in a litter – some peasants go up on their knees.'

The Duchess looked down at her knees under the silk shift, and rubbed them in foreboding. 'If it brought me a son, I'd do it.'

'If your Grace really wants such a wish granted, you want La Feconda.' The speaker was a swarthy, secretive woman, whose superlative skills at hairdressing and sewing had so far outweighed the Duchess's sense of unease in her presence. Marina was one who knew all kinds of little spells to be said over everything from a cut finger to an indifferent lover and, worse, the spells often had an effect.

'La Feconda?' The Duchess turned round. 'That sounds appropriate. What is it?'

'Before I came to Court, your Grace, I used to live in Montesacro. Near there, the Pantera family had a cross that gave prosperity – and children.'

The Duchess put her arms through the bodice sleeves without turning her eyes from Marina. '*Children?*'

'There's a jewel in the cross, called La Feconda because of that – and the cross itself has that name too, but it's the jewel, I heard. Anyone who has it can count on fertility of all kinds.'

'They must sell it to me. They must. Pantera, you say? They must be sent for.'

The Duchess would have liked to know that several Panteras, and the cross they did not possess, were at the moment within Rocca's walls.

The Duke's cooks were anxious to impress the Abbot. A great deal of sweat had gone into the dishes before they were satisfied with their work. It had been decided that, Pietra being a port, the Abbot no doubt lived on fish all week as well as on fast days, and they had determined to show him what could be done with the beasts of the field and the fowls of the air. Meatballs of pork had been prepared, with currants and cloves and ground almond, fried and sprinkled with sugar and topped with tiny flowers of marjoram. Chickens stuffed with parsley and bacon were stewed in white wine and coloured with saffron. Pheasants were roasted to be served with ginger sauce, geese simmered in wine, their flesh then fried with minced onions and given a sauce of garlic and crab apples. A peacock, the *pièce de résistance*, had been roasted and then clothed again in its feathers and served, *regnant*, on its golden dish, ready to sail in to the sound of trumpets and give everyone indigestion. White roses had been gathered, with the Duchess's permission, from her garden and used to create rose pudding – blanched, pressed under heavy weights and mixed with cream, chopped dates and pine nuts. Cherry pottage was made with wine, sugar, butter and breadcrumbs and was decorated with the flowerheads of clove pinks, gilded at the edges.

Abbot Bonifaccio honoured the occasion with a cloak of cloth-of-gold which shimmered on the expanse of his shoulders and, as he intended, set off all the more the austerity of plain white robes beneath. However, no one contemplating his generous bulk would be immediately struck with the thought of a life of fasting, self-denial and devotion to spiritual matters.

Duke Ludovico looked the man he was, hard to amuse and dangerous to provoke, and his clothes of green and white brocade, liberally embroidered with pearls and emeralds, made the same point the dinner made: Rocca was short not of money to pay the Abbey dues, but of inclination.

The Duchess looked delightful as always in her rose and gold, the gauze of her undersleeves puffed out through the slashes in the rosy silk so that the sleeves emphasized the slender delicacy of her figure, but there was not a Roccan present who would not have preferred her to be clumsy, sallow and pregnant. All three took their chairs of state at the high table on the dais and, with another fanfare from the hard-worked trumpeters, the feast began.

It was tacitly understood that the dinner was not to be sullied by discussion of what had brought the Abbot to Rocca. Such a thing would be uncivilized and discouraged by any physician with respect for his patient's digestion. Such matters would be dealt with later in a private chamber with the Duke's advisers and the Abbot's treasurer, Brother Filippo, to add their voices. One might hope that the magnificence of the food and drink, both of which were being obviously appreciated by the Abbot, might soften his attitude over the taxes. The Duke ate far less, though perhaps more than might be expected from one so lean; he drank as much. The Duchess picked at her food, sipped at her wine. The Roccans, again, would have been glad to see her in a condition to pig it outrageously or demand strange foods for which the Duke would willingly ransack the world.

She spoke little, too, in return to the Abbot's elaborate compliments, which were reinforced, as her ladies had predicted, by an assessing scrutiny which made her cast her eyes down, not in modesty but from a desire to poke her chicken leg in the Abbot's face. The Duke luckily had missed the Abbot's lubricious stare and settled on a subject for conversation which might both flatter the Abbot and also imply that he had no need for further revenue.

'A magnificent cross, my lord Abbot! One of the treasures of Pietra?'

Abbot Bonifaccio engulfed a meatball whole without difficulty, wiping away a trail of sauce from his chin with the damask napkin.

'An offering to the Abbey, your Grace.' The Abbot smiled, his underlip shining with grease. 'Our Lady sent it.'

The Duke raised his eyebrows. 'Did it appear one morning on the altar?'

His tone nettled the Abbot. It implied a lack of faith.

'She sent it by the hand of a thief.'

The Duke looked up sharply. Thieves and crosses had recently been put into his mind by the young man Gian Pantera, who had sought to make him believe that Sigismondo, to whom he owed his life, was a common murderer.

'A thief? What did this man look like?'

The Abbot was picking out a morsel and was oblivious

to any oddness in the question. 'A rascal with a shaven head like a wrestler. I would have had the Marshal string him up but he escaped on his way to jail. Your men should keep an eye out for any such fellow in Rocca in case he comes here.'

Duke Ludovico, his eyes on the shifting lights in the jewels, nodded and, to the Abbot's surprise, gave a bark of harsh laughter.

'Oh, he will, he will, I'm sure of that. He'll be here. So that's the famous Pantera cross.'

Abbot Bonifaccio was engaged in tearing the flesh of a pheasant's side with his teeth, but his eyes came swiftly towards the Duke as his mind informed him that this news was not to his advantage. If the cross on his chest was famous for belonging to someone else then quick thinking would be required if he were to avoid its surrender. While the word 'Pantera' had this unpleasant resonance for the Abbot, it produced a more startling reaction in the Duchess. She leant forward suddenly, staring.

'Then that's La Feconda!'

Chapter 21

'I Must Have the Cross!'

'La Feconda?' The Abbot, holding a partridge away from his chest, made a bulbous wimple of his secondary chins as he squinted down at the jewel. The Duke watched his wife with keen attention but she at once straightened up and looked vague.

'No. I was mistaken. The jewel resembles one I had heard of at my father's court – but I see now it is nowhere like. La Feconda was a sapphire.'

There was no denying that the glittering centre of the Abbot's cross was a ruby. Its wearer relaxed and smiled, as if yet another claim to ownership was put out of question. He dismembered the partridge with gusto. The Duke, however, remained thoughtful. He was not a fool nor had he married one. He expected to hear more about this when the feast was over.

Of course he had to wait longer than that. Business must come first. He and his advisers retired to the Duke's private study, a magnificent chamber paved in black and white marble with, in the centre, the Roccan arms in a mantle of green and white supported by small enthusiastic leopards, with tongues and claws much in evidence.

The Duke's advisers showed their claws too, threatening, with infinite discretion and tact, to withdraw the Duke's trade entirely from Pietra in face of these exorbitant dues. It was then Brother Filippo's turn to display polite menace as he questioned the geographical possibilities. Was another port to appear suddenly on the Roccan coastline? If the Duke were considering negotiations with his neighbour Duke Gioffredo of Vallebruna he might find the dues more calamitous than those of Pietra, not to mention the increased cost of transport. Brother Filippo had a narrow, pale, slightly asymmetrical face, and a smile with closed lips and no effect in the cold, watchful eyes. He used this smile when he had descanted on the charming fancy of God creating a new port for Rocca from its mountainous shore. The Duke, playing with a tassel on his chair-arm, reflected how satisfying it would be to smash that smile with a well-planted blow – regrettably as much of a fantasy as the vision of a port. He glanced at the Abbot who, for the moment, sat somnolent, hands clasped across the stomach that had been given a momentous task at the feast so recently. It would be interesting to hear from Sigismondo, whom this venomous glutton had failed to hang. From Sigismondo he would hear more about the cross which was obsessing everyone, if he didn't hear more about it first from his Duchess.

He was right. The conference over the tax broke up with no concessions from either party and fresh discussions promised for the next day, when both would probably make side-steps in this diplomatic dance and reach a compromise. The Abbot had got out of his chair, with the necessary help of Brother Filippo whose narrow shoulders looked scarcely up to the task, and his secretary Torquato, handsome and sly. The blessing bestowed by Abbot Bonifaccio on the Duke in parting was a little impaired by the loud rumble from his stomach, a thunderous borborygm that seemed to echo round the room and made his secretary suppress a smile.

When the Abbot and his train of obsequious monks had left, and the Duke had dismissed his advisers, his real problems began. He was leaning on the sill of the window embrasure, looking down at the people in the dusk passing to and fro in the great square, soothing his mind with idle curiosity about them, their gossiping groups, the purpose of their errands. The door-curtain squealed on its rings as a page hastily drew it back and, bowing, announced the Duchess. He came to greet her and kiss her cheek; she drew back with a look he knew well. Tiny though she was, she had a determination that did not match her size, and her will was set on the one thing only God could provide.

'That cross, Ludovico. I must have the cross. Did you know it was a jewel that gives fertility? I must have it! You must pay him, you must get it for me.'

She twined her arms round one of his and looked up at him with huge dark eyes, head tilted so that her small mouth parted, showing the little teeth that might have belonged to a child. When he first married her, he had supposed that she was fragile. Now he knew better. It would be easier to bend an iron rod than to make her change her mind.

'Carissima, you know that old fox won't let anything out of his clutches. He's a greedy man: would he let it go?'

She pouted, touching his lips with her forefinger. 'And you? Will you let the chance of another son go?'

Ludovico was silent. Before the feast, he had visited his little son, had watched his pale face and listened to the physician's opinion, so tactfully delivered, so carefully ambiguous but still clear. At any minute, if the fever came again or if the boy's appetite did not recover, Rocca would find itself without an heir.

'I will not pay his taxes, sweetheart. The world would laugh at me after all that has passed.'

'If you pay him enough for the cross he will forgive the taxes.' Her finger caressed his cheek.

Ludovico snorted. 'He will never part with it unless I pay more than Rocca can afford *and* the taxes. He's not a man amenable to reason. To know that I want the cross will rouse all his avarice.'

She snatched away her hand. He saw her lips press together, then she spoke. 'What use is Rocca's money with no heir to leave it to!'

Ludovico watched her turn with a swirl of skirts and make for the door, the page just managing to open it in time. If she were to meet Abbot Bonifaccio at this point, he thought, she'd snatch the cross and pay not a penny. If only Sigismondo *had* stolen it!

Chapter 22

Murder!

Benno was delighted to be back in Rocca again, and told himself that after all his foreign travel it was really true that being at home felt good to the heart. By home he meant the city and the country surrounding it, for he had never had what some might call a home, not even a peasant hovel, nor had he loving parents to hug him on his return, yet he recognized where he was with a deep satisfaction. He hoped he might see the young lady in whose father's stables he had once worked. She must be nearly twenty by now and a rich wife, and, he had heard, the mother of two sons.

He even managed to conceal his respectful alarm at the sight of his Duke again. He had met a few dukes since he left Rocca, and princes too, but none had inspired quite the same feelings as Duke Ludovico. He was relieved that the ducal gaze – so disturbingly blue – had ignored him and fixed upon his master.

'I have been told, Sigismondo, that you are a thief and a murderer.'

The tone was uncompromising but it was answered first by a long, disclaiming hum. 'Indeed, your Grace, I have heard princes called so.'

'We are not talking of war and of the killing of soldiers and the taking of lands, but of innocent citizens and their property.' The Duke, ranging away up the room, cast this over his shoulder. 'What have you to say to that?'

Sigismondo, left elbow propped on right hand, drew the left forefinger thoughtfully across his upper lip. 'Your Grace, may I know who accuses me? Whom have I murdered and what stolen?'

The Duke came back and flung himself into his chair of state, still drawn up to the table where the discussion over taxes had taken place. The Turkey carpet over the table, with its glowing lozenges of amber and gold brilliant in candlelight, was rucked where the Abbot's waistband had caught it when he rose from his chair. The Duke leant forward.

'Do you know Gian Pantera?'

'I have heard of him, only. Is he my accuser?'

There was silence for a moment. Benno, pressed against the tapestry by the door, thought: now we're in trouble. My master's done a lot to make Duke Ludovico grateful but dukes do have a way of hanging those who kill, even if it was an accident. And you can't pretend my master didn't take the cross. Who's to believe he meant to do right?

'The young man spoke of an uncle you had killed, and a cross, treasure of the family, that you took. Is this true?'

'I killed Bernabo Pantera, though not by design. His last wish was to offer the family cross to the Virgin of Scheggia. His family's desire is to keep it, to bring them prosperity and sons.'

'The gift of La Feconda. Do you believe it has the power?' The Duke's gaze was intent, so forceful that one might expect to feel it on the skin.

'Your Grace, I believe such things are only in the power of God Himself. Any object that engenders hatred and greed may bring success in this world but never in the next.'

The Duke paused before he spoke. 'Then, *without* hatred

111

and greed, such an object, if revered as any cross should be, might yet have the power that relics have . . .'

Sigismondo bowed, spreading his hands in agreement. The Duke's chair grated as he got up and thrust it aside, and he strode away up the room. At the window he stopped, and wheeled.

'I must have sons.'

Sigismondo waited. Benno thought: he's not expecting my master to tell him how they're got?

The Duke beckoned with an imperious arm, and Sigismondo crossed the floor to him. He put a hand on Sigismondo's shoulder and spoke in an abrupt low voice while his hand tightened its grip until his knuckles were white. Whatever it is *now* that the Duke's telling my master to do, he's going to have to do it no matter what, Benno thought. As they left the study, Sigismondo's face said nothing to Benno, who had anyway been only vaguely hopeful that it would provide a clue. In the anteroom, Sigismondo paused to speak to Durgan, a senior among the Duke's dwarves. Benno paused by a bench where a page had left a dish with the remains of someone's meal, and when he moved on the dish was empty. Biondello became frantic in Benno's bosom and had to be put on the floor, where he kept close to Benno's ankles as Sigismondo led the way out into the labyrinth of the palace.

There had not been room, here on the citadel of Rocca, to build a modern palace separate from the old fortress so the two parts of the building co-existed and led into each other. Sigismondo walked with his usual air of knowing where he was, and Benno followed. They traversed a couple of rooms, went down wide marble stairs and emerged on a paved terrace, arcaded at one end, a little above the garden. It was dark here and, although there were people in the garden, Benno had more a confused impression than actual sight of them. The rooms behind the arcade were ablaze with candlelight.

'Benno – can you find our room from here?'

'No.'

'Up the spiral stairs beyond that small door, then to the right. Bring my scrip.'

On the stairs the smell of wax candles and lamps burning olive oil gave way to a choke of pitch, and the only light was a flaring torch in a wall-holder at the first bend. The half chicken inside Benno's shirt was uncomfortably slippery and he was glad to cache it on the shelf in their small room. He found the scrip on the bed and had nearly got back to the terrace when he heard a cry, a hoarse unearthly howl. After it, the flap of sandalled feet and a wavering shout that echoed in the stairway, this time with words.

'*Murder*! Father Abbot's been murdered!'

Chapter 23

'*He* Is the Murderer.'

Benno pelted down the stairs and came out on the terrace. The shouting came from the left, but to the right, a door stood open in candlelight, and a monk, his hands to his head, was staring in. Benno saw Sigismondo push past him and go into the room, and Benno crowded behind the monk to peer round his arm. All he could see was the back of another monk wrestling with something. There was a strong smell of blood. Benno scooped Biondello up as the dog pattered forward to investigate.

Then the monk turned, giving up what he had been trying to do, and they saw a tall, gangling man with ruffled white hair and an apologetic smile. It was the prophesying brother from Pietra, and what he had been wrestling with was the handle – the short, curved, black handle – of an axe still embedded high between the shoulders of Abbot Bonifaccio collapsed forward over what seemed to be a prie-dieu. The fine robes of the Abbot, the rough ones of the monk, were lightly spattered with blood, and the monk held his hands, red palms out, towards them as if in demonstration.

'The Devil. The Devil was here.'

As he spoke, several things happened. Uproar burst out at the far end of the terrace, where a quick glance showed Benno that torches were being carried down the steps; the body of the Abbot, its weight having shifted as the

114

monk relinquished the axe, fell sideways with grotesque slowness, taking the prie-dieu with it; and a monk, pushing aside Benno and the cataleptic brother in the doorway, exclaimed, 'Brother Ieronimo! What have you done?'

The monk daubed in blood raised his arms out sideways and let them sink. He still smiled. 'I came to tell Father Abbot that the Devil was here.'

Benno knew the priest who had just arrived, and he drew back into the shadows. He had met Father Torquato before, when he had struck Benno as a particularly slippery customer, and one who had excellent reason to regard Sigismondo without any affection at all.

'You. I might have expected to find *you* here.'

Sigismondo had been standing, observing the scene, and had made no effort to approach the Abbot or question Brother Ieronimo, as surely most people would do. He now bowed slightly. 'Father Torquato.'

Whatever Sigismondo might have been going to add was cut off by another monk who erupted past Benno, pointed at Sigismondo and cried, 'The thief! The man who stole the cross! He is the murderer!'

By now the room was being invaded by a crowd. Benno pressed back against the wall by the door as courtiers who had already retired for the night came in, reefed in bedgowns of furred brocade or velvet, avid for sight of what sounded like the most promising murder since the Duke's second wife had been found with a knife in her. There were pages, still on duty, sent to find if the shouted news about the Abbot's death were true, and under orders to report back every detail. There were guards, who naturally imagined that if murder had been done there might be somebody they should arrest.

This idea was also in the minds of the Abbot's secretary and treasurer. What made them hesitate a little was whom to point out as the one to arrest. Here was Brother Ieronimo, hands red with the Abbot's blood, brightly interested in events whereas, if he were the murderer, he could be expected to writhe in guilt and beg forgiveness. Here was Sigismondo who, as they knew, had been arrested for stealing the cross and who would have been dead by now if he had not so dishonestly escaped. Now the Abbot was dead, and one need look no further than this shaven-headed villain for the murderer. Brother Filippo saw logic in this.

'Arrest this man. He is a fugitive from justice.' At least, if Sigismondo had not murdered the Abbot, and he was distressingly unspotted by blood if he were to be culpable, Brother Filippo could be sure of his facts here, and he gave the order with confidence.

What he had not expected was that the palace guards would show reluctance to obey him. He could not have known that some of them remembered Sigismondo from some years ago as the favoured confidant and agent of Duke Ludovico. Curious things could happen to past favourites, true, but not one of the guards was going to risk the anger of their Duke by so much as laying a finger on the supposed criminal. There was also the factor that the man would not be a pushover to subdue, should he object to the arrest.

'What is happening here?'

It was the harsh voice of the Duke himself, still in his green brocade, very wide awake. All present drew back, bowing, as he came striding to view the body which seemed, piled in an ugly heap on the green marble floor, to be even vaster in death than in life. Benno wondered whether the Abbot, now translated into spirit, found the lack of weight a relief, or whether he was condemned to carry his bulk into the next world. This metaphysical reflection was interrupted by Duke Ludovico's wheeling to survey the throng in the room, and his question, with the quiet of menace:

'Who has done this?'

Secretary and treasurer had their answers by now, but they diverged. Torquato had taken Brother Ieronimo by the bloodstained sleeve, which the monk obligingly surrendered to him. Brother Filippo had seized Sigismondo's arm but with less co-operation. The Duke stared at both, and drew his brows together over the fierce blue eyes.

'*Two* murderers. And did both strike the blow?'

Benno dismissed a sudden horrific vision of Brother Ieronimo, that innocent smile on his face, pinning the Abbot helpless on the prie-dieu while Sigismondo used the axe. All the same he felt sweat on his brow. It could be half true. He'd seen the Duke speak in secret to his master, could easily guess it concerned the cross. Sigismondo had stolen it once. Abbot Bonifaccio was so conveniently to hand and was now so conveniently dead. One of Sigismondo's preferred weapons was the hand-axe, and though Benno could not see this one clearly as yet, he could not remember seeing, recently, the one Sigismondo usually carried. Indeed Angelo had had to procure a sword for him, whether bought or stolen Sigismondo had not asked, when they came to Rocca. It didn't mean Sigismondo hadn't got a spare axe stashed among the many mysterious things he travelled with. Yet if he had killed the Abbot . . .

No one answered the Duke. No one had seen the murder committed, it seemed. Brother Filippo had evidence as good as an eye-witness, however. He approached the gross heap of bloodstained robes and pointed.

'See, your Grace. The axe. It belongs to that man. It

was on him when he was brought before the Abbot as a thief. He is the murderer.'

Benno craned to look. Everyone looked. It was a distinctive weapon because of the short, curved black handle with a thin strip of metal inlaid at the end. Benno perfectly recalled asking Sigismondo about this and being told it helped the balance of the axe for throwing.

If the Abbot had not been killed by Sigismondo, he had been killed by Sigismondo's axe.

Chapter 24

The Prayers for the Dead

'Is it your axe, Sigismondo?' The Duke's voice was more harsh still as he wheeled on Sigismondo with a speed that made two courtiers next to him flinch. Benno thought: he wants it not to be, because it'd look bad for him once it's known he wanted the cross; and it'll be known – this is a *court*, it'll be all round in no time.

The Duke watched Sigismondo move unhurriedly to the object that had been the Abbot, observing the axe. 'Certainly, your Grace. This is the axe that was taken from me in Pietra when I was ill.'

The Duke had come to stare down at the unpleasant sight and at the handle, bloody, dumb to tell them whose hand had gripped it to bury its blade in Abbot Bonifaccio's spine.

'How did it come to be here?'

Brother Filippo came forward, directed a glance full of venom at Sigismondo and spoke.

'It came here because *he brought it*. Is it likely that Father Abbot had this weapon conveyed here from Pietra? Why would Father Abbot have such a thing in his room?'

Sigismondo shook his head slowly. 'A good question. With your Grace's permission I would ask it of those who had charge of Abbot Bonifaccio's luggage and his room furniture.'

Benno saw that, in the spheres inhabited by dukes and

119

by princes of the Church, not everything could be provided by host for guest. You must bring religious things with you like the right prayer books, and robes for Mass. The prie-dieu, lying forlorn on its side, might have been custom-built for the Abbot's kneeling weight, and perhaps to aid him from getting up off his knees, which after all he couldn't have seen for years.

Torquato was now at Brother Filippo's side. 'Has your Grace considered that this man, already found to be a thief, may have planned revenge upon Father Abbot?' The suggestion came with oily gentleness and he glanced sidelong at Sigismondo under his eyelids.

Both men stepped simultaneously backwards as Duke Ludovico turned on them with a feral glare. 'This Sigismondo, whom you accuse of theft and murder, is a man to whom I owe my life and state. Should I think he lies? May the murderer not have stolen it at Pietra, planning to inculpate its owner, if he planned to kill the Abbot?'

No one, thought Benno, ever said Duke Ludovico was a fool. Let's hope he's guessed right; and that neither he nor my master has a hand in this. He's given that slimy Torquato and the monk a nasty shock – they can't have known the favour my master's in with the Duke. Shut yourself from the world in an abbey and you miss the important gossip ... Benno liked Father Torquato's obsequious tone as he replied:

'Your Grace, we spoke only of what Father Abbot believed. Perhaps the Father could have misinterpreted the situation from what it seemed at the time ...'

'It was a misunderstanding,' Sigismondo rode in, genial, relentless, 'that might seriously have affected my breathing. But had I been hanged, my axe would not have been used.'

There was a murmuring as the spectators puzzled over the meaning of this remark. Did Sigismondo admit guilt, or mean that one who wanted to implicate him would not have had the chance?

The Duke got the point at once. 'Then the villain who did this planned it in Pietra.' He lifted a hand at a page who had pushed through the crowd to bow before him, and turned to the still figure of Sigismondo. 'We invest you with full powers, Sigismondo, to make your inquiries wheresoever you see fit and of whomsoever.' He was tugging from his finger a heavy-shanked ring with the sardonyx intaglio of the crest of Rocca, a ring that had been entrusted to Sigismondo before. As Sigismondo bowed and touched it to his lips, the Duke was staring with a grimace of sudden revulsion at what had been Abbot Bonifaccio. 'Let this be removed and what is proper be performed for it.' He lent his ear to the page's discreet murmur and told him, 'Say to her Grace all is well and I will be with her.'

As he strode to the door, all falling back before him, the first part of his message seemed to strike him as questionable and he stopped in the doorway, the curtains held up behind him framing the haggard, handsome face, and he surveyed the company. 'Be very sure that all will be well. This murder of my guest is a blot upon my honour and the honour of Rocca. The murderer has struck at me as well as at him. He shall be brought to my justice, and shall suffer the severest penalty man can devise. By giving this into the hands of Sigismondo I ensure that all will, as I say, be well.'

With a valedictory glare from the blue eyes, he was gone, to reassure his Duchess. The crowd in the room was edging forward to get a thoroughly good look at the fascinating conjunction of axe and Abbot. Torquato and Brother

Filippo, seconded by other monks, were trying to usher them out so that the operations of lifting and laying out the Abbot could begin. Unexpectedly, Sigismondo took this in hand, his courteous request that the room should be cleared sounding distinctly beneath the hubbub and, perhaps because of the authority the Duke had so conspicuously vested in him, he was obeyed. From the sliding glitter of Torquato's eyes, this was unwelcome. As the room emptied, someone – was it Sigismondo? – started the prayers for the dead.

Chapter 25

Death from Above

'There is no place for you here, at this time.'

Though Sigismondo had rid the room of the assorted crowd of courtiers and servants earlier, Torquato and Brother Filippo were determined that he should now go. A vast linen sheet had been draped over the Abbot before he was raised from the floor, perhaps to spare the feelings of the monks who had known him, to prevent horror from clouding their minds and distracting them from the prayers the Abbot undoubtedly needed. Sigismondo had added his strength to the challenging exercise of getting the huge body on to the bed. It was not only heavy with the inertness of death but inclined, appallingly, to let its limbs roll beyond the controlling grasp of the lifters as if Abbot Bonifaccio struggled to escape the finality of his laying-out.

Now the Abbot was supine upon the bed under the shrouding sheet, which had accumulated smears of blood and had dragged tight across the corpulent mound. Huge candles of beeswax brought by the Duke's *maestro di casa*, stood in iron holders at foot and head. Monks knelt and kept up a continuous murmur of prayer, and two, with a basket and basin and linen towels, now picked their way past their brethren to remove the sheet and perform the necessary offices. There should be no strangers at such a time.

123

Sigismondo, ushered bluntly to the door by Brother Filippo, made no protest. He carried the axe which, watched by fascinated monks uttering shreds of prayer intermittently, he had dislodged from the Abbot's spine. Though he had cleaned the blade, some eyes still could not leave it. Benno was ready to follow Sigismondo out when a penetrating low cry stopped them both.

'The cross – the cross is gone!'

The cry came from one of the monks washing the corpse. Brother Filippo was instantly at his side, bent and searching among the bloodstained robes that had been removed.

Sigismondo, who had immediately turned back, was intercepted by Torquato with unnecessary drama, spreading his arms, his face a mask of enmity.

'Perhaps, sir, it is *you* we should be stripping. You stole it before, did you not?' Then, a memory of the Duke's words evidently visited him and his expression changed. His tone had moderated as he added, 'The Duke should be informed. Will you do it, sir?'

Sigismondo did not reply. He advanced, Torquato giving way, and looked down on the Abbot's bared neck and chest, naked of chain or cross. In spite of protest, he bent to heave up the shoulders; the head, which even with jaw tied up and eyes closed, had the look of being under restraint rather than dead, rolled to one side. Benno felt that the Abbot might at any moment open those eyes, tear off the bandage and demand to know what they were about, to handle him so.

'The axe severed the links. Indeed it drove a piece into the bone. You see?'

Brother Filippo, peering, turned to look up at Sigismondo with revulsion and even fear.

'The *murderer* took the cross? Father Abbot died

124

because a thief coveted a sacred object?' Contempt came into his voice. 'The torments of Hell are too good for such a man.'

'The Devil claims his own. The Devil will come again.' Brother Ieronimo had knelt, unnoticed till now, with the rest, bloodied hands raised in prayer. He spoke now with mournful certainty, drawing all eyes. Brother Filippo moved to confront him – this, after all, was the one found with his hands on the axe, and only the presence of Sigismondo as a more likely murderer had distracted them. Sigismondo intervened: 'By your leave, Brother. I would speak with Brother Ieronimo very soon. Until then, no one should do so.'

A protest might have come to the treasurer's lips. This was an affair concerning the Church . . . The sight of the Duke's ring gleaming dully on Sigismondo's hand reminded them all that they were, without an authority at their head, in the Duke's palace. He might have spoken but there was a commotion among the lingering crowd outside, the curtain was rattled back and a large man, in leather and steel-studded burgundy velvet, appeared and made a contemptuous scan of the room full of kneeling monks. His face changed when he saw Sigismondo. One fighter knows another. He raised his voice over the lugubrious chanting.

'Sir. You're wanted.'

Out on the terrace the man introduced himself as Captain of the Duke's guard. He knew Sigismondo, he said, by reputation although he had been away from Rocca when Sigismondo was last there. The murder of the Abbot he evidently felt as a reflection on his own security measures.

'One of the guards who patrol the palace has just been reported to me as dead in the garden beneath the terrace here. His Grace has put you in charge of investigations, and so I told my men to touch nothing until you come.' He tapped the side of a broken nose with a scarred forefinger. 'The huntsman studies the lie of the land, eh?'

Benno, trotting after them both down the spiral stair, reflected that Sigismondo was always insistent on looking before touching, saying that breaking threads destroyed connections. Benno saw these as gossamer threads insubstantially connecting evil-doers to their crimes.

They came out in the dark garden. A flambeau spluttered and flared in the hand of one of the Duke's guard.

Sigismondo knelt by the long shape on the ground, and the quick-witted torch-bearer came to crouch alongside. The dead man seemed to have dug himself the beginnings of a grave; his body was pressed into the ground between two trimmed bushes of myrtle. Sigismondo's hands went over him, touching lightly and then more forcefully. That the body was strangely soft, giving unnaturally under Sigismondo's probing, occasioned Benno's stomach a qualm. Sigismondo looked up at the terrace balustrade, then all round. He rose, took the flambeau, stepped round the body and bent down near the wall.

'Is this your man's sword?'

The captain joined him. 'It is.' He pushed forward the similar hilt of his own. 'He had drawn it, then.'

'So he had challenged someone.'

'The Abbot's murderer?'

'Perhaps.' Sigismondo picked up the sword and returned to the body, handed the torch back and knelt to prise the dead man from the earth. He turned him over, the body more slack than was natural even in the dead. He laid the sword along the bloody torso and put the man's hands on the hilt and held them there.

'It may be that the man he challenged killed him, but I believe that his death came from above.'

Chapter 26

'My Hands on the Axe!'

'From . . . ?' The captain, startled, tilted his face towards the stars.

'From the terrace. While he faced one man, the other fell upon his back. If he'd been looking up, seeing the man come down, he would have been knocked backwards. He has told us all he could.'

The captain's men took up the body and carried it away. Benno put Biondello down to roam the dark garden. Light came indirectly, from a flambeau at the stairhead, a lantern on the terrace. A small night breeze brought a smell of plants and broken earth.

'How easy is it, Captain, to enter this garden from the city?'

'Too easy, sir. The place is a warren and although I have brisked up the discipline there are still those who take bribes at the doors and the gates.'

Sigismondo had taken advantage of this when he was here last. 'And the city? The gates shut at dusk? Are they well kept?'

'They are, sir,' the captain admitted.

'The City Marshal has an easier job than yours.' Sigismondo smiled, wagged his head in sympathy and made for the stairs.

Benno pattered up the winding stairs again. The Duke was in a proper fix now, his guest murdered when the whole world would know – and very soon – that he and the Abbot weren't just each other's favourite person. Whether Sigismondo were involved, Benno did not care to think about, but Brother Filippo and Father Torquato would not be alone in calling him the murderer in spite of that wild-eyed monk grappling with the axe when they came in.

It was the wild-eyed monk to whom Sigismondo was talking on the terrace. Brother Ieronimo, extracted from the praying throng of monks, had been brought out here among the shadows and fluttering lights. Sigismondo leant in relaxed fashion on the stone balustrade, his back to the garden below, and Brother Ieronimo stood, hands linked loosely before him, wearing a vague smile, for all the world as if the subject under discussion were a scholarly argument over the scriptures.

'You say you saw the Devil tonight, Brother. Where was he when you saw him?' Sigismondo spoke conversationally, as if demons were as common as donkeys, and Brother Ieronimo responded in the same casual fashion.

'I was coming along here, to see if I could speak to Father Abbot.'

'Here? When was this?'

Brother Ieronimo lived by the Offices of the Church. He had no need to think of time, it was measured out for him.

'Before Vespers.' His smile had a tinge of apology. He had quite large teeth, and a faint lisp suggested that they got in his way.

'Why did the Abbot bring you to Rocca?'

'He wanted to know at once if the Virgin told me anything further.'

'What had Our Lady told you already?'

The monk shook his head. 'I am to tell no one.'

'And has the Devil appeared to you before?'

'Never. Our Lady had warned me that terrible things were to happen but I didn't expect the Devil.' He sounded cheerful and interested.

'Where was he?' Sigismondo indicated the terrace about them, and Brother Ieronimo turned, pointing.

'Just there. I was coming along from our lodgings and suddenly I saw him. Dark against the sky – it was still twilight – huge! – his wings out, flapping.'

Benno felt a cold tingle at the back of his neck and crossed himself. That bit about the wings . . .

'What did you do when you saw him?'

'I made the sign of the cross against him,' the monk's arm swept in a big formal gesture, 'and I called on Our Lady to protect us all.'

'And the Devil?'

'He reared up, threatening – ' Brother Ieronimo raised his hands overhead in imitation, clearly unaware that they were still marked with the Abbot's blood – 'and then he gave a terrible cry and flew away.' Brother Ieronimo, modestly pleased at this triumph over Satan, added, 'Thanks be to God.'

'Amen!' Sigismondo was jovial. Benno mused: Brother Ieronimo blamed the Devil – in a way you could blame the Devil for everything that went wrong in the world, but not everyone was left holding the axe.

Brother Ieronimo was going on with his story from when he had put the Devil to flight. 'I hurried to Father Abbot's room to warn him of the Devil.' He stopped, groaned, and struck himself on the forehead with such force that he staggered a little. 'And alas, you know what happened then.'

'Tell me again,' prompted Sigismondo, interrupting a

singsong of prayer into which Brother Ieronimo had launched, rocking to and fro.

'The Devil! It was the Devil all along.'

'He had flown away.'

'But not before he had entered into *me* . . . I found myself there with my hands,' and Brother Ieronimo examined them, obviously for the first time since then, and saw them dark in the shadows and caked with dried blood, 'my hands on the axe! For my sins and for his, the Devil made me slay Father Abbot! *O mea culpa, mea culpa, mea maxima culpa!*'

Chapter 27

Was the Devil Satisfied?

Brother Ieronimo struck himself on the breast, lamenting. Benno felt nervous. If the Devil was on the prowl and entering such an innocent-looking religious, he surely might take a fancy to a shabbier soul.

'How did the Devil make you strike the blow, Brother? Show me.' Sigismondo held out the axe.

Brother Ieronimo shrank and then, with a visible effort, grasped the haft, stood uncertainly for a moment and Sigismondo repeated, 'Show me. Here is the Abbot.' He pointed to a spot two feet in front of the monk. 'His back is towards you. Approach and deal the blow.'

Brother Ieronimo obeyed. He put one foot forward, hefted the axe in his hand and cut the air with it; he lost his grip as the blow descended and Sigismondo swept the axe away before it hit the flagstones.

'Sir: the Duke sent us to take this man to the cells.' A guard in the Duke's green and white livery had arrived, three others at his heels, pikes ready, expecting trouble, surprised at the tall, angular monk with the wild white hair, who bent his head meekly and held out his wrists to be bound. Like most of the Duke's subjects, they had strongly resented the Abbot's demands over the Duke's goods. The man who removed the Abbot was therefore a benefactor. They bound the wrists firmly but not so as to cause pain, and led him away.

Sigismondo stood thoughtfully regarding the axe in his hand

'Pity it can't speak to give evidence,' Benno ventured. He could not entirely shake off his idea that Sigismondo, from loyalty to Duke Ludovico, or even perhaps at the Duke's command, had killed the Abbot himself. Nothing he knew of Sigismondo led Benno to believe his master would do such a thing; he knew Sigismondo could be ruthless, but this was different; he had been angry and disgusted at killing Bernabo Pantera. However, if there was one thing Benno was sure of about Sigismondo, it was that he was unpredictable.

And if Sigismondo had used his axe on the Abbot, and this questioning were all a pretence, had he also got the cross? Was he just protecting the Duke? Here was the dead man, who had tried to extract money from the Duke and who was in possession of an object the Duchess badly wanted. Would Sigismondo baulk at being used for the dirty work by the Panteras but do it for a Duke?

'Dreaming?' Sigismondo cupped a hand behind Benno's head and bore him forward, stumbling at Sigismondo's pace and so producing a faint, surprised yelp from Biondello inside Benno's doublet.

In the palace chapel, in cloth of gold and clouds of incense, the Abbot lay, with chanting monks either side of his bier. He had a dignity now – even the mound of his belly had a grandeur; though his face was not yet wholly relaxed. It still suggested not peace but a shocked astonishment at being forced from life so unexpectedly. Benno could not help thinking of the terrible wound hidden from sight.

'Father. I must speak with you.'

Torquato, in the middle of crossing himself, finished the

movement while turning a look of anger on the interrupter.

'Remember where you are: in the presence of death. Now is not the time, sir.'

'Now *is* the time, Father. It is about this death that I come. The Duke requires me to question both you and Brother Filippo.'

The Duke's name once more had power. It modified Torquato's manner; his sharp, discontented face tried to assume amiability.

'You understand – we are greatly disturbed . . .'

'It would be strange if you were not.' Sigismondo inclined his head, as if in sympathy. 'If you would ask Brother Filippo to come as well, I have a place where we may speak.'

The place was a room off the chapel, perhaps once a private oratory but now evidently used for storage. Sigismondo shut the lid of a long chest where vestments were laid flat, and sat on it. His shaven head shone in the light of a candle Benno had borrowed from the chapel. Torquato and Brother Filippo, standing before Sigismondo, were absorbed in resentment: here were religious summoned to stand before a layman for inquisition. Father Torquato voiced their shared feelings.

'Why are we here? Brother Ieronimo, may God forgive him, has confessed. What can we add to that except our prayers for a penance that will save him from the torments of Hell he so terribly deserves?'

'May God have mercy on all our souls.' Sigismondo took them by surprise, forcing them to imitate his sign of the cross, taking the wind from their sails. 'You can add, Father, that which will help me in my report to the Duke. Who was in charge of packing the Abbot's effects for this journey to Rocca?'

Brother Filippo spoke. 'I was. Why do you ask?'

'To whom did you allot the task of packing things from the Abbot's study?'

Brother Filippo waved a hand as if the question's triviality pestered him as would a fly. 'What is the point of that?'

Sigismondo smiled broadly, cocking his head to one side. 'My axe, Brother. When I was brought before the Abbot for questioning, my axe was laid on the desk in front of him, in proof that I was no harmless merchant. Perhaps no one thought to have it removed. If you ordered that what was in the room was to be packed, it may be that in obedience the brother never questioned whether the Abbot would need an axe but packed it with the rest.'

Benno thought of the monk, trained to obey and not to make judgements for himself, packing up the Abbot's death.

Brother Filippo was frowning. 'Whom did I delegate . . .' His face cleared and he brought out a hand from his sleeves to snap the fingers, drawing a frown in his turn from Torquato. 'It was Brother Ieronimo. Father Abbot, God rest his soul, instructed me to keep him busy . . .'

'Yet the Devil was not to be resisted. He had work to be done here in Rocca.' Torquato seized on the point to which this led: the Devil had prepared for the Abbot's death already in Pietra. Benno's picture now was of Brother Ieronimo happily busy, wrapping up everything that came his way, methodical among candlesticks and inkwells, axe and prie-dieu, his mind afloat on some holy private vision, unaware of the Devil's choice of two of his instruments.

'Why did you, Father Torquato, come tonight to see the Abbot?'

Benno saw the swift glance between the two men. Sigismondo would not have missed it.

135

'We came to give our counsel on the meeting with his Grace tomorrow.'

'Today,' put in Brother Filippo softly, as the sound of the Cathedral bell reached them over the castle roofs. 'It is past midnight. Soon we must go to Matins.'

'You found the Abbot alone. Brother Ieronimo was not to be seen.'

'Perhaps he heard us coming and hid.'

'We found Father Abbot dead.' The fastidious grimace of Brother Filippo showed how one would feel on making such a discovery. 'I could not touch the axe.'

'Our first thought was to inform his Grace of the dreadful deed performed under his roof. We returned to be told by Brother Marco that he had seen Brother Ieronimo with his hands on the axe—'

'Why, do you think, did Brother Ieronimo risk discovery if he had killed the Abbot and got away unseen already?'

'What goes on in the whirling brain of a madman?'

'Brother Ieronimo himself foretold a rain of blood, before we left Pietra. He warned Father Abbot not to come to Rocca.' Brother Filippo shook his head sadly. 'Perhaps even then an angel strove in his soul to resist evil. The Devil seeks everywhere to destroy us, particularly those who seem favoured, as our brother was by the Virgin.'

Sigismondo suddenly rose, so that they backed. He inclined his head to them. 'I must thank you for your time, and let you go about your duties. The Abbot ought not any longer be deprived of your prayers.'

Both Torquato and Brother Filippo looked disconcerted by this sudden dismissal. In the dungeon chill of the small room, the musty smell of old hangings and of the dried herbs laid among the vestments, and the flicker of the candle as the men bowed to one another, Benno felt uneasy. Was the Devil satisfied with what he had achieved? Was he lingering hereabout to do more? Whom would he enter next when the Virgin herself could not protect a monk to whom she had appeared? Benno shivered. Even Sigismondo might not be safe.

Chapter 28

A Missing Pantera

'The man must be in the city, sir. The gates were shut and I can trust the guards.'

Sigismondo regarded the City Marshal. With his burly build and broken nose, he had plainly been in quite a few fights and not lost by being a fool or a coward. If he trusted the guards at the gates it would be because he had tested their honesty. There was a rumour spreading sibilantly through the palace, that the Devil had flown in and snatched the Abbot's soul for his unholy greed over the warehouse dues. The Marshal had seen death and, when axes were used, he was not inclined to blame the Devil despite the crushed guard below the terrace. The Duke's captain had shown him footprints in the earth there, even the handprint of one levering himself up, obviously with no wings to help.

'You have lists of strangers lodging in the city, Marshal?'

'At hand.'

This hand was the inkstained one of a grubby clerk, roused to find and bring the lists. He looked as if he would kill any number of Abbots if he could only get back to his pallet.

The list was comprehensive: each lodging-house keeper put down the names of those under his roof, and the towns from which they had come – or claimed to have come – and also their destinations and occupations.

The Marshal held out a second paper.

'His Grace insists that families who have relatives or guests lodging with them should also provide their names. Danger may lurk anywhere.'

'I'm looking for a name, Marshal—' Sigismondo ran a finger down the precise, cursive writing. 'Here! Staying with the Bandini; merchants with merchant, Olivero and Ferondo Pantera. And the lodging-house list, if I may . . . Pantera again. In the Via Corsa at the Dolphin, Gian Pantera, here this last week. These are the men to visit, Marshal.'

Benno followed Sigismondo like a small, untidy shadow, while he and the Marshal and his men crossed the city to the Palazzo Bandini. Benno knew the way well. He had grown up in Rocca and lived there until Sigismondo entered his life, and he had many times engaged in a running fight with Bandini servants pursuing the feud between their master and Benno's. He was fondly remembering pushing a Bandini groom into some pigshit just as he was about to gain the sanctuary of the Bandini gates, when those same gates loomed overhead, lit by the flares of the Marshal's men. Two muscular statues, hoisting a shield with the Bandini arms, frowned down at them; the flickering light making them seem to grimace at this intrusion on Bandini privacy.

Their annoyance was nothing to that of Bandini himself. Swathed in a bedgown of furred velvet, every fold on his bloodhound face trembling with indignation, he stared at the Marshal.

'Why am I roused at this hour?'

He hasn't changed, thought Benno, as Sigismondo spoke.

'Perhaps, my lord, you remember me. It is his Grace's wish that your guests, Olivero and Ferondo Pantera, should answer for themselves. Abbot Bonifaccio has been murdered.'

Bandini's change of manner was swift and ludicrous. He had started at seeing Sigismondo; though expressing shock at the Abbot's death, he was now all smiles and he called for wine and seats, brought by sleepy servants.

'They shall be roused, sir. They are my fellow merchants, no more, and lodge here at their request. They told me nothing of their business in the city – indeed I have spoken little with them. They arrived late in the day, requesting hospitality, and were too fatigued to take more than wine and a light supper.'

'From where had they come?' asked Sigismondo. Benno thought that signs of drunkenness in Olivero might be taken for fatigue, but if he were drunk how could he go to the palace and kill the Abbot?

'They told me, Pietra. They told me they are on their way to join their wives at Rome.'

'What is all this?'

Olivero and Ferondo, surly and tousled, came on the scene showing either astonishment or a nicely calculated appearance of it. Olivero in burgundy brocade, Ferondo in grey silk, displayed their importance as rich merchants, but their bedgowns toned strangely well with each face, Olivero's with a bruise on his chin, Ferondo's with pallor. They showed no pleasure whatever on seeing Sigismondo.

'Sirs.' The Marshal took the initiative, as his was the authority in the city. 'The Abbot of Pietra was murdered this night. Where were you three hours ago?'

'God's Bones! The Abbot of Pietra? Three hours ago? We were in bed, where else; why come to *us* to ask?'

'You are not surprised at his murder?'

'No more than you, sir. A man may have enemies anywhere.'

That's an expert talking, thought Benno – his own family's crammed with them. But my master wouldn't seriously think he could get that Olivero on the hop.

'How did you come by your bruise?' Sigismondo's question was almost friendly. Even under Olivero's short close beard the purpled swelling showed, and he touched it, tenderly. He shot a glance at Ferondo, who had done nothing yet but hold his bedgown to him and look confused and apprehensive.

'An argument. A brotherly difference of opinion.' Olivero smiled though his eyes did not, and nudged Ferondo who quickly grinned as well. Benno reflected on the likelihood of Ferondo delivering such a blow and not getting laid out for it; and having done it without grazing his white hands.

'So, sir,' the Marshal took up, 'you are prepared to swear that you know nothing of this deed, that you were not abroad in the city tonight?'

'I and my brother are innocent of the deed. We will swear it on any relic you produce.'

Sigismondo murmured to the Marshal, who now beckoned his guards forward. Bandini coughed fretfully, as if in protest at the night air, and the Marshal addressed him.

'My lord, it is the Duke's wish that the baggage and room of your guests be searched.'

Bandini's cough nearly choked him. Benno speculated: did he wonder if the Panteras had not just killed the Abbot but also dismembered him and brought bits back? Benno knew a story of someone made into a pie and his family tricked into eating it. The Abbot would have run to a great many pies and a prime roast into the bargain. Bandini was eyeing the Panteras as if they were quite the least welcome guests he had ever had under his roof. He said hastily, 'The Duke's wish is my command. Search!' He made a grand gesture and nearly lost his bedgown. Hauling it back over his shoulder, he added, 'Search all the house if you desire.'

'It may be necessary. Certainly these gentlemen's servants and any baggage they may carry . . .' The Marshal was matter-of-fact, not threatening. Bandini glared again at the guests who were causing such upheaval.

The brothers seemed uncertain how to react. Olivero grumbled indignantly, but in a manner almost tentative. Ferondo chose grieved dignity. If they had got the cross, Benno decided, they were pretty sure it couldn't be found. At this point he was distracted by a Bandini servant, going by with candles to light the way to the Panteras' room, recognizing Benno and giving him a vicious pinch in the side.

Benno's involuntary whoop brought Sigismondo's gaze to him and made him smile. This enraged Olivero, who of a sudden strode across to Sigismondo and thrust his face close to his.

'You shall pay for this! I do not forget!'

Unwise, perhaps, to threaten a man in the Duke's favour, yet it was a move that might be made by a man confident of his innocence who suspects he is persecuted for personal reasons, and so perhaps it was clever. Sigismondo preserved his smile and did not draw back. It was Ferondo who took hold of the burgundy velvet and pulled his brother away.

Bandini was drinking wine, wine that had been offered also to Sigismondo and the Marshal but not, significantly, to the Panteras. None quicker than servants to know their master's mind.

The Marshal's men returned eventually. Nothing had been found to incriminate either brother, and they left the Palazzo Bandini and its owner, who was obviously keen to get rid of guests who had brought such trouble. Benno was the only one satisfied with the visit, having managed to get in a hefty kick on the shin of the man who had pinched him – the very one, he realized now, that he had pushed in the pigshit a few years ago. Some memories never die.

'Well, Marshal! For the Via Corso and another Pantera.'

The Via Corso was in a good part of the city, and the Dolphin was the kind of inn a rich merchant might well patronize, an inn not accustomed to having its doors knocked on around midnight by the Duke's Marshal. The innkeeper, however, escorted them to the room Gian Pantera had hired. He tapped on the door and the Marshal, reaching past him, thrust it open.

The room was empty.

It was a small room, with a large bed – no doubt Gian had paid extra to avoid sharing it with anyone, but it had not been slept in. Sigismondo pointed out some baggage lying in a corner and the Marshal had it tipped out on the bed and rummaged through, while the innkeeper stood by and looked on, shaking his head. Sigismondo's fingers felt the seam of a doublet, and the silk lining of a pack was gone over minutely by the Marshal himself. It seemed that Gian Pantera was travelling light, for the search did not take long. The Marshal straightened his back, frowning.

'Well, he'll be in the city. Somewhere.'

If he *had* murdered the Abbot and stolen the cross, he naturally wouldn't come back to the Dolphin afterwards.

Where, in a Rocca mostly shut up for the night, could he be hiding?

Benno had a sudden hope that they might have to search the brothels.

Chapter 29

Still Missing . . .

Disappointingly, it proved not necessary to search the brothels for Gian Pantera. The innkeeper of the Dolphin volunteered that the young man claimed to have a friend at Court who was to get him an audience with the Duke that day. It may have been Sigismondo's prompt and prompting coin, or the need to keep on the right side of the Duke's Marshal, but the innkeeper also miraculously remembered the name of the friend at Court, a name that Gian Pantera had let drop, perhaps to impress him: Roderigo Ranieri; the Marshal, who knew everyone at Court, was not impressed.

'At least we know where to look next,' the Marshal remarked.

The streets were dark and deserted still. The only people they met were some noisy revellers suddenly sobered by the unexpected sight of the Marshal. The palace was another matter. Anyone who had missed the excitement of the Abbot's murder by being asleep had been kindly woken and brought up to date by the luckier ones, eager to impart their impressions of how the Abbot had looked wearing an axe. They could retail just what the Duke had said, and how the mysterious Sigismondo, remembered by most from a few years ago, had turned up again out of nowhere, to be given the task of clearing the Duke's honour.

The busiest conveyors of the hottest news for years were the palace dwarves, legacy to the present Duke from his father who had sought out anything human and close to the ground for miles around. Quite distant potentates had sent dwarves in, so to speak, the diplomatic bag as presents. This palace élite was now typically first with the news because of their habit of standing around under people's elbows, observing without being noticed. One of them greeted the Marshal as his party entered the palace, capering crabwise before them across the marble slabs of the great hall.

'Do we get to see a hanging yet, Marshal? Have you got a present for us?'

This was impudent, as the Marshal clearly had no prisoner, and he ignored it, striding on. Sigismondo, however, stopped to ask a question. The dwarf was delighted to oblige and went ahead to lead them to Roderigo Ranieri's room. It was no bigger than a cupboard with a window, and just broad enough for a bed where two men were sitting in earnest talk when the dwarf scratched on the door and simultaneously flung it open. Both looked up in astonishment at the Marshal.

'Sir, is this Gian Pantera?'

Ranieri had a soft, affronted face like a petulant lapdog. He inquired in a high, complaining voice, 'Why, Marshal? What is wrong?'

His companion rose and, flinging back his head, he said, 'I am Gian Pantera and I answer for myself. Does the Duke send for me to restore to me what is mine?'

The Marshal's reply was forestalled by Sigismondo who smoothly put in, 'By your leave, Marshal, I would question these two alone.'

So Sigismondo shut himself into the cupboard with Gian and an alarmed Ranieri, leaving outside the impassive

146

Marshal, his guards, a disappointed dwarf and Benno, who at least hoped to hear later what had been said.

'Later' turned out to be no more than half an hour after that, in their own room, to which a sleepy page brought cold chicken, olives, plums, and wine. When at last they were alone the question burst explosively from Benno.

'Did he do it?'

Sigismondo, pouring wine into a silver cup chased with the Roccan ducal arms, laughed. He drank before replying.

'Mmm. Hey, as you know I left the Marshal supervising a search of both those two and the room. Ranieri's ready to have a seizure at the mere thought of being implicated. He was willing not only to swear his innocence on his mother's head but to remove it if we felt the need.'

Benno saw his question had not been answered. He veered. 'Did he have a chance to kill the Abbot?'

'Mm-hm . . . Certainly a motive. He admitted he'd seen the cross this afternoon on the Abbot's arrival in Rocca. His Grace told me that Gian had pleaded for it to be returned to him should anyone, such as the villainous Sigismondo, offer it to the Duke, but that was before the Abbot came.'

Benno was considering the prospect of the Abbot, when alive, returning the cross to anyone however prettily they asked, when Sigismondo added, 'Ranieri got him the audience with the Duke yesterday. Apparently they were friends in youth and Gian came to him and asked the favour.'

'But why wasn't he at the Dolphin?'

'After he saw the Abbot wearing the cross, Gian meant to offer a price for it. He's not short of money, it seems — he attributes this to his father's ownership of the cross —

and the Abbot is known to be short of it this year, so he believed he had a chance.'

'Not if the Abbot knew about La Feconda.'

'No. But Ranieri offered Gian a share of his room for the night so that he could waylay the Abbot before Prime in the chapel here.'

'This Ranieri was with him, then, when the Abbot was killed?'

'Did I say that?' Sigismondo offered a piece of chicken to Biondello, who was sitting between him and Benno, turning palpitating attention from one to the other. 'Ranieri was with the Duke when Torquato and Brother Filippo burst in to say they had found the Abbot murdered.'

'So where was Gian Pantera?'

'He says he was praying to the Virgin for success with the Abbot. In the palace chapel.'

' – Next to the Abbot's lodgings. You mean he *could* have done it.' Benno incautiously lowered a piece of chicken and had it instantly mouthed from his fingers.

'Hey, *I* could have done it and plenty of people think I did. Even his Grace may have hoped I did. But I've produced no cross, so far, to please the Duchess, and I think the Duke does not believe I'd sell it elsewhere.' He expelled an olive stone into his hand. 'But yes, Gian isn't in the clear. He says a priest can bear witness to his presence in the chapel but a priest in a chapel is like a woman in a house; there are always jobs to be done, tending to candles, sweeping, setting things to rights, prayers. No priest watches a man praying in a chapel; he could have gone out and come back.'

'But wouldn't there be blood on his clothes?' Benno remembered with disgust the pool that had crept from the prie-dieu as if ashamed of the horror propped on it. 'Was there blood on the Panteras' clothes?'

Sigismondo made a cleaving motion with his right hand, startling Biondello. 'You sever the spine, the blood needn't spurt. It was on the axe; a certain amount was on Brother Ieronimo. The Abbot bled into his own clothes. What the Marshal is looking for is the cross – and even that wouldn't prove its possessor was the murderer.'

Benno took this in with the last of the chicken. 'Somebody killed the Abbot, somebody else took the cross . . .'

Sigismondo shrugged. 'If Brother Ieronimo killed the Abbot, courtesy of the Devil, d'you think *he* took the cross?'

'Even if the Devil can make you do anything he wants, I can't see that he'd want to meddle with a cross. I mean, so the Abbot wasn't exactly a holy man, still a cross is a cross.' Benno was disturbed. He had always thought that if the Devil were to go slumming and appear to him personally, making just the sign of the cross was an infallible protection. You were also supposed to say something in Latin to tell the Devil to get behind you, but he'd never been able to see the point of that – surely better to have the Devil where you could see him than where you didn't know what he might be up to.

'A cross that's stained with blood already.' Sigismondo's face had darkened. 'I don't forget why Bernabo Pantera wanted the cross to go to the Virgin at Scheggia. Two of his brothers had died for it before he did.'

Benno wiped plum juice from his hands on his doublet, where the marks were invisible in a patchwork of stains, and was tactfully silent. He was sure his master still intended to carry out Bernabo's dying wish but, with the cross missing and the Duke requiring the Abbot's murderer to be found, it was hard to see how even Sigismondo could achieve it.

And if the cross was found on Gian Pantero's person, or

149

in his belongings, that handsome young man would shortly have bits of him, carefully parcelled out, nailed to four gates of Rocca, his head reserved for the palace gate, so that the world should see how the Duke Ludovico treated those who impugned his honour by slaying his guests.

Unfortunately, too, the Duke would keep the cross.

Chapter 30

Permission to Go to Rome

The Duke sent for Sigismondo early next morning just when he had completed his comprehensive shave, leaving the brown head shining like oiled new leather. Benno helped him on, quickly, with a fine cambric shirt with drawn-thread work at the throat, and a plain black velvet doublet over that; anxious not to be left behind, he then scrambled into his own best doublet, a nondescript affair in brown homespun, over his old one, and combed his beard with his fingers as he followed Sigismondo's stride. Biondello, unable to don a fresh ear in honour of the occasion, scampered innocently after.

It was already hot, with promise of a scorching day to follow. The Duke was out on the loggia of his room, leaning over the stone balustrade and surveying his city beneath and the hills beyond, touched with the rose of sunrise while mist lay thick in the valleys. He was already dressed, in green brocade edged with white silk, the colours of Rocca. The Duchess, who was walking restlessly up and down the loggia, still wore a bedgown, her hair in a plait down her back. She turned to look with evident curiosity as Sigismondo made his bow, a long look, and she understood why her husband trusted him.

Sigismondo for his part saw a girl barely more than fifteen, pretty enough to make it credible that the Duke sought to please her by giving her La Feconda, even

151

without his concern for a future heir. His present one, as Sigismondo knew, had caused immense anxiety by a fever during the spring, from which he had not yet made a full recovery. La Feconda, if it brought the blessings the Panteras thought it did, was very much needed in Rocca.

'Your Grace.'

The Duke fixed his rather manic blue stare on Sigismondo, giving his hand to be kissed.

'What have you found?'

'Neither cross nor killer yet, your Grace. All three Panteras have been searched, they and their rooms, their baggage, even their hosts.' Sigismondo spread his hands and heard the stamp of the Duchess's soft slipper.

The Duke's stare did not diminish. 'What, then, do you advise? Torture?'

'Mm . . hm. It will gain us nothing. Pain makes men lie as much as tell the truth. My advice is to let them go.'

'Let them *go*!' The Duchess had swept forward, small and furious. 'When we have them in our hands?'

'Your Grace. If we let them go, they will run or bide. Where they run to will be interesting and they can be followed. If they bide, they may be waiting to recover the cross if they have hidden it where we have failed to search. Then your Grace will have them, and the cross as well, in your own hands.'

The Duchess's eyes sparkled. 'Let them go, let them go!' She ran to the Duke and clasped his arm, looking up into his face. 'Set your men to hunt it down.'

The Duke put his hand over hers but did not share her glee. He had another aspect to consider. 'How can I let men go who may have murdered my guest? What will be said of me?'

Sigismondo, about to answer, closed his mouth as a page came up to bow and murmur to the Duke, who dismissed the page and addressed Sigismondo.

'The Abbot's treasurer and secretary are asking audience. I am reminded that I have a murderer to hand. Do you believe that this mad monk did the deed?'

'Your Grace, nothing at this stage is certain. He claims the Devil caused him to commit it but he could not show me a stroke that could have severed a gnat, never mind the Abbot's spine.'

'That could be cunning.' The Duchess was pleased that her husband had, after all, a scapegoat even if the goat in question was a frail-witted religious. If this matter of the Duke's honour were only out of the way, he could attend to such things as ensuring his line with the help of La Feconda.

'Mm . . . He does not strike me, your Grace, as capable of cunning. But he is subject to visions and he may not always be sure what is happening in this world.'

The Duchess had no opinion of monks so out of touch with reality that they took an axe to their superior, and she was about to speak when the page returned with Father Torquato and Brother Filippo. The Duchess, regarding them with distaste, thought how crow-like they were in their dark robes. She noticed the slide sideways of Torquato's eyes as he checked whether Brother Filippo would speak first; monks could certainly look cunning. Brother Filippo reminded her of her confessor at her father's court, a man she had taken pains not to bring with her – one of those inclined to think breathing itself sinful; his face had the same tortured intensity.

The Duke gave them leave to speak.

'Your Grace, we are here to seek your permission to start for Rome at once. The Holy Father must hear from our lips what has happened, and decree the punishment for our wretched brother.'

'Where is he now?'

'Your Marshal's men have him in a cell below.'

The Duchess became suddenly aware of the layers of the palace she lived in: the rooms here, light, airy, elegant, marble and gilt; but deep beneath, like the murk of nightmares, the ancient stone dungeons in the foundations, where so many had lived, and died, forgotten. She tightened her hands on the Duke's arm.

'What of the obsequies for the Abbot? Do you not mean to attend them?'

It was Torquato's turn. 'Your Grace, it is fitting that Father Abbot be buried in his own chapel at Pietra. Father Prior will head the Chapter. We have too urgent a task ourselves – the consideration of Brother Ieronimo's soul – for it to be possible we should attend, and we are sure that Father Abbot looking down on us from Heaven will understand and bless us.'

This, presuming hugely on the whereabouts of the Abbot's soul, and on a benevolence for which he had never been famous in his lifetime, struck an uncomfortable, false note even in ears accustomed to the lies of courtiers. The Duke frowned. If these monks went to Rome with their story, what version of events might they offer to the Pope? They would be unlikely to play down the quarrel between Duke and Abbot; what poison might they distil against Rocca? Ludovico still owed the dues on his goods warehoused at Pietra, and these two would not only urge the Abbey's point of view unopposed, but they might even suggest that the Duke had suborned the crazy Brother Ieronimo to solve his problem for him, in the hope that a new Abbot might prove more amenable. He mentally surveyed his court for a man of both presence and diplomacy, and glanced at Sigismondo, standing watchful by a jasper pillar.

'We grant permission, Father, but stipulate that you go

to Rome with an escort. This is the man – ' he gestured to Sigismondo to come forward – 'who will ensure your safety and that of your prisoner. He will inform the Holy Father of last night's events, and speak of my grief at such a crime against the Church, grief doubled by its having occurred here in my Court.'

Sigismondo alone showed no change of face at the Duke's programme. Torquato and Brother Filippo were openly taken aback. Torquato, who had known and much disliked Sigismondo in the past, wore a face so sour as to be nearly comical, before he recovered himself. The Duchess grimaced, although she was quite unable to look other than pretty; from what she had seen in this brief interview she had become confident that this quiet man was able, if anyone was, to get La Feconda for her, and she must have it. If the Panteras were the most likely thieves (for the jewel was not theirs however long it had been in their possession) then if he went to Rome with these horrible monks, how was Sigismondo to watch that family and seize the cross for her?

A noise of distant cheering arose in the city and the Duke turned, putting a hand to the sill to look out. 'Cardinal Pontano has returned. I sent a message to him last night at Colleverde to ask if he would break his retreat and return early to give us his advice and help. He must have travelled by moonlight.' The Duke wheeled and surveyed the men before him. 'He will guide us in the wishes of Holy Mother Church.'

Such are the devices and desires of the human heart: the monks looked less than grateful to have their own wishes submitted to a higher authority for approval. Sigismondo was not asked what his wishes might be. Men who offer their services to dukes must put their own honour beneath that of their employers.

Chapter 31

Who Goes Where

Cardinal Pontano, though he could not have slept the previous night, showed no signs of fatigue when dealing with the situation. The killing of a priest is sacrilege; the killing of an abbot is no more in principle but, in practice, the scale of retribution will acknowledge the rank. In any case, the monk who admitted to the murder must go to Rome. The Pope must hear about the appalling deed and decree the punishment.

The Cardinal, straight-backed in his chair beside the Duke's, gave his approval also to the scheme of the Abbot's secretary and treasurer escorting Brother Ieronimo. They were of sufficient importance to accord with the seriousness of the event and they had discovered the Abbot's body, which gave them an extra, if gruesome, significance. Regarding the Abbot's obsequies, he himself would go to Pietra and conduct them.

It grieved him to find, after questioning Brother Ieronimo and hearing from the other brethren about his visions, that the Abbot's murderer was not as overcome by remorse as he should be. Brother Ieronimo claimed the Devil to be at fault, not he, and he even inclined to excusing the Devil for acting according to his own infernal nature. So far from being plunged in tears and remorse, Brother Ieronimo was looking forward to his first visit to Rome – and that it would be his last did not seem to weigh upon him. The Virgin, he assured the Cardinal, had come to him just that morning, quite early, just after Lauds, and had told him to be of good cheer – all would be well.

As for Sigismondo as escort to the party, and bearer of the Duke's messages of regret to the Pope, the Cardinal was not in doubt. He had first met Sigismondo a few years ago, and now, as he extended his hand for Sigismondo to kiss the ring, he bestowed his blessing for the journey. There would be, he promised as Sigismondo rose, letters which he would immediately dictate and which would assure them of a proper reception at Rome, and the help of his friends in the Curia to obtain audience of the Holy Father without delay.

Naturally nobody asked Benno for his opinion about the journey, but, as he saddled up the huge roan Sigismondo would be riding, he whistled between his teeth the refrain of the bawdy song Angelo had been singing when they met all those days ago in the tavern at the crossroads. Never in his life had he thought he would go to Rome! And although Benno knew that not the devoutest of prayers, even could they be said before the High Altar in St Peter's itself, could restore Biondello's ear, they would surely safeguard the one he had left. And if a cat may look at a king, then Biondello, hidden in Benno's jerkin, might certainly view the Pope and come away the better for it.

Whistling Angelo's song might have been a conjuration. As Benno turned from the roan, a slender hand extended a worn velvet cap and jiggled it invitingly under his nose.

'A ducat from the Duke? Where's my travelling expenses, then? I'm going to need a horse too until the Devil teaches me how to fly.'

Alarmed, Benno pushed the cap away and looked round. 'Don't say that! Haven't you heard about the flying Devil that possessed the monk and made him kill the Abbot? You don't want to give people ideas.'

'That's my profession,' remarked Angelo, replacing his cap at a jaunty angle on his long blond hair. 'People are deadly short of ideas and will pay for quite a few of mine. As for the Devil and the monk, Rocca's talked of nothing else since dawn. And now I hear you're off to Rome to see the Pope and no word to me.'

'No word to you,' Sigismondo's voice, deep and amused, broke in from the shadows, 'because I count on your having ears as sharp as your knives. What does the city say?'

Angelo gave his crooked smile. 'The best place for the Abbot is in the river, they say, with a few monks tied to his ankles to keep him from floating. They want the Duke to take the cross and shut himself up with the Duchess until she asks for out-of-season medlars and chews charcoal.'

'They think his Grace has the cross?'

'Why else,' asked Angelo sweetly, 'did you axe the Abbot?'

Sigismondo wagged his head. 'Mmm. There was also the matter of the taxes due. Hey, I give *value* for money.'

'Tell that to the Panteras. They're talking compensation payments from the Duke for being searched and found innocent. I think Ferondo fears that's pushing their luck, though. They were arguing outside the Palazzo Bandini and I saw Olivero hanging on to his horse's bridle so as not to sit down in the street – at this hour of day. If Bandini didn't have dealings with the Pantera bank at Rome, his doorman says, he'd have turned them out last night after the Marshal's visit.'

'Gian Pantera lost his bed here at the palace at the same time, *and* a childhood friend into the bargain. Not all the scent at Court can cover a whiff of disgrace. Here.' Sigismondo sent a gold coin spinning towards Angelo, who snatched it from the air. 'For a change of clothes as well as the horse. I need to know about the Panteras and I can't watch them for myself.'

Angelo rang the coin and raised his eyebrows, an amazed seraph. '*All* the Panteras? Should I suggest to Gian that he ride pillion with Olivero so I can watch them together?'

'Then you would have done what the Church has failed to do.' Sigismondo tossed another coin to Angelo. 'You may have to hire someone. I leave it to you.'

Angelo nodded and slid into the shadows as a groom came past the stable yard leading a grey, caparisoned in green and white with a fringe of gold bullion. The man bowed at sight of Sigismondo – by now there was no one in the palace unaware of the name of the man in black with the shaven head, and that his axe, whoever had wielded it, had rid the world of the Abbot.

Sigismondo put out a hand to smooth the silken neck. 'The Duke rides out, then?'

'He goes to escort her Grace to the gates.'

'Her Grace is leaving the city today?'

'She has decided, this minute, to leave for Pietra. She travels with the Cardinal.'

Sigismondo put a useful hand to the bridle as the grey tossed its head and sidled, irritated by the cold rasp of bullion. 'An honour for the Abbot,' he commented. Funny, thought Benno, that the Duchess should go for the Abbot's funeral and not the Duke, but perhaps he couldn't be spared. It was always tricky, too, leaving your capital city if you were a ruler – people had a nasty habit of getting up riots, even revolutions, in your absence.

The groom, though, knew and was eager to tell them the true reason, although since it was gossip he lowered his voice and looked about him as he spoke. 'There's been

a quarrel, sir. I have it from one of her maids. Her Grace
is angry that the cross which brings luck hasn't been found.
She's off to Scheggia to pray to the Virgin to send her sons
if she can't get the cross. His Grace is against her going.'
He shrugged. 'When a woman wants her way . . .'

'Hey, it's men's business to see that she gets it!'
Sigismondo clapped the grey's neck cheerfully and turned
to Benno. 'Be ready. His Grace is sending soldiers with us
against brigands on the road to Rome, and his secretary
is finishing the letters to his Holiness for the Duke's
signature. Bring the horses to the piazza as soon as you're
ready.'

Sigismondo entered the palace and made his way
through a turmoil of bustle. Normally, several days were
spent in preparing for the journey the Duchess had this
minute decided on. Tempers were being lost as fast as
belongings. The Duchess's ladies had been instructed to
pack dresses suitable for a pilgrimage but, tiresomely, no
one had thought of such a purpose when her wardrobe
was designed. One lady, with all her own dresses and
possessions to pack as well, was driven to suggest they
could pick up the appropriate sackcloth from the Abbey
at Pietra, while ashes could be supplied from anyone the
Duke happened to scorch with his glance.

Quarrels in palaces spread downwards and few ladies
were on speaking terms when at last the chests were
waiting to be corded and carried down to the mules. After
all, pilgrimage or no, her Grace would make the right
impression in Pietra, and the majority of ladies carried
the point that black velvet sewn with pearls demonstrated
dignified sorrow at the Abbot's fate. What she would wear
for the further journey must be left to her Grace to decide
but, if the crossing to Scheggia were as choppy as it was
rumoured to be, nobody would much care.

In the piazza, the scene was as confused as that inside the palace. The Duchess's baggage was still being roped to the string of mules, the horses and litters for her ladies mixed with those of the Cardinal's retinue, the monks of Pietra getting under everyone's feet, and the soldiers who were to escort Sigismondo and the man popularly called the 'Mad Monk' trying to form up. Nothing at all could be heard clearly and everyone was convinced of the prime importance of his own undertaking, and most of Rocca had come to see the fun. Benno, up on his own wiry little black, struggled through with his master's great roan and wondered if Angelo were in the crowd. That, he supposed, would depend on where the Panteras were.

As it turned out, they were there too. The brothers had come to take their leave of the Duke; perhaps they imagined they might establish their innocence still more firmly by putting themselves into the jaws of the lion for the second time. Unfortunately the lion was not interested. Duke Ludovico was wholly absorbed by the problem of establishing his own innocence in the face of a city comfortably sure that he had ordered the assassination of the Abbot. Where the Mad Monk fitted into this scenario, no one was prepared to say, nor did they care: cells were no novelty to a religious and it was high time monks had to perform a few penances as well as handing them out.

No crowd where there was the Duke was ever short of petitioners, eager for the Duke's attention and no more likely to get it than were the Panteras. One, more persistent and of respectable, even affluent appearance, managed to seize the Duke's bridle and, before his grip was broken by the Marshal's staff on his wrist, gasped out his wish, impatiently granted by the Duke: a rich merchant just obtaining permission for himself and his wife to travel to Rome under the protection of the Duke's soldiers. Sigismondo did not know him but would certainly have recognized his wife Felicia, having spent several hours in her arms at Pietra not so long ago.

Chapter 32

Departures

Agostino da Sangallo had a ruling passion in his life: greed. When he was a small child his nurse had noticed how, once he got hold of something – even a pebble whose glitter attracted him, or a ball another child had been playing with – it was almost impossible to make him let go.

As he grew older, the things he grasped were larger and more expensive, such as estates or jewels, but the difficulty in making him let go had matured: it could not be done.

His father left him a house in Pietra and a villa in the country, a business and a great deal of money. Because money attracts money he was able to enter into an excellent marriage with a young rich widow, who brought him more property and a collection of antique coins and engraved gems her husband had made. The reason he was now travelling to Rome, in the protection of Duke Ludovico's guards, was to offer, at a shrewd price, certain fine things from this collection to the Pope himself who had an inexhaustible enthusiasm for, among very many other things, antiquities.

The reason he was taking his wife Donna Felicia along was that he couldn't trust her. On this journey there'd be no chance for her to make an assignation with anyone and he meant to make sure she kept to her curtained litter rather than her horse, so that no man could picture her in his fantasies. As for her fantasies, it is not possible fo man to control the wickedness in a woman's heart; but a least, as he examined the features of this Sigismondo wh was in charge of the party he had asked to join – savin the cost of an armed escort – and as he took in the Roma nose, the column of neck like a wrestler's and, worse, th unsightly head of a wrestler shaved for combat, he though it a grotesque fancy indeed if Felicia's eyes should ligh on him with favour.

While Agostino congratulated himself on his trave arrangements, the Pantera cousins were making their in considerable haste. The brothers set out, impeded i the streets by citizens come to see off Duchess, Cardina and Abbot; the latter in a much more satisfactory conditio than yesterday when he had arrived so full of himself an so confident of besting their Duke. It would have bee impious actually to cheer the departing coffin, especiall under the stern eyes of Cardinal Pontano; but smilin faces lined the route. They were sorry to see their Duches go, and certainly they cheered her part of the procession but she would soon be back and the Virgin of Scheggi would take pity on Rocca and send her sons.

It was against the homeward surge of these citizen that Olivero and Ferondo were making their way, whe they had to draw aside. The Duke, in no good mood, wa riding with his escort back to the palace, a tide of gree and white through the canyon of the street. The brother might not have been noticed, for Ludovico's thoughts wer divided between regret for the departure of his prett young wife, and anger at the crowd's covert approval o the murder they believed he had ordered. The Marshal however, riding by his stirrup, dourly drew his attentio to the brothers, whereupon the Duke remembered tha Sigismondo had said they should be under observation

The simplest way would have been to put them behind bars, but simplicity was not the first consideration: the Panteras beside being merchants were also agents for the Pantera bank with its branches in Florence, Venice, Genoa and Rome; dukes rarely have enough money even to finance weddings or wars and the Panteras were well able to be useful to Rocca. Also of weight was that these two, taking their caps off to him now, one very sulkily, were undoubtedly related to Cardinal Pantera, reputed to have the ear of the Pope.

All these factors mitigated the Duke's glare as Olivero levered himself up from a bow with his hand on the pommel. Also, if he knew his Marshal, these Panteras already had men following and marking them. He inclined his head almost graciously.

'You're leaving us, I see. You are going home to your wives?' It was in his mind that they might be returning with or without the jewel guaranteeing riches and heirs. The reply, however, surprised him.

'Your Grace has hit on it exactly. We are travelling to join our wives at Rome.'

Ferondo had a more conciliatory air than his brother and was anxious, slyly, to impress. 'They lodge with our cousin, Cardinal Pantera.'

The Duke's horse, responding to some movement of its rider, tossed its head with a shimmering dazzle of gold bullion in the sun. Ludovico was smiling, and he could smile with charm. 'Why, sirs, you must haste on your way. Take advantage of our guard that goes with Sigismondo to Rome. There are such dangers on the road and we would wish you to arrive safely and bear our greetings to his Eminence. Our Marshal will ride with you as escort until you join the party – they are but just gone.'

Olivero and Ferondo, with the Marshal wheeling his

horse alongside theirs, were forced to improvise thanks, put on their caps and ride off to join the party led by a man whom they distrusted more than any other man alive. What was surprising was the look of grim satisfaction on Olivero's dark face as they rode away.

Another Pantera left Rocca shortly after his cousins. He, too, had Rome as his destination and, like all sensible travellers who did not wish to fall victim to the robbers – masterless men, discharged soldiers, bands of beggars – who preyed on everyone, particularly on the road to Rome, he had hired some sturdy men for protection. Of course, it would have been safer to travel in numbers, but Gian had no wish to be saddled with a lot of pilgrims wanting to visit every church on the way; he was glad to be accosted at the gates by a quiet young man who asked for a share in his armed escort. He was also going to Rome, and his serious, beautiful face reminded Gian of the archangel Gabriel in a painting of the Annunciation he had recently seen in Florence. He did not, however, give the impression of one who would be boringly pious, and he might even be of use should bandits attack.

Gian was not to know exactly how many knives, concealed about his person, the young man would have available in such a crisis.

Chapter 33

We All Make Mistakes

Benno was delighted and surprised to see a face he knew among the three people and a groom permitted by the Duke to join their party. Agostino da Sangallo he had never seen in his life before, and was sorry to see now – eyes close together as if neither eye trusted the other, and lips so thin they might have been stitched into a line. His clothes were plain but good, and his wife's brocade seemed familiar to Benno somehow. Her face was heavily veiled, which must be stifling, poor lady, but the way she moved persuaded Benno that she was worth being seen, particularly since her husband didn't want her to be.

Then he saw the face he knew. It certainly was not a pretty one, resembling a long slab of cake with currrants for eyes, and it showed no sign of knowing him in return. He realized at once when he had last seen it, rousing him from sleep in the house in Pietra and driving him out to look for his master on that terrible morning. It was Perpetua, riding pillion behind an uncouth groom, and their mistress must be the woman his master had spent the night with, and the brocade was the stuff he had seen her buy, and this man was the jealous husband. Benno had been thinking of speaking to Perpetua, and now knew it was the last thing he must do. He kept his usual expression of hopeless stupidity, and was sure of one thing: there'd be no funny business on this journey, with da

Sangallo scrutinizing everyone with such bitter suspicion

Barely a mile out of Rocca, the City Marshal caught up with them and handed over, in the manner of one delivering prisoners rather than companions on the journey, the Pantera brothers.

Both of them appeared happy with the arrangement; it might be, thought Benno, that Sigismondo too did not mind having them here under his eye; but very certainly Agostino da Sangallo was violently displeased. He barely acknowledged Sigismondo's introduction of them and immediately snatched his wife's mare's bridle and dragged her away to ride alongside the monks instead.

Sigismondo had got the soldiers to change the cords round Brother Ieronimo's wrists for plaited linen; the cords had already chafed the skin and in a week of travel would have produced running sores. Benno could hear the monk's voice raised, as they rode along, in a penitential psalm which would have been more appropriate if sung in a less joyful manner.

Sismondo rode ahead, either alone or with the sergeant of the guard. Behind them all came the Pantera groom and the other four men of the escort.

They made better going once they were out of the valley where the wide road had been all iron-hard mud trenched with wheel tracks and pocked by hooves. The worn expanse crossing the hillside gave better footing even on slabs of rock. Still, they had not come within miles of the first hospice as dusk came on, and they made camp by a wide stream above a ford, built a fire, and the sergeant posted a watch well out of the firelight on the outcrop of a rocky hill.

The Sangallo party kept an unsociable distance, eating and drinking on their own. The groom kept edging closer to Perpetua, who kept edging away until she edged against her master, who scolded her furiously. Benno wondered how fast the four of them would join the main party if there were sudden danger.

Olivero produced wine, which he offered even to the soldiers, and, as if he had suddenly made up his mind, passed to Sigismondo.

'Fill your cup, man. It's good stuff. Drown our differences, eh? I bear you no grudge for killing my uncle!' Something about Sigismondo's face made Olivero hurry on. 'All that was a misunderstanding and he brought his fate on himself. As for the search at the Palazzo Bandini, that was the Duke's doing and none of yours. You and I fought side by side and against bandits once. If we have to do that again, let's do it as comrades.'

Sigismondo inclined his head. To Benno, his expression by the fire's light looked demonic rather than acquiescent, but it did not deter Olivero. He leant across Brother Filippo who was sipping his wine as if enduring a penance and, seizing the flagon from Ferondo, sat back and tilted it over Sigismondo's cup. 'Drink up, drink up, I've brought plenty.'

For all his good humour or perhaps because of it, Olivero himself appeared to be drinking less than usual, in his role of generous provider of wine. Brother Ieronimo took his share with perfect simplicity. He made no attempt to join in the talk but sat looking around in the gathering dusk as though everything he saw gave him pleasure. Suddenly he pointed.

'What's that on the hill top?'

They all turned to look, Benno not the only one with premonitions of a band of robbers surveying them before riding down to the slaughter. The pale green of the evening sky was bitten into by the jagged outline of a ruin. One of the escort satisfied everyone's curiosity.

'That was a hermitage. My auntie used to go up with food for the hermit, she told me, till he died. People came from miles around, he was such a holy man.'

'I'd like to pray there.' Brother Ieronimo started to scramble to his feet and Torquato pulled him down with a sharp tug on his sleeve.

'Out of the question. You'll say the Office with us before we sleep.'

There was no protest from the monk but he went on gazing at the hill top as everyone got ready for sleep. Agostino busily constructed a barricade of packs and belongings round his wife. She had of necessity lifted her veils to eat, but he had made her turn from the firelight even at that distance, and had propelled Perpetua forward to intercept the flagon-bearing Olivero before he could reach their little group and pollute it with his inquisitive stare. Agostino seemed to fear intrusion by their own party almost as much as any attack by bandits, and Benno saw that his behaviour was making his wife an object of speculative comment with the Panteras, something which caused Brother Filippo to withdraw in disgust.

The soldiers had spread in a ring round the camp, the one linked to Brother Ieronimo being the one left on first watch. Under the sergeant's stern eye he had accepted only half a cup of Olivero's wine but, as if in compensation, Olivero lingered now to speak to him, putting a friendly arm round his shoulders before joining Ferondo and their groom in the comfortable huddle they had created by the fire. Benno saw to their own horses and carried their saddles to the foot of the hill, where Sigismondo had elected to sleep. Olivero's wine had been rich and heavy, of a quality Benno was not used to, and he yawned as he spread Sigismondo's cloak. Biondello had already made a few quick turns on Benno's cloak and now, curled up nose to tail, rolled an eye to see what was taking his quilt so long to come to bed.

'How far – ' Benno's yawn nearly dislocated his jaw – 'how far is it to Rome? Will we get there soon?'

Sigismondo had explained to him a little about the immensity of the world, and Benno had a hazy idea of many leagues stretching beyond the horizon; some he understood to be covered in sand or snow all year round, but surely Rome, not being beyond the sea, was only a night or two away? When he had gone into France with Sigismondo a year ago it had taken weeks to arrive but that after all was in another country. His master now lay down and wrapped the cloak round him, saying, 'Too soon for some.'

With this ambiguous pronouncement, he closed his eyes and almost immediately was breathing more deeply. Benno settled down round Biondello, sheltering him from the night breeze, and heard the sounds of the countryside about them, the river's soft talking, the crackle as someone fed the fire; he wondered if 'too soon for some' meant poor Brother Ieronimo who, in spite of his complete lack of anxiety, must be travelling towards a very nasty fate indeed. It was all very fine to blame the Devil for what happened but it wasn't the Devil who'd be taking the punishment.

Brother Ieronimo's face floated in Benno's dreams, and more than his face as he capered about singing resonantly and swinging an axe at random, among flying monsters all veiled. One monster hovered over Benno with claws poised to tear the veil from what would, Benno knew, kill him if he saw it, and he woke, sweating and trying to shout, to find Brother Ieronimo's face still before him in the moonlight.

'May God be with you, my son. What is wrong?'

What indeed? Benno sat up, in the grip of his nightmare. Behind Brother Ieronimo two figures were struggling against the night sky, but in a dream-like silence. The next moment, an axe landed at his feet, making Biondello execute a backwards jump that would have done credit to any acrobat.

Brother Ieronimo, apparently unaware of what was happening behind him, picked up the axe and examined it in the moonlight. He was just remarking something when one of the struggling men cried out and fell to his knees, one arm twisted behind his back by the other whom Benno, coming to his senses, saw to be Sigismondo.

Brother Ieronimo, axe in hand, ran to intervene.

'This is no bandit, my son. He is your friend.'

As the man on his knees threw his head back and was discovered by the moon to be Olivero, the statement lacked credibility. Sigismondo, however, not only released his grip but helped Olivero to his feet, dusting him down with bruising geniality and saying, 'A mistake! We all make mistakes—'

Olivero pointed to the axe in Brother Ieronimo's hand, which Sigismondo swiftly took from him. 'I caught him with that, stealing up on you and I'd just got it from him when you woke. Fool that I was, I'd taken pity on him! I took him up to that hermitage where he wanted to pray, and he went on chanting for ever. I dozed off . . . he must have had that axe hidden on him . . . I woke and saw him wandering off to murder whom he could find!'

Odd that Brother Ieronimo had bothered to wander off with his axe, Benno thought; why not bash Olivero, who was handy? Perhaps the Devil was cunning enough to make him go for the man in charge of taking him to justice. Brother Ieronimo, his hair on end, looked far from cunning himself. He was gazing at Olivero as though he were the madman, and he made no resistance as Olivero seized him by the wrists and began to drag him away. People by this time were stirring. Benno hoped they'd have been quicker if robbers had attacked.

'Wait.' Sigismondo's voice had something of the arresting effect of a drawn sword. 'Where is the guard who should have been with him?'

He arrived, now, at a rush, as did others of the escort. The rest of the party had started up. Weapons gleamed in the moonlight. Olivero took the rope of plaited linen dangling from the guard's wrist and began to lash Brother Ieronimo's wrists together brutally hard. Sigismondo stood, focus of all as he waited, and it was to him and not to the furiously demanding sergeant that the guard, his arm jolting at Olivero's exertions, spoke in excuse.

'I only let him go because Signor Pantera said he would be with him and see he didn't escape. I thought there could be no harm.' From the fear in his voice, he had changed his mind about that. Sigismondo merely nodded at the sergeant, who marched the man away, Brother Ieronimo shambling after on his umbilical cord. Benno wondered if the monk would remain alongside during the beating the guard was in for, or if the sergeant would untie Olivero's handiwork and attach him first to a more reliable keeper.

Sigismondo was embracing Olivero and speaking with a cordiality so false as to be offensive. 'I must, I *must* thank you for saving my life, sir. What I owe to the Panteras! But I will repay. Never fear, I'm not a man who owes a debt for long.'

Olivero came out of the bear hug with the look of a man who needs to count his ribs to make sure they are all there. He probably appreciated the true meaning in Sigismondo's statement. Benno thought the scheme of procuring Brother Ieronimo's release so as to have him for a scapegoat for attacking Sigismondo was quite clever. Olivero must have carried one of the firewood axes up to the hermitage, and have brought Ieronimo carefully down the hill past where Sigismondo lay.

Muffled cries came from downstream where the guard was being beaten, and someone was praying quite loudly. Benno picked up Biondello and held him close while he watched Sigismondo arrange himself again to sleep. There were mutters from those disturbed by events – Ferondo would be getting a disappointing account from his brother – but the moon, sailing high, shone on a serene Sigismondo.

Benno whispered, 'Tried to kill you, din' he?'

'Hey, that was a question you didn't *need* to ask. And yes, he'll try again. But not tonight.'

Benno hoped fervently that Rome was not too far away.

Chapter 34

'He'll Live, if God Permits'

The word came at midday. It was hot enough now to raise a blister if you touched a rock, but these were men who had long known not to do anything so foolish. Their wisdom might have come to them from Nature herself for they lived so close to her. Like her, they were ruthless. Harvests fail, sheep and cattle die, people starve to death. To survive, take advantage of everything that comes along.

Coming along now, reported by a child who was lookout, rode a very promising party on the winding track below, promising because it was not too large and because it had only two or three as escort. The leader of the peasants, his face in shadow under his hat of plaited straw, considered the plan of action as he lay gazing down between boulders. One of the party at least was well dressed, he should have rings and a chain they could sell, and of course the clothes. He was young, could likely handle that sword of his, best take him out first. The other, seemingly his companion, should be easy, a slender creature pretty as a girl, might as soon scream as fight, and that blond hair would get a good price from a wigmaker.

He rose soundlessly to his feet, put a stone in his sling, and lifted a hand in signal to the others. They would be eating well soon.

The first and only thing Gian Pantera knew of the ambush was a stunning blow on the side of the head. Even from that he might have rallied if his horse had not bolted, and this was as well because it carried him far from the scene. When his hold on things began to slacken, it threw him, and stood circling and trembling for a while. Then it began to browse from a bush nearby.

In the rocky defile it had left behind was a trampling shouting confusion. The stones and boulders thrown and bowled down had hit some and missed others. Surprise had been lost and now the whole thing must be done quickly before blood spoiled any good clothes. They could catch up with the runaway later.

Scrambling down the hillside, two launched themselves on one soldier, three at another, snatching at bridles, cudgelling at sword arms, pulling a foot from a stirrup. One alone was judged sufficient for the frail blond. He gripped the bridle, a mistake that left his fingers still gripping the bridle and the rest of him lying dead under the hoofs. A knife flew in a silver arc and lodged in a peasant's neck; another, still in Angelo's hand, sliced into a cudgelling arm. The peasants' leader, seeing the odds were suddenly against them, led the retreat as vigorously as he had the attack and, scrambling up the rocky scarp, received a knife between his shoulder-blades, tumbled backwards, and came to rest at the foot of the slope, hat over face, as if sleeping.

One of the escort was down and dead, a peasant had been kicked under the chin by a rider and sprawled over a boulder, twitching. A peasant fell to a sword blow, another trying to catch the loose horse succumbed to one more of the deadly flying knives, and one fled full pelt back along the track. The remaining guard wheeled his horse, set off and rode him down. The last of the robbers, on his knees by the fallen leader's body, clasped his hands towards the blond angel and cried for mercy. At that moment he remembered, vividly, a traveller who had done that to him not long ago and whose bloodstained doublet he was now wearing. It still surprised him that the calm angel leant from his saddle and knifed him.

Angelo collected the three knives that had hit and, for he had been dealing with targets moving among valuable horses, two that had missed. He was considering a robber who crouched trying to stem the blood that poured from his right arm, when the guard rode back, sagging over his saddle-bow and holding his ribs.

'I'm not waiting,' Angelo said. 'I'm off after Pantera.'

The guard looked at him and saw he was not persuadable.

'Help me get my mate across his horse,' he said. 'The robbers' women will come, and you know what they'll do to his body.'

'If you hang about, they'll do the same to you without waiting for you to die first. Leave him and save yourself.'

With this bleak advice, Angelo applied spurs and set off, kicking up dust in the face of the robber bleeding over the stones. He, at least, was grateful Angelo had no more time to spend at the scene.

The sergeant in charge of Sigismondo's escort was the first to hear the drumming of the hooves behind them. He had assumed the responsibility of the rearguard while Sigismondo led, and on this last day or so before they reached Rome everyone was aware that their chances of being attacked were high, lucky though they had been till then. Among the vast numbers of robbers and cutthroats who lived in the city it was customary, to make a pleasant change, to roam outside its gates and come back happily with some booty at dusk. They were far more to be feared than the peasant gangs because, as professionals, they were less daunted by numbers.

Calling a warning to the party ahead, the sergeant wheeled his horse and drew his sword, and the two rearguard soldiers did the same. Whoever was on the road, past a spur of the hill and therefore still out of sight, would have seen their dust and the traces of their passing and sounded, for whatever reason, anxious to catch them up.

When the guard saw their pursuers, they stared and, cautiously, lowered their swords. The wild advance checked its pace and the two horses came slowly forward. One was ridden by a golden-haired young man, soberly but well dressed, and the other, which he led, carried a young man, his head bandaged with strips of shirt, who lolled in the saddle, tied to the leathers by more strips of cloth. His eyes were shut and, though the sergeant knew very well that a decoy was possible, he also knew from experience that the colour of the face under that bandage was one not easily faked. Still with drawn sword, he rode forward.

'We need protection into Rome. I can pay.'

The sergeant saw he was dealing with a man who did not waste time. 'You must ask him,' he said, jerking his head towards Sigismondo who was riding back towards them. 'He's the one in charge.'

Sigismondo arrived. He looked like the man in charge.

As he reined in and inclined his head courteously towards Angelo, it could not possibly be guessed that Angelo was in his hire. Angelo's explanation was brief: 'Robbers attacked us. We need help.'

Sigismondo was already alongside Gian Pantera, steadying his horse, looking him over.

'He should lie flat and no longer be jolted like this. His wound must be tended soon if he is to recover.'

'But he can – he must – ride in my litter. He can lie flat there, poor creature.'

It was a woman's voice calling out, a voice not heard until now by most of the party, though Sigismondo knew it well. The party had ridden back and grouped as near to the newcomers as the path, and the escort, allowed. Agostino da Sangallo cried out angrily over the murmur of approval, 'No, no. My wife needs the litter. She ought not to be riding in this heat.'

'Let the lady judge for herself,' Sigismondo said, dismounting. So far, in spite of her husband's urgings, the lady had refused to make use of the litter whose curtains would have concealed her so much more effectively than veils. The grooms, now, were leading the horses round with it, close to the young man drooping in the saddle.

'It is gracious of you, my lady.' Sigismondo, pulling undone the strips of cloth that kept Gian from falling headlong, spoke with impersonal calm. He took Gian's weight and, lifting him down like a baby, carried him and laid him down on the green silk mattress and cushions of the litter. Sigismondo lifted, first, the makeshift bandage and examined the wound, where the hair was matted with blood over a lump the size of a hen's egg. Then he looked under the young man's eyelids, into which he let the sun shine for a second before allowing them to close again.

Two more travellers jostled in front of the rest at this point, to find out how much more delay there would be, and there was a sudden shout as Sigismondo drew back.

'God's Bones, it's Gian! Is he dead?' No one could mistake the excited hope in Olivero's question.

Sigismondo drew the curtains shut against the sun and

all inquisitive eyes. 'He'll live, if God permits and we get him to Rome and a quiet bed soon.'

Up on his great roan again, he gave a sweep of the arm forward for the party to move on. This time the sergeant took the lead and Sigismondo rode by the litter. Agostino, after a question to Angelo about payment for the litter's use had been coolly rebuffed, chivvied his wife away; she was still clouded with veils but a thick plait twisted with ribbons hung free and bounced on her back as she rode off. Olivero and Ferondo urged their horses ahead, close together, and they bent towards each other as they talked.

Benno, riding beside the second litter horse, watched his master conversing with Angelo and wondered if he were thanking him for adding Gian Pantera to the party. If the party containing Angelo had been attacked by robbers, Benno fancied there would not be very many robbers alive back there to sit around regretting their mistake. Fortune might be smiling after all. If any of the Panteras had the cross, despite the Marshal's search, they were at least all here under Sigismondo's eye.

On the other hand, Sigismondo could not easily search them again, and soon they would reach Rome and be out of his power to watch. His first concern must be to present Brother Ieronimo for justice and to present Duke Ludovico's letter to the Pope. The Panteras would be swallowed up in the immensity of Rome – which Benno tried to imagine from having seen Paris – and they would be free, if they had the cross after all, to do what they liked with it. Benno had slept badly during the few nights since Olivero's attack on Sigismondo. Now Gian was another burden for Sigismondo, to be protected against his cousins. Olivero's father had been killed by Gian's in their mutually fatal struggle and Benno, seeing in his mind's eye that steady blank stare, did not credit Olivero with any scruple about killing an unconscious man. Benno sighed.

Somewhere up in the front of the party, Brother Ieronimo began joyously to chant a psalm of praise.

Chapter 35

Rome

Rome was terrifying,

Benno smelt it and heard it before he saw it. They had passed squalid little groups of hovels and he had kept thinking these would conglomerate into the outskirts of the city, but it was quite different. When they finally rode in over one of the bridges he felt his stomach turn. The river they crossed was not the turbulent sort he knew at Rocca but was sluggish, as though it had to make its tired way over unspeakable obstacles. The water was low and the banks filthy, and the people who seemed to be searching the shores looked like part of the mud. On spikes at the end of the bridge, a row of faces welcomed them to Rome. They were faces their owners had long finished with and even the bird pecking at one of them looked dissatisfied. The smell as they rode beneath made even the soldiers cough and brought a muffled exclamation from Felicia's veils as she raised a pomander to her face. Perpetua, with no such resource, put a hand over her mouth and shut her eyes. Agostino's groom, Nuto, who had not been discouraged by her continual repulses, took her mule's bridle and tenderly led her along. The monks started a low chant of prayer. Biondello, after extruding a working nose, turned and burrowed under Benno's armpit. Only the man in the litter entered Rome with no response to its powerful stimulant.

Beyond the bridge they were in narrow streets whose dust and stones were padded with rubbish amd crowded with vociferous people. Buildings rose all round, pierced with dark windows from which came more noise and once a shower of vegetable parings. The travellers' bridles were pulled at, unsavoury people with extraordinary accents offered incomprehensible things – although two girls in pink and scarlet, with yellow ribbons in their hair, who raised their skirts at Brother Filippo with shrieks of laughter, were giving an unambiguous message.

Agostino da Sangallo was the first to announce his intention of quitting the group. He might have gone without farewell except that he must claim his wife's litter in spite of her protests.

'We are in Rome now. Some convent will take the young man in and tend him.' Agostino wrenched back the litter's curtain, revealing Gian Pantera trying to rise on one elbow and trying to make sense of his surroundings. 'You see, he is recovered enough to ride.'

'Stay.' Sigismondo's voice as before had the power to arrest action. 'Gian Pantera comes with me and he is still in need of the litter. I will send it to your lodgings, and I am sure the young man will recompense you for its loan, when he is able.' He smiled, widely. 'Your Christian charity shall not go unrewarded, sir: you shall have our prayers as well.'

'You need our permission, Sigismondo.' Olivero had thrust forward on his big black horse, forcing Agostino aside. In the litter Gian Pantera's eyes fixed on his cousin with what might have been disbelief. 'You need our permission to remove a Pantera from the care of his kin. This is a time when he needs his family about him.'

To ensure he never gets better, Benno supposed, and watched in astonishment as Sigismondo bent his head in

183

assent. 'The care of his family is a man's right and I shall see that he gets it. But first—' He wheeled his horse and Olivero was prevented from reaching the bridle of the leading litter groom. 'First we must see our charge is fulfilled. Father, where do you take Brother Ieronimo?'

Torquato pointed to a dark mass, dark even in Roman sunlight, looming at the end of the street. 'Our brothers will receive us. Brother Ieronimo will be guarded day and night until his Holiness can pronounce judgement on him.'

Brother Filippo gave an austere nod at this, and Brother Ieronimo, recalled to the present by the sound of his own name, redirected his smile from the street crowd about them to Father Torquato. Some kind matron, attracted by his air of tranquillity, had given him an apple from her basket. He crunched at it heartily as he listened to the plans for his disposal. Their party, half-blocking the street's entrance, had drawn this small crowd to watch, with the usual percentage of beggars into one of whose outstretched hands Brother Ieronimo suddenly deposited his apple, only a quarter eaten. Three more girls with yellow ribbons ornamenting their hair had appeared and Benno saw that, in thinking the first two, because of their matching ribbons, were sisters, he had been right in a way. He remembered now Olivero a few nights ago telling Brother Filippo, to his revulsion and protest, that there were fourteen thousand prostitutes in Rome, though how he knew, Benno could not imagine.

Sigismondo and the sergeant of the guard were talking, while the Pantera brothers chafed to take possession of their cousin. He had sunk back pallidly on the green cushions with his eyes closed, consciousness plainly not to his liking. Da Sangallo, finding the litter was being requisitioned now by Olivero, tried arguing with him until the dangerous blank stare made him falter. Behind him,

Perpetua the maid looked at the prostitutes with guarded curiosity, as if debating how a yellow ribbon in her own lank hair might transform her appearance and her life. Beyond her, Angelo remained indifferent to all that passed. He might have lived in Rome always, and it was noticeable that no one pestered him for alms.

It turned out that the soldiers were to escort the monks and their prisoner to the monastery of their order which Torquato had pointed out, and the sergeant received a purse of Duke Ludovico's money from Sigismondo to pay for their lodgings and their journey. Tomorrow they were to set out for Rocca, and in that moment of hearing it, Benno longed to be going too. Rome was so crowded, so foreign that, for all his wishes to see it, he was cowed by it. When he had been in France he had not expected to know what was going on, but in a country where people were supposed to speak his own language, it was a shock to feel so confused. Where did Sigismondo mean to spend the night in this alien place? His master was giving orders to the litter grooms.

'To the Palazzo Pantera. I am right, am I not?' he added, turning to Olivero. 'You lodge with the Cardinal?'

'Certainly.' Olivero gave Sigismondo one of his dismayingly false grins. 'And you, sir. Where do you go?'

'I, sir? Oh, I follow you. I have letters from the Duke to Cardinal Pantera.'

Chapter 36

'You Have a Story to Tell Me'

'Useless trash. Done by an amateur.'

The intaglio stone twirled on to the marble table, with a sharp sound eloquent of the speaker's disgust. He leant on blunt, scarred fingers and blew out his lips, dismissively.

'They are antiques, you know.'

'Doesn't matter *when* they were done, y'Eminence. They're still trash. Antique trash.'

Cardinal Pantera sighed. Sometimes being a patron was truly hard work, and one of these times was when you'd picked Brunelli. Brunelli, in the modern manner, could turn his hand to anything; he could get you out plans for a palace, oversee its building – if you did not mind the occasional problem with the construction teams – decorate the inside, paint you frescoes, design and make your tableware in gold and silver and, when he had provided sufficient objects for you and your friends to admire and your rivals to envy, he could execute a bronze of you to remind posterity that you had both the funds and the sense to employ a genius. This he was about to do for the Cardinal.

Like most geniuses, Brunelli did not care for other people's work, his utter confidence telling him that if a thing was not done *his* way, and no one but he could do that, then it could not be worth looking at. Now he was scanning the walls of the Cardinal's magnificent reception room, with its long windows overlooking the entrance courtyard and its frescoes of nymphs and satyrs at play in a romantic landscape. He folded his arms over his barrel chest and snorted.

'Leconti's work. Know it anywhere. Insipid rubbish.'

Cardinal Pantera was examining the rejected intaglio for chipping, and he raised his head and looked around at the frescoes with mild approval. 'No, I think they're quite charming. But,' he went on blandly, seeing a slight, ominous swelling in Brunelli's features, 'I haven't asked you to come here to discuss frescoes. His Eminence Cardinal Sforza has shown me the surpassing bronze you did of him this spring. I would like . . .'

A noise of hooves and clamorous shouting in the courtyard interrupted his wish. He crossed to the nearest window, the stiff silk of his robes whispering across the marble floor. He observed with interest the foremost rider, at that moment swinging from his horse, a man he had not seen before but a man one would remember. There was a soldier's build, with shoulders able to take armour or blows, but a face of quiet intelligence less often seen on soldiers. The Cardinal was reminded of a certain bust of a Roman emperor in its look of command, containment and thought.

The next man was making most of the noise, and Cardinal Pantera knew him. He turned back to Brunelli, who was improving his time by scraping with a ridged fingernail at the plaster of one fresco, bearing with his assumption about Leconti's poor preparation, and by chance damaging the winsome smile of a nymph. The Cardinal's tone held apology, however, rather than irritation.

'I fear you will have to return another time. Kinsfolk have arrived and I must receive them.'

Brunelli was not pleased, but he had been taken by the Cardinal's face and had already been mentally modelling its planes. Such a bronze would moreover be paid for on a generous scale and Brunelli, who had a habit of keeping money that he earned in wicker baskets for those who visited his studio to help themselves, was always short of the stuff even though he lived as frugally as a peasant. Assistants had to be paid, and colours and materials bought, and one had after all to eat. He managed a not unamiable scowl and let himself be led away by the servant who answered the little gold bell on the table among the intaglios.

Benno had seen cardinals before. He was in suitable awe of Rocca's Cardinal Pontano and he had been envisaging this one as Olivero in scarlet, an alarming vision. Now, as he followed Sigismondo so closely, with his cloak and the packet of letters, that he gained entrance to the reception room, he saw he had been wrong. In a way, the Cardinal did resemble Olivero. The eyebrows were as thick and black but they curved up, plaintively, in the centre. The mouth was as wide and, when he spoke, showed small close-set feral teeth but his voice was soft where Olivero's was harsh. In spite of his air of having been battered by life, Cardinal Pantera was gently courteous. As Sigismondo mentioned the letters from Duke Ludovico and Cardinal Pontano, Benno handed them to him, and he knelt and offered them.

Cardinal Pantera looked very keenly at Sigismondo as he stood up; breaking the big seal on its green ribbon, he said, 'You are welcome, my son, to stay here as my guest. My cousins, I suppose, have gone in search of their wives, who have been with me some weeks . . . you will wish to remain in Rome while this dreadful affair of Abbot

Bonifaccio is under consideration. His Holiness will certainly wish to hear the full story from you. His Grace, here,' and he tapped the parchment, 'asks that I use what influence I have,' the dark eyes looked deprecating, 'to see that His Holiness gives audience to you soon. Of course, His Holiness has already received the news by the Duke's special dispatch and he is very shocked. Very shocked.'

At this point Olivero thrust through the door, Ferondo after him. Perhaps they had visited their wives, however briefly – Olivero's collar was turned up on one side, Ferondo's hair ruffled – but they appeared to be as anxious to greet their host. His eyes roved speculatively over the pair, as they bowed, and he gave them a brief display of the lower teeth, more like a cat snarling than a smile.

'You are in Rome on business, cousins, as well as to collect your wives? We must,' he went on, smoothly stifling Olivero's reply, 'we must speak at length, and soon, about family matters, must we not?'

His gaze returned to Sigismondo and the eyebrows became more plaintive. 'My son, Duke Ludovico recommends you to me as one who has served him, and others, well in times of need. You shall take wine with me now and tell me what I am to say to His Holiness.' He rang the table bell.

Benno was entertained to see Olivero and Ferondo given their cousin's ring to kiss and another, rather pained, view of his teeth but no more. Servants surrounded them, steering them out of the room, and Olivero's attempt to speak was lost, like the first, as the Cardinal turned from him and gestured for the wine to be poured.

'Your Eminence,' Sigismondo's voice sounded very deep after the huskiness of the Cardinal's, 'you have another relative below, in a litter, who needs tending for a head wound. Gian Pantera.'

'Indeed.' The dark eyebrows were raised. 'It shall be done.' The Cardinal nodded to a servant who had been bringing a gilded stool, covered in brown velvet, to set near the desk. As the man hurried out and the door was shut, the Cardinal said, 'Sit. You have a story to tell me.'

Chapter 37

Absolution for Anything

That night, in a room of noble proportions as befitted the envoy from the Duke of Rocca, Sigismondo relaxed. He drank the excellent wine provided by the Cardinal's major-domo, poured by Benno into a silver-gilt cup chased with the Pantera arms crowned with a Cardinal's hat. Benno, incurably unkempt, was an incongruity in these surroundings, but as always made himself perfectly at home.

'Suppose you was to pack that cup in your baggage – ' Benno was thinking of Angelo's method, a couple of weeks ago, of delaying Olivero and Ferondo – 'everyone would know where you lifted it from.'

He hesitated. He eyed Sigismondo. Was he in a good enough mood to answer questions? He fetched his own pewter cup from the baggage, poured himself a little wine and sipped thoughtfully before trying a question. Sigismondo laughed.

'You want to know what I think, Benno. Hey, I don't *know* what I think. Soon – with luck – we'll be finding out what His Holiness thinks.'

'Will they hang Brother Ieronimo?'

'You know as well as I do Mother Church doesn't kill. Brother Ieronimo will be handed over to the secular arm if the Pope judges him guilty and, after that,' Sigismondo shrugged and spread a hand, 'he'd meet death better prepared than some.'

'D'you think he did it?'

'He had the opportunity; he says he did it. That will be enough for most people.'

'But so many others had the opportunity, din't they? There's all the Panteras. Gian was in the palace and nobody knows where he was at the time the Abbot was killed and Olivero and Ferondo were in Rocca and you said if the Devil *did* land on that poor guard that was crushed in the garden then he had a man's weight, so couldn't it be Olivero or Ferondo . . . ?'

'Mm . . m.' Sigismondo was sampling one of the sweetmeats, sugar crystallized with rosewater and gleaming with a thin skin of gold leaf. 'These *manus Christi* are the best I've ever tasted. Olivero, if he was there, is the one more likely to have wielded the axe. With, as I'd guess, Ferondo keeping watch below.'

'But he couldn't've counted on finding an axe. He couldn't've known yours'd be there. I mean he'd have used his dagger more likely, not an axe even if it was lying about.'

'You tell me: would a man who is so afraid of Holy Church that he dare not kill for fear of the Bishop's excommunicating him – would he murder an abbot?'

Benno scratched his beard furiously. 'Well – if he thought nobody'd find out.'

At Benno's feet, Biondello stretched on his side luxuriously. Sigismondo leant back on the red brocade bolster on his bed, eclipsing the gold-thread Pantera arms that were repeated on the bed-head, the tassels of a Cardinal's hat framing a lean gold panther courant.

'You're saying that any of the Panteras would have killed the Abbot to get the cross in their hands again. Think: they might have killed him and not got the cross. All three were searched very thoroughly, as were their belongings and, when I was tending Gian's head wound, I searched him again.' Sigismondo offered a sweetmeat to Biondello, who sat up to take it but with a contempt for worldly vanities proper to a Cardinal's guest, gulped gold leaf down no more avidly than he would have gulped a scrap of offal. Sigismondo lay back and went on. 'Remember, the blow that severed the Abbot's spine severed the chain that held the cross. It would slip, I fancy, and have been caught in his robes or have fallen to the floor. Suppose the murderer to be groping for it, then hear Brother Ieronimo singing as he came along?'

Benno was silent. The Devil had appeared to Brother Ieronimo, rushing out from the Abbot's room and, poised on the parapet, flashing out great wings and diving off into the sky. Benno had been immensely reassured by the more human idea of Olivero, all but overbalancing in a great dark cloak, and then jumping on top of the wretched guard. But then if it wasn't the Devil, what had given Brother Ieronimo the impulse to kill? The monk seemed a remarkably peaceful soul, ready to see good in everything – not one to raise a finger, let alone an axe, against his superior, no matter how corrupt or tyrannical that superior might be . . .

'Well, but then if Olivero or Gian killed the Abbot and then they couldn't find the cross, who do they think has got it?' Benno saw Sigismondo's broad smile and thumped his own knee with his fist. 'Right! *That* was why Olivero attacked you, not because he just can't stand you. He thinks you took the cross. But what about Gian?'

'He may have come to kill the Abbot and found him dead and the cross gone. Suppose he, like Ieronimo, saw Olivero but recognized him, and thinks he'd taken the cross. He didn't leave Rocca until after we did; suppose he hoped that by travelling light he could reach Rome before we did and persuade our host to take his side against the brothers. Threat of excommunication is powerful; it could have made them yield up the cross.'

Benno tried to picture Cardinal Pantera threatening Olivero, and failed; yet the Cardinal had put the brothers in their place when they arrived, with no difficulty at all.

'If those brothers have got it, they'd come here because their wives are here. I mean . . .' His suggestive jerk of the head was misinterpreted by Biondello, who snuffled round the floor thinking more gold had fallen from above.

Sigismondo laughed again. 'Mm . . mm. Of course you're right. Making children under a Cardinal's roof might gain from the sanctification of a cross but, if they have blood guilt on their souls . . .' he turned a hand palm upward. 'Can you think of another reason, beside getting heirs, that could bring the Abbot's murderer to Rome?'

Benno's beard refused all inspiration. 'Why?'

'Benno, Benno, Rome is where you can buy absolution for anything, anything at all.'

Chapter 38

'Your End Is Near'

'We count on you, my son, to explain this situation to Us.'

The plural the speaker used was magisterial. The ring Sigismondo knelt to kiss was the Fisherman's Ring. He had been granted this special favour after first kissing the foot in its slipper of white brocade resting on a red velvet cushion fringed in gold.

Cardinal Pantera had been too modest about the influence he possessed; the Pope granted an audience very soon to the envoy of the Duke of Rocca. Sigismondo, in his doublet of black velvet embroidered in silver, remained on one knee, head respectfully bent, while the Pope surveyed him. His Holiness had spared scarcely a glance for the others admitted to his presence and they stood eclipsed in their dark robes against a dark tapestry, Torquato and Brother Filippo pale and anxious and the criminal himself, Brother Ieronimo, smiling serenely. Benno had only passed the Papal chamberlain's gold-tipped wand, extended to bar his way, by showing the letters he was carrying, dangling the seal of Rocca and that of Cardinal Pontano. Now that his master had taken them from him and offered them to the Pope, he had nothing to do but to stare.

The Pope was worth staring at. There was plenty of him to see because, like Abbot Bonifaccio, His Holiness was built on a large scale, his portliness accentuated by the cape of crimson velvet lined with ermine, over the robes of white corded silk. The face, under the crimson biretta fringed with the same fur, might some time ago have been handsome in a florid way, but good living had hung pouches under and along the jaw and beneath the eyes, blurring the features. The mouth was generously full, however, and the expression one of good humour.

Cardinal Pantera, standing to the side between Sigismondo and the Pope, had taken the letters and put them in His Holiness's hand; they were given to the chamberlain to have their seals broken and to be spread out, and His Holiness took the Duke's letter back without, it seemed, much interest. That was reserved for the man still kneeling before him.

'A terrible thing, this murder. Terrible.' The Pope shook his head, his jowls following the movement obediently. He spoke as a connoisseur. Rome was the city for murders, running at an average of fourteen a day. The murder he spoke of, however, had a horror all its own, that eclipsed common-or-garden murders. This was the murder of a cleric, no less in importance than the superior of a great abbey; a murder committed, moreover, by one vowed to obedience, himself in the Church.

The Pope, glancing down at the letter, held out his hand and his chamberlain put something into it, a thing revealed, as the Pope raised it to his eye, as a large emerald hollowed out, which gleamed like a fragment of summer sea.

'His Grace says here that he wishes to clear his honour of all taint of suspicion of the blood of his guest. Surely,' the Pope lowered the emerald and addressed Sigismondo, 'surely no one could suspect his Grace? We have heard of his differences with Abbot Bonifaccio, but how can his Grace be suspected of so horrific a crime when the murderer has confessed? Is he supposed to have suborned the murderer?' He made a brusque gesture which brought Sigismondo to stand up before him.

'Your Holiness, the case may not be as simple as it appears.'

The real point, Benno thought, is whether Brother Ieronimo is as simple as he appears. The Pope beckoned and the monk was brought forward, a Papal guard gripping either arm as if fearful that a man who could murder an abbot might ambitiously set about the Pope. Brother Ieronimo, on his knees, beamed while the Pope considered him. Again, the abrupt gesture, and the monk was hoisted to his feet.

'You did this terrible thing, my son? How was it possible?'

'The Devil entered into me, Holy Father. It was his work.'

'So might all evil-doers say. Yet they are hanged for it, and go to meet their master in Hell.'

'I shall not go to Hell.' Brother Ieronimo's confidence was untroubled. 'Our Lady promised me.'

The Pope's eyebrows, mere lines above the heavy lids, rose into the ridged forehead.

'Our Lady! You pretend to have heard Our Lady promise you that?'

'By your leave—' Sigismondo's deep voice intervened. The Pope's hand sketched a permission. 'Brother Ieronimo has had visions of the Virgin of Scheggia. Abbot Bonifaccio knew of them.'

'The Virgin of Scheggia!' The Pope held out his hand once more and his chamberlain placed in it a gold goblet set with pearls, from which he sipped, eyeing Brother Ieronimo over the rim. 'Are we dealing with a madman here? The Devil can assume even holy disguises. Have you not thought your visions came from the Devil, who drove you to kill?'

Brother Ieronimo made a movement which caused the guards to tighten their grip, as though he would raise his hands, as he did his face, towards heaven; or at least to the painted ceiling from which a group of frolicsome putti winged as cherubs looked down inquiringly at him. Taking the guards by surprise, Brother Ieronimo suddenly flung himself on his knees, dragging them stumbling down with him.

'O my Lady, merciful Mother of God, pray for us . . . She is here! She is here! O Mother of God, pray for us!'

This was an invocation all present were used to, and an automatic murmur rose while more than one pair of eyes searched the ceiling with dubiety. Brother Ieronimo's face of rapture, however, was fading. By the time the guards had hauled him to his feet, there were tears in his eyes and he was babbling incomprehensibly.

The Pope shrugged massive shoulders and pointed to the doors, which pages instantly swung open. Brother Ieronimo was borne towards them, his feet barely touching the ground; but before he reached the doors he flung the guards from him with an impossible strength and turned, arms outstretched to the Pope.

'Our Lady warns you, repent! Your end is near!'

Chapter 39

The New Bishop

Well, that's torn it, thought Benno. We start with Brother Ieronimo seeing a rain of blood just as the Abbot leaves Pietra, and he provides the rain himself with an axe. Now he predicts a bit of the same for the Holy Father. People don't get much fun out of being told they're going to die shortly. Trouble is, it does away with hope. People can live on hope when there's nothing else left. But what hope is there for a man whose death has been foretold by the Virgin?

'Away with the man. He's mad.'

The Pope had no need to give the order. The guards had already got a fresh grip on Brother Ieronimo and they ran him out through the doors, which pages immediately shut. Outraged whispers had started up among those grouped by the tapestries. Cardinal Pantera's face customarily expressed an aristocratic deprecation of events, and it did not alter now, nor did the Pope seem unduly perturbed. In fact he was laughing, which made his jowls jump and the silk of his robes crepitate.

'Mad, mad. Next thing, my son,' he said to Sigismondo, 'the Virgin of Scheggia would have put it into his head to strangle me.' The laugh subsided to a jovial chuckle. 'A man must make sure his prophecies come true, eh? Well, the world will be no worse without one mad monk. He can be tried in consistory tomorrow, handed over at once to the secular and hanged the day after. The Devil will be pleased to see his servant delivered to him so promptly – will give him a warm welcome, eh?'

Deferential laughter and clapping greeted the Holy Father's joke, while Benno felt his stomach turn. He hadn't realized how much he liked poor Brother Ieronimo who was to be hurried into eternity in a day or two just as he'd been hustled through those doors. And Sigismondo had hinted that the poor man might not be guilty either, but just confused. A much more apt place for the rope would be round Olivero's neck, but men like him with plenty of money and a Cardinal for cousin were the sort that died in their beds of old age or, at worst, of a surfeit.

What Sigismondo thought of events, you couldn't tell. The Pope, with a slight circling of the hand, had beckoned him closer and motioned those nearby to stand back. Their colloquy was secret and Benno wondered if he would ever get to hear what was said. He let his imagination go. What if His Holiness, impressed by what Duke Ludovico had written, and by Sigismondo's appearance, was offering him a position in the Church? Sigismondo had told Benno of men who were in favour with the Pope, or were the Pope's relations or such, who had been priested one day, made bishop the next and cardinal the day after. Of course it would be an immense honour and Sigismondo would look magnificent in the robes, but Benno did hope it wouldn't happen.

The conversation proved quite short. The Pope again gave his ring to kiss. If Sigismondo had refused a bishopric, it was being taken in good part. He had to stand by, however, not dismissed but waved a little way off, and he backed until his broad shoulders obscured Benno's view of the Papal throne. Father Torquato and Brother Filippo were having a private audience as well, although everyone had heard the Pope say, 'The new Abbot of Pietra.'

Benno shifted. He could see an unwonted animation on Torquato's face and the interest on the Pope's. Maybe Torquato or Brother Filippo would like to be the next Abbot?

The announcement, when it came, was a surprise. The Pope, extending his hand for Torquato to kiss the ring, looked around at the assembled company, smiling genially.

'The new Bishop of Canigallia! He shall be enthroned next week after the funeral of Bishop Odo.'

More polite clapping and, suddenly and visibly, the Pope was bored. The hand made a series of the quick dismissive waves and his chamberlain began to clear the chamber. The audience was over.

In the corridor, walking between bronzes of centaurs, fauns, martyrs and warriors that lined the walls, Benno hissed, 'What'd he say to you? Did he ask *you* to be the Bishop?'

Sigismondo smiled broadly. His answer was so quiet that the St Sebastian they were passing could not have heard. 'He asked me if I'd kill someone for him.'

'His *Holiness* asked you that?'

'Don't yelp, Benno. It seems the Holy Father felt he could trust me. I was flattered.'

'*Who* did he—'

'Questions, Benno? Haven't I heard questions? I remember someone proposing himself as my servant because he didn't ask questions. What you should be considering is Bishop Torquato of Canigallia.'

'I thought he might be asking for the Abbey of Pietra.'

'Oh, too far from Rome where the action is. Canigallia is just outside Rome; he need spend no time in his bishopric. Bishop Torquato doesn't mean to linger on the ladder, I'm sure. Have you thought, Benno, why the Holy Father made Torquato a bishop when, so far as I know, he has no money to pay for preferment; and no contacts or he'd have left off being secretary to Abbot Bonifaccio ages ago? Bishoprics are a steep price, I believe.'

'How'd he do it, then, if the Pope wants money?'

'Popes, like all sovereigns, want money. Or, what is even better, they want what can breed money.'

Benno stopped abruptly and Biondello, who had been so overcome by awe in his audience with the Pope that he had fallen asleep inside his master's jerkin, woke up and stuck his head out inquiringly. Sigismondo patted it.

'You mean—'

'I mean, if Torquato has been made a bishop, he has the cross. Until he gives it to the Pope.'

Chapter 40

A Lightning Bolt

'Tell your fortune, sir? You've a lucky face. See if the Fates have sent you a lucky hand to match.'

In the lowering heat of evening, under a sky livid with impending storm, the crowd was shifting and parading about the square. The thin hand held out to Sigismondo had a scar across the back; Benno had sometimes thought that the person who gave that to Angelo couldn't have enjoyed the triumph for long. A mystery was solved, too: after their party had split up, how on earth Sigismondo would find Angelo in this crawling ant-heap of a city.

Angelo had recently been seen as a ballad singer in a tavern, then as a pilgrim with a widowed mother (Sigismondo was always formidable masquerading as a woman), then as a respectable young merchant; and now in a rôle familiar from the past, in a patchwork doublet of blues and greens, and a flat velvet cap, this time of faded scarlet. It was all he needed to go into business. His seat was the stone coping of a fountain basin, his customers the Roman crowd, ever curious, ever sceptical but ever ready to be amused.

This time he was not using a pack of cards. His customers sat by him and submitted their palms, for him to trace the lines with a long finger. He had just dismissed a satisfied client, and called out to Sigismondo, attracting local attention. Also attracting attention to the fortune-teller, by beating an intermittent tattoo on a small drum, was a large man with a gingery beard, whom Benno, staring with his usual vacancy, also recognized.

'Hey, I need all the luck you can show me. My girl's my cross – she's been stolen by another and I haven't the money to lure her back to me, how's that for a fortune?'

This pleased the crowd; a girl promptly offered herself as substitute and was towed away by her young man.

Sigismondo, in shirtsleeves for the heat, sat by Angelo and surrendered his palm.

'The luck of the very Devil!' Angelo's hair draped Sigismondo's sleeve as he pored over the hand. 'You'll get your girl back ... I see riches too. You must have been born laughing, sir, with Venus ruling your house—' He prodded the base of Sigismondo's thumb. 'And here, the trident of Neptune for treasure.' Glass-grey eyes looked up into dark brown. 'But I see danger too: swords wait for you in the dark. There is something I should tell you in secret, for you have enemies to whom the very birds of the air might carry word.'

Angelo's warning provoked the crowd to demand details of this fortune, but when Sigismondo rose to go with him for a private consultation, suddenly no one cared to press the point.

Benno hitched Sigismondo's doublet, folded inside out to protect the velvet, more securely into his grasp, for he supposed Roman thieves would be no less smart and sudden than any others, and he followed Angelo and Sigismondo and the man with the drum, idling after them as if by chance, looking to see if anyone followed or showed particular interest. Biondello kept close to him.

The light, or coming darkness, made Sigismondo's shirt and all pale colours seem luminous. A hanging basket of flowers almost shone. Benno was struck by how the grander-looking houses were next door to what were really only tenements. Naturally, it was at the door of one of these that Angelo led them in. Higher on the wall, a wicker cage hung, with a linnet, not singing but hopping about fretfully in its tiny prison. Benno felt a sudden pang for Brother Ieronimo in his cell, with so little life left to him; but he was not likely to be fretful.

A little white and orange cat came up the stairs with them, causing Biondello, hastily stuffed into Benno's jerkin, to growl like an angry bee.

They went up stair after stair, the place smelling as if its function had been misunderstood by some of the inhabitants. Doors, left open for the heat, showed ramshackle beds strewn with clothes. On one of them two people were engaged in an occupation generally regarded as private. The girl raised an arm to wave at them as they passed. The little cat bounded up the stairs ahead of them, while Benno's jerkin vibrated.

The top rooms were like an oven under the roof. The cat jumped on the windowsill to monitor the street; the big man hung the drum on the wall and turned and embraced Sigismondo with a vigour warmly reciprocated – a hug that would have cracked any other's ribs.

'You rogue, Angelo told me you were in town. Seeing the Pope, no less . . . I last saw you in Rocca robbing a nun; did you nick the Holy Father's slipper when you kissed his toe?'

'If I had, you'd be sure to know a fence I could pass it to. Barley, you brute, how are things with you?'

The room was darkening still further as they spoke; a rumble of thunder taught Biondello how his empty threat to the cat ought to sound. Barley raised one of the cups Angelo had been filling and said, 'Here's to the hair you had in Switzerland, Martin.'

They drank, companionably, in the small, stuffy room, lounging on the pallet bed. Benno, on the floor, his feet out before him, speculated on Sigismondo's past, where he had acquired a variety of names, a different one, it seemed, for each old friend or comrade-in-arms they met. He was happy to see Barley's familiar face after so many strange ones, and hoped he could be a help to them. Sigismondo explained the situation to him while Angelo, elbows on the sill, watched with the cat what went on in the street. Beyond them, a line of washing crossed to the opposite building. Dark patches appeared on the sill as if the house sweated and the cat withdrew quickly, shaking its fur. Angelo merely turned round, leaning back with elbows on the sill, and let the rain fall on his closed eyes.

'If that cross is all you say, the slyboots priest could have asked for a red hat, not just a bishopric. How much time have you got to get it off him?'

Sigismondo shrugged. 'Who knows? His Holiness will want the cross in his hand, I'd say, before Father Torquato gets enthroned next week.'

Rain fell faster now, thunder prowled the sky, women's voices yelled from over the street and the washing danced out of view.

Footsteps came up the stair and Barley cocked his head, listening. Were they to be interrupted? Benno wondered, but the footsteps turned in at the room next door. Someone else lived under the roof and the hammering rain.

'You think this priest wears the cross round his neck? Suppose I bump into him in the street and kiss his cross away? Suppose Angelo slips a knife into him – the cross is ours. This is Rome, Martin. Priests are two a penny.'

Benno almost shook his head. He knew his master for a fighter, not a murderer. Sigismondo said, 'I can't tell if he killed Abbot Bonifaccio. I believe he has the cross.

Too many men have already died for that. I'll not be responsible for another death.'

The sombre emphasis was so like his manner to the Pantera brothers in the hour after Bernabo's death that Benno was chilled. Barley had not heard it. He was listening for something, through the pounding of rain and the rumour of thunder. A sharp bang on the wall from the room behind this dislodged a flake or two of plaster and fetched Barley to his feet to seize a cudgel propped in the corner by the door. It must be an attack only Barley was expecting; but he was meeting it in a strange way: he opened the door, crept out with quite ludicrous caution and shut the door silently. Sigismondo and Angelo smiled. Rain still came in a drive across the roof so that Benno was surprised Barley could have heard the approach of enemies at all.

Yet here they came. Footsteps pounded, booming up the rickety stairs and, as Benno was expecting Sigismondo to prepare for the assault, the door of the next room was burst open, they heard a roar, a shout and a simultaneous scream. Angelo's smile extended. Footsteps scrambled on the landing, slipping, rushing, retreating down the stairs while Barley bellowed obscenities down the stairwell and a girl pitifully wailed. For a moment Barley's voice seemed to attain superhuman proportions but it was a crack of thunder overhead that shut their hearing and sent Biondello trying to bury himself in Benno's ribs.

Unheard after that thunder, their door opened, and Barley was there, ushering in a girl with disordered golden ringlets and a dress as disordered as her hair. Her olive skin and dark eyes showed the gold of her hair to be spurious; but she was very pretty. Sigismondo rose, smiling, to take her hand, which she gave with some coquetry although her sleeve was sliding down her arm.

Barley raised his voice in the din of rain and thunder. 'Gemmata, my neighbour,' and to her, 'How did we do?'

She delved into her décolletage, leaning forward and rummaging until Benno's eyes bulged and he swallowed. The hand emerged, together with part of herself which she stuffed back negligently. She opened the hand to Barley, showing a palm full of glittering gold links.

'He won't miss that for a bit, not until he gets home and stops sweating. Let's see his purse.'

Barley picked the chain from her hand and held it this way and that, judicially. She nudged him with her open hand and he produced a purse – dark green Florentine leather stamped with gold. He poured coins into her hand, and grunted.

'He did have enough to pay you, anyway, even if your husband hadn't come home. Let's drink to the foolish of this world who help to keep the wise from starving!'

Benno appreciated the dodge they were working. Automatically, he raised his cup to the toast, while the girl put her wine back with a fling so wholehearted that the sleeve did part company from her bodice. Sigismondo gallantly retrieved it from the floor and she extended her bare arm to him. He slid the sleeve on and bent to tie the frayed ribbon through the eyelets.

Barley propped his cudgel against the wall and was sharing out the money with Gemmata, remarking in a pause after a roll of thunder, and when the rain was merely tapping overhead, 'We could cut you in on this, Martin, any time you cared. More fun than kissing the Pope's arse, and I could do with a rest for my cudgel.'

'You never have to use it,' Gemmata said. 'They start pissing cash when they just set eyes on you. Though,' she flapped her eyelashes and peeped sidelong at Sigismondo, 'your big friend would do fine, I'm sure.'

'You're generous, Barley; I'll bear it in mind. Now we have to go out in the wet or we'll be late for dinner at the Palazzo Pantera.' He nodded at Barley. 'I know where to find you now—'

An appalling crash somewhere outside, a noise more alarming than the thunder, seemed to reverberate even through the floorboards and made Gemmata rush to the window to peer out. 'God and the saints protect us! Sounds as if the city was coming down!'

The noise, a gross jarring clangour, was still echoing in their ears.

'A belfry's been struck,' Sigismondo said. Barley pulled a cloak off the wall.

'I'm going to see. There's always pickings from a disaster.'

Angelo took a sienna-red cloak from the bed and silently enveloped himself in it, setting off down the stairs without further ado, so they were all going out except the cat who had taken over the warm patch left by Sigismondo on the pallet, and Gemmata who, declaring she wasn't going to get wet, waved them goodbye from the top of the stairs. Doors on the way down were still half-open. The couple had disappeared and a small child huddled under a wrap sheltering from the lightning. From one room came energetic prayer, a patter of words as fast and furious as the pattering rain.

The sound of rain on the tiles changed as they reached the stairfoot, to the hiss of rain from the street. They came out to find it almost totally awash; only by the walls was there any footing, the rest was a brisk stream rolling down, to meet another at the corner with a plume of spray and make a river down the side alley. Sigismondo set off up the other stream, coming out on a square. The rain gusted suddenly, pouring over Sigismondo's head and shoulders, dancing on the ground churning up mud. The far side of the square vanished in a curtain of rain.

Benno gave up the effort to keep Sigismondo's doublet dry and trudged after Angelo's swathed form. Along another flooded street, water spewed from gutters and unspeakable rubbish swilled round their ankles, including a dead dog on its back, all four feet in the air, revolving with dignity. Benno made sure Biondello could not slip from his jerkin and be borne away for ever.

There were a few others out in the dwindling storm. Barley beat one of them to the rescue of a lute, trailing drowned ribbons, floating like a little boat. It might have fallen from some sill under a driving gust. The man who also tried for it gave up when he saw Barley's size and scowl. A boy, covered in mud and worse, and all but naked, had been luckier. He clasped a pig's head and a handful of offal; he ran plashing out of sight. A basket drifted by, some rags, a bench in the same attitude as the dog. Barley scooped up the basket but after a look threw it away.

A great square opened before them, the distance still now and then lit by a white glare where lightning made vast jagged rents in the black of the sky. Where they stood, daylight had returned. Sigismondo suddenly stopped and pointed. 'Look there.'

More people than they had so far seen were gathered on the steps of St Peter's. What had brought this crowd was not the hope of salvage because what they were seeing was beyond salvage: a tower like a great broken tooth stood up, rubble at its foot.

Their way to the Palazzo Pantera led them closer and they met a priest scampering over the puddles with his skirts kilted up, who greeted them with all the joy of one with bad news to impart. He paused a moment, nodding back at the ruin.

'That's a bell will not be tolled again! I'm off to give word to the sacristan of St Jude's and he will pass it on to the city by the mouth of the great bell there.' He still paused, as if he had not told all.

'Someone's dead,' observed Barley, 'if you want a bell to toll. Was it the lightning struck them?'

The priest, his face radiant with his news, let go his skirts to gesticulate. 'It was like a lightning bolt, for they say he fell like a slaughtered beast. It's just happened! Just as the mad monk prophesied!'

Sigismondo stepped forward. 'Then—'

'The Pope is dead!'

Chapter 41

Cousins Together

Things were happening too fast for the papal chamberlain. This was not the first time he had had to prepare a Pope's body for burial and he was expecting to have little help with this one. The great bedchamber had emptied of physicians and servants – all had fled to find patrons, as fast as they could, elsewhere. And of course not only had everyone vanished, but everything portable had vanished with them. There were now no bed hangings, no coverlet, no sheets even. He washed the body, but he had to dry it with the Pope's own nightshirt which no one had cared to remove in the pillaging rush. The whore who had been with him at the moment of death, who had perhaps precipitated that death, had taken the rings, such as she could drag off, from his hands before she fled. They had been missing when the rest arrived.

The chamberlain sighed, and pondered how to clothe the Pope since chests and garderobes gaped empty. Hangings had been stripped and carried off. His voice echoed strangely in the emptiness when, following the ritual, he called the Pope three times by name, his baptismal name, not heard since he became Pope, supposed to summon him back to life if any were left, though in this case there was palpably none.

While the bells of every church in Rome tolled the message to the city, and couriers already spurred to take the news to all the cities of the Christian world, the papal chamberlain was absorbed in the problem of borrowing a pair of slippers and a cassock.

If he had his problems, so did others, and of a far more complicated kind. When Sigismondo and Benno arrived at the Palazzo Pantera – Angelo, with a promise of keeping in touch, had slipped away – they found confusion. Cardinal Pantera, living so near to the Vatican, had heard the news very soon. A servant had run through the downpour and appeared on the threshold, a saturated and panting rat, to herald a time of intense activity. Already there were other servants in various liveries, waiting in the antechamber as Sigismondo strode through, and more were arriving. Benno trotted after his master, shaking his head like a dog, the drops mingling with the mud everyone had traipsed in over the marble flagstones. He hoped there'd be time to dry out his master's doublet before dinner at the Cardinal's table.

There was no Cardinal's table that evening. The city was in a ferment, all attention being directed at the cardinals present in Rome. Cardinal Pantera, with petitioners, messages and visitors arriving constantly, sent courteous excuses to his guests and retired to his study to receive the steady succession of people. A long table in one of the reception rooms had been laid for dinner, the silver dishes piled with fruit, peaches scenting the air, beeswax candles already lit in the gloom after the storm. The servants clustered in groups, whispering, excited, arguing, one woman in tears with her apron pressed to her face. Benno could see no sign of Olivero or Ferondo – or their wives whom he'd never set eyes on.

'D'you think Gian is dying or something and they're at his deathbed getting reconciled . . .?' Benno faltered. Not only was he asking questions again but he was running into fantasy. Sigismondo had tended Gian's injury and not said he might die of it, and as for reconciliation, it would take more than a cardinal to force that on men whose fathers had killed each other. He was lucky, though; Sigismondo was ignoring him and bowing, with the suppleness of a courtier, to the two women who had just come in. The Pantera wives at last, advancing with the rustle of expensive silks, extended hands to be kissed and introduced themselves to the interesting stranger.

'Our husbands have spoken much of you, sir. I am Elisavetta, wife to Ferondo Pantera; this is my sister-in-law, Lydia.' Olivero's wife might have been the one expected to take the lead, but Ferondo's wife was the more imposing, in build and in height, black hair piled high in thick braids, black eyebrows and glittering eyes; her whole appearance made yet more impressive by a dress of burgundy silk slashed with sage green and embroidered with gold – a person to be reckoned with: and her eyes assessed Sigismondo as if she saw the same quality in him.

Lydia was very different. Slender, with pronounced cheek-bones, she was more obviously good-looking, her silver-blonde hair, teased into kiss-curls in front of her ears, half hiding and half resembling her earrings of gold filigree. Yet her face had a bitter, hungry air as though nothing she saw satisfied her. Blue watered silk in voluminous folds demonstrated the money and status of her husband. Her eyes looked over Sigismondo as she said, 'You brought the mad monk to Rome, who foretold His Holiness's death. What is happening in the city?'

Sigismondo stood with his customary stillness. 'The storm has kept most people indoors, but the news of the Holy Father's death will be spreading fast.'

Lydia made a face. 'We were to have had audience of

him next week – his Eminence our cousin had arranged it. Now we must wait Heaven knows how long . . .'

'However,' Elisavetta intervened, with a trace of humour, 'we shall have all the more time to buy clothes and jewellery, bankrupt our husbands and finish visiting all the churches in Rome.'

'You are here for pleasure, ladies?'

The women exchanged glances, and Elisavetta had just opened her mouth to reply when three more people entered the room. Amazingly, they completed the family party for, following Ferondo and supported on Olivero's arm, Gian Pantera came pallidly forward.

Chapter 42

Bolt the Door and Sleep Light

Benno pulled the pallet bed from beneath Sigismondo's grand one, and prepared it by spreading his cloak over the straw mattress and rolling his jerkin for a pillow, whereupon Biondello jumped up and, after circling, lay down in the middle with the sang-froid of one who slept in cardinals' palaces every night of his life.

Sigismondo was silent, leaning out of the tall window to observe the courtyard below. Benno, although his muscles reminded him that it had been a long day, joined him there, to see the cobbled expanse lit by torches and filled, even at this late hour, with a mosaic of horses, mules and grooms. The shouts and the clatter of hooves on the stones came up to them on the night air. Benno sniffed the cool of it and the homelike smell of horses. 'Rome doesn't go to sleep at night, does it?'

'Mm. I doubt if our host at least will get much sleep tonight. Nor any other cardinal in the city for that matter. They've only ten days in which they can negotiate.'

'Ten days?'

'That's how long they must wait for other cardinals to get the news that the Pope's dead and to come here. Then they're shut up in Conclave to decide on the next Pope.'

Trampling and squealing below heralded a line of mules, ushered into the torchlight, protesting about their loads, their grooms, and life. The servants with them began to unrope their burdens, helped by men in the Cardinal's livery. One of the packs slipped its moorings too soon and crashed to the ground with a strange clangour.

'Sounds exactly like a load of pans,' Benno observed. Sigismondo hummed, smiling.

'You've hit the mark. Hey, if not pans, then dishes. I don't think Cardinal Pantera means to be Pope.'

Benno's scratching of the head, diligent though it was, produced no meaning for this. 'I'd have thought he should be as good as any other. Better than some, surely? I thought really he's a lot nicer than His Holiness.'

Sigismondo was watching the violent recriminations among the torches. Two grooms were nearly at blows over the blame for the fallen load. He shrugged without looking round.

'Nice, Benno? *Nice*? We're talking about the chair of St Peter, not a mother choosing a nursemaid. You get elected if you have, first, the money; second, the influence; and if the rest of the cardinals can stand you. These next ten days will see hundreds of bribes changing hands.'

Benno peered down into the chaos. 'That's a bribe, is it? A load of dishes?'

'Those dishes are silver, and worth a lot more money than you'll ever see.' Sigismondo's tone was detached. 'I doubt if they're a bribe. They'll have some other cardinal's coat of arms engraved on them.'

'Then why are they here?' Benno followed his master back across the room and took Sigismondo's doublet as he shed it, folded it on the chest at the bed's foot and said, 'Cardinal Pantera's not borrowing someone's dishes for a party?'

'His party won't come until the Conclave is over. No, Cardinal Pantera must have let it be known already that he's not standing for election and that he's prepared to store his brother cardinals' silver in his cellar – the silver of those who think they've a chance of election.' Sigismondo lay down and linked his hands behind his head. 'This is Rome; a place with its own customs, one of which is that when a cardinal gets elected, the mob sacks his palace. Perks, you might say. They're telling him: now you're Pope you won't need this. Mm . . m. They've been known to take the doors and windows out.'

Benno, amazed, sat down on his pallet and stared at the candle. In his mind he saw a horde of people surging into a palace like this, taking the bed hangings, the bedding, the bedstead, the wash basin, the chest, the pallet, the panelling . . . He could see the avid faces. In his mind he suddenly saw the Pantera wives. They could lead a Roman mob all right. If the big one wanted a carved door and couldn't carry it on her own, she'd make someone do it for her. As for Olivero's wife, she looked as if she'd tear down anything she wanted and tear the face of anyone who thought they'd got it. He did not seriously imagine they'd be part of a Roman mob, but both women had provided an entirely new image of the brothers.

'I'd reckoned those Pantera ladies'd be all meek and mild, doing just what their husbands said. They didn't get much of a say at dinner, right?' He leant to snuff out the candle and lay down. Biondello rearranged himself by his shoulder.

The deep voice in the dark was amused. 'If those ladies are in Rome to get sons, they will get them whether or not their husbands can. I doubt La Feconda will be necessary.'

Benno mused a moment on this, thinking of the faces at the dinner table. Standing behind Sigismondo he'd had a good view. 'Their cousin – Gian Pantera – he didn't seem to be on bad terms with them, after all. D'you think he'd made it up with those brothers? He didn't seem a bit well yet. Could he have thought he was dying and ought to forgive them?'

'My belief is that he's lost his memory. I've known it happen from a blow on the head. What will be interesting is to see if it comes back. I've known that happen too.'

'He doesn't seem to remember the feud, does he? Olivero was talking to him about their childhood and racing through their grandfather's house and their competitions as to who could eat the most plums and how ill they were . . . I mean, *Olivero* remembers the feud. Why is he acting so nice? Is he just waiting to kill Gian when he doesn't expect it? Can't see him not killing his cousin just because he's ill.'

There was a pause and the sound of a pillow being thumped and resettled. 'This is Cardinal Pantera's roof we're under. Olivero'll wait until Gian's able to go out of doors and the Cardinal's in Conclave.'

'What about the cross, though?'

'He may still think I've got it, so we bolt the door and sleep light. As for Torquato, who *has* got it as I imagine, he has to wait too. Everything is in suspension now. The next Pope will have to confirm his bishopric, so he'll have to market La Feconda all over again.'

'That gives us time to get it, then?'

The silence was not broken this time, save by a small snore from Biondello. Benno realized he was not going to have an answer to that or to his next question: did Torquato kill the Abbot? If he had, getting the cross off him was going to carry quite an added risk.

Chapter 43

Problems

Brother Porter was having a difficult stint. Before dawn he had been brought to the wicket by insistent hammering at it. There he had found not one but about twenty people outside and anxious for admittance. Of course it was impossible – several of them were women, for a start – but they refused to go away. Now, at Prime, there were at least twenty more and none showed signs of going.

It was a matter for the Prior.

The Prior, though he came from the North, had an unhealthy respect for Romans. He commanded that Brother Ieronimo should be brought out. Brother Ieronimo had been confined to a cell, a circumstance so usual that he could not be said to have noticed it, while he awaited the consistory court where, everyone expected, he would be handed over to the secular arm; which in this case would be swinging a noose in its hand. While the murderers of abbots might be accorded warm sympathy in this city of anti-clericalism and liberal thinkers, the free spectacle of a monk being hanged, or perhaps broken on the wheel, would amply compensate for any feeling that a man who had done a public service deserved better. A vast number in Rome had heard of the Abbot of Pietra now because of the prophecy, though hardly anybody had ever seen him, but most had formed a remarkably accurate picture of a corpulent, overbearing cleric whom an axe could only improve.

The Prior's problem stemmed from this fame. A growing number of Romans were clamouring to see Brother Ieronimo well in advance of his execution. He had prophesied the Pope's death just as he had foretold that of the Abbot of Pietra; that he had been personally involved in that death showed him only as an instrument of Divine justice. He was said to have been blessed by visions of the Virgin of Scheggia who, it was well known, could ensure many blessings, particularly children, to those who prayed to her devoutly.

Credulous peasants might have come crowding to touch his robe or beg his prayers. Sophisticated Romans wanted a bit more action. A vision on the spot would fill the bill. He might tell them who was to be next Pope; since betting on the subject was already in exuberant progress, this would be of practical use. Or if more deaths were on the programme, these Romans were keen as mustard to be the first to hear. For one thing, a palace is more vulnerable to looting when its owner is dead or absent, as the papal chamberlain, and the cardinals sending their treasures by night to safe storage, were so well aware.

Not everyone in the crowd packing the street was influenced by such mundane perspectives. A proportion were women who, lacking means to visit Scheggia, hoped for the visionary monk's intercession with the Virgin there.

The Prior considered the factor that Brother Ieronimo would not be at the monastery for ever. The court to try him might be convened less briskly than the late Pope had intended, a more urgent business having superseded his intent; but after the new Pope had been elected, things might move fast enough. The interim, therefore, really ought to be profitably used.

So Brother Ieronimo would appear and say a few words. What he said was not important – everyone would put a separate interpretation on it anyhow – and if he had a vision, so much the better. The real point was that Santaporta should be, however briefly, a focus for the faithful and the inquisitive, that it should attract alms along with attention. It might be rabble outside at the moment, but this was Rome; soon would come inquiries from higher up the social scale. Cardinals might pose discreet questions as to who might shortly swap the red hat for a triple tiara, and one did not ask such questions for a few pence. Then, if the mad monk were executed after all, the sentence might be annulled in years to come and the creature made a saint, and this place where he had spent his last days might become a shrine, a scene of pilgrimage . . . As for possession by the Devil – might it not be the Abbot who was possessed? The Prior knew an abbot or two whose lives made it perfectly likely.

Either way, Santaporta would be visited by hundreds, thousands . . . the Prior began to calculate. The chapel's roof . . . the refectory's dangerous floor . . . those frescoes were in a dreadful state – they might even be able to afford that fellow Brunelli.

Among those outside the monastery, Goffo Puzzo was one with an aim in life. He had heard of the mad prophet but his own concern was more immediate. He was going to kill someone. As it was someone he had never met and for whom he had no hatred, he had stipulated good pay for it.

The six of them, for he was not alone in spite of his statement that he'd never needed a back-up before, spotted their subject emerging from Santaporta's pillared doorway, and with easy nonchalance they waited until he had passed them before detaching themselves from the bench and the wall and loafing after him. Their casual indifference became hard to maintain when they found they had to loaf at quite a pace. Goffo looked at the subject's shoulders and the column of his neck, and his bearing, and thought, well, perhaps six of us is about right.

'Wish we knew where the swine was going,' Zucco remarked. 'Could have put someone ahead to slow him down.'

Squalo Scorreggia, labouring, snarled, 'Well, we didn't.' They hurried up a populous street, skirted a group of black-clad women on their knees before a shrine, pushed aside a man with a tower of finches' cages on his back, avoided the puddle round a fountain, and saw their subject turn aside down an alley.

'That's our boy,' said Goffo inaccurately. The man was somewhat more than full-grown. However, they put on a spurt and were not far behind him when they reached the alley. In fact, he must have loitered; he was closer than they expected. The half-wit at his heels must have annoyed him, for he was in the act of shoving him at the wall; but he prolonged the movement into a turn that brought him face to face with Squalo.

For all his bulk Squalo was quick. He had his dagger out and made play with it, letting Goffo circle round their prey and ignoring the half-wit gaping by the wall. The next moment he was doubled up and howling, had dropped his knife to clutch his privates. The half-wit felled him with a cudgel blow to the nape.

The subject had whirled on Goffo, who for the first time met the level dark gaze, which yet did not quite distract him from the falchion in the man's hand. He leapt nimbly back and fell over a dead dog in the mud.

Supine, struggling, he watched the brief fight. The

entrance to the alley was blocked by a hairy giant. Somewhere in the mêlée Goffo glimpsed a swirl of golden hair and a cool seraphic face above a knife. Someone trod Squalo's head into the mud. Zucca Pomello soared from the giant's hands along the alley four feet or so above Goffo, and landed inert. Otto Lancia came stumbling, a hand pressed to his midriff, fell and reddened the mud beside Goffo.

Fear spurred Goffo to struggle to all fours. He had to get out of here. They should have sent twice as many men. If only he could kill the man and run, all the money would be his. He put a hand down on the dead dog for better purchase to get his feet under him, it slipped into the mud and he found that Otto had been holding a knife when he fell. At this moment an almighty kick on his rear propelled him forward. His head hit the wall and he sank obliviously back into the mud.

Sigismondo surveyed the littered alley. At the far end a child sucking a rag had appeared and watched them. A shutter slammed overhead. Already a couple of pigs, on whose scavenging track this was, advanced cautiously from the street to investigate a possible feast.

Barley and Angelo had wasted no time before frisking the bodies strewn in the mud, though the most valuable thing recovered was probably one of Angelo's knives from Otto's midriff. Benno looked on, fascinated, clutching his cudgel.

'Thank God! You're safe!'

Olivero stood at the alley's entrance, scattering the pigs, sheathing his sword. He gazed at the strewn figures with something approaching admiration.

'I saw you turn down here and a gang of cutthroats seemed to be tailing you. I thought you'd need some help if they were after you, but I see you got help already.' He stared at the burly giant and at the slight man in the faded parti-coloured doublet, his face half-masked by long fair hair as he looked round from Zucca Pomello's unconscious form. Olivero gave him a second heavy-lidded stare. 'Don't I know you?'

Angelo shook his head and if Olivero thought he had recognized the respectable merchant who had turned up with the wounded Gian, he was silenced by the unlikelihood of his being here dressed as a vagabond. Barley beamed, which did not make him less alarming. Sigismondo, by contrast, was serious.

'I owe you much, my friend. How can I ever repay? You are my guardian angel ready to protect me against all-comers.' He put an arm round Olivero's shoulders and gripped the far one, leading him back to the street. 'You saved me from the monk and now you do me further favours. Your time will come, sir, I vow it.'

Olivero had no word in return but, with a salute, left them and joined Ferondo, who stood at the corner and seemed surprised by what he saw. Bemused, he returned Sigismondo's cordial wave.

Benno watched Barley and Angelo heading away down the alley, and turned to look up at Sigismondo, who shook him by the arm and led him onwards.

'If you want a couple of guardian angels, Benno, tell them what route you're taking, as I did. With any luck one flap of their wings will scatter those who are anxious to give you a free pass to the next world. And yes, Olivero was waiting till his crew had done their job before he came to get the cross. D'you think he'd trust that lot to search my corpse?'

Back in the alley, Goffo had returned to consciousness with the help of a pig sampling one of his toes that protruded through a slit in his boot. A man with a tower

225

of finch cages was bending over him, in a dazing flutter of wings and discordant twitters.

'You've been in a fight,' he said helpfully.

Chapter 44

The Prior Gets Lucky

In a remarkably few days, thanks to some foundered horses, sore bottoms and bloody thighs, most of Europe had received news of the Pope's death. Various things were therefore set in motion, notably those cardinals able to travel to Rome for the election. Some were too aged or infirm even to contemplate the journey, and resigned themselves to dying at their leisure where they were, rather than on a dusty road or the stink and heat of the city. The rest took to mule or litter, with attendant train as befitted their dignity – which some hoped would increase in triplicate by means of the Conclave. Many others, who had little hope of election themselves, were at least confident of enrichment by the bribes of various factions enlisting their votes. A few were looking forward to the jaunt. It is always interesting to observe the decay of one's contemporaries.

Kings, princes and dukes prepared embassies to wait on the new Head of Christendom when he should be declared, and sent these out with letters of congratulation, wanting only the insertion of a name, to be delivered after the Pope's coronation. Ludovico of Rocca put his splendidly flourished signature to a second letter to a Pope while he was still ignorant of the effect of his first one. Cardinal Pontano returned from Pietra where the Abbot had been buried and set off immediately for Rome, taking this letter with him. In the stifling heat of late summer, many envied those such as the English cardinal, completely unable to make the journey in time, who could stay comfortably at home.

One cardinal with not far to go was Cardinal Bufera, which was lucky because his health, or lack of it, enforced travel by litter. He lived from choice in his ancient villa in the cool of the Alban hills where, everyone knew, he was likely to die at any moment. Nobody knew from what he was suffering although everybody hoped it was not infectious. His villa, where he lay surrounded by books, was reported to be a poky little place rebuilt from an old Roman house, and he would certainly not be storing silver with Cardinal Pantera or anywhere else. Not one cardinal among them all was less likely to be elected, partly because he was too unworldly to rule Christendom – his famed eccentricity was considered no bar although anecdote made it sound almost like dementia – and partly because he was unlikely to survive the Conclave, let alone a coronation.

Cardinal Pantera had emerged from the frenzy of business that had absorbed him since the Pope's death, to pay attention to his guests and show a reserved pleasure at the mending of the feud. Gian, still in a dazed state, submitted to escort his cousins' wives on their constant expeditions to spend their husbands' money. As he had no recollection of his purpose in coming to Rome, neither he nor his cousins had any objections to this.

The man he had intended to visit was his uncle, or rather his father's cousin, Piero Pantera, head of the illimitably wealthy and influential Pantera bank. Olivero and Ferondo had paid visits there already, several visits as their cousin was too busy at first to see them. They explained that Gian would wait on the banker when he was less engaged in enjoying himself about town. Piero Pantera was even more busy than his cousin the Cardinal and for much the same reason. The movement of money among the members of the future Conclave was already crucial. He brushed away Olivero's false excuses for Gian, either ignoring, or ignorant of, their subtler intention.

'Let him enjoy himself, he's young and he's had his sorrows. So have you all. And for some superstitious nonsense . . .' He tapped one of the great steel boxes on his table. 'You don't need some rubbishy jewel to make money, and as for sons, you'll just have to keep trying. Now, if you'll excuse me, I've people to see.'

One of the people who arrived to see Piero was a man they were more sure of recognizing than Angelo. Agostino da Sangallo acknowledged them in the antechamber with only the curtest of nods, a nod which conveyed that he would be quite happy never to see them again. He was remembering, no doubt, that Olivero had caught an inflammatory glimpse of his wife's features on the journey, thanks to a busy wind. Indeed, if he had had better luck among the other bankers he had been seeing, he would not now visit one called Pantera. The money Agostino needed was hard to come by when suddenly the richest men were husbanding their resources against the contingencies of the election.

'One thing,' remarked Olivero to his brother as they made their way towards the Palazzo Pantera, 'that old fox will not do, is to ask Cousin Piero to dinner with that juicy wife of his. He'll keep her under wraps until it's time for a shroud.'

What answer Ferondo might have made was lost as a sudden current of people, swirling ahead regardless of anyone, swept them apart and carried them through a stone archway leading into the Santaporta monastery. It took all Olivero's force of resistance and Ferondo's sly sharp elbows before they could extract themselves. Ferondo had heard some shrill exhortations among the women, and commented, 'It's that mad monk they're after. He's not hanged yet, then.'

'Now they've heard he's killed an abbot they'll put an axe in his hand and point him at a few cardinals – reduce the competition. The red hats are coming into Rome every hour, like leeches looking for blood.'

The weary and dust-stained Princes of the Church were certainly unaware how many who might have gathered at the city gates for their blessing had gone instead to beg blessings from a crazy murdering monk. However, as Princes of the Church they had seen more of human nature than was entirely comfortable and they would not have been surprised.

Brother Ieronimo had first, by kind permission of the Prior, appeared on the balcony above the inner courtyard, by now packed with the faithful and with sightseers but, instead of usefully having a vision, he had gazed down in slight surprise at the faces lifted towards him. Brother Filippo, his escort, had given him an impatient nudge with no more effect than to make him start an Ave, in which the crowd respectfully joined. If they were expecting this to be the prelude to more stirring stuff, they were sadly disappointed, for Brother Ieronimo, having ended his prayer, gave a benevolent wave to the crowd and wandered indoors, followed by a scolding Brother Filippo.

The Prior, behind the shutters at another window, had observed the crowd and was disturbed at its reaction to this. Romans expect value for money, and the donations these people had made in order to be allowed into the courtyard were good for more, they felt, than just a prayer and a wave. The mood was darkening. A mutter rose into shouts. A monk blamelessly traversing the arcade was hustled and hit and pushed indoors to say that Brother Ieronimo must come down and give his blessing or they would come and get him. Women hoping for sons from the Virgin of Scheggia were no less forceful than the men.

The Prior deliberated. Brother Ieronimo, were he to mingle with that crowd, was likely to be pulled about; he could not be relied on to satisfy them – but even if he did, they might tear his clothes, or even his limbs if either enthusiasm or rage escalated. The Prior was responsible for his person but, as the shouts rose below, he recalled that the monk had already been condemned by the late Pope and, if he died at the hands of that mob, it would just be ahead of time. Then, should he prove to be a saint . . . There would be those pilgrimages to the scene of martyrdom; there was only the question of relics. It would be a pity if there was nothing left . . . Nevertheless, action was needed.

'Take him out there. Now. Let Father Torquato and Brother Filippo take him out to the people.'

Neither of those named found this a welcome task but in fact the crowd had no eyes for them. They were instantly parted from Brother Ieronimo, who was seized and tugged about by a group of brawny women, assailing him with demands for blessings. He was dragged to his knees, while their hands snatched at his habit and at his ruffled hair that stood up like white feathers around his tonsure. One had got a knife and was ready to hack a piece from the hem of his habit, and she was pulling at the cloth when, throwing them all off with a startling access of strength, Brother Ieronimo rose to his feet, flung up his arms and, in a voice that rang above all the babble, he cried, 'She is here! Oh, Our Lady is here!'

Chapter 45

The Husband Dodge

The noise died. Silence came, an awed silence only disturbed by the sound of people all over the courtyard getting to their knees. A baby burst out wailing; every face was raised towards the sky. Brother Ieronimo held up his hands, and his face was joyfully transfigured.

'Rome is blest! See where Our Lady looks down upon the city. . . She wishes all to live at peace with one another. Restore all to whom it rightfully belongs and all will be well with you.'

Sobs and awed murmurs succeeded the silence, as everyone vainly attempted to see what the monk saw. A pickpocket who had just relieved a woman in front of him of her purse crossed himself and pushed it forward to lie by her knee. In one corner a boy was having a fit, barely noticed by those near him, who shuffled away from him but kept their eyes on the sky or on Brother Ieronimo. Others, weeping, embraced those next to them and vowed friendship. One beggar, who had painted his stumps artistically for the occasion, nearly fell off the wooden shutter he poled himself round the streets on, when he was hugged by the most beautiful whore he had ever seen, who left the mark of her kiss on his cheek like an extra wound.

For of course there were professionals there, as in any crowd. Those who have come to gawk at a murderer or a visionary are open to temptation of all kinds, and this is what a professional of a different kind should have remembered; but when Torquato caught the eye of a young woman at the front of the crowd he did not stop to ask himself what kind of woman had the determination to gain so conspicuous a place, or whether he himself had any business to be giving her his attention.

What a face! Torquato had a sense he might have seen it before, perhaps in dreams. He might have seen it in one of the Abbey's illuminated manuscripts. The arched brows, large eyes, straight nose and finely shaped mouth, those perfect features framed in luxuriantly ringletted blonde hair, all this belonged, or should belong, to an angel; but this was not a sexless angel but a woman, with a disturbing physical presence, and the regard those grey eyes gave Torquato made it clear that her thoughts were more concerned with the priest as a man than any angel could conceive of. He was flattered that this creature should be giving attention to him and not to the skies.

It was Brother Filippo, therefore, who had the presence of mind to hurry Brother Ieronimo indoors while the crowd was still in a confused state and on their knees. The Prior, still watching, was delighted that not only was the chief performer saved for another day but also that the performance had left the crowd in an euphoric state. Most of them were convinced by now that they too had seen the vision and were ready to describe the details of the Virgin's robe and her expression to those who had not seen. The promise that all would be well was taken both personally, for each one, and for the city, which was now bound to have an excellent Pope. The conditions mentioned by Brother Ieronimo, on which the felicity rested, were largely forgotten, though one or two serious souls made private vows and one decided to call at once on his lawyer and make such restitution in his will as would dismay his heirs and pleasantly amaze his enemies.

Torquato stood still in all the chaos of the departing crowd, and Brother Filippo, having delivered Brother Ieronimo to his cell, returned to the courtyard in time to see him in conversation with a tall, slender blonde, her hair both fetchingly dishevelled around her face and also in copious braids at the back, perhaps a brighter blonde and almost certainly false – and tied with the yellow ribbon that marked the prostitute. True, there was no obvious décolletage to disgust, but Brother Filippo trembled with the intensity of his revulsion as he stared at the wretch. Surely his colleague would turn from her, would know it was beyond the call of charity even to exchange words with someone so foul her very presence could pollute? Yet, as he watched, Torquato allowed his sleeve to be taken by the whore – began to go with her among the people leaving by the great stone archway.

Of course there were reasons – she might be fetching him to a dying man in need of confession and, even more, absolution: but the last rites required certain objects Torquato had not got. Brother Filippo's mind, having provided one good reason, refused more, and that was because he had seen the look Torquato had given to the thing tugging at his sleeve. Becoming a monk did not prevent lust – embracing chastity did not mean you forgot what it was like to embrace anything else. Brother Filippo had enough burning within him, despite all discipline, to recognize what had shown in Torquato's eyes.

Torquato, unaware of being observed, incapable indeed of noticing anything but his enticing guide, followed her so close that even in the smell of gutters and ordure that permeated the heatstruck alleys he breathed the strong musky scent she wore, as intoxicating as the glances she cast back to lure him on.

Brother Filippo had been uncannily correct in supposing a dying man wanting a priest; it was with just such an excuse that the blonde had begged Torquato to accompany her through the huddle of narrow streets and tenements. Whatever Torquato chose to tell himself, he did not expect to find a dying man at the top of the rickety stairs he had to climb. He kicked out of his way a little orange and white cat on the landing. He was sweating, and not because the room she had gone into was under the roof, baking despite the closed shutters.

In the twilight it was hard to make anything out even had he wanted to or if she had given him time. The girl's arms wound round him tightly as with one foot she skilfully kicked the door shut. She drew him down on the bed. If there ever had been a dying man on it there wasn't one now, unless Torquato in the throes of desire could be called one. How hard and strong her arms were, how hard and insistent her mouth! Torquato, panting, felt her fingers explore his hair, caress his neck, clamp his face against hers as he struggled to find his way into her dress. Thrashing on the bed, his skirts hauled higher than hers, his heart hammering, her urgent breath hot on his face, beseeching her to pull up her skirts, he quite missed the footsteps thudding up the stairs.

He couldn't miss the noise the door made when it crashed back against the wall, or the deafening shriek from the girl clasping him so tightly.

'My husband! He'll kill you!'

The chances of the bed after all containing a dying man increased dreadfully. Torquato, pushed away by the strong arms, fell from the bed and thumped to the floor; from there he had an excellent view of the man in the doorway;

although from that angle the man would seem even taller and larger than he actually was, in Torquato's eyes this bellowing, ginger-bearded man was a giant. Worse, he carried a cudgel and menaced him, bringing it down an inch from Torquato's toes with a rending thud that made Torquato scramble back on his bottom in ignominious haste. He could not spare a glance for the blonde, but he was peripherally aware of her pulling her clothes straight and cowering against the wall.

'You bastard priest, you'll pay for this!' The cudgel came down again, missing Torquato's head and splintering the window sill.

And pay, of course, was what he did. Luckily he still had much of the money entrusted to him by the Abbey for expenses in Rocca. He fumbled, panting still, with burning face, rooting under his robes like any washerwoman until he found his purse, and untied it, and poured its contents into the giant's huge palm. Then he was allowed to get up and escape, falling over the cat in the doorway and hearing the caged linnet burst into triumphant song as he reached the street. He hurried away, muttering curses rather than prayers, and then tried desperately to look composed as people turned to stare at him.

In the attic room Angelo, still in Gemmata's dress, was admiring La Feconda.

Chapter 46

Preparations and Invitations

On the eve of the Conclave a spirit of excitement pervaded Rome. The cardinals were about to become prisoners, for an unknown time, till the election was over, and many were bent on celebrating their last night of freedom. There were those who dedicated the night to prayer or even to sleep, but theirs were largely neglected pastimes. Cardinal Tartaruga, who lived in the city anyway, was in the best position to entertain the rest, and his aim was to show that, of all those to be locked up next day, he was the one best fitted to be displayed to the crowd at the end as their Pope.

In particular he wished Cardinal Lepre, his closest rival for St Peter's chair, to be dazzled, overwhelmed.

Invitations had been carried to all whom his Eminence considered influential or useful: relations, like his cousin by marriage Agostino da Sangallo (wanting a loan he would certainly get when Tartaruga had the papal treasury at his command) had to be asked as they were family, but he chiefly wished as many of his fellow cardinals to attend as were able. Cardinal Pantera was to come, along with his guests and relatives, the three nephews and the wives. Another guest was one Sigismondo, who came from no city whose name could be attached to his, but who had had audience of the late Pope as envoy of the Duke of Rocca. Cardinal Tartaruga promised himself a few words with *him* before the evening was out.

Not all his colleagues could come. The French cardinal had only arrived today from Avignon and, being elderly, was too fatigued to attend. Cardinal Bufera had made the journey only from his villa outside Rome in the Alban hills but for him the invitation was a formality – everyone knew he wouldn't come; it could be called a miracle that he had survived that short journey. Tartaruga certainly didn't want a guest dying at the dinner table and putting people off the food.

This had been planned like everything else – to impress. The Cardinal's cooks had all but taken their knives to each other and with great difficulty had been persuaded to a truce and to rational discussions of the dishes to present. Swans, served to look as if swimming, ate better than peacock though they lent themselves less well to display; there was wild boar with sultanas and pine nuts, there were roast geese stuffed with herbs, quinces, pears, garlic and grapes. There had to be the Cardinal's favourite little pies of fried chicken liver with hard-boiled eggs and ginger. The cook whose speciality these were had become melancholy with perpetually making them.

Pheasant with white truffles and cream was a dish that generally went well, but the main piece would be the subtlety brought on at the end to inspire universal admiration. It was the sole task of one of the master cooks to produce this, in a small room of his own almost like a private chapel. The Cardinal's coat of arms must figure prominently, so a tortoise was the centrepiece, grounded on a base of wafer biscuit and made of sugar paste and jelly, the shell of flat coloured comfits gilded, stuck on with sugar, and the whole frosted with sugar and rosewater so that it shone like ice. Between the tortoise's front feet the cook had managed to secure a long gilded pole which carried a crucifix atop, a suitably religious object, as the tiara at first contemplated was considered bad luck. It was bound to be applauded politely when it was carried in, though Cardinal Lepre, whose coat-of-arms showed a hare's head caboshed – full-face, under its red hat – would unquestionably get the message that in the race for power, the tortoise won.

Apart from the frenzy in the kitchens, there was hubbub in the great dining hall. Trestle tables, laid with damask linen, were decorated with sprigs of bay and box; the garlands, with flowers – of all extravagant things – were to come later to ensure their freshness would last. The credenza was carefully piled with the Tartaruga silver dishes embossed with the family tortoise crest, surely destined soon for Cardinal Pantera's cellars. All this work took place, however, against the hammering and sawing of a group of carpenters at the far end where the tapestries had been taken down and stood, neatly rolled, against the wall. Supervising the confusion and din was his Eminence's *maestro di casa*, who was driven by the inspiring thought that if anything went wrong with the entertainment that night, heads would roll, starting with his. The Cardinal had planned more than one surprise for his guests but not the one he was actually to get.

Agostino da Sangallo was pleased with his invitation and with himself. He had told his wife that the invitation was not inclusive of wives, it was a political occasion at which the strategies of the Conclave would be discussed and women would be a frivolous irrelevance. Felicia had taken the news meekly, he was glad to see. He had no intention whatsoever of allowing her to attend a dinner where so many religious, notorious for their eye for attractive female – as a rule – flesh, were to gather.

Suppose she were to be noticed again by a Prince of the Church! He had not forgotten the Abbot. The greater power a man had, as Agostino well knew, the easier it was for him to seduce.

Even a priest had unfair advantages: still in his mind was what he had seen yesterday. It had been a grim moment. He had accompanied his wife and her maid to church and, coming out, had engaged in conversation with some merchants he knew. Turning around in the confident expectation that Felicia would have heeded his commands and be waiting meekly, heavily veiled, what was his furious consternation to see her, bare-faced, talking animatedly to a priest whom he identified with no pleasure at all, Father Torquato; who had, no doubt, like that damned Olivero Pantera, seen Felicia's face on the journey when her veil blew off. He was hurrying forward when she kissed the man's hand, put down her veils again and came to meet him, the priest vanishing into the throng. He waited until he got her home to show her what a mistake she had made, and now she was not going to have the opportunity to make another.

Some go to feasts because they are specifically invited, others because they accompany the guests. Benno's appetite for feasts never flagged, and he was sure a Roman one would be special. He was the more ready for this one because his master appeared to be in a good mood in spite of Torquato still having the cross. He entertained a mind's-eye picture of Sigismondo's taking the priest by the throat and choking him till he produced it, but he supposed that to walk into a monastery and start strangling one of its inhabitants might, even in the strangely secular city of Rome, not be taken well.

'D'you think he'll be there tonight? Torquato, I mean?' This was surely a question safe to ask, and Sigismondo did not appear irked by it. He looked down at Benno carefully lacing the gold cords across his black velvet doublet.

'As a late abbot's secretary – ' Benno thought: late abbot's murderer? – 'I doubt that he's important enough for Cardinal Tartaruga. Yet something tells me he'll be there.'

'What?' asked Benno daringly, arranging the gold dags to hang properly on the broad chest.

'Hey, what should I say? A little bird with blood on its beak? There are things I don't know, Benno, but I *feel* them. Like a breeze on the skin. I'll wear that chain tonight.'

That chain was one given by Duke Ippolyto of Altamura, a token of his gratitude for the services Sigismondo had done him. It was both massive and delicate, a heavy chain holding in its links gold leaves of filigree and emerald flowers; a chain, Benno thought, to make Cardinal Tartaruga stare and know he'd made no mistake about the importance of this guest at least.

Chapter 47

The Host with the Most

The guest who made everyone stare, however, was a quite unimportant one. She owed her presence there to her husband's being a cousin by marriage of the Cardinal, and to her having recently made the acquaintance of the Pantera wives at church. It was Elisavetta Pantera who had revealed to Felicia da Sangallo that wives were in fact invited to the Cardinal's feast. Felicia, who understood her husband perfectly, waited until he left, in his best clothes, and then threw off her wrapper, removed her swathed turban, dressed in her best, and followed.

This meant that the guests were all assembled when she was announced, and all eyes turned to her entrance. Felicia had tinted her hair, with Perpetua's help, and arranged it in long braids twisted with lilac ribbons fringed in gold, and with long curls to lie on her breast on the mulberry velvet slashed with lilac satin. She was *not* wearing a veil, unless the nonsense of lilac gauze twisted round the crowning braids counted as one. Her dimples, as she curtseyed to her host and apologized for her lateness, were enough to melt the hearts of everyone present except her husband, who was speechless with rage and frustration.

Cardinal Tartaruga, generally rumoured to think of women as a necessary nuisance who should be kept in their place, which was bed, came forward with something very like a smile on his austere features. It was the first time, he realized, that he had seen his cousin Agostino's wife. He expressed himself delighted that she had recovered so soon from the malady from which her husband had reported her to be suffering.

Luckily for Felicia, because she had arrived so late and so unexpectedly, the *maestro di casa* did not find her a place near her husband but, perhaps unluckily, next to Torquato who, as Sigismondo had prophesied, was certainly present. She could not have found anyone more prepared to devote his attention to her, for he was still smarting from his wretched experience at the hands of what he believed to be a whore and her pimp. He had come straight on to the Cardinal's dinner, where he had been promised a moment or two of private audience when it was over. His clothes still smelt of the whore's scent and Brother Filippo, who sat round the corner at the end of the table, had recoiled from him as if he stank of a midden.

Brother Filippo also, although Torquato was too absorbed in Felicia's dimples to notice, neglected his food to glare at them both. Brother Filippo was not of the Cardinal's opinion, that women were necessary; if it had not been for Eve, Adam would still be in Paradise. If a mistake could by any stretch of possibility be attributed to the Almighty, it must be His creation of woman, the downfall of so many.

Most of Cardinal Tartaruga's guests were too busy enjoying the food and the genial atmosphere to entertain bitter thoughts, although Cardinal Lepre might have been the exception. Just as his rival Tartaruga bizarrely resembled the tortoise of his crest, with his bald head, ropy neck and reptilian glare, so people affected to see something of the hare of *his* crest in Cardinal Lepre. Perhaps the name had been given, in ancient days, to a member of the family who had bequeathed his features to this descendant, but he had slightly protuberant eyes, and large front teeth above his grey goatee beard.

Tonight the hare was fussed. The tortoise was putting on far too good a show before the gathered College. The food was excellent, the chamber of considerable grandeur, the silver-gilt plate revoltingly abundant – was there nothing to criticize? If this creature became Pope his head would explode. It would be Christian charity to prick his vanity now. He remarked, smiling, and loud enough to be heard by many, on the state of the tapestries at the far end of the chamber.

'Hercules, I see, is cleaning the Augean stables; but should someone not have cleaned Hercules himself? Yet these old tapestries that have faded are hard to clean, I've heard. You must let me recommend a firm of weavers I employ – expensive but they *are* the best – unless of course you feel such things are of no importance.'

It was nicely done. Sigismondo, at the high table by virtue of his chain and his recent position as the Duke of Rocca's emissary, and as Cardinal Pantera's guest, smiled. Benno, behind his chair, saw that Cardinal Lepre implied his host had no appreciation of detail and would leave a dirty old tapestry up when he was entertaining – for all his display of silver-gilt and swans he was too mean to replace an old hanging. Cardinal Pantera, courteously anxious to dispel ill-feeling, said, 'Surely what is old gains from being seen to be so. We value the antique. And this chamber is unmatchable for size and splendour. I have seen no room more princely in the Vatican itself.'

Cardinal Tartaruga seized the chance for which he had been waiting all evening. He beckoned the *maestro di casa* and said, 'His Eminence Cardinal Lepre finds the tapestry of Hercules distasteful. Have it removed.' The *maestro di casa* sped away, signalling servants who stepped forward with poles to lift the tapestry off its hooks. 'You must forgive me,' Tartaruga said, 'for not entertaining you in my finest chamber.'

The tapestry was swiftly gathered up and carried away. 'This is really, as you see, part of my stables.'

A row of stalls, complete with mangers full of hay, with bridles hanging up, with buckets and brooms but no horses, was revealed. The silence of the astonished guests was broken by a storm of clapping, for a host whose careless magnificence could apparently have quarters for his horses that could double as a place for Princes of the Church to dine in. A few could see that there were no marks of shod hooves among the straw scattered on the floor there, and could sniff out the smell of new wood under the perfumes that servants continually scattered everywhere, and the heaviness of great wax candles burning in their huge silver-gilt sconces and on the tall torchères. But it must be said that most of the company appreciated the conceit of the Cardinal.

Cardinal Lepre had clapped with painful slowness, and some of his adherents were muttering in assumed indignation at being invited to dine in a stable; Cardinal Pantera, still the peacemaker, reminded everyone that the Saviour Himself had not disdained a stable, and that Cardinal Tartaruga had certainly sought to put this in their thoughts before the sacred responsibility of next day's Conclave. This unfortunately convinced many that Cardinal Pantera must have accepted massive bribes from Cardinal Tartaruga already, and that any mule-loads of tortoise-marked silver to reach the Pantera cellars would be there to stay.

The subtlety was now carried in, to more applause. The comfit-strewn tortoise, with the gilded pole topped by a crucifix, seemed to wear a smirk on its primitive features, and quite a few guests wondered how soon they would be bidden to a feast to celebrate a Tartaruga pope. The subtlety was dismantled and consumed, the crucifix lying on the gilded dish on the sideboard among ruins of crushed paste and jelly. The cloths were removed, the tables taken down and carried away, and sweetmeats and dessert wine handed round. The predominance of purple in the room – cardinals in their robes of mourning for the late Pope – became more noticeable as the company dispersed to talk, or wandered to the loggia where some breeze, little more than a shifting air, came off the river – the smell that came with it being overlaid as fast as possible by assiduous sprinkling of scented water and the burning of incense. The Cardinal's Chair had been standing at the far end of the chamber on its dais, a chair only used when the chair of St Peter was empty; Cardinal Tartaruga, a man not given to losing opportunity for display, assumed his place on it.

He had private words now with this guest or that, one of them being a priest and another the mysterious man with the shaven head whose appearance and bearing had given rise to the usual speculation. Among those who knew nothing of him, the most popular theory was that he was an important member of the Eastern schism – look at that chain – and was here in disguise to spy on the most intimate business of the Catholic Church, or even to influence the election towards a pope who might be in favour of the Patriarch of Constantinople. Certainly if the man was a priest he did not look a celibate.

Celibacy had a bearing on the interview Torquato had with his host, and he kissed the Cardinal's ring with rage in his heart as he was dismissed. Sigismondo's interview was peripatetic, strolling the length of the chamber, but there was nothing to be deduced from his expression when he raised his head from the ring. Benno, watching from the dark of a doorway among servants of the other guests, with his dish of assorted broken meats, longed to ask a rash question for which he was luckily too distant. Then the main entertainment arrived.

The Cardinal's *maestro di casa* was accustomed to produce jesters, jugglers and jongleurs; he had in the past ushered in conjurers, dwarves and dancing whores. He had never until now had to take delivery of a monk in manacles. His wand of office kept Brother Ieronimo at a sanitary distance as the guards pushed him forward. He had his orders, however and, reassured by the sight of the manacles before Brother Ieronimo clasped his hands in his sleeves, the *maestro di casa* permitted the mad monk to advance into the great chamber.

The orchestra, small but skilful, which had been discoursing soothingly on harp and flute, now struck up an altogether more rousing strain, to which a hand drum added dramatic effect. Conversation hushed as all eyes turned on the tall, gangling figure with the white halo of hair round the tonsure. People came in from the loggia and stood, brushed by the lawn curtains, to stare.

Scarcely anyone in Rome had not by now heard of the murdering monk who prophesied. His success with predicting the death of the late Pope had brought him instant stardom, and several of the cardinals present had sent privately to the Santaporta with donations and inquiries as to their future. The donations had been accepted but the inquiries were not answered. Brother Ieronimo, explained the Prior, had received no word from above as yet.

Word from above was what everyone wanted, and it was a measure of Cardinal Tartaruga's confidence that he believed he would obtain a favourable answer. If the prophecy was adverse, or ambiguous, he thought of the priests at Delphi giving meaning to the Sibyl's inspired ravings; he could come up with an interpretation that would convince these guests from the Sacred College that in voting for him in the days to come they would be carrying out the will of God.

The trouble at the moment was in getting Brother Ieronimo to perform. He stood there, looking about him with lively interest, smiling at faces he knew, but perfectly silent and with no sign whatever of imminent utterance.

Cardinal Tartaruga took the initiative. He beckoned a servant carrying wine, and himself filled a goblet and advanced towards Brother Ieronimo. Something had however caught the monk's eye: the little gilded pole with the crucifix at the top, abandoned on a dish, and he strode to it and rescued it reverently. He turned, holding it out to Cardinal Tartaruga as if to exorcise him. Brother Ieronimo had found his inspiration.

Chapter 48

Fishing for Men

It was very nearly cool at dawn. Benno, his shirt open and Biondello panting at his heels, fanned himself with his cap as he ambled at Sigismondo's side. The pearly light in the dome of the sky, deepening to rose low in the east, was not echoed in the sluggish yellow of the river beneath their feet. At the far side of the bridge, the heads on their spikes were almost old friends by now. Benno spared a glance for the features that seemed to stir in recognition as the flies on them shifted. His mind was still full of the events at the Tartaruga supper he and Sigismondo had left not so long ago.

'Brother Ieronimo let him have it, din' he? The coming glory of Rome and all that, and Our Lady wanting people to restore things.'

'I feel that did not appeal to the Cardinal quite as strongly as the part about the next pope.' Sigismondo had been walking with his doublet slung down his back by one finger hooked in its neck. He leant on the parapet and brooded over the slow current beneath. A solitary fisherman sat unmoving in a boat not far off as though the river had infected him with its inertia. Perhaps he doubted any fish would be worth the catching. 'That part appealed to him without doubt.'

'What exactly did Brother Ieronimo say? People all

249

round were saying what the Latin meant but I still couldn't make out, about the next pope being *happy*. After all, goes without saying, right?'

Sigismondo wagged his head gently, quoting, 'I see the man who shall be pope. Happy shall he be called.'

Benno pulled at his beard. 'All very well; but I din' think he was looking at Cardinal Tartaruga. Seemed to me he was looking *through* him. And if he was having a vision, we don't know who it was of.'

Sigismondo did not reply. Instead, he nudged Benno, who shifted to see what his master was seeing. On the river bank to their left, where the Tartaruga palace loomed over the water, there were figures moving on the low stone quay under the jutting loggia.

'You reckon they're going to throw anything else out? I couldn't believe it, could you?' Benno was reliving his astonishment when the Cardinal's servants had piled up all the silver-gilt dishes into baskets and, passing through the guests scattered on the loggia, tossed the lot over the balustrade into the waiting Tiber. That really was a gesture – designed to impress, even more than the revelation about the stables. The Cardinal was demonstrating now that he had the resources to put as much silver on the table again or to commission a fresh set. It was a gesture of reckless magnificence, made with great calculation.

'Mm . . . Perhaps I am less credulous than you, when it comes to cardinals.' Sigismondo was watching the figures at the waterside, busy twitching cords free of poles buried up to their heads in the riverbed. 'And no, they are not likely to throw anything more out. For one thing, nobody who matters can be watching.'

True, the servants had looked about before they started, but only in a perfunctory way. The world, for Rome at that hour, was empty; the moribund fisherman and two figures on the bridge hardly counted. Sigismondo could hear a shout from the man in the centre who seemed to be co-ordinating their efforts; and everyone hauled. Were they getting fish for the Cardinal's breakfast? Their catch came up gleaming, tumbled together in shoals, but Benno, staring, doubled up and broke into silent laughter. After a moment he could speak.

'It's his dishes! He'd got those nets waiting all along. The artful old—' Benno stopped. He had still a provincial sense that it could be blasphemous to refer to a cardinal in pejorative terms. A practical idea made him add, 'They'll be all bashed about and messy. This river has all sorts in, you can bet.'

Apparently it had. The servants drew the nets halfway on to the low quay and some were already reaching for the silver to stack it into the baskets. A cry came suddenly across the water, and one end of the net began to slip. It was retrieved, to a jabber of scolding and justification, succeeded by an abrupt silence.

Sigismondo whistled between his teeth and stood upright. The net held, in a jumble of dishes, a long, black object with pale extremities, dripping like weed.

'Cardinal Tartaruga's practising to be Pope, indeed. He's already a Fisher of Men.'

Benno gulped. Now, as the servants examined the black object, he could see what it was, the limbs lolling helpless, caught up in the netting. Probably it happened all the time. That fisherman in the boat was unmoved by the find, as used to corpses as to fish.

Sigismondo, however, had gone striding back across the bridge and was descending the steps to the waterside, Biondello in full scamper at his heels.

The Cardinal's servants were still arguing when

Sigismondo reached them. Was the body to be brought in or thrown back? One servant, looking up, discovered it was a guest of the night before, a face and head not easily forgotten. It was too late to conceal the Cardinal's deception even if they could, and the man appeared relieved to see him.

'Sir, what should we do? His Eminence goes into Conclave in a few hours – he'll be hearing Mass shortly. How can we bother him with this?'

This was the body which, on closer viewing, had dark hair – or dark from the water – clinging to a bald patch. The gown, also black but muddy, was long and belted at the waist. Attached to the belt and snagged taut to a strand of net was a rosary. Sigismondo helped to drag the prone body on to the quay and, as the servants drew back, he turned the head in order to see the face.

The mouth was open, the features soft and bleached with immersion. There were small nicks in the skin of the throat. It was lucky the man had no further use for his eyes as fish had breakfasted on them. Yet the face was familiar. That had been not a bald patch but a tonsure. It was Torquato.

Sigismondo, hands under the corpse's shoulders, dragged it free of the net and laid it, streaming water, on the quay. Most of the servants, mindful that they must answer to the *maestro di casa*, and perhaps not unused to the sight of bodies in a city of more than a dozen murders a day, went on retrieving, shaking, and stacking the dishes in the baskets. The rest watched in fascination as Sigismondo pulled aside the cape and scapular and opened the priest's torn gown. Benno knew it could not be in search for La Feconda, which Angelo had handed over not half an hour ago.

The reason for Sigismondo's curiosity was soon revealed.

Swollen, everted, one sporting a leech, gashes in the pallid flesh of Torquato's chest and midriff showed that he had not just slipped into the Tiber and drowned.

Chapter 49

Spoilt for Choice

All the company signed themselves and Sigismondo spoke
a prayer, the servants and Benno providing the amen.
Now that it was clear that the man dragged up with the
Tartaruga dishes had been murdered, there was increased
argument over whether they should disturb the Cardinal.
Sigismondo was the one they turned to for a decision,
Benno noticed, and when appealed to he did not hesitate.

'Take me to the *maestro di casa*.'

They were spared the trouble, for he was here, emerging
from the high flood-door and demanding to know where
the dishes were. He viewed the body with fastidious
disgust but no surprise. This was Rome. Priests were as
common as murderers and not always more welcome. By
no means was his Eminence to be disturbed. The *maestro
di casa*, trained to observe, had known again the priest
he had brought to his Eminence for a private word after
the dinner and, of course, he recognized the guest with
the shaven head and the commanding air who had also
had a private word with the Cardinal. It was his pleasure
to accede to that guest's suggestion and order two servants
to take up the dripping body, wrap it in a black cloth which
he could supply – it would figure anonymously in next
month's expenses – and carry it on one of the little
stretchers used for bringing in set-piece dishes, to
Santaporta. If only all his problems could be so painlessly

solved! He gave Sigismondo one of his lowest bows as the little procession started on its way in the strengthening light.

Few of the people now up and about the streets paid any attention to the shrouded burden. Sigismondo attracted glances, but, apart from a mechanical sign of the cross, his followers were ignored.

At Santaporta, the monks were at Lauds but the porter, horrified by the unorthodox return of Father Torquato, let them into the first courtyard and sent his assistant to waylay Father Prior at the chapel door. The Cardinal's servants deposited their burden on a stone bench beneath the arcade bordering the courtyard and left, exclaiming at the generosity of Sigismondo's tip. The others waited, Sigismondo relaxed, leaning against a column of the arcade, studying the sky across which some birds flew purposefully towards the east. Biondello had lowered his rump to the cobblestones and sat, taking in the scene while Benno watched the thin ooze of water seep from under the black swathing and make its way across the flagstones; he fairly itched with questions he did not dare to ask yet.

The Prior, apprised of dreadful things, approached down the arcade at the measured pace of one who has the philosophy to deal with them. All the same, when Sigismondo nodded to Benno and he twitched the cloth from Torquato's face, the Prior recoiled and Brother Filippo, who had accompanied him, crossed himself and groaned. Benno, enjoying the chance to make an effect, twitched the cloth still further, revealing the wounds on Torquato's neck, chest and midriff.

'Stabbed! May the Lord have mercy on his soul! Who could have done such a thing and why?'

'Say rather, who could be surprised!' Brother Filippo spoke with force. 'I have to tell you, in charity, Father

Prior, that this our brother was an evil-doer before God. Let us hope he offered penitence in the moment of death or I fear he must even now be enfolded in the flames of Hell!'

'An evil-doer, brother?' The Prior, bringing his hands together under his long sleeves, looked dubious. 'Which of us is not a sinner before God? Do you know, sir, how he came by these wounds?' The Prior studied Sigismondo as though suddenly aware that here was a man who might be familiar with wounds; who must indeed have caused not a few before now. Perhaps he thought, however, that murderers do not commonly produce their victims and stand by to take the consequences.

'I am as much in the dark, Father, as you are. Like Father Torquato I was a guest at the Palazzo Tartaruga last night; and also as you were, Brother, if I don't mistake.' As Brother Filippo inclined his head, Sigismondo continued, 'Then can you tell us what happened afterwards? Did you not accompany Father Torquato back here?'

A flush spread on Brother Filippo's thin face. 'I would not accompany that man one step of his way lest I pollute my soul. I took no heed of where he went – doubtless to some whore or other.'

'Speak no ill of the dead, my son. Avoid evil speculation.' The Prior kept the monks of Santaporta under strict control, but Torquato was outside his jurisdiction. 'Our first concern must be to have the body washed and a Mass begun. Sir, our thanks are due to you for bringing him here, and we shall inform the prefect of police for this quarter. I much fear that the villain who killed him will never be found; this is an evil city. No doubt he was slain for what he may have had in the way of money. Brother, do you know if he was carrying any?'

Brother Filippo shrugged, not concerned about money. 'He had gold from our Abbey for expenses in Rocca, which was not spent.' He watched while the Prior felt for, and found, a sodden purse inside Torquato's scapular. It was empty, as Sigismondo and Benno very well knew from Barley – 'he coughed up the lot' when Barley burst in upon the wretched priest in Angelo's grip – and Brother Filippo drew up his lip and said, 'He spent it all in a brothel. May God forgive him.' Clearly this was not something Brother Filippo was inclined to do.

'But it is proof,' said the Prior, 'that he was murdered for money.' Sigismondo did not say that those who murder for money do not put the purse back. 'If only he had given it to me for safe keeping.' The Prior, seeing two monks passing silently along the arcade on the far side, clapped his hands once, bringing them gliding across at speed.

Sigismondo left to them the decent disposal of Torquato's body. In the street people were about their business. Some – a group, mainly women – were waiting quietly outside the doors, at their beads, in hope of seeing Brother Ieronimo. A blind beggar at the wall gave a theatrical start as Sigismondo placed a coin in his outstretched hand, and blessed him with fervour. Someone sent a bucketful of water curving out of a shop doorway and, further along, someone emptied the night's slops from a window into the street. A bell from Santaporta behind them began to toll and Benno thought of Torquato. Had he really been killed by a thief disappointed at an empty purse? By a thief who discovered too late that the purse was empty? People could get very resentful if a robbery wasn't worth their trouble. 'Suppose we'll never know who did it,' he said. His master had a miraculous power, Benno believed, of knowing things, and he hoped to provoke him into answering without asking a question. Sigismondo laughed.

'Hey, now I'm going to tell you? How many hundreds of people in this city could our friend have come across last night, who'd have taken a knife to him?' Then he was silent, thoughtful, his face dark, and he went on in a different tone. 'Yet he may have been unlucky in a way we do know about. I watched him talking to Cardinal Tartaruga last night and I believe he meant to drive the same bargain with him as he seems to have done with the late Pope. A jewel like La Feconda would adorn the next Holy Father, whether or not it filled his treasure chests and granaries; and poor Torquato would have got his bishopric.'

Sigismondo paused to buy a handful of ripe figs from a girl with a pannier of them and, giving some to Benno and biting into another, he strolled down the next street, a series of shallow cobbled steps. Benno groped inside his shirt, where from long habit in former deprived times he kept a larder, and found a piece of cheese, and ate it with the fig as he listened.

'I saw Torquato at the moment he realized he hadn't got the cross to show the Cardinal. He fished at his neck, he patted his chest, then his stomach in case it had slipped its thong and then,' Sigismondo's mouth curled at the corners and his voice warmed, 'then he gave himself a beating like a *mea culpa* and then he had to pretend, so I thought, that he'd left it behind.'

'He must have felt stupid! What'd he mean to do? Get Angelo arrested?' The very idea was pitiful, like trying to arrest a wind.

'That doesn't matter now. I think he could have been killed for La Feconda, like so many others.' From Sigismondo's voice Benno as good as knew he was thinking of Bernabo. 'I was in a position to see Torquato and the Cardinal, but there may have been others less well placed, who may have thought he still had the cross.'

'Like who?'

'Someone who was standing near the Pope the other day when Torquato had audience. Standing near enough to hear, probably, what was being said.'

Benno stood still to picture it, and Sigismondo waited, regarding him gravely. Benno saw the fleshy face of the late Pope, bent to listen. Another face, a profile beside the Pope, came into his mind's eye, and he exclaimed. It was Cardinal Pantera's dark brow and sad eye that he saw. 'D'you think *he* heard Torquato say he had the cross?'

'He was near enough and we haven't noticed him to be deaf.' Sigismondo had come to the end of the shallow steps, and stood looking about, as if undecided which way to go. 'And we know that he likes harmony to prevail. He may have told his cousins that the cross was shortly to go to the Pope, thinking it would settle the dispute once for all.'

'Reckon he don't know his cousins, then.' Benno darted forward to rescue Biondello who was backing hastily before a large scavenging pig asserting rights over the gutter. He turned, clasping a rather smelly little armful and looked up into Sigismondo's face. 'Was it *Olivero* killed Torquato then?'

Sigismondo shrugged, and chose a side alley, decorated with banners of washing overhead, and the sunlight and crowds of a square beyond. 'When he thought I had the cross he tried to kill me. Torquato would be an easy target. Olivero was at the Tartaruga supper too, and Torquato knew him from the journey and could easily be got into talk or approached. Don't let's forget Ferondo either. It helps to have another pair of hands when you're heaving a body into the river.'

'But—' Benno trotted alongside, the alley just allowing two abreast, 'if it was Olivero, he knows now Torquato hasn't got it. Isn't he going to think *you* have it?'

The trouble was that Sigismondo did indeed have it, and was a target for a man who had just shown how ruthless he could be. 'Or could it be someone who thought Torquato killed the Abbot and has only just caught up with him, so to speak?'

'Count how many people you think could have loved Abbot Bonifaccio enough to kill for him.' Sigismondo stepped up into a doorway to accommodate a donkey, with baskets either side stuffed with cabbages and ridden by a man whose toes scuffed the ground. When Benno in his turn had flattened himself to the wall for the donkey, Sigismondo added, 'And there was another last night who, if looks were daggers, would have destroyed Torquato long before we reached the subtlety.'

No need to ask. Agostino da Sangallo had made his feelings quite plain. 'It's a wonder his wife dared turn up like that, looking marvellous when he'd said she was ill. After all, he beat her that night you'd been there because he thought he'd seen a man leaving the house.'

'It seemed like a challenge to him to beat her again.' Sigismondo shook his head. 'I don't know why she did it.'

'*And* Torquato was making up to her at dinner.' If Agostino had killed Torquato for so obviously finding his wife attractive, it was certainly lucky he didn't know who'd actually visited her that night. While Agostino himself was no match for Sigismondo, he had the money to hire bravos and he was obsessed enough to keep trying. Madmen could get lucky.

In the square they had to stop for a procession. A purple, fringed canopy, swaying erratically, advanced above the man in purple silk, with a cardinal's hat carried before him. He rode on a white mule whose tassels swayed to its pace and whose trappings were purple and gold. Priests flanked him, choristers sang a processional, censers were swung sending blue drifts of smoke to and fro, and the onlookers cheered. As the procession passed, the rider turned his head, purple glove raised in blessing. In the weary face came recognition as the eyes lighted on them, and he smiled. It was Cardinal Pantera.

'Wish *he* was going to be Pope.' Benno held up Biondello to get as much of the blessing as he could. 'That horrible old Tartaruga's dead sure *he* will be, right? What was he talking to you about all the time you walked up and down his fancy stables?'

Sigismondo cuffed the side of Benno's head. 'Questions! Too many for one morning, mm? Cardinal Tartaruga's practising to be Pope so he asks the same thing the last one did.'

'To *kill* someone?' Benno, exceeding his quota, got his head jolted the other way, making Biondello yelp. Sigismondo laughed.

'No guesses now. Cardinal Lepre is on his way to be locked up and I've missed my chance.'

261

Chapter 50

'He'll Kill Her'

Now that the cardinals were gathering into Conclave, Rome simmered in the heat, restless with expectation. Nothing would happen at once, Conclave was unlikely to be unanimous and come up with a pope on Day One. Still, it could be hoped that a result would be announced in the shortest possible time since anarchy would rule now until the next pope did, with everyone in authority surrendering office in the interregnum. Criminals would seize their chance, feuds be pursued without check and murders go off the scale.

In the past, squabbles among the cardinals had gone on interminably. Nearly two centuries ago, Sigismondo told Benno, a Conclave had dawdled about in Viterbo enjoying themselves for two whole years, until the magistrates shut them up in the Bishop's Palace there and blocked all the exits. Even then they were comfortable enough, or had got into such a habit of procrastination, that they produced no pope; so the people took the roof off the place and sent in only bread and water, and the Conclave, so encouraged, achieved an election; the cardinal who got elected had also got the message. As Pope, he ordained that future Conclaves were to be enclosed, with no opportunity for luxury, no visiting about or talk to foreign emissaries of influence. Each morning and evening the crowd would assemble before St Peter's and a procession of clergy would demand '*Habemus Pontificem?*' Any excessive delay would be likely to incur the bread-and-water treatment again.

One of those indifferent to the outcome, because whoever sat on the papal throne her profession would not suffer, was Gemmata. She was on her bed at the top of the tenement, sewing a sleeve that one of her customers had torn in the heat of the moment, when she had an unexpected visitor.

He had stopped in the street below to check that this was the right place. There was the pink-painted house opposite, with the carved balcony, over his head the linnet drowsed in its cage and, although he had not been informed about the little white and orange cat, it duly appeared to inspect him. He did not know about the stairs save that what he wanted was at the top.

Gemmata, hearing a tread unlike the heavy thud of Barley or the almost noiseless whisper of Angelo, put down the sleeve and came out on the landing to see who it was. The visitor, not seriously out of breath, returned her gaze with an opaque dark stare that made her unaccountably nervous. Barley was out at some tavern, Angelo earning money by singing in some square or wineshop or telling fortunes. If he had told hers before he left, it might not have looked so good. She backed away as the man came up the last few steps, and edged towards the room where her knife lay with her sewing. She knew from his bearing that this was no ordinary customer and that he was dangerous.

Barley felt at peace with the world. He and Gemmata were still living comfortably on Torquato's money. The excellent late dinner it had bought for them the night before had been as enjoyable for them as any Tartaruga feast to a cardinal; and it would buy them plenty more as well as a new dress and earrings for Gemmata. Barley had also won a bet that morning on a dogfight and a scowling fellow who had been sketching the dogs in action had asked Barley to come to his studio the next day and pose for an eventual painting of Goliath. He had offered a small downpayment in advance, and named a useful fee, so Barley had bought two flasks of wine and hurried home to tell Gemmata.

Had he arrived a minute later there could have been no Gemmata to tell, unless he felt like confiding in a corpse. Luckily for her, the shifting tread and trample of their struggle, her cries muffled by the stranger's hand, and his growled threats, both masked the sound of Barley's climbing feet and alerted him. Once suspicious, he could move like a cat and the first thing the stranger with a knife to Gemmata's throat knew about Barley was a yank at his own throat that nearly strangled him. His knife fell to the floor where Gemmata put her foot on it, Barley jerked him backwards by the chain he wore while clouting him round the head until the chain broke and he fell downstairs. If the chain had not been of gold and therefore delayed Barley in an exercise of valuation, the damage would have been far greater, but as it was the man reached the bottom of the stairs badly bruised, temporarily deaf, with a sore neck and an anxiety to be out of there before the giant caught up with him.

It was in a very poor mood indeed that Olivero limped into the courtyard of the Palazzo Pantera. He could not report his failure or consult Ferondo because his sister-in-law had commandeered her husband as escort to her and his own wife, Lydia, to go and watch the cardinals' procession into Conclave. Elisavetta, annoyed that, thanks to Cardinal Pantera's distaste for the hurly-burly of politics, she was unlikely to be a close relative of the next

Pope, was still not to be denied any fun that she could find. For a moment, as Olivero caught a glimpse of the woman hurrying across the courtyard, he thought the party had returned from their expedition. He quickly moved behind a pillar; his sister-in-law's comments on his present appearance would be totally unwelcome. His wife Lydia might notice the absence of the neck-chain. Olivero had too much pride, even were he to conceal the actual facts, to admit he had been robbed in broad daylight.

The woman turned her head and moved into the sunlight. He saw the drab clothes of a servant, and that long horse face, so dauntingly plain, he knew very well. What did Perpetua, the maid of that very tasty wife of Agostino da Sangallo, want here? Olivero entertained the random hope that the very tasty wife had taken notice of him at Tartaruga's and wanted an assignation; he was even beginning to emerge from concealment when he saw, beyond her in the shadow of the colonnade, the man to whom she was talking. As she talked, Olivero forgot the bruises still swelling on hip and head, forgot the burning neck and ringing in the ears. Sigismondo's theft of the cross was the ultimate cause of those pains and to a Pantera revenge cures all ills.

Bruises were, so it happened, what Perpetua was talking about, while Sigismondo listened darkly.

'She's covered with them. And *both* eyes black this time. I knew how it would be. I told her it wouldn't be worth it. I said, you *know* what he'll do! But would she listen? Go to that feast she would, and looking like a princess too, and Devil take the consequences! But . . .'

Perpetua hesitated. The long horse face took on a mottled flush. Her hands clamped themselves together. 'That's not why she sent me. It's a thing she daren't tell him. He's been punishing her, you see, since that night he caught sight of you leaving, not that he knows it was you, he thought it was someone quite different, but he was convinced she'd been unfaithful. My poor lady!' Perpetua was as exasperated as if her mistress had been innocent. 'To punish her he stopped being a proper husband to her.' She looked demurely down, a maidenly mare. 'My lady was more than pleased at that, I can tell you, only now, well, this week she's had confirmation.'

'Confirmation?'

'She's with child. And he'll kill her.'

Chapter 51

Dodge the Husband

Inside the Vatican Palace where the Conclave was in session, the atmosphere was more restless even than in the city around. It had been forbidden by Clement V, he of the extended Conclave in Viterbo, for the cardinals to live separately at this time, and so the horrors of communal living were forced on these Princes of the Church; although used, like everyone else of whatever rank, to having no privacy, they rarely had to consider the wishes of anyone else. Here they were allowed only a secretary and one servant each – unless, like Cardinal Bufera, they were ill and allowed an extra servant.

Cardinal Bufera had been carried into the palace in a chair. His brother cardinals had on first sight supposed he would be carried out on a bier. He had been reluctant to leave his physician Master Valentino, whose fees were said to be as amazing as his cures, but the rules must be kept. His secretary had been entrusted with the medicines Master Valentino said were essential, together with a scroll of instructions and he duly fussed about with phials and decoctions while the two servants alternately propped their master up and laid him down. Cardinal Lepre and Cardinal Tartaruga were particularly assiduous in waiting on and discoursing to him, but it was Cardinal Pantera who came to sit and read prayers with him.

All was proceeding as it should: the vote in the Sistine

chapel, morning and evening, the counting by the rota of scrutineers, the burning of the papers with a little straw the first evening so that quantities of smoke would show the waiting crowd that a Pope had not, with unnatural celerity, already been chosen. The crowd, which had in any case come without expectation of a useful answer, listened to the choir sing the *Veni Creator*; the question '*Habemus Pontificem?*' had been asked and answered and they dispersed. As days went by a shade more impatience would enter the proceedings, but no note of urgency for a while.

It had with Sigismondo. Benno had seen Perpetua leaving the Palazzo Pantera, but though he supposed her visit had been to Sigismondo he judged it altogether unwise to ask in view of his master's abstracted air. He could not imagine what Sigismondo planned to do next. Now that he had the cross, why did he not leave at once for Scheggia, to fulfil the obligation to Bernabo Pantera? Bernabo had wanted to heal the feud, to put an end to the deaths that came from fighting over the jewel. If Sigismondo didn't get a move on, there'd be more for sure, because although Gian Pantera was wandering about like a dazed lamb shepherded by his cousins' wives, Benno believed that when Olivero and Ferondo were good and ready, Gian would suddenly be lacking more than his memory. The protection of the Cardinal's presence had perhaps restrained the brothers but now, in the lawlessness of the interregnum, what might they get away with? The picture of Torquato's eyeless face and the gashes in his body haunted Benno.

They should start for Scheggia! Olivero, once he knew Torquato had not got the cross, would suspect Sigismondo all over again, and already owed vengeance on him for taking the cross in the first place. For sure, something really effective, more than a poor bunch of hired bravos, would be set on him soon?

Sigismondo had come to Rome on behalf of the Duke of Rocca, to assure his Holiness that the Abbot's death under his roof was no fault of the Duke's; Benno now suspected that Sigismondo thought right from the first that Torquato had the cross and had seized the opportunity to travel with him. Had Sigismondo undertaken to the Duke to find out who had killed the Abbot? Was that why he delayed in Rome? If Torquato was the murderer, how could Sigismondo ever find proof now?

There were far too many questions.

Several things occurred on the second day of the Conclave. In the Vatican, Cardinals Lepre and Tartaruga quarrelled violently before all the Sacred College, and Cardinal Bufera took a turn for the worse after drinking copiously of the water his servant brought him in the stifling heat.

In the city, Barley in his turn quarrelled with the artist Brunelli because he got cramp and changed position while he was being sketched, and was pelted with abuse and charcoal.

Elisavetta and Lydia Pantera finally did what they had been putting off since they first came to Rome: they spurred each other on, got up their courage and climbed the steps to the church of Santa Maria in Aracoeli on their knees, to ask the Virgin, as Roman women had asked their Queen of Heaven, Juno, in the same place, to grant them the sons their husbands longed for.

Gian Pantera went to Confession and found he couldn't remember any sins he had committed.

Piero Pantera the banker gave a supper to which only Agostino da Sangallo was invited. The same evening,

Sigismondo also prepared to go out.

Felicia received him in a small room with the shutters pushed nearly to, and the windows above them wide to let in the gentle breeze from the west which often alleviated the heat at this time of evening. In the shadows, she still sat with her back to what light there was, conscious of her blackened eyes and a bruise on her cheek that rice powder could not conceal. All the same she was a woman whose voice had dimples in it and whose presence gives off allure as a flower gives off scent. Sigismondo sat close to her, with her hands in one of his.

'What can I tell him? I've not slept with him for over two months, not since I last saw you. He's said before that he'll kill me. Now he has the perfect excuse. What can I do?'

'What is it you want to do? I will try my utmost to help you do it.' Sigismondo's voice was deep and calm and she took comfort from it, tightening her hold on the broad hand.

'Perhaps a convent? I want this child, and the nuns will look after me till it's born. But Agostino must not know where I am or he'll find a way to destroy us both.'

The way had already been found. A shout on the stairs announced it, a second before Agostino himself burst into the room.

Chapter 52

What Sort of Trouble?

Agostino was not alone — two ruffians followed him. Sigismondo had drawn his sword and put Felicia behind him. He had another moment of advantage as Agostino turned immediately towards the bed. Even in that dimness he saw its smooth surface where he had expected a naked unarmed man and a woman; and then he saw the gleam on the sword and turned towards that. There was murder in his heart and he laid on with fury but he was not a swordsman; in half a minute he had a wound in his forearm and his sword fell to the floor. He staggered, which gave the ruffians a chance of getting into the small room and engaging Sigismondo, shouting to intimidate their victim. In the trample and clash, Felicia saw that she might reach the jib door and get help but Agostino, lurching forward, let go his grip of his wounded arm and struck her violently. She caught her foot on the bedstep and tumbled with a crash between bedpost and wall.

Sigismondo backed and pivoted to protect her from further attack; the ruffians shifted with him, hampered by lack of room and light. One of them reached for a shutter and pushed it open, revealing Sigismondo vigilant behind his sword. The other ruffian was revealed as Goffo, horribly surprised at meeting Sigismondo a second time; he faltered, but his companion pressed on.

Into this, unexpectedly, came Olivero; the poor light

271

showed him the scene: the ruffians swearing, attacking as they could even if only one of them seemed in earnest; Agostino bent over his arm; no sign of the lady. There were feet on the stairs, voices echoing in the stairwell. If Agostino had been Olivero he would have picked up his sword and attacked Sigismondo on the flank, but he was not and he merely got in the way, and he was still crouched and moaning when the arrival of more men, bursting into the room, forced Goffo unwillingly forward behind his comrade already too close to Sigismondo's sword. Olivero was in the shadows, bent over Agostino whose moans had stopped.

'Put up your swords.'

The man who stood in the doorway, tall, grey-bearded – more men crowding behind him – had authority in his voice and manner. 'I am the owner here. Who disturbs my peace? I warn you, sirs, I am a magistrate – was, till His Holiness died – and I shall bear witness when the new Pope is elected, that you came like thieves and robbers. Who are these men?'

It was Olivero who answered.

'That is Sigismondo, a noted assassin. He came to betray my friend here, Agostino, with his wife. Agostino discovered him.'

Olivero displayed Agostino, who lolled against him, mouth agape and blood running from it.

'And see, he has paid for it with his life.'

'As I see it,' Angelo shook his head fastidiously at the brilliantly coloured sweetmeats Gemmata was offering round, 'you've bound yourself on oath to appear before the Pope – when we've got one – to answer for a murder you didn't commit.'

Sigismondo held up, as a reason in his turn for refusing

the sweetmeats, the chitterling he was exercising his teeth on. 'I'm not fool enough to contradict you, Angelo. It's true I didn't kill da Sangallo, unless he died of shock; and equally true that I intend to appear before the next Pope to say so.'

Barley scooped a pawful of sweetmeats and spoke through four or five of them. 'Suppose he won't believe you?' He chewed for a moment to render his speech more distinct, and went on, 'There are you visiting this man's wife, he pops in with some hired help and a friend and goes for you with a sword – they're not going to think the friend did it, are they?'

'How could they, not knowing Olivero Pantera as we do?'

'And don't forget,' Barley leant forward, sugar spangling his beard, 'that he has a cardinal to cousin, you say. A cardinal can get the ear of a pope, no trouble, and,' Barley with a twisting gesture gave force to this, 'you end up on the scaffold.'

'No rescue job guaranteed,' added Angelo. 'We'd come to watch, of course.'

Shouts from the street made Gemmata turn to push back the window shutter and lean out. Shrieks followed the shouts and she clapped her hands as at a show. 'Oh go on, go on, *kill* him!' Benno got up from his stool beside her, grunting as his bruises hurt him. Agostino had thrust him off the stairs and his ribs and side were sore; he wore a poultice and no doublet. Gemmata shifted along the sill to let him see. Down in the street people were going to and fro with torches, though it was after midnight, and a knot of them had gathered round a brawl. A sturdy woman in a torn dress, her black hair streaming, was getting the better of a man attacking her with his fists. When Barley had thought it wise to move lodging in case Olivero came back with reinforcements, he had not moved to a better district.

He sprawled now on the mattress, speaking persuasively. 'Why don't we deal with that bag of offal before he tries anything else on? If he hadn't been wearing a bit of glitter I fancied when he called on Gemmata, I'd have hammered his head to a pulp. Or Gemmata here would've slipped her own knife into him, wouldn't you, love?'

Gemmata turned to nod vehemently. 'Sure, I'd have put his tripes on view. There he was going to slit my throat unless I gave him your blessed cross; but Our Lady saved me.' She pushed past Benno to genuflect at a clay figurine of the Virgin, her robe a vivid blue, which had been put in a niche in the plaster wall. Before it burnt the room's only light, a lamp whose cloth wick gave off a smell of hot olive oil, reminding Benno of cooking and making him hungry in spite of his fair share of chitterlings and a bowl of cabbage soup. Biondello chewed, with great application, in a corner, a wary eye on the orange and white cat, which had philosophically adapted to the move and was making a home on Sigismondo.

Angelo reached to put a finger under the cat's paw, and asked, 'You think it was Olivero slung Torquato in the Tiber? After getting our address out of him?'

'Hey, do I know? Will anyone ever know? But it's likely. Olivero wanted the cross, Torquato hadn't got it and believed the lovely girl had taken it. Olivero may have killed Torquato in the course of finding where you lived or in rage at being disappointed of the cross.'

'Poor litle priest, he wasn't born with luck,' Gemmata sank on the mattress beside Barley and leant across him to tickle the cat under the chin. 'How did he come by a jewel like that in the first place?'

Sigismondo smiled at her warmly. 'A *long* story and one we don't know the truth of yet. He may have killed an abbot to get it—'

'He? Kill an abbot?' Gemmata pulled the corners of her mouth down, 'That one'd have had to struggle to kill a flea. How's he supposed to have done it? Poison?'

'With an axe, in the back while the Abbot prayed.'

Shocked, Gemmata crossed herself. 'Then he'd be in the warm place now, that's for sure . . . But no, he hadn't the guts. I was watching through the crack when Barley went for him. He was scared pissless. I tell you, I know men.'

This could scarcely be denied, as a professional statement, and there was silence in the little room for a moment. Angelo broke it. 'Would he have taken the cross off the Abbot when the murderer scarpered? That's more his style; though I thought the Abbot was murdered *for* the cross.'

'What's that matter?' Barley, his chin tucked down, was searching his tunic for an escaped sweetmeat. '*He's* got the cross now.' He gestured at Sigismondo. 'La Feconda brings wealth and sons, right? Is that what you're after?'

Sigismondo's mouth moved thoughtfully but he made no immediate reply. Benno thought of the magnificent chains of gold and jewels, even bags of gold, that grateful employers in the past had given Sigismondo. They were usually lodged with bankers in various cities, for Sigismondo to draw credit when he needed. As for sons, Sigismondo might have a selection of those in every city too. Then a thought struck him and he gasped, making him put a hand to his bruised side.

He thought of Agostino's lodgings, an hour or so ago. He had got himself up the stairs and looked in, and there had been Felicia, a widow so suddenly, sobbing on the floor by the bed, and Perpetua wailing and lamenting –

not for her late master but for her mistress's plight. The owner of the house had sent for his wife and her maids to help, and Felicia had been carried off with all the fuss and secrecy women use when female matters come before men's eyes, though Benno had gathered she was having a miscarriage.

Sigismondo, when he spent the night with her in Pietra, had been wearing La Feconda.

'I intend to take the cross where it belongs.'

'And where might that be? I thought it belonged to the Panteras.'

'It first came from Germany, I was told, carried by a pilgrim who wanted to give it to the Virgin at Scheggia in gratitude for his prosperity and his children.'

'So how'd the Panteras get their hands on it?' Barley found the lost sweetmeat and smeared it on his tongue. 'Did they rob him?'

'In a manner, yes. He fell ill on his journey and they took him in and heard his story but, when he died under their roof they somehow failed . . .' Sigismondo hummed cynically, 'to carry out his wishes. Donna Irina, Olivero's aunt, told me that her father, who had been kind enough to tend the pilgrim with his own hands and pay for the physician himself, had just lost his only son and his business was on the verge of bankruptcy. Perhaps he thought he was owed; perhaps he meant to take the cross on to Scheggia after it had worked its blessing . . .'

'But perhaps – eh? – you can never have too much money or too many sons.'

'The strange thing is that, although he had three sons after that time, all are dead because of the cross.'

They pondered on this for a moment. In the street, a flautist strolled away to a dwindling melancholy tune.

'My question,' said Angelo, 'is, what became of that

Pantera I delivered to you with a bash on his head and we brought to Rome? From what you say of this cross-purposed feud, he should be dead by now.'

Sigismondo frowned; and the cat's purr, rasping softly under the voices, hesitated as his hand stopped stroking. 'That's one reason why I'm sorry I had to leave the Palazzo Pantera. If Olivero is the man we so appreciate, now the Cardinal's in Conclave he'll move on him.'

'Why doesn't this Gian fellow leave if he's in such danger?'

'Hey, he's had a blow on the head. His memory's left him. Let's hope it comes back before he loses the head itself. At the moment he's under the impression that his cousins are friends and always have been.'

Benno shifted. 'I don't begin to see how he could forget *his* father was killed by their father. It's just not the sort of thing you forget.'

'Lean this way,' said Angelo, 'and I'll try what a tap on the skull will do for you, shall I? I'll get the exact spot he was hit. I remember it perfectly.'

Sigismondo flung up a hand. 'I need that head. If it hadn't been for Benno's shout, Agostino might have got his sword into me.'

Benno knew this for a kindness. The likelihood of anyone's taking his master by surprise was demonstrated by the fact that he was still alive, but all the same Benno glowed. He had managed only a shout before Agostino violently hurled him off the stairs but, now he thought about it, he was glad Agostino hadn't tried out his sword on him first. Any of the experts in this room would have done that.

Gemmata yawned and stretched her arms, having to sit upright to miss hitting Barley. 'I'll be glad when we have a pope again. Anything goes in the street now, you

277

can get your throat cut for just looking at someone. We need some law and order.'

When people who earn a living from thievery and prostitution yearn for the return of law and order, you could see the pass things had come to. Benno heartily agreed; the anarchy of Rome without a pope frightened him. Yet, if they got a pope and it turned out to be Cardinal Tartaruga as Brother Ieronimo seemed to predict, what sort of trouble would Sigismondo be in then?

Chapter 53

'We Are Pope!'

It was the tenth day of the Conclave. With all exits barred and what air there was slowly and hotly drifting through the top of the tall windows, the atmosphere inside was suffocating. Although the chapel was large, this atmosphere was of men living in close proximity, sweating in heavy robes, and of the food passed in each day through a guarded window. One cardinal, fatter even than the late Pope, was so much afflicted that he lay flat on his back being fanned continually by the sole servant permitted him. He had scarcely energy to join the twice-daily ritual of voting. However, the other and more serious invalid, Cardinal Bufera, had progressed to being propped up on pillows and was able, languidly, to contribute his share. Cardinals Lepre and Tartaruga, seeming now the best of friends, spent their days canvassing their colleagues for votes against each other. It was stalemate.

The suddenness of the Pope's death had caught everyone unprepared. They needed more time, but were aware that outside their doors the crowd was getting seriously annoyed. The heat, the sudden and violent storms that gave only short relief, and the lawlessness, had brought an ugly note into their waiting voices. If the cardinals didn't come to an agreement soon it might be not only the palace of the future Pope that would get sacked.

Cardinal Pantera may have had the idea originally,

although it was not original; Cardinal Pontano of Rocca was his ally immediately and together they proposed the plan to each of the rest, making an opportunity to speak in comparative privacy with all of them, except for Cardinal Bufera. He might be supposed to have no significant interest in the proceedings, terminally ill as he was.

Cardinal Lepre and Cardinal Tartaruga refused to consider the plan at first, but Cardinal Pantera gently sketched the advantages for them both and they finally, with many stipulations and demurrals, gave way. It was the moment, they saw, to take a breather, marshal their forces with greater attention, gather more funds than there had been time for, and play the game another day.

That day would be soon, after all.

On the evening of the tenth day, the usual procession of clergy entered the square before the Vatican Palace, singing the *Veni, Creator*, jostled now by what was nearer to a mob than a devout crowd. Inside, the three scrutators, who happened today to be Cardinals Lepre, Pontano and a small cardinal from Naples who looked like a weasel in purple, solemnly cast the papers on the fire, and the smoke ascended, curling up ghost-like against the sky, and the watching crowd gave a roar. The priest at the head of the procession approached the window hopefully and almost whispered '*Habemus Pontificem?*'

The answer brought another, deeper roar from the crowd, the roar that must have been heard in the Coliseum when gladiators depended for their lives on the favour of the Roman mob. Caps flew into the air, people embraced strangers, crossed themselves, wept and held up children to see.

What they saw was a window, opened at last, on the palace loggia, and three figures step out; two, that is, supporting between them another, who raised a diffident gloved hand in blessing. He was not recognized for some moments, as he had hardly visited Rome more than once a year and then only to say Mass at his titular church, where his arms were carved above the door and his portrait hung, according to custom, just inside. Only the sharpest eyes would have distinguished the original of the portrait now standing at the loggia balustrade, his arms gripped helpfully by two other Princes of the Church. Now Cardinal Pantera, whom they did recognize, stepped forward to announce the new Pope. The name by which he wished to be known had been respectfully inquired, and as the crowd fell silent, craning to hear, he proclaimed it in a surprisingly resonant voice.

The new Pope was Cardinal Bufera. The name he had chosen for his reign was Felix. In the room behind the loggia many other cardinals looked at one another. Most of them had been at Tartaruga's feast and had heard Brother Ieronimo's prediction: *Happy shall he be called.* Cardinal Bufera had not been there, nobody had told him about the events of that feast or the prediction, and here he was calling himself 'Happy'.

Tartaruga, oddly enough, was comforted by this. True, he had been convinced that the monk was looking at him and that he was the fortunate one, but if the mad monk had got it right this time because of some quirk of old Bufera's, all the more hope of a luckier casting of the future next time. Had they not prayed every day for Divine inspiration? God had chosen, through the medium of His devoted servants, an eccentric invalid confidently expected to last only a few months in this life – if indeed he survived the coronation.

Listening with a smile to the cheers of the crowd, Tartaruga forgot the history of the papacy, forgot times when election had acted as such a stimulant to ageing and exhausted cardinals, particularly to those elected as stopgaps, like Bufera, that it increased their life expectancy by, in one case, two dismaying decades.

Quite as though he were illustrating this tendency, Cardinal Bufera who had tottered to the loggia supported by Pontano of Rocca and the sacred weasel from Naples, politely declined their help and, as Pope Felix, walked slowly back unaided. How tall he was! He smiled round joyfully, raising both hands, and Tartaruga wondered if they had been wise to choose a Pope who looked, one had to face it, irredeemably silly. Those eyes like a mad owl's, that grin that could scarcely accommodate all those teeth! Rome would have been better off with the dignity of a Tartaruga. And what was the creature chortling?

'We are Pope! And with God's will We shall enjoy Ourself!'

In the street, people found themselves baffled. As intent as their new Pope on enjoying themselves, they ought to do the traditional thing and sack the palace of the successful cardinal. They were faced with the problem: where was it? Hardly anyone had heard of Cardinal Bufera. Then one or two, who *had* heard of him, managed to disseminate the bad news: it passed from mouth to mouth with accelerating rage.

There was no Palazzo Bufera in Rome. Their new Pope had his private residence in a clapped-out villa far up a steep hill outside Rome, a tedious journey and a worse climb.

By common impulse, they decided it was only fair to sack the palace of the man they had expected to be chosen, the man most had laid their bets – lost their money – on. They surged, yelling, good nature restored, through the streets to the Palazzo Tartaruga.

Chapter 54

Too Many Murders!

Although the new Pope's intention of enjoying his office soon became widely known, he had at first not a great deal of opportunity. The coronation once over – and His Holiness sustaining it with amazing verve – there was far too much business to be got through. His predecessor had left affairs in a vast muddle despite all the efforts of the papal secretaries. When they could get him to consider business, he would attend first to such cases as would bring in revenue; for instance a tidy proportion of the money reaching the treasury had been paid in for pardons of those various classes of murder for which only a papal absolution had the power to excuse from many thousands of years in Purgatory, if not from the eternal flames of Hell itself.

It was Cardinal Pantera who, at the urging of his cousins, brought a case before the new Pope almost at once. The Cardinal had seen too much of the world to be surprised, but he was grieved, that a guest of his whom he had immediately liked and trusted should have revealed himself as an adulterer and a murderer. Olivero, whom although he was family the Cardinal neither liked nor trusted, also assured him that Sigismondo not only slew husbands but had also stolen the cross, that cause of the unhappy feud which had brought so many Panteras to death.

Olivero's account of this theft and of the death of Bernabo was curiously specious; nor was the Cardinal anxious that the cross should be returned to Olivero and Ferondo. Yet he was grateful for the apparent amity among his nephews, and it was this sign of grace that prompted him to bring up the matter of both the Sangallo murder and the missing cross, before the Pope.

Olivero also told him that whoever had taken the cross was probably the murderer of Abbot Bonifaccio of Pietra, a sacrilege that could not go unpunished. The problem was, how to get hold of Sigismondo? It did not at all surprise the Cardinal that Sigismondo had left the hospitality of his house before he had to ask him to go; he was only surprised when Olivero said that the man had promised to appear before the Pope to answer the charges. If he were guilty, he would have taken advantage of the interregnum to flee the city – unless he relied on such great men as the Duke of Rocca to speak for him against a sentence of death. Yet there is little satisfaction in having a friendly letter arrive by ducal courier when your head is already in a basket.

Pope Felix was ornamentally signing his old name, Teodoro, to a Papal Bull, the only place it would be used until the papal chamberlain should formally summon him by it to check that he was dead, and that looked to be somewhat later than anyone had thought. A secretary came to say that the Sigismondo of whom Cardinal Pantera had told him was waiting to see His Holiness. Would he grant audience? Pope Felix cast down his quill – hastily rescued by the secretary who scanned the vellum for ink-splashes – and rubbed his hands.

'Let them summon the witnesses, and we shall hear it forthwith.'

Those concerned were assembled with all the efficient

speed of functionaries trying to please a new Pontiff. They gathered in the antechamber, some fidgeting and looking about; but the accused stood, both composed and imposing, his shaven head a strange contrast to the ornate gold and green brocade of the hangings. Olivero, almost as unmoving, stared at him with his dark blank gaze, Ferondo more uneasy at his side. Gian, summoned by his cousin the Cardinal because the Pope had promised to address the family feud, was pale, and still as if he moved in a dream. Benno was there by courtesy of his master; he was no witness, having spent the vital time concussed and winded at the stair-foot. Nuto the groom stood beside Perpetua, in fact as close as he could get, his fingers stuck through his belt, rocking on his heels and, although his eyes roved to take in the coffered gold ceiling, the hangings, the portraits, he sniffed loudly as if in comment at the grandeur of it all. The widow was not present, being still ill. Benno reflected that at least she wouldn't get beaten up any more by that brute of a husband.

A disturbance at the outer doors made even Olivero glance round. Pages were opening them for others summoned to audience. The Prior of Santaporta entered, hands in sleeves, eyes cast down, and behind him, flanked by a guard on one side and Brother Filippo on the other, came Brother Ieronimo with his usual air of cheerful interest. He beamed when he saw Sigismondo and also, oddly, when he saw the Pantera brothers. Benno, seeing this, was in the middle of a serious thought about Christian charity when the chamberlain ushered in the magistrate who had rented a floor of his house to Agostino da Sangallo and had arrived at the scene of his death.

Then they were all ushered into the presence.

A good many people were already in the chamber where the Pope sat in a great canopied chair of scarlet velvet fringed with gold. Benno caught a glimpse of Cardinal Pantera among the cluster behind the Pope, and another man he knew from the past, Master Valentino the doctor; but his real attention was for the man sitting there. While the others were called forward, named, and sank to their knees to kiss the red velvet slipper on the red brocade step of the throne, Benno was absorbed in the difference between this Pope and the last. His master's fate depended on this man's whim.

It was by now generally known that Pope Felix was not expected to live long. His expressed wish of enjoying the papacy had been taken as a desire to make the best of that short time, but there was no sign of approaching death in that face, strongly constructed, with a beak of a nose, large round eyes and a wide mouth showing, as he greeted them, a quantity of teeth that would have graced a horse. Pope Felix looked not so much ill as a bit mad.

Signs of derangement made no appearance at first. His Holiness evidently knew exactly what had been happening and, after a long thoughtful look at Sigismondo, he said, 'Let me see the cross.'

Sigismondo felt at his neck – Olivero making a convulsive movement he at once checked – and in a moment laid the glittering La Feconda in the palm of the outstretched scarlet glove. The Pope brought it close to his eyes and then held it at arm's length.

'Very pretty.' He closed velvet fingers over it so that it vanished from sight. 'Now, about the murder.' He looked round at the attentive faces with a sudden grin of quite manic benevolence. 'Who saw it?'

The magistrate had taken upon himself the ordering and presentation. He put forward Olivero, who knelt to speak.

'With my own eyes, Holiness, I saw him kill my poor friend Agostino, in front of the wife he had seduced.'

The Pope looked levelly at Olivero before glancing round again. 'Who else saw the man die?'

'Holy Father, I did.' Perpetua, plumping on to her knees, had all the advantage of extreme plainness in looking honest with it. '*I* saw my master die. *He* killed him!' Her outflung arm swung past Sigismondo and pointed straight at Olivero. 'I came in at the jib door when I heard my lady scream, and I saw him drive his sword into my master.'

'What do you say to that?' The Pope's tone to Olivero was one of curiosity.

'I say it is nonsense, your Holiness. The slut's in league with her mistress to protect the lover.'

The Pope smiled brilliantly at Olivero, as if he pleased him. 'And did anyone else witness what occurred?'

'Holiness, it was me.' Nuto dropped to his knees. Awe was foreign to him. He spoke in a tone almost amicable. 'It's like this. I was coming after, to help the master, hearing swords, like, and the mistress yelling out, and I saw him stick his sword in, just like she said.' He got to his feet and made an illustrative, forceful little gesture and smiled, gap-toothed, at the Pope. The uncouthness also was convincing. The Pope slowly nodded.

'Two to one, two to one, Pantera.'

'Holy Father, these are *servants*. A groom, a maid. They can be bribed or bullied to say anything.'

'And others cannot? Oh, oh.' The Pope looked round at the company and an obedient small laugh sounded. Corruption is too close, in any court, to be the subject of unforced mirth. The Pope, however, seemed satisfied with the reaction and turned again to Olivero. 'The cross. We hear that you claim it was stolen from you by this man. Did you see him take it?'

Olivero cried, 'Holiness! You saw he had it! What more proof than that?'

'You, sir.' The Pope turned the gaze of his large round eyes on Sigismondo. 'You say nothing yet you stand accused of theft and murder. Speak.'

Sigismondo went on one knee beside Olivero, and replied without haste or heat. 'I took the cross, Holy Father, but I did not kill Agostino da Sangallo. The cross may be said to have caused many deaths, but not that one.'

Olivero turned his head to fix the unblinking dark stare on Sigismondo so close beside him. 'And the Abbot of Pietra? You murdered him to steal the cross back when it was taken from you.'

'Murdered the Abbot of Pietra?' The Pope was genially interested here. 'I thought another did that. Was it not you, my son, who confessed to this terrible deed?' The velvet finger located Brother Ieronimo, who had been watching all that passed, as absorbed as if he were at a play. He shambled forward with eager obedience, dragging his guard by the chain to his wrists' manacles, and taking him off balance as he too fell to his knees.

'Yes. The Devil entered into me, most Holy Father, and I killed Father Abbot.'

The Pope contemplated him with lively enjoyment. 'The Devil? How did he look?' It sounded somewhat like an inquiry after the Evil One's health, and Brother Ieronimo responded in much the same manner, flinging his arms wide, jerking the guard's arm with his.

'Winged like a bat, Holy Father! He fled from the belvedere at the castle of Rocca.'

'You killed Abbot Bonifaccio with an axe, I am told. Did the Devil put the axe in your hand?'

Brother Ieronimo paused, as if trying to recollect, while the Pope watched him. 'I don't know, Holy Father. I found my hands on the axe, and the axe in Father Abbot's back, so the Devil must have given it to me. Father Torquato and Brother Filippo found me with it.'

'And where are they?'

Cardinal Pantera stepped forward to murmur in the Pope's ear, while Brother Filippo fell to his knees, humbly announcing himself. The Pope, listening to Cardinal Pantera, shook his head with a sudden change of expression to deepest melancholy.

'Too many murders, may God have mercy. Our Saviour dies for us and still we kill each other every day. The saying is that the Devil rules Rome and takes so many thousand souls in rent. A bitter saying! While We rule also, We must save all We can from his claws.'

He paused, his eyes shut; and then opened them, wide so that the whites showed round, on Olivero. 'You, my son. What would you do with this beautiful thing?' He opened his left hand and showed La Feconda glittering in his palm.

'My brother and I will take it back to our family house, your Holiness, where it will have a place of honour and safeguard us all.'

The manic smile returned. 'I hear it protects wealth. Are you poor?'

Olivero looked stunned. After a moment he said, 'Holy Father, I have enough to make a donation to the Holy See in gratitude for the restoration of our family treasure.'

'And your sons. If La Feconda brings you sons, will you give them also to Holy Mother Church?' The Pope was leaning forward in earnest inquiry. As Olivero tried to find an answer, the Pope turned his gaze on Sigismondo. 'And you, my son? What would you do with this?' Rainbow flashes spiralled about the room from La Feconda held up by the velvet hand.

289

'Take it where it belongs, Holy Father. Where I have vowed to take it.'

Before the Pope could speak, Brother Ieronimo had scrambled upright, the guard pulled down on all fours. The Pope's upraised hand stopped the guards at the doors as they made ready with their pikes to rush in. Brother Ieronimo had both his arms and one of the guard's raised towards heaven and, from his face, lifted too, it was clear he saw more than the painted ceiling and its beams damascened with gold.

'To Scheggia! See where Our Lady holds out her hands . . . Blessed is he who restores to her what is hers, blessed shall you be all your days.' Then slowly Brother Ieronimo brought down arms and eyes, and turned to the Pope, who had been scrutinizing the ceiling.

Everything depended on whether this eccentric Pope thought the mad-looking monk saw the Virgin or an evil delusion; and whether he would take the word of a self-proclaimed murderer on anything at all.

Chapter 55

Farewell for Ever

'Scheggia.' The Pope regarded La Feconda once again. He swung a little in his chair and extended his smile at Olivero. 'How much better there than where only a few can benefit! You will rejoice in Our Lady's blessing. You, my son,' he directed the beam at Sigismondo, 'you shall fulfil your vow, in penance for such deeds of blood as you have committed. Olivero Pantera, you and your brother—' Again the Cardinal murmured and the Pope nodded, '—and your cousin Gian, shall go with Sigismondo da Rocca to offer this cross to the shrine of Our Lady at Scheggia. You shall go as pilgrims, and endure such mortifications as you meet for the good of your souls.' His round eyes looked at each brother for a short while, as if he made a brief scan of those souls and their needs, and he went on: 'We accept, Olivero Pantera, a donation of twenty thousand gold ducats to the Holy See.' The Pope continued to smile benignly at Olivera's face of shock. 'It will in some degree expiate the sin of greed that has led you into the deeper sin of murder. Brother Ieronimo!'

The monk clasped his hands, smiling, as if sentence of death would be accepted gladly, and the Pope tapped his finger to his lips, considering.

'The Devil does not tempt unless God permits him. I have been informed about Abbot Bonifaccio; it may be that you were chosen as the instrument of God's punishment on a sinful shepherd. You too shall go to Scheggia and there you shall stay, serving Our Lady there all your days, never returning to Pietra. And now, my children, embrace one another as the sign of the love Our Saviour has for each of you and that He wishes you should have for one another.'

Sigismondo and Olivero rose and, under the Pope's still watchful eye, formally cast their arms round each other and kissed cheeks. Benno caught sight of Olivero's face over Sigismondo's shoulder; too clearly he would sooner bite out Sigismondo's throat than kiss him.

The Pope had risen. Two pages came forward to support him but he waved them back and descended the steps towards the two men, who turned towards him. His face was heavy with authority as though no smile had ever visited it. He lifted his right hand. 'Keep the peace that We have laid on you. The cross is to go to Scheggia, to the Virgin's shrine and you, my sons, will suffer excommunication if you hinder this.' The hand traced a cross in the air over their heads. He raised his other hand to his lips and kissed the cross in which La Feconda was embedded, and held it out to Sigismondo. 'This is your charge. Go, all of you, with God, and may Our Lady protect you on this mission.'

The audience was over.

Benno, shuffling out at the rear as they were ushered from the room, reflected that although his master was not about to die for a murder he didn't commit, he yet had been sent on a journey with a man who hated him, with the purpose of putting eternally out of reach a jewel that the true murderer believed was his own. Certainly, Olivero minded the threat of excommunication, or he wouldn't have set up Sigismondo to kill whichever Pantera should come to steal the cross. Now that the ban on killing his own kinsfolk had been extended to murdering Sigismondo, it was a step up. Only, come to think of it, there were ways of making murder look like accident or, going by past events, getting someone to do it for you; and if Olivero wasn't to keep La Feconda, he would hunger to visit vengeance on the man responsible for that.

This was to be the second journey with the Panteras as companions, and it promised to be even more delightful.

First, there were the women to deal with.

Elisavetta and Lydia were already displeased that their husbands had obtained audience of the new Pope when they had waited over a month, in spite of having a Cardinal to cousin, for an audience with the last one. When they heard that the famous cross was found and at once permanently lost to them, they expressed their feelings with passion. The family feud had always imperilled their husbands' lives and therefore their own status and prosperity. Elisavetta was of the opinion, and stated it, that if Ferondo spent more time attending to business, the wealth he expected La Feconda to supply would be theirs from his own efforts. Lydia, more afraid of her husband than Elisavetta was of Ferondo, did not suppose that Olivero would settle to be more accommodating, whether or not she could provide him with sons. As to that, now they had prayed in all the churches at Rome for sons, what better than to accompany their husbands as supplicants to Our Lady of Scheggia? Here they were, giving her their family treasure – what might she not grant them? Elisavetta and Lydia went to pack immediately.

There was some question of Felicia, still indisposed as she was, also having to pack immediately. The magistrate had feared for her life after the loss of the child and the death of her husband, and he had conveyed her to a nearby convent of nursing sisters. It was there that Benno heard his master describe himself to Sister Portress as Sigismondo Minola, brother to the Lady Felicia. The lady in question, they were informed, would receive her relative in the visitors' parlour. Benno was left to wait in the lodge, where Biondello won the heart of Sister Portress and received far more kisses than he wanted.

Felicia was pale, Sigismondo grave. This was the woman he had as good as made a widow, through the design of others; whom he had nearly made a mother. It was not a time for superficial regrets.

'You are better.'

She nodded but could not smile. He stood against the window, still, looking at her.

'What will you do? Do you know the terms of his will?'

She made a face. 'Oh yes. He told me when it was drawn up. The business is to go to a nephew in Montesacro – I've never seen him. My portion as a widow—' She stopped and looked out of the window into the corridor, where beyond the grille came the sound of a nun on her knees patiently washing the stone flags. – 'is to go as my dowry to any convent that will have me.'

'Can he do that? Do the laws of Pietra allow it?'

She turned her eyes back to him and he noticed the dark shadow around them. 'He went to the best lawyer in Pietra. For that, he didn't spare the money. I am sure the man would have told Agostino if it couldn't be done.'

Sigismondo was silent for a moment and then came and took her hands in his. 'You shall have all you need. Where do you want to go?'

She looked at him seriously for a moment and then said, 'Oddly enough, Pietra. I had no friends there – he saw to that – so I won't have lost any. I might make some now; and I like the place. I want to run his business my way. I know a lot about cloth, how it is made and sold; where it is made and about quality. It interests me. There are men who worked for Agostino and would, I think, be willing to work for me. The nephew in Montesacro might be willing to sell.'

For the first time Sigismondo smiled. He bent his head to kiss her fingers.

'You shall have what you want.'

A knock at the door made them turn. The elderly nun in charge of guests, who had brought Sigismondo from the portress's lodge, was smiling happily there, all radiant wrinkles.

'A surprise, my children! A family reunion! Your other brother, daughter, has also come to see you.' She stepped back, put her hands in her sleeves and glided away.

Brother Filippo stood in the doorway, staring.

'Adulterer! You dare to defile a sacred place with your lusts!' The monk advanced, one thin finger pointing at Felicia. 'And *you*. Have you not done with your shame? He murders your husband and still you allow him – *lure* him – to touch you. Agostino's blood is on those hands!'

Felicia threw back the wings of her veil that shadowed her face on either side, and faced Brother Filippo without flinching. In the light from the passage window the bruises showed yellow and green round her eye and on the swollen cheekbone.

'You have no longer the right to speak to me so. You gave up your family when you entered the order. You renounced me then, you cannot denounce me now. Agostino would have killed me but you don't condemn him for that.'

Brother Filippo's face quivered as though he felt physical pain. 'He should have killed you long ago. It was his right to chastise you for flaunting yourself before men. He did all that he could to preserve you from further evil, you whore!'

He wheeled, to spit in Sigismondo's face. 'Devil! His Holiness should have had you hanged; you pollute this earth. Mother Superior shall hear of your conduct under this roof—'

'You are the one who should leave.' Sigismondo, without heat, wiped his cheek and, by stepping forward, forced Brother Filippo back, away from Felicia. 'Your sister needs peace to recover from what has happened. You bring only anger and lack of charity.'

Brother Filippo gripped his hands together under his sleeves; his eyes were bright with triumph. 'I came here with good news. My sister is to move from here at once. I have arranged with a convent here in Rome to accept her widow's portion as her dowry.' At the door he looked back. 'Make your farewell for ever, adulterer. It is an enclosed order.'

Chapter 56

The Prettiest Pilgrim

'You mean he's really her *brother*? He never said anything nice to her on the journey.'

'Brother Filippo finds it difficult to say anything nice to anyone, Benno. And he doesn't speak to any woman unless he has to.'

'I suppose the Mother Superior doesn't count as a woman. What'd he say to her, though? I mean, the nuns would have had a job to get rid of you if you didn't choose to go.' Benno was busy rolling up his master's best doublet on Barley's mattress, to go in the pack, and Gemmata took it from him, flattened it out, smoothed away the creases carefully, folded it and rolled it up again.

Barley, leaning against the rough plaster of the wall, his feet sticking out off the edge of the bed, whittled at a piece of wood and rumbled with laughter. 'I can see a pack of them tugging at your sleeves and getting nowhere. So what did she say? Hope you told her you were on a mission for the Pope.'

'Mm . . m . . . You're a diplomat, Barley. At first she wasn't prepared to listen at all. She was too angry at her convent being used as a house of assignation as Brother Filippo had told her. But she was a great lady in the world before she took her vows, and this is Rome after all. She disliked my lie that I was Felicia's brother; and I said that I had come there *as* a brother to a woman I believed

297

to be without friends. And when, as you say, I spoke of His Holiness and the fact that I was on a pilgrimage to Scheggia, things calmed down a bit.'

'What's to become of the poor lady?' Gemmata delicately avoided the name, as she took Sigismondo's cloak from the wall and shook it out.

'The Mother Superior agreed to offer her shelter until we leave Rome. She accepted that I was not da Sangallo's murderer, in spite of Brother Filippo's tirade. She disapproves of women being forced into the conventual life, and I don't think she cared to be told what to do in her own convent.'

'You and she must have had a great chat,' Barley said. 'What's to become of the lovely widow when we leave Rome? I take it her brother's not to be allowed to wall her up as he wants.'

'He has not the power to do that. No . . .' Sigismondo handed a small bag of herbs to Benno to fold into the cambric shirt he was packing. 'She comes with us.'

'To *Scheggia?*' Benno could not believe Felicia could want another child when the last had caused such trouble. Particularly now she was a widow.

'Pietra is the port for Scheggia. We're giving her escort as far as that. She means to take over her husband's business there and I think she'll do well.'

'Us. You said "comes with us".' Angelo's light, hard voice struck in. He decorated the doorway, watching Sigismondo. 'Who are *us?*'

'Don't count me in.' Barley squinted down the piece of wood and blew shavings off it. 'I'm doing all right here.' He nudged Gemmata's leg with one foot. 'Rome suits me. When I've had enough I'll move on, but not till then. Besides, that cross you're carrying – people die round it. There'll be more corpses before you get to Scheggia.'

'So you want me along,' said Angelo coolly. 'I'm to be a pilgrim, am I?'

Sigismondo gave him a measuring regard. 'The prettiest of the lot. Olivero's seen you twice, once on the journey here and once in a street fight. Next time he might even know you, and I'd rather you were a card up my sleeve than on the table.'

Angelo pulled Gemmata to him. 'Can you find me another dress? Respectable this time, so not one of yours. And a wimple and the fittings.' With his free hand he screwed back his long blond hair and gave a fanged simper. 'It must be Rome; I'm feeling ever so religious.'

Benno was surprised at himself: he found he was glad to leave Rome. Their stay had been exciting, perhaps too exciting so that he was glad to be going.

There were new faces on the spikes at the end of the bridge, fresh ones as Pope Felix had rather smartly restored law and order after the chaos – executions were now official instead of private. The party now leaving Rome past these trophies of justice was not greatly different from the party that had arrived only a few weeks ago. Here was Brother Ieronimo, free of manacles and riding his donkey next to Brother Filippo who looked sourer than ever.

One good reason for sourness was certainly his sister Felicia, riding with the company, sober in widow's black but with a veil which made no pretence of hiding her face. Brother Filippo had tried hard to carry out her husband's wishes but here she was, riding back to Pietra, where he hoped she would find herself destitute and probably forced on to the streets. Worst of all, she was travelling with the man who had widowed her, who might either be Olivero Pantera as she and her maid and the groom insisted, or

Sigismondo who had only escaped judgement because the Pope believed all that farrago about the wretched cross and the shrine at Scheggia.

The party was lumbered, moreover, with a shrew in the person of Lydia Pantera and, a worse thing than that, the obnoxious virago, epitome of all things abhorrent in her sex, Elisavetta Pantera – assertive, finely dressed, handsome. At least one of the women conducted herself properly, a quiet pale creature extinguished between a hood and a wimple, drably dressed, a pilgrim to Scheggia anxious for their protection.

Hardly anyone thought about the one omission from the former party. Torquato had been given a decent burial in the Santaporta graveyard. It was Benno who wondered, as they left the stink and noise of the city behind, whether the murderer of Abbot Bonifaccio had been buried there, and whether Sigismondo had found out enough to clear the Duke of Rocca's name of the death. Had Olivero killed Torquato? It was likely. He wouldn't have thought twice about it. It was possible he had murdered the Abbot too and been scared away, before he could get hold of the cross, by Brother Ieronimo singing, as he was doing now, as joyfully as the lark rising high overhead. Poor Brother Ieronimo had probably taken hold of the axe with some idea of the Abbot's being more comfortable without it.

Torquato of course could have come by the cross at any time after the Abbot's death. Brother Filippo, who was also on the scene, wouldn't concern himself about jewels. Sigismondo would certainly get La Feconda to Scheggia, but Benno felt sure that someone would try to get it off him before then.

Chapter 57

Coat-of-Alarms

Amazingly, the journey was uneventful until they actually reached Scheggia itself. No robbers offered themselves, for all the loudly voiced fears of the Pantera ladies; no quarrels erupted – even Brother Filippo refrained from lecturing the women, although he did not eat with them and took care that Brother Ieronimo kept away from them. Everyone was taking the Pope's injunction to treat the journey as a pilgrimage very seriously. There was no gambling or swearing – Olivero could in any case convey as much by glowering as by cursing. There was complete chastity even between husband and wife; this, in view of the brothers' urgent anxiety for heirs, must have come as a relief to Lydia and Elisavetta. Felicia, once they reached Pietra, made the decision to come on to Scheggia in pilgrimage for her husband's soul, a piece of generosity he would not have been likely to reciprocate.

An ordinary pilgrim party, of the sort they met at the inns and hospices, would devote their evenings to either religious occupations such as prayers or holy legends or, if they were treating their pilgrimage as a holiday with a bonus at the end, to story telling and jollity. Benno envied this. He dearly loved a good story and would hang close to any party telling one. Brother Filippo offered to instruct their party in the lives of the saints but, after hearing of St Agatha, martyred by having her breasts cut off,

Elisavetta declared that she would hear no more; everyone else agreeing with her, Brother Filippo became even more taciturn and austere. Angelo, who had clutched his chest in horror at the story, was already particular friends with Felicia, in whom he confided that he sought to surprise a straying husband by producing a child to bind him fast. Where, as was usual, they shared beds, Felicia usually shared with Angelo, and Benno thought that if Angelo were not so reliable it might be a quite other child which would surprise everyone.

When they reached Scheggia, however, there was plenty of room; not in the village hostel, nor inland, which seemed to their dazed eyes, after a rough passage from Pietra, to be no more than a hideously lofty mountainside, its outline blurred with wild olives and juniper. A winding path visible here and there led steeply up to something half-visible at the top, which was no doubt the shrine. The room offered in abundance was in a castle almost on the shore, which gave hospitality to pilgrims needing to recuperate after the sea journey and before the rigorous climb ahead, and which was where the Duchess of Rocca had stayed.

Benno, legs out of control and stomach rebelling, looked up towards this castle as the party made for it in the gathering dusk. They crowded thankfully in, Lydia half fainting and supported by her sister-in-law. Sigismondo brought up the rear, and lingered as the rest were welcomed. Benno saw he was looking over the coat-of-arms, carved in weathered, sea-bleached stone, above the great arch of the gateway. As always, Benno wondered at the way in which some things, like writing, made sense to his master. They followed the others through the big doorway out of the evening light.

Their host was there in the great hall to greet them, while his servants took charge of their baggage, and wine and food were handed to refresh them after their voyage. A fire burnt with green and blue flames in the huge hearth like a giant's mouth, for here inside the walls the air was chill. There was a smell of salt from the sea, of damp stone, of rosemary from twigs thrown on the fire to scent the place. Vast faded tapestries hung on the walls and a stone staircase on the same monstrous scale wound up to the shadows beyond.

The man who owned all this was tall and thin, with a long, reserved face and dark hair under the cap of black velvet which he now swept off as he spoke to them.

'Ladies, gentlemen, you are in your own house. It is my privilege to welcome pilgrims within these walls.' He paused and regarded them all, a dark mournful gaze. 'Until the Virgin of Scheggia opened my eyes, I was abandoned to a life of sin. She gave me hope that I might pass my days in penance for that life. At the top of this castle, as near as it can be to the shrine above, I have built a chapel, where is a statue of Our Lady blessed by the late Pope himself. We will hear Mass there before supper, when you have rested.'

He replaced the cap, and came courteously to greet each one in person and inquire after their health and wishes. Benno saw that he spent more time with the fair Lydia, almost prostrate in a tall-backed carved chair, than with anyone, and Olivero, as though jealous, walked him off to have words alone. The two monks, however, were the pilgrims to whom their host accorded the greatest respect, speaking to them uncovered, kissing their hands.

Benno muttered to Sigismondo, 'He's so religious now it makes you wonder what he got up to before. Pity he can't give us a few stories after supper, moral tales like, bet they'd beat Brother Filippo's saints hollow.'

Sigismondo smiled, and Benno wondered if perhaps the

servants couldn't be got to be a bit forthcoming about their master's former life when they got to chat in the kitchens.

Lydia had risen, and the party was ready to disperse to the various rooms, when the host halted the servants and once more commanded attention.

'After supper, I trust you will all honour me by sharing in a loving-cup, to signify that you come here to this island in charity with each member of your party. It is a tradition here, to remind us all that Our Lady's mercies are for those who are at peace in their hearts and without malice towards another living soul.'

Once more his glance touched each in turn, lingering significantly as though he knew the story of the feud. Olivero could hardly have been telling him about it; nor was Olivero going to enjoy sharing a loving-cup with his cousin Gian and with Sigismondo. Benno could not fancy, either, that Brother Filippo would care to drink with an adulterer and murderer. All the same, if it was a castle tradition he would have to do it or look very unChristian indeed.

There was that about the castle which made one uneasy: the chilly vastness of it, the vistas of endless rooms, the twisting stairs, stone walls and floors, the shadows and the sound of the sea, breathing continually on the rocks of the shore. Benno felt threatened in that curious inexplicable way he knew from nightmares. Also, if no one had attempted to get the cross off Sigismondo yet, time was running out for them to try.

The kitchen hearth was big enough for an ogre to roast a whole family at; Perpetua and Nuto and the grooms were listening open-mouthed to a tale of their host's past, but Benno, gaping with his customary incomprehending face, heard something else, something that made him desert the story, sweep up Biondello and the meat he was chewing, and hurry up the worn steps and across rooms and landings and up crumbling spiral stairs with the slap of the sea on the rocks coming through window-slits from below. He made his way to the room allotted to his master, where Sigismondo sat on the bed among dark curtains so filmy they resembled cobwebs and gave Benno the horrible sense that the spider that had woven them might be splayed on the dark ceiling over the bed. Sigismondo looked up as Benno's precipitation almost made the lamp go out, and smiled.

'Hey, you found your way again. And what else have you found?'

'It's not a tradition at all – the loving-cup. The castle servants were saying it's the first they'd heard of it and one of them was grumbling 'cos he had to clean this thing the size of a little cauldron, all beaten silver with the coat-of-arms on.'

'Mm . . m. I had a good look at that coat-of-arms before we came in. Our host's name is Giovanni Falcone, and sure enough he has a falcon with wings addorsed – back-to-back to you, Benno – but he has interesting quarterings too. I'll pass over the bee on one side, which shows industry, and he seems to have worked hard at his life of sin. Let's look, instead, at one quartering you may have seen before.' Sigismondo had swung to his feet, and carried the lamp over to the deep, recessed window. Above it was a carving. 'You see?'

Benno peered. The damp had eaten away the stone and, although he could make out a bird with wings sticking out at the back, and a knob that could be a bee, the thin object at the foot, to which Sigismondo was pointing, looked somewhat like a greyhound running flat out. His master's hand descended to cuff the side of his head.

'I knew you'd see it. A panther, Benno. A panther.'

'So . . .'

'Our host is related to the Panteras, yes. They could afford to wait until we reached here.'

'But why did you come in here if you saw it? And Olivero was talking to him – and this loving-cup! He'll poison you!'

Sigismondo wrapped his fingers in Benno's hair and wagged his head to and fro. 'Think, man. *Everyone* must drink. That means Olivero as well as Gian and I. Unless he's decided to commit suicide, or unless our host wants to ruin his reputation by having to bury a whole party of pilgrims, I don't think there'll be poison in the loving -cup tonight. No . . .' Sigismondo leant on the sill and looked down at the sea, heard now rather than seen, punishing the rocks. 'I think there'll be a sleeping draught which all will drink. We shall sleep soundly enough not to know when we're searched.'

Benno stared. The shadows in the room were deepening. He could believe in the huge spider that lay in wait.

'What will you do?'

'I'll drink it.'

Chapter 58

Fire!

The chapel high above the waves, reached by a final steep flight of steps, was big enough to take a far larger party of pilgrims than this small band. Giovanni Falcone had hung it with his grandest tapestries and, in the warmth of many candles burning, it seemed to give more of a welcome than the draughty spaces of the rooms and stairs below.

A finely carved crucifix hung against the marble wall behind the altar. By the door on a pedestal was a statue of the Virgin, almost life-size, with hands extended palm upwards as though asking Heaven for a blessing on them as they went by. The statue was beautifully painted, and dressed in a gold tissue gown and blue velvet robe sewn with pearls. Falcone, or perhaps pilgrims who passed through here, had shown reverence and gratitude by decorating the statue with necklaces, chains and badges, hung round her neck and arms, pinned to her robe. A necklace of pearl and garnets was loosely tangled over the fingers of one cupped hand, while the statue's eyes, turned upwards, seemed to offer to Heaven all the tributes bestowed on it.

Brother Ieronimo was struck into almost a trance before it and had to be hustled forward by Brother Filippo as people pressed after them up the stairs. Each pilgrim kissed the hem of the blue velvet robe, and reached up to touch the hands that asked forgiveness for them. Angelo distinguished himself by bursting into muffled weeping and having to be led into chapel by Felicia.

Benno stood sweating with fear. The idea of Sigismondo drinking something which would render him helpless while strangers turned him over and searched him, shocked Benno past belief. Although, as Olivero must drink as well, he would be as helpless as Sigismondo, who could know what this sinister relative of his would do? And where was Sigismondo to hide La Feconda – where, if his room and his baggage were to be searched? Benno, gazing vacantly all this time at the gilded crucifix while the familiar, incomprehensible Latin was spoken, consoled himself with the fact that his master did not appear in the least disturbed.

Another thing on Benno's mind was that Angelo too must drink. Benno had been sent to warn him, but if Falcone couldn't find the cross and was driven to search everyone in case Sigismondo had passed it on to someone else as a safeguard, Angelo's gender would be discovered and a very vicious cat would be among the pigeons.

Falcone's chaplain lingered to speak to Brother Filippo, but most of the pilgrims left the chapel quite briskly, thinking of the supper ahead and talking cheerfully to one another. It was Felicia this time who good naturedly steered Brother Ieronimo past the statue at the door when he showed signs of becoming enraptured.

Recently she had constituted herself the guardian of Gian who had, from time to time, periods when he would stare at nothing and require a friendly hand to restore him to the world. He had told her that Brother Ieronimo said the Virgin would restore his memory. Once she had come upon him struggling on the ground, his limbs out of control; when he came round she asked him about what had occurred, and he said that something must have happened to him when the robbers injured his head. He thought he might have the falling sickness, and he begged her to tell no one or people would say he was mad. Now, she reached the foot of the second flight of stairs and, surveying the group ahead, she saw he was not among them; nor was he following. She wondered if he had stayed behind in the chapel, or was even now lying in a spasm in some corner, unable to help himself.

She turned and, gathering up her skirts, ran back up the stairs. She paused at the foot of the steep flight to the chapel. At the top she could see the great wooden door, partly open. She listened. Was there scuffling, moans, something that would tell her help was needed?

Someone else, unseen by her in the dark under the overhang of the staircase, had stopped and was watching her. Felicia, although she still heard nothing, made up her mind and quickly climbed to the chapel. She opened the door wider.

Expecting to see Gian, she was surprised to see Sigismondo. He was there by the statue of the Virgin, head raised to look at her, hand raised to touch hers, the strong planes of his face gilded by the candlelight, serious and concentrating.

She stopped short, being almost upon him, and he turned his head swiftly to look at her, when a hoarse shout, full of horror, came up from below.

'Fire! *Fire!* Get out, get out before it's too late!' Panicking, she turned to the door, but Sigismondo seized her arm and drew her the other way, past the statue into darkness which changed to a cool twilight, full of the smell of thyme and pine and the sound of the sea. She had not noticed the small door that led to the roof terrace; she stumbled on flagstones, feeling his strong arm's support,

309

and cried out, 'Gian! I think he's in the chapel! Look on the floor . . .'

'Wait here.' Without asking the reason for her strange instruction, Sigismondo was gone, back into the castle and, perhaps by now, into the flames.

The chapel was being infiltrated by smoke in ghostly wreaths from the open door to the stairs. Sigismondo did not stop; he followed his ears, not his eyes. The moment he entered the chapel, a shout echoed in the stairwell beyond the door and a succession of thuds followed. Sigismondo reached the door in one stride. The smoke was thick out here but a vagrant gust of air blew it aside and showed him, at the foot of the stairs, a figure slumped among folds of the tapestry which hung now from one hook, torn from the wall.

The noise brought others. Angelo, engaged in intimate conversation with Elisavetta on the way down to supper, had perceived all at once that Felicia was not of the company, made an excuse and come back. The cry of 'Fire' gave him speed and he arrived among the smoke just as Sigismondo was peeling back tapestry from the body at the stair-foot.

'What happened?' With the tapestry off his face, Gian stared up at them. Next moment he was sitting up, fanning away smoke with one hand, rubbing his head with the other. 'Is there a fire? Where am I?'

Sigismondo spoke swiftly to Angelo, who fielded his skirts with practised ease and ran up the stairs to the chapel and the terrace where Felicia waited. Sigismondo felt over Gian's limbs, discovered no injuries save for severe bruising, and gave his attention to the source of the smoke. He had seen, on the flags in the shadow of the chapel stairs, a torch from one of the wall brackets smouldering on the damp rushes that thickly strewed the flags. He picked it up, scattered the rushes and stamped out the dull embers, until the smoke ceased to rise. Gian, wincing and groaning, had got to his feet. His eyes narrowed as Sigismondo turned to replace the flambeau in its bracket.

'You're Sigismondo! You had me searched in Rocca.'

With this demonstration that memory was on its way back, Gian wheeled to face others arriving on the scene. Smoke had found its way downstairs as well, as had the cry of 'Fire' more distantly heard; Giovanni Falcone arrived, ahead of servants labouring with buckets of water half of which had splashed out in their haste. With them was Benno, with wet legs and anxiety for his master, and behind them the men of the pilgrim party, Olivero to the fore.

Gian, focusing on him at once, lunged past a servant whose bucket voided itself incontinently on Falcone's feet, and got the startled Olivero by the throat.

'You son of blood! My father's death! God will not let you live—'

Gian was not about to leave God any choice in the matter; Olivero's hands tore at Gian's without breaking their grip and Gian had run Olivero back against the wall violently before Sigismondo and Ferondo between them dragged the cousins apart. Ferondo was expostulating, but it was Brother Ieronimo, white hair on end, who advanced, with arms flung wide and with beatific face, on Gian who still struggled to free his wrists from Sigismondo's grasp.

'Rejoice, my son! The Virgin has blessed you.'

From Gian's expression, as Brother Ieronimo bestowed an embrace he was unable to resist, the monk formed no part of his returning memory; nor was an enthusiastic kiss from this religious lunatic in the least to his taste.

Falcone, seeing that the threat of fire was not real,

waved away his servants who went grumbling and
slopping water down the stairs, and turned to his guests;
one of them at least seemed confused about his vocation
as a pilgrim. The monk, still clasping this one in his arms,
beamed round at the watching faces.

'Our Lady came to me two nights ago and promised she
would of her mercy bless this young man. He went to the
chapel to pray and lo! – he remembers!'

Benno, gaping at the scene, thought that Brother
Ieronimo, in his innocent way, had no idea what the
restoration of Gian's memory involved. Had he missed
Gian's attack on Olivero?

Sigismondo had released the baffled Gian but kept close
behind him as Brother Ieronimo seized his right wrist and
held out the hand towards Olivero, standing scowling and
easing his throat. 'Our Lady has done this so that you
may not forget but remember and forgive.' He spoke in an
affectionate tone to Gian. 'Had you approached her shrine
with such hatred lying on your conscience, in whatever
way the Devil chose to hide it from you, she could have
offered you nothing.'

Reaching for Olivero's hand, he took it and joined it to
his cousin's.

'Make peace, children, before God takes from you the
chance in this world. Blood, alas, has been shed. Shed no
more.' He held their hands in both his as the cousins stared
at each other. 'If Our Lord is to forgive your fathers' sins,
you must forgive their sons.'

Angelo, who had materialized at the top of the chapel
stairs with Felicia beside him, put his hands together at
this and, in his best counter-tenor, broke into the first
verse of a hymn very popular with the pilgrims they had
been meeting on the way.

> 'O as no soul is free from sin
> The Lord's forgiveness ye would win.
> Pilgrim sister, pilgrim brother
> First forgive ye one another.'

When the singing, taken up heartily by Brother Ieronimo, Felicia's warm contralto and Perpetua's moo, had ended, Falcone put an arm round each of the two cousins as they stood reluctantly joined.

'To supper, dear friends. After that, you shall pledge your pardon for each other in the loving-cup, to seal your bond. I am blessed that the Virgin has brought about this healing of bitterness under my roof. Let us go down to supper.'

Olivero and Gian suffered Falcone's shepherding as they had Brother Ieronimo's uniting their hands, with an air more dazed and resentful than reconciled. Everyone followed them downstairs, Angelo with eyes piously cast down as he passed Benno, who clasped Biondello tightly to cover the fact that he was wagging his tail. Disguise was immaterial to that intelligent nose. Only Sigismondo was left, on the chapel stairs now, and coming down them coiling a thin cord in his hand.

'You going to strangle someone?'

'Mm . . . I fancy it's done its dangerous work already.'

Benno hastily looked about him for evidence of bodies in the dark corners, and Sigismondo's laugh, quiet and deep, reassured him. 'No one's dead yet. I found this lying across the stairs halfway down, fixed to the far side of that ornamental ironwork.'

Benno, jaw sagging, swung to survey the precipitous flight. 'Like a snare?'

'The shout of "Fire" was an invitation to someone to break their neck.'

'But,' Benno thought back, 'it wasn't Olivero; *he* was downstairs when we heard someone yell "Fire"! I know because he shoved me out of the way. Ferondo was there too. Does anyone else want to kill Gian except his cousins?'

Sigismondo looked thoughtfully at the stairs and the chapel doorway golden within. 'There were three of us up there when "Fire" was called. Ask yourself who knew who was there and who wants whom dead.'

'But the people who want to kill you were downstairs, like I said . . . Lady Felicia? Who'd want to kill Lady Felicia?' The only person who seemed to hate her was her brother; he had tried to shut her up in a convent, meant as a sort of living death, but it wasn't the same thing as trying to break her neck. 'Surely . . . her own brother?'

Yet Sigismondo was shaking his head as he held up the cord to the torchlight, and ran his fingers along it. 'There's a part in the centre here darkened by sweat and grease; and either end of that it's kinked where it's been knotted. Men who seek to mortify the flesh wear such a cord round the waist next to the skin. It works like a hairshirt, as a constant reminder to purify the thoughts.'

He blew softly between parted lips. 'The trouble is, it doesn't always work.'

Chapter 59

In the Open

Benno woke, with a dreadful thick head, to Biondello
licking his face anxiously. Sigismondo was already up,
stripped to the waist, dashing water over his head from
the earthenware basin, and shaking it till the drops flew.

'Hey, come and put your face in this. It'll clear your
brain.'

Benno rolled off his pallet and laboriously to his feet.
Only his master, and Angelo, credited him with a brain
to clear, and as he obediently put his head down and felt
cold water shock his face, some of the cloudiness did
disperse. If losing your memory made you as muzzy as
this, poor Gian couldn't have enjoyed it. His own memory
of the night before was returning.

The loving-cup . . . apprehension had almost interfered
with his appetite at the supper. If Benno hadn't a peasant's
sense of the sacred obligation to eat heartily of any food
going he could not have made such a good meal, even of
the remainder of the great pie filled with pears cooked in
wine, boiled salmon, figs and apples, even the pastry with
dates stuck to it – the kitchen dinner, as the guests
upstairs finished their dessert. He had hoped that the
pilgrims' servants would be overlooked, that Sigismondo
might at the last moment hand him La Feconda to hide.
Not that he'd know where . . . but he had scarcely wiped
his beard after the last gloriously greasy mouthful when

word came down, a summons to the great hall where the loving-cup was to be shared by all the pilgrims of whatever rank who were to visit the shrine next day. Benno had followed Nuto, Perpetua and the others with a full stomach and a sinking heart.

'What happened last night?'

Sigismondo was shaving his scalp, among coils of steam rising from the hot water some Falcone servant had delivered before Benno was conscious. The long blade of the razor glittered as Sigismondo scraped it past one ear.

'You tell me. I drank from the cup before you. It was strong – it had to be, after a meal like that.'

That had been the worst part: watching Sigismondo take the big cup of beaten silver, with the wretched falcon and sly panther embossed, take it by both handles and dip his head to drink, knowing he was putting himself at the mercy of anyone who cared to do him harm. Benno was saying an Ave when it came to his turn. Herbs swam in what remained of the wine, it smelt of thyme and tasted rough. Benno nearly gagged on it.

One thing had given him hope. Angelo had refused the cup. It seemed he had not eaten the supper either. When Falcone brought the cup to this pale, shrinking female, so shrouded in her wimple and head-veil that it was hard to tell whether she were worth masculine attention or not, she had put up a thin, forbidding hand.

'I must not. I must fast until I have made my devotions at the shrine. I have vowed to keep vigil tonight in the chapel.'

At that point everything had become beautifully clear to Benno: Angelo had devised the perfect way to escape both drug and search. Falcone could not have afforded any witness from their party to what was going to happen, so Angelo had located himself conveniently out of the way,

316

up in the chapel. There had been no connection on the journey between the shrinking pilgrim and Sigismondo, so that Olivero would have no suspicion of her. Sigismondo had clearly given La Feconda to Angelo, and it would be perfectly safe in the chapel while they were being searched. Falcone, however frustrated he might be in his efforts to find the cross, was not likely to burst in on the devotions of a pious female to insist on searching her.

Once Benno saw all this, he had followed his master up the stairs after supper with a lighter heart, even though he was disliking the idea of the search. As he pulled off his master's boots he felt clogged with drowsiness. Sigismondo had propped himself on the bolsters and closed his eyes, his head rolling slightly on the strong neck as though the muscles could no longer support it. Benno had pitched full length on his pallet, just aware of Biondello leaping out of the way.

Now he sat on the pallet drying his face and beard with a towel and slowly regaining his wits.

'How will you get the cross from Angelo?'

'He hasn't got it.'

Benno stared. 'Then where . . . ?' Had the plan gone wrong? Sigismondo went on lacing his doublet, quite unconcerned.

'Come on. We'll be late for Mass.'

Biondello gave a brief admonitory bark before scampering after Sigismondo, leaving a baffled Benno coming last.

Mass in the chapel was briefer than that of the evening; the chaplain knew that the pilgrims were anxious to start though perhaps it surprised him how many yawns there were, stifled or open, and Lydia had twice to be shaken awake by Elisavetta. The responses were slow this morning from everyone but Angelo, who had been on his knees before the altar when they all first arrived.

Above the sound of the chanted Latin came another sound, not the wash of the sea on the rocky shore below but a distant pervasive rumble. Their host had spoken again last night of the sudden storms of which they had also been warned in Pietra, a feature of Scheggia at this time of year. A fair sky would from nowhere gather thunderclouds and there would be brief but torrential rain. Pilgrims had slipped on rocks streaming with water, and been injured; more than one, in the history of the place, had been washed from the crag and one had fallen into the sea and never been found. It was necessary to approach the shrine with a clear conscience.

Benno, as the growl came again and Biondello shrank against his leg, hoped he hadn't done anything wrong he didn't know about. He didn't fancy landing in the sea from a great height, though probably the falling part would be worst. The Panteras had better watch out – if Olivero actually *had* killed the Abbot he might be in for a nasty surprise: and what about Brother Filippo, who had planned to break his sister's neck on the chapel stair?

Benno respectfully waited for the gentry to leave the chapel, each one pausing to kiss the hem of the robe and reach up to touch the fingers of the statue at the door. The servants went out. Sigismondo was still kneeling, his head bent. He rose, genuflected and came towards the door, Benno shuffling and yawning after him.

Sigismondo raised the corner of the blue robe to his lips and then put up his hand to touch that of the Virgin. The necklace of garnets interlaced in her fingers swung as he brushed it and then, suddenly visible for a moment before it vanished into Sigismondo's palm, glittering, brilliant, unmistakable, was La Feconda.

Benno was speechless. Sigismondo had often said, if

you want to hide something, put it in the open. People had passed and touched, and all night long the Virgin had held it in her cupped hand.

Chapter 60

You, Here?

After Falcone's renewed warning, given to the party as they breakfasted on bread and wine, it was a surprise to them to emerge into a bright day. They scanned the sky, but what clouds they saw were peacefully white, a flock of lambs on blue pastures. Still, when Elisavetta asked Falcone if this guaranteed freedom from storms, he shook his head.

'It's as God wills. Scheggia makes its own weather.'

They were not the only pilgrims on the road. Even at this early hour, a party who had spent the night at the bleak hostel in the harbour village were already on the path, some calling out encouragement to each other as they began to negotiate the steeper slope, others singing hymns to the Virgin while they still had breath to spare.

Their own party, thanking Falcone and declaring they had enjoyed an excellent night's rest, by contrast resembled a band of sleepwalkers at the start of the climb.

Benno had been told by Sigismondo to keep an eye on Gian, this morning feeling stiff after his fall down half the chapel stairs, and limping. Pilgrims who were invalids, here to beg the Virgin for health rather than offspring, as well as the frailer of the female pilgrims, had the option of an easier path that wound more at leisure right round the hill, thus dispensing with the steep zigzag up the hill's face. It was a path that could be taken by donkeys and also, before the ways diverged, Benno saw an elderly woman piggyback on a wizened man; no doubt on the way to pray for grandchildren.

The females of their own party were more heroic, though none of them imitated the women who were padding their knees with rags, preparatory to climbing the hillside on them. Felicia had recovered from the indisposition she had suffered in Rome, her loss of the child, and with kilted skirts and the help of a staff she set out in determination. Angelo accompanied her, moderating his steps. Benno hoped he had used his skills at sleight of hand to secrete some food at last night's supper, since he had piously refused breakfast.

Watching Brother Filippo stride along after them, Benno had another moment of revelation: Sigismondo, suspicious of that monk's intentions right from the start, had brought Angelo not to protect his own back at all; with Angelo always at her side, the monk's chance of giving his sister a push off the crag was negligible. Benno could still hardly believe in such hatred.

After the monk stomped Perpetua and Nuto. He was already trying to offer his arm, and she shrugged it away but without the scoldings she had heaped on him during the journey to Rome. During this latter journey she had been very nearly flirtatious with him, until now when perhaps she felt it was not the time for earthly distractions.

Lydia and Elisavetta too had chosen the hard path, which now took a sharp swing upward from the smoother track and rose on a strong incline, among juniper and stunted pines whose scent mixed with the salt air from the sea. Elisavetta declared that nothing could be more arduous than their effort in Rome – going up the steps of Santa Maria in Aracoeli on her knees. Lydia appeared too sleepy to contradict her. Their husbands, oddly enough, had suggested they take the easier way. Olivero had hired donkeys from the village through a Falcone servant, before Elisavetta rejected them. Both brothers seemed insouciant, almost high-spirited, this morning. Benno could not make it out; they must be furious and frustrated that Falcone had not managed to find La Feconda. Had they given up at last? Could Scheggia possibly have worked a spell of reconciliation on them?

Ahead on the track, barefoot over the stones and singing away, went Brother Ieronimo. Condemned by the Pope to live on Scheggia, he was going to his destiny with transparent joy and gratitude. He was going at last to see the Virgin of Scheggia, she who had blessed him with visions, at her own shrine, and to serve her there for the rest of his life.

Among those at the rear was Sigismondo, watchful but withdrawn. Benno, toiling after Gian, thought of his master bringing La Feconda at last, after all the struggles and distractions, in a species of penance for killing Bernabo Pantera; perhaps a penance for not having seen what the Pantera brothers were up to.

Finding that Gian needed no help, having soon walked off his stiffness, Benno paused at the head of another steep stretch to look around. The sea glittered below, the shore of the mainland blue in the distance. His legs ached already. Biondello, who had scrambled valiantly after him, sat down abruptly with lolling tongue and small ribs heaving, and Benno picked him up before turning to face the next stretch.

Here a flight of steps had been hacked in the rock, steep and uneven. He could see the backs of the others ascending slowly, and set out. Someone, perhaps Brother Ieronimo, had started a series of processional Aves; Benno took it up automatically, but he found the chant got him up the steps

322

more easily. At the next turn, posts and a rail had been set up, for the hillside fell sheer and vertiginously to the sea. Benno took one glance and averted his eyes. The party in general had slowed, and Olivero was quite tenderly helping Lydia – surprising Benno, who had not seen him show her the slightest consideration so far. The influence of the place had no limits . . .

Benno rubbed his legs and looked upward, with misgiving. More stony stretches had followed more steps; the climb was said to get steeper at the end. Stunted pines, all leaning one way and shaped by the prevailing wind, hid the top; the shrine itself had remained mysteriously obscured all through the climb, each twist in the path offering no glimpse of it more than the rest. On the path just below, Sigismondo came steadily on among other pilgrims. Benno straightened his back and followed Gian, letting Biondello walk the rest, to get what merit he could.

Here they came to a little bay in the hillside, strewn with pairs of shoes, sandals and boots. From here most pilgrims went barefoot up the last stairway to the shrine itself. Benno pulled off his boots and put his hot feet down on the roughness of the rock. Ahead were the labouring backs of all the others and, surprisingly, Brother Filippo sitting on a boulder by the path, head sunk between his shoulders, panting and muttering to himself what, from his face, were not the prayers they should have been. By the time Benno passed him, the monk had his head in his hands and was rocking to and fro. Biondello gave him a wide berth.

Many of the party were on hands and knees by the end of this last rocky stretch. Benno, almost crawling, raised his eyes towards the shrine. He had formed an idea of a place rather like the Falcone chapel, with a statue, only bigger, filled with marble, glitter of candlelight on jewelled offerings, with gold leaf and all the sumptuousness of a church he had visited in Rome.

The shrine of Scheggia was no more than a cave.

There was a large opening, as though the crag had a gaping mouth at the top. This was not dark, though, but blazed with candles. A monk stood there controlling the flow of those who went in to the inner shrine; they passed through the antechamber whose uneven surfaces held hundreds of objects on walls and roof: pictures, carvings in wood and wax, plaster moulds of limbs, of ships, and of babies. Everywhere were small figures and pictures of babies. Tiny cribs of wood or wicker swung from the roof, papers of prayers fluttered, and, as the candles, stuck in pools of wax on any spur or ledge, wavered as the pilgrims passed, the tiny features of the multitude of babies seemed to smile.

They had to wait as a small crowd of pilgrims came out. Then they were allowed to go forward.

The entrance to the inner rock chamber was narrow, and pilgrims could enter no more than two abreast and Elisavetta on her own. Within, all the candlelight was gathered at the far end, leaving the rest full of shadows shifting far up into the smoke-blackened roof as if bats nested overhead. The air was dense with the smoke and incense, and Benno could follow only the silhouette of his master's head and shoulders. When Sigismondo reached the altar step and knelt, Benno on his knees behind him could look up at the painting beyond the little altar. He had expected a statue. It was a picture, almost too dark to see and shimmering in the heat of the candles. The Virgin and Child were visible from their haloes of gold leaf, gold showing on their robes. It was only a small picture, and not even hanging quite straight, but Benno could not take his eyes from it. After a while he could make out the faces, dark, mysterious, both with the same indefinable power.

All round the picture was a blaze of offerings: necklaces, chains, brooches, the jewels flashing rainbow sparks as the candle flames dipped and quivered.

After Mass the priest came forward – he had only to take a step to be able to touch the pilgrims in the front – and waited to receive any offerings. Elisavetta and Lydia kissed the necklaces they handed to him, the Pantera men had brought purses. Benno yielded up a silver ring he was very proud of but never liked to wear; Perpetua, sniffling, gave a lace scarf. Felicia reached over Lydia's shoulder to give a pair of pearl ear-drops, Angelo a thin gold chain.

When the priest came to Sigismondo kneeling next to the wall, and waited, Sigismondo held up La Feconda glittering and glowing. Reverently, slowly, as if he sensed something of what the cross stood for, the long and bloody journey it had taken to reach here, the priest received it in both hands; admiring, seeing it as at least of exceptional worth, he turned to bow before the picture and hang the cross by the hook at its back on the foot of the frame. La Feconda was where, perhaps a hundred years ago, it was meant to be.

Benno had covertly watched the three who must surely resent this sacrifice of La Feconda deeply. Gian was the one who looked suddenly disturbed and angry, and almost got to his feet. The brothers both wore smug faces as if the deed pleased them immensely. Scheggia was certainly having the most salutary effect on them.

But where was Brother Ieronimo who, like the cross, was to remain here? Benno could not see either of the monks. Brother Filippo might still be sitting by the path, but Brother Ieronimo had been ahead of everyone – where

was he? The chapel was emptying. Perpetua came ou
with tears running unheeded down her large, plain face
Nuto looked actually impressed. In the porch the nex
group was waiting, examining the dolls, cribs and prayer
slips. An old woman crouched on the ground, the one whe
had come up on the man's back; she looked as light as a
sack of feathers. A young woman, clearly no peasant ir
her gown of good cloth and head-covering of gold
embroidered linen, watched the priest hang up a little
woven crib, bought at the place where shoes were left.

Suddenly Gian Pantera pushed between Benno and
Lydia, and grasped her.

'Elena – why – what – *you*, here?'

They were both astounded. After their first exclamation:
she smiled, blushing in a way that extremely became her
and pointed at the tiny crib swinging over their heads.

'We are to have a child in the spring. I would have sent
to tell you only no one knew where you were.' She looked
from the circle of his arms, at cousins she knew by sight
but, because of the feud, had never spoken to. She made
polite acknowledgement of their greetings while her
husband was covering her hands with kisses. One Pantera
at least had managed to get a child without La Feconda's
aid. But the true surprise was that the brothers showed
every sign of pleasure at this meeting; one would think
the cousins had lived in each other's pockets all their lives
Kissing and congratulating held everyone up so that the
priest had virtually to turn them all out. As they emerged
it was to a growl of thunder far louder and closer than the
one they had heard that morning.

Scheggia was changing its weather.

Chapter 61

The Devil's Answer

They hurried out, looking up at the sky, anxious to get
down before the worst of the storm; putting up hoods,
wrapping cloaks tighter against the sudden wind. The sky
was now piled with thunderclouds, one a long anvil
presaging lightning. The women lost no time, climbing
down the rocky steps to where their shoes were, threading
their way among pilgrims coming up. They found their
shoes, crying out at a flicker of lightning; the donkeys
tethered for hire got up a commotion.

There was a stall, sheltered under an overhang of rock,
where a monk offered for sale lead and pottery statues of
the Virgin, seals and badges with the crag of Scheggia in
dizzying outline, woven cribs of rush or wicker, little clay
babies, and rather bad copies on wood of the painting in
the shrine. He was not selling successfully at the moment,
only Elisavetta hesitating over a purchase before being
dragged away by a nervous Lydia.

The descent was officially by way of the wide track that
circled the crag, and far ahead already Benno could see a
donkey led by Angelo, with Felicia on it, skipping nimbly
down the track, pursued by Perpetua, and Nuto still
carrying his shoes. Lydia, not far behind, gave a shriek at
a brilliant, shimmering white flash from the sky, followed
by a sharp crack of thunder overhead.

The first drops of rain were descending, huge, spotting

the ground with a sudden dark. Benno trod into his boots, pulled up his hood and tucked Biondello firmly inside his jerkin. Was there time to buy a pilgrim seal? Sigismondo stood at the shrine entrance still talking to Gian and his wife. When the two turned and went back together into the shrine, Sigismondo came down the rock steps. Benno hastily bought his souvenir while Biondello, poking his head out, shrewdly surveyed the goods for sale and withdrew instantly at a flash and crack right overhead. Rain cascaded from the stone ledge that sheltered the stall.

Sigismondo arrived smiling, the rain pouring sleekly over his skull; he had a sprig of rosemary from a bush by the head of the steps, and he stowed it carefully in his scrip. That, it seemed, was his memento from Scheggia – he passed the stall without stopping. He found his boots, rubbed his feet and pulled the boots on, and almost in the same movement set off down the path – the path, not the easy track.

When Benno hurried after, as fast as aching legs and mud on the path let him go, he found it was harder going down than up, and was glad that some pilgrims coming up were not blocking his way but sheltering under an overhang; more cowered under bushes or in any refuge they could find. Beyond lay a dark sea almost invisible beyond great shifting curtains of rain. Sigismondo went on down as effortlessly as though rain were an element he could swim in, sluiced head shining. A zigzag of the path took him out of sight, and Benno, sliding and only stopped by getting an arm round a distorted pine trunk, reached the bend precipitately.

There he came upon three figures lit dramatically against sea and rock by a blaze of lightning.

Brother Ieronimo was shouting at Brother Filippo, who was shouting at the sky, but neither could be heard in the crash and reverberation of thunder. Sigismondo stood watching them both. The rain showed like silver rods in the lightning, Heaven chastising sinners.

Brother Filippo raised to the sky a face contorted with rage. He was capering as if demented, his feet plashing mud and dislodging stones.

A short lull in the thunder let Benno hear some of what Brother Filippo was howling, though it made no sense – a wild address to the Devil whom he accused as agent of this storm. Brother Ieronimo also seemed to be addressing the Devil – but in the person of Brother Filippo. Benno, with rain running into his mouth, gazed from one to the other.

'God warns you!' Brother Ieronimo, slipping on the mud, managed to grip the flailing sleeve of Brother Filippo's wet habit. 'Do not approach the shrine! Our Lady will not permit those with blood on their hands to pray there!'

Brother Filippo hurled Brother Ieronimo from him with such force that he made him stagger backwards till he hung for an awful moment on the edge with the pitiless drop beneath. Sigismondo moved and seized him and flung himself back on the inward edge of the path among ferns and broken stone. The rain slashed down, lightning flared in one long shiver and the thunder's explosion drowned Brother Filippo's raving though spittle flew from his lips as he screamed against the storm. In both hands he held up the iron crucifix he wore, as if defying his Devil.

The Devil answered. A white sword of lightning and a thunderclap that seemed to shake the world came together. Benno, blinded, fell in the mud, clutching Biondello, sure they were both dead.

He must be in Hell because he could smell burning, a worse smell of burning than he had ever smelt before. He opened his eyes. There were no demons. Brother Filippo had apparently vanished. Benno blinked, his eyes full of after-images, and saw Sigismondo bending over something while Brother Ieronimo scrambled up to his knees and put his hands together in prayer. Still the rain dashed down on them. Benno made his painful way – heels, one hand and seat, holding a shuddering Biondello – to the something his master knelt by.

It was Brother Filippo, but barely recognizable. Benno retched at the twisted, blackened face and the smell of cooked flesh. More horrible than all, when Sigismondo got an arm under the monk's shoulders, his mouth fell open and smoke, visible even in the rain, came out. Benno crossed himself again and again.

Sigismondo did a thing that seemed blasphemous. He took the iron crucifix from Brother Filippo's neck and threw the distorted thing into the sea, moved to Brother Ieronimo, lifted the crucifix off over his head and sent it after the first.

As if this were a signal for the storm to let up, the rain lost its violence and the thunder trampled away into the distance. The dark clouds began to shred, and a pale finger of light touched the charred thing that had been Brother Filippo.

Brother Ieronimo was weeping. He had got to his feet and came to stand beside them.

'The mercy of God is infinite. It may be he repented before it struck.'

'We may hope so.'

'You took the crucifix from me.'

'Iron calls to fire in a storm; I've seen it. There are more reasons than you know, why we should leave weapons behind when we go up to the shrine. Do you want to be struck too?'

Brother Ieronimo, tears and rain running down his face,

looked bewildered. 'But he was punished. God punished him. I have done my penance and I have to live to serve Our Lady. Why should I be struck?'

Sigismondo only shook his head, heaved Brother Filippo's dreadful body on to his shoulder and started down the path again.

Chapter 62

Temptation for a Saint

They sat in the evening sunlight at a table outside a tavern. Down in the valley the river ran through the little town that climbed the hill almost to where they sat. The tavern was well placed to refresh those about to enter the town or those who had just left it.

They had finished their business there, and could afford to relax, to enjoy the region's excellent wine and raise their faces to the autumn sun; it no longer scorched but was warm enough to banish any lingering chill of Scheggia's storms from their bones, enough almost to make up for the summer's unnatural rains.

'So that's over.' Angelo, his severe beauty gilded by the light, leant back with an arm along the stone wall, looking at the houses clinging to the hill. 'You reckon he's satisfied now? Cosier in Purgatory?'

An hour ago Sigismondo had laid the sprig of rosemary from Scheggia on Bernabo Pantera's tomb. Donna Irina had unlocked the vault, and suddenly, passionately, embraced Sigismondo when he left. Sigismondo now stretched out his legs and pushed his cup to be filled by Benno from the big brown jug.

'I don't know if he's satisfied. I know I am.'

Indeed Benno thought the shadow had left Sigismondo. It had cast its darkness over him all these months since Benno had seen him with his right arm soaked in

332

Bernabo's blood. That stain he had washed off as soon as he could, but the stain in the mind was harder to be rid of.

'*You* may be satisfied. I'm not.' Angelo turned from the view and fixed his regard on Sigismondo. 'You still have things to explain. You delivered La Feconda as you intended, but why was that lovely pair of brothers so smug about it? Anyone would think *they* had the cross and not you.'

Sigismondo laughed, a sound that ended in a contented hum. 'They thought they had.'

Angelo imitated Benno's dropped jaw, and Sigismondo went on, 'You remember when I asked you to keep an eye on them in Rome – you reported that Ferondo went several times to that goldsmith after the Pope had ordered us to Scheggia? While we were getting ready for the journey? I believe he had a replica made of La Feconda, for a plan they had.'

Angelo had closed his mouth on the crooked teeth that made a devil out of the angel, and was nodding slowly. 'So that was why they didn't make a push to slit your throat on the road to Scheggia. They planned to cheat the Pope *and* the Virgin, counting on Falcone and a sleeping draught, to do a switch.' He paused, nodding, and aimed a long finger at Sigismondo. 'There *wasn't* a switch. Falcone couldn't find La Feconda where you'd put it. What did he do?'

Sigismondo smiled broadly, picked up a piece of bread and dipped it in his wine, drizzled oil on it from the jar, sprinkled salt on it and ate with relish. 'Hey, the man's no fool. He's family, he's obliging his kin. He's also a Pantera; he can't find the cross, is he going to tell them he's failed, have a quarrel that'll last his lifetime and bring the castle round his ears? No, he gives them a cross in the morning

– the one they'd given to him but he doesn't say so. Everyone's happy.'

Angelo regarded Sigismondo thoughtfully. 'What did Falcone think would happen at the shrine if you had no cross to offer?'

Sigismondo shrugged. He had half-shut his eyes against the evening sun and the lashes shadowed his cheek. 'I don't suppose he thought I hadn't got it, only that I'd hidden it better than he'd thought possible.'

'He'd looked everywhere,' put in Benno, 'my spare shirt and everything.'

'It's the one you were wearing he might have been shy of.' Angelo looked down his elegant nose. 'It's a wonder he didn't slit the linings on doublets and packs.'

'If he did, he got them sewn up after. He had all night.'

'Biondello gave him something for his trouble, didn't you?' Benno lavished a large crust on the little dog, who, with forepaws on the table, made more than one effort to bolt the crust whole before he got it down. 'Our host had bandaged fingers next day and he gave me and him some dirty looks at breakfast.' He patted the still gulping Biondello. 'Those Panteras must have been wanting to laugh out loud when they watched you hand over what they thought was a fake at the shrine. They'll never be able to show the one they've got, though, will they? Suppose the Pope got to hear they were flaunting La Feconda! Bet you they won't even tell their wives.'

'Would you tell Elisavetta Pantera she'd climbed Scheggia for nothing, that you had La Feconda all the time . . .' Sigismondo shook a hand loosely from the wrist and turned up his eyes ' . . . and that it'd bring her sons anyway?'

'But it won't, will it, because it isn't? And *Gian* didn't need it.'

'It may not be a son they're having. And children so easily die . . . but hey, faith can move mountains. They *believe* they have La Feconda.' Sigismondo drank, and turned to gaze down into the valley where evening shadows were pooling. The river still reflected the brilliance of the sky, and birds were swooping after the insects, cutting the air overhead, twittering, flashing down past the three who sat there. A bell in the church below started to ring for Vespers, the sound clear and sweet in the stillness. 'At least now, as Bernabo wanted, they can live in peace with one another. For the moment.'

Biondello received another piece of bread and, mindful of his trouble with the last one, dumped himself off the bench to wrestle with it on the ground and gag in comfort. Benno, as his master called for more wine, was, as usual, grateful to Angelo for asking questions he had not even thought of, let alone hoped to get answers to. There were still far too many things he wanted to know, and hadn't cared to ask, even though Sigismondo's mood had changed so entirely. He waited until the girl from the tavern, divided in her attention between Angelo's beauty and Sigismondo's head which evidently fascinated her, had put down another big jug and a plate of chestnuts. Then he asked.

'Did Brother Filippo kill the Abbot? I mean, Brother Ieronimo told him he had blood on his hands and mustn't go up to the shrine. And he seemed to be in a state about something on the way up. And it was him with Torquato who found the corpse, he could not-so-much have *found* it as *made* it, and rushed off to tell the Duke before they came back and were told Brother Ieronimo had been trying to get the axe out . . .'

'Which is *very* likely.' Angelo chose a chestnut. 'You stick an axe in someone, wander off and then think, oh, must

335

get that back before I need to trim my nails again . . .'

'Yet you could believe Brother Ieronimo would. I mean, he didn't seem to know what he was doing half the time. Wonder how he'll manage at Scheggia; perhaps he'll do all right because he knows it's for the Virgin.'

'I think,' Sigismondo's deep voice rode in, 'that he always knew more than anyone realized. He's not the man, however, to condemn another, even for murder. He would prefer to take the blame himself. Nor do I think he was sure which of them did it.'

'Which of them?' Benno, shading his eyes against the low sun, looked at Sigismondo.

'Torquato or Brother Filippo. But Torquato had not the courage. He was one who peers round doors at violence. Nor had he the motive. The Abbot was a tyrant to others besides his secretary, but that wasn't the reason he was killed. In fact *I* killed him.'

Benno coughed his wine over the table.

'Mm-mm, what a *waste*. Angelo will tell you how I killed him.'

Angelo raised his eyebrows. 'I know?'

'What did you say Felicia told you? About Agostino's jealousy?'

'Ah. Of course.' Angelo gave his harsh laugh. 'In our womanly confidences. We talked long hours in bed.' After a glance at Sigismondo he went on more quickly, 'It seems when her husband came home one night he saw a man leave by the back way. He caught a glimpse of what he thought was a tonsure,' Angelo's glance skimmed Sigismondo's head, smooth and golden in the light, 'and a cloak billowing out round a large man – a fat man, he thought, and he didn't stop to think how much was cloak and how much was man because he thought he knew. Felicia had unwisely let out to him how she'd reverently embroidered an altar frontal and she took it to the Abbey, and the Abbot made an ecclesiastical grab at her. Agostino was sure it was the Abbot she had been entertaining that night.'

Benno remembered: the night Perpetua had sent Sigismondo out into the pouring rain, which had brought back his fever and, worse, had caused the collapse in the marketplace which led to the Abbey infirmary.

'But *Agostino* surely didn't kill the Abbot?'

Angelo tapped his winecup on the table and Benno pushed the jug across. 'You're forgetting, mooncalf, that Agostino had a brother-in-law who might think of avenging the family honour. I expect he hurried over to the Abbey with his suspicions. Brother Filippo wasn't one to think well of any living soul and you're not telling me monks don't know the gossip about their superior.'

'But Brother Filippo was such a strict religious . . .'

Sigismondo took up. 'A religious who quite recently tried to kill his sister. It appalled him that men don't act as they ought; nor women, though that surprised him less, for women repelled him. If they could not be brought to judgement here, they must be dispatched to be judged in another place.'

Benno was silent. What judgement had been passed on Brother Filippo himself, whose body had looked as if the flames of Hell had rushed to meet him?

Sigismondo too was silent for a while, then he spoke. 'As I see events, Olivero and Brother Filippo both followed Torquato from Cardinal Tartaruga's banquet. Olivero must have seen, as I did, Torquato's confident smiling and touching his breast turn into panic when what he expected to touch, the cross hanging under his habit, was gone. He caught Torquato up and threatened him: remember the dagger-pricks on his throat? So Olivero found out where

Gemmata lived and that she, Torquato thought, had the cross. But it was Brother Filippo who found Torquato and finished him off.'

'Just for making eyes at his sister at the banquet?' Benno was astonished.

'For visiting whores,' Angelo said. 'Didn't you smell that scent of Gemmata's on you after we left her lodging? A tomcat's spray isn't more powerful. I reeked of it, and Torquato must have stunk like a brothel to Brother Filippo. Torquato could go and explain *that* to God.'

'Besides, the hold Brother Filippo had on Torquato was gone.' Sigismondo spread his hands wide. 'Say this is what happened: Brother Filippo, when his sister's husband comes to tell him the Abbot has seduced Felicia, bides his time. My axe was taken from me then, when the Abbot chose to think I had stolen the cross, so it was in his room. Brother Ieronimo was told to bring everything in the study to Rocca. Brother Ieronimo, under obedience, would have packed the walls if it occurred to him. At Rocca, the axe is Brother Filippo's temptation; when the Abbot's alone at prayer—'

'Bad move,' Angelo interrupted. 'Gives the Abbot a better chance in the next world.'

'Mm . . . he can't afford to be *too* picky. Then I think Torquato walks in on him. He wanted that cross to back his ambition. With that to sell, he could make his way up in Rome.'

'A deal, was it? I thought they were on edge with each other on that journey to Rome . . . Then killing Torquato for whoring removed the only witness to the murder.'

'And Torquato without the cross,' cried Benno, 'could have told on Brother Filippo!'

'The bargain was broken,' said Angelo, nodding. 'Brother Filippo was no fool.'

Sigismondo took up. 'The man they thought was a fool, Brother Ieronimo, was the one who understood all along what had happened—'

'But why,' and Benno did not even notice that he too had interrupted Sigismondo, 'why did he take the blame? Why'd he say the Devil had entered him?'

The bell in the valley had ceased to ring, and Sigismondo, looking up as a bird swooped past his head, went on surveying the sky. 'I can enter into the mind of a villain but I hesitate at that of a saint. Perhaps he wished to give Brother Filippo time to repent. He may have been truly tempted. The path of martyrdom may be the final temptation for a saint.'

'I can see I am not ever going to earn a halo,' observed Angelo, taking the last chestnut.

More Crime Fiction from Headline

DEATH OF A DUCHESS

AN ITALIAN RENAISSANCE WHODUNNIT

ELIZABETH EYRE

When a deadly feud beween two wealthy families threatens the life and rule of the Duke of Rocca, he decrees a marriage between them. But this is a Romeo who despises his Juliet, a Juliet who runs away from her Romeo.

The girl is kidnapped – or has she run away? – and the Duke employs one Sigismondo, the man from nowhere, quiet, enigmatic and observant, to find her. Sigismondo sees a number of things that don't add up: a dead dog, a servant lying in the fire, but finds little enlightenment. He is present at the fatal banquet which ends in fireworks and the murder of the Duchess of Rocca in circumstances which point to the son of the feuding family.

Whilst the boy awaits the scaffold, Sigismondo sets out to unravel the mystery, foil a conspiracy – and reveal the murderer lurking behind a courtly mask . . .

DEATH OF A DUCHESS is set in the danger of a time which feeds on poison, the days of the Medici and the Borgias, but spiced with humour as Sigismondo, a man as good with his brains as he is with an axe, stalks through, followed by the shrewd half-wit, Benno, and his little one-eared dog.

FICTION / CRIME 0 7472 3748 4

The White Rose Murders

Being the first journal of Sir Roger Shallot concerning certain wicked conspiracies and horrible murders perpetrated in the reign of King Henry VIII

MICHAEL CLYNES

In 1517 the English armies have defeated and killed James IV of Scotland at Flodden and James's widow-queen, Margaret, sister to Henry VIII, has fled to England, leaving her crown under a Council of Regency.

Shallot is drawn into a web of mystery and murder by his close friendship with Benjamin Daunbey, the nephew of Cardinal Wolsey, first minister of Henry VIII. Benjamin and Roger are ordered into Margaret's household to resolve certain mysteries as well as to bring about her restoration to Scotland.

They begin by questioning Selkirk, a half-mad physician imprisoned in the Tower. He is subsequently found poisoned in a locked chamber guarded by soldiers. The only clue is a poem of riddles. However, the poem contains the seeds for other gruesome murders. The faceless assassin always leaves a white rose, the mark of *Les Blancs Sangliers*, a secret society plotting the overthrow of the Tudor Monarchy . . .

FICTION / CRIME 0 7472 3785 9

A TAPESTRY OF MURDERS

P. C. Doherty

Chaucer's pilgrims, quarrelling amongst themselves, are now in open countryside enjoying the fresh spring weather as they progress slowly towards Canterbury. A motley collection of travellers, they each have their dark secrets, hidden passions and complex lives. As they shelter in a tavern from a sudden April shower they choose the Man of Law to narrate the next tale of fear and sinister dealings.

In August 1358, the Dowager Queen Isabella, mother of King Edward III, the 'She Wolf of France', who betrayed and destroyed her husband because of her adulterous infatuation for Roger Mortimer, lies dying of the pestilence in the sombre fortress of Castle Rising, where her 'loving' son has kept her incarcerated. According to the Man of Law, Isabella dies and her body is taken along the Mile End Road and laid to rest in Greyfriars next to the mangled remains of her lover, who has paid dearly for his presumption in loving a queen. Nevertheless, as in life so in death Isabella causes intrigue, violence and murder. Nicholas Chirke, an honest young lawyer, is brought in to investigate the strange events following her death – and quickly finds himself at his wits' end trying to resolve the mysteries before a great scandal unfolds.

FICTION / CRIME 0 7472 4588 6

By Murder's Bright Light

THE SORROWFUL MYSTERIES OF BROTHER ATHELSTAN

PAUL HARDING

In the winter of 1379, a sea of troubles besets England. French privateers are attacking the southern coast and threaten London itself. Sir John Cranston, the portly, wine-loving Coroner of the City, also has problems. Not only does he have to sit in court and listen to allegations of witchcraft but he is puzzled by the crimes of a skilful felon.

Cranston's clerk, the Dominican monk, Brother Athelstan, is preparing a mystery play – and trying to placate the members of his church council, all of whom want to play God. But these mundane concerns pale into insignificance when an English flotilla of warships, with *God's Bright Light* in its number, drops anchor in the Thames; during the first night the entire watch of the ship disappears without a trace.

The series of murderous and strange incidents leads to Sir John and Brother Athelstan being summoned to resolve the mysteries on board the ill-omened warship. In particular, they must search out the truth behind the death of Sir Henry Ospring who was viciously stabbed in a tavern chamber. Their investigations uncover scandal, sexual misdemeanours, murder and even treason – and they find themselves in the thick of a bloody battle on the Thames.

FICTION / CRIME   0 7472 4461 8

CONTUMACIOUS

A selection of bestsellers from Headline

OXFORD EXIT	Veronica Stallwood	£4.99	☐
BOOTLEGGER'S DAUGHTER	Margaret Maron	£4.99	☐
DEATH AT THE TABLE	Janet Laurence	£4.99	☐
KINDRED GAMES	Janet Dawson	£4.99	☐
MURDER OF A DEAD MAN	Katherine John	£4.99	☐
A SUPERIOR DEATH	Nevada Barr	£4.99	☐
A TAPESTRY OF MURDERS	P C Doherty	£4.99	☐
BRAVO FOR THE BRIDE	Elizabeth Eyre	£4.99	☐
NO FIXED ABODE	Frances Ferguson	£4.99	☐
MURDER IN THE SMOKEHOUSE	Amy Myers	£4.99	☐
THE HOLY INNOCENTS	Kate Sedley	£4.99	☐
GOODBYE, NANNY GRAY	Staynes & Storey	£4.99	☐
SINS OF THE WOLF	Anne Perry	£5.99	☐
WRITTEN IN BLOOD	Caroline Graham	£5.99	☐

All Headline books are available at your local bookshop or newsagent, or can be ordered direct from the publisher. Just tick the titles you want and fill in the form below. Prices and availability subject to change without notice.

Headline Book Publishing, Cash Sales Department, Bookpoint, 39 Milton Park, Abingdon, OXON, OX14 4TD, UK. If you have a credit card you may order by telephone – 01235 400400.

Please enclose a cheque or postal order made payable to Bookpoint Ltd to the value of the cover price and allow the following for postage and packing:

UK & BFPO: £1.00 for the first book, 50p for the second book and 30p for each additional book ordered up to a maximum charge of £3.00.

OVERSEAS & EIRE: £2.00 for the first book, £1.00 for the second book and 50p for each additional book.

Name ....

Address ....

....

....

If you would prefer to pay by credit card, please complete:
Please debit my Visa/Access/Diner's Card/American Express (delete as applicable) card no:

Signature .... Expiry Date ....